BLOOD
ON THE
LANCE

Other novels by Alfred Dennis

Chiricahua

Lone Eagle

Elkhorn Divide

Brant's Fort

Catamount

The Mustangers

Rover

Sandigras Canyon

Yellowstone Brigade

Shawnee Trail

Fort Reno

Yuma

Ride the Rough String

Trail to Medicine Mound

Arapaho Lance: Crow Killer Series - Book 1

Lance Bearer: Crow Killer Series - Book 2

Track of the Grizzly: Crow Killer Series - Book 3

Bear Claw: Crow Killer Series - Book 4

Blood on the Lance: Crow Killer Series - Book 5

Slocum

To see more books by Alfred Dennis visit
www.alfreddennis.com

BLOOD
ON THE
LANCE

Crow Killer Series - Book 5

by

Alfred Dennis

Walnut Creek Publishing
Tuskahoma, Oklahoma

Blood on the Lance: Crow Killer Series - Book 5

ISBN: 978-1-942869-35-1
First Edition, Paperback
Published 2020 by Walnut Creek Publishing
Front cover painting: derivative work of Alfred Jacob Miller/Encampment of Crow Indians /AAC/CC-BY
Library of Congress Control Number: 2020949806

Books may be purchased in quantity and/or special sales by contacting the publisher;
Walnut Creek Publishing
PO Box 820
Talihina, OK 74571
www.wc-books.com

This book is dedicated to my daughter-in-law
Gayla Christine Dennis, (Li'l Annie Oakley).
She's game for anything… horses, hunting,
and a pretty good poker player to boot.
Yes sir, she'll do to ride the river with.
She's always in my corner.

CHAPTER 1

The long, harsh winter had finally succumbed at last, giving up its death grip on Jedidiah Bracket's high lonesome valley. As with every year, the passing of each season was welcomed, bringing a new generation of life and growth. The past winter had been the worst Jed had ever witnessed since he first discovered this beautiful valley, serene and undisturbed, surrounded by high majestic lofty mountains. The winter storms had been relentless with tentacles of ice-like fangs hanging from the eaves of the roof. The frigid cold penetrated even into the normally snug cabin. The freezing ice and snow, with the cutting, gusting winds, had covered the valley in a death grip of intense cold for days on end. Huddled around the roaring hearth for warmth, Jed, Bright Moon, and Ed Wilson had bided their time, waiting for the weather to break.

Most days and nights had been a constant struggle as they tried to keep enough snow melted beside the blazing hearth so the horses could have water. The frigid cold had caused the animal's hair to grow much longer and thicker than normal. Jed smiled as he thought the thick hair made them look like shaggy buffalo as they stood underneath the barn overhang where they were protected from the wind. Jed couldn't do anything about the cold air, but at least the animals were dry. One thing he had learned early in life was if a large animal like a horse or cow could be kept dry, the cold didn't affect them as badly. Wilson often said his milk cow would give more milk in the cold months than she would in the hotter, stifling summer months.

The past winter was harsh, but luckily, Jed's stepfather, Ed Wilson, had come to live with them two summers before. The old hunter and scout, Lige Hatcher, had kept his word and guided the farmer with his cow and belongings across the rivers and back into the isolated mountain valley Jed called home. The second winter that Wilson was in the mountains, with Jed and Bright Moon, had been an ordeal. The winter had been a chore alright, but with both men working and Bright Moon stoking the fires and keeping the coffee hot, they had survived one of the most bitter winters in anybody's memory. Jed remembered Hatcher's last words of warning in the spring before he headed back to Bridger to hook up with Chalk Briggs and his wagon train. The old trail scout had sensed something in the air, even though it was still early summer. Like Bright Moon, he had warned of a possible severe winter ahead. How the old scout or Bright Moon had known the fierce storms were coming, Jed would never know, but they had been right.

The old-timers like Hatcher and the Indian tribes had learned to watch the movements of the ants, grasshoppers, and even the fur-bearing animals. They looked for signs such as heavier winter coats, the side of the trees where the animals built their mounds, and even the early disappearance of some species sounded the alarm. The animals couldn't speak, but with their inherited instincts, in someways, they were more aware of the elements than the human species. Like the native Indians, living in the wild, Lige Hatcher had watched and learned from the wild animals of the mountains.

Many times, lying awake through the long, frigid nights with the terrible shrieking winds, Jed wondered if Hatcher and the wagons had made it safely across the high mountains on their way west. The cold was so intense he could hear the huge trees along the mountainside cracking and splitting as the cold froze them solid and the heavy snow snapped their big trunks and limbs like twigs. They were constantly at work, keeping the deep drifts of snow cleared away from the cabin door and a clear path to the horse corral.

Finally, the storms had vented their wrath and had blown themselves out. After weeks of keeping them cooped up inside the cabin, the storms finally subsided. Through the long winter days and nights, Wilson and Jed had fought back cabin fever. They dared not venture outside to face the terrible gusting wind, the blowing sleet, and the quick death it could bring. Now with the break-up and the deep cold desisting, letting the ponds and waterways thaw, Jed reset his traps and finished adding to his cache of furs. With the penetrating and terrible cold, the fur bearers had burrowed deep, staying holed up in their dens. Even hungry as they were, the smaller animals were not coming out of their snug burrows. Jed's bales of furs wouldn't be as plentiful as they had in the past, but he still had a respectable amount of prime pelts to trade at Bridger. As soon as the rivers finished their spring runoffs and were passable, it would be time to make their yearly trek to Fort Bridger.

Jed sat before the warm hearth sipping hot coffee and thinking back on the beginning of the vicious storms. He remembered fall had come, but it was still far too early for the harsh winds and snow to begin. Looking to the dark sky, Bright Moon had sensed the impending storm and warned the men of the bad weather approaching and perhaps the severe winter to come. Even the horses seemed nervous as the ominous thick clouds moved in from the northwest. Having learned to listen to her, Jed dropped his axe and grabbed a halter, bridle, and his rifle. Quickly haltering the black mule, Jed swung up on the paint horse and started toward his farthest traps, strung out along the south end of the valley. He was in a race against the elements. He had only a few precious hours to bring in his traps and prepare for the onslaught. Luckily, Ed Wilson was there to help with the horses and stack firewood to the rafters inside the cabin.

He knew Bright Moon was rarely wrong about the weather, but he had no idea the storms would be so severe. Jed had noticed the horses had put on a heavier layer of winter hair than usual. The storms raged unrelenting in their fury for days on end, keeping them trapped inside. The small cabin seemed smaller as stacks of wood completely lined the whole north wall. Before the vicious storm had swept over the valley, Jed had Wilson bring in an immense supply of wood. By storing the wood inside, they wouldn't have to be out in the hard-driving winds and ice, digging the precious life-giving logs from beneath the drifting snow.

Earlier the previous summer, after arriving in the valley, Jed and Wilson had built the farmer his own cabin only a short distance from the main cabin. Finally, they had finished the cabin, then added on a corral and shelter for the cow plus a small barn for her hay. As the storms and heavy winds had built up and screamed across the valley unchecked, Jed had convinced Wilson to bring the livestock into his corrals. With the frigid, blustery winds, it was much too dangerous to walk the short distance to Wilson's corral to feed and water.

For a few days after the norther hit, the men had been able to chop down through the ice to the water, but with each passing day, the task had become much harder. Finally, the deep ice became unbreakable, freezing the creek solid all the way to the bottom. Plus, the walk to the frozen stream was much too dangerous to navigate in the blinding sleet and wind. Just the short distance to the creek would leave their faces and eyes almost frozen, blinding them as their eyebrows became covered in ice. Now, the only way of watering the animals was to thaw snow in copper buckets by sitting them alongside the fireplace. Taking care of the water was a tiring chore, but there was no recourse. Even in the worst of the storm, the horses and the cow had to have the life-giving water.

As he carried water to the animals, Jed grinned when he noticed the black mule and the cow huddled together against the cold. Out of necessity, they had become bosom buddies, leastways they would be until the frigid cold subsided. When Wilson had first turned the cow out on the valley floor with the horses, the little mule endeavored to show the cow who was boss. She would lay her ears back and charge if the cow ventured too close. In the first few days, the farmer had sat on a horse most of the time, protecting his pride and joy. Finally, after the first week, the black mule had given up and seemed to enjoy the cow's company. Jed would laugh as the mule followed docilely when Wilson led the cow into the corral to be milked in the evening. With the wild night animals lurking in the valley, Wilson always kept her locked up safely during the dark hours for her protection and his peace of mind. The little mule and jersey cow had become fast friends, sharing the small corral together.

Jed studied the long stick he had been notching, where each notch represented a day the winds and snow had howled across the valley. For two days, he hadn't made a single notch, the fierce storms were apparently over. Watching the skies, Bright Moon admonished Jed to be careful, telling him to be ever watchful of the building clouds. She feared another storm could strike the valley without warning. Her worries had been partially right, as one last small norther had passed across the valley, but it only lasted for two days, dropping less than six inches of snow across the valley floor. The storms were terrible, but the valley was carpeted beautifully, completely covered in glistening snow and ice. The glare from the valley floor was severe, causing them to squint their eyes against the glare. Many a trapper had learned the hard way, becoming snow blind from the bright rays from not protecting their eyes from the glare.

At last, the snowstorms stopped and most of the deep snow melted with the returning sun. Jed was relieved as the storms had quit none too soon. The stacks of firewood inside the cabin were almost depleted. He had more split wood outside, but to dig it out from under the iced in snowdrifts would have been difficult.

Finally, released from the confinement of the corral, the horses frolicked out on the meadows. Their pent up energy burst from them as they ran and bucked through the deep snow with their new freedom. Wilson fretted as he watched the black mule trying her best to stampede the cow into running with them.

"If this running keeps up, all she'll be giving us is buttermilk." The old farmer sat at the outside log table grumbling over a steaming cup of coffee. "That little mule is a caution."

"She's about gone dry anyway, Pa." Jed laughed as he watched the cow trotting after the mule. "Let 'em have their fun."

"It's no wonder she's about gone dry." Wilson shook his head. "As cold as it was, all the poor thing was giving was ice milk anyway."

"It was downright cold for sure." Jed agreed. "This was a bad winter. I've never seen the likes of these storms."

"Well, Old Beauty will have her calf soon and we'll be swimming in fresh milk again, I reckon." The farmer stated.

"Yes, we will." Jed nodded. "Don't know if it was worth the long ride back to Carter's bull though."

"When you get your belly full of milk, cream, buttermilk, and real gravy, you'll be glad we took her there." Wilson laughed. "I'm sure hoping it's a heifer calf this time."

"What did she have the last few years?"

"Bull calves, every blasted one of them." The farmer shook his head in disgust. "Three in a row now."

"Well, keep your fingers crossed." Jed smiled. "She's long due a heifer this time around."

"I need a plow to plant a small cornfield." Wilson studied the meadow. "Beauty needs grain to give good rich milk."

"You could do that alright, but everything would be eating on it soon as it broke the ground." Jed looked across the valley floor. "Deer, elk, coon, and even the wild horses would eat the corn as soon as it sprouted."

"Reckon you are right about that, boy." Wilson agreed. "Well then, maybe we could pack a few sacks of grain in during the summer."

"I reckon we could do that before trapping season."

"That would be good."

"It sure seems like years ago when she followed the wagon all the way out here." Jed recalled.

"She was just a heifer when we left the east." Wilson nodded sadly. "Hard to believe, she'll be coming on six years this spring."

"She's had a fine calf for you every year."

"Yes, she has." The older man looked out at the horses. He was thankful the cow and all the horses had come through the severe winter in good shape. "What's your plans now?"

"The rivers will be dropping soon. I've got to get my pelts to Bridger." Jed looked worriedly at the cabin door. "They'll bring better prices if they're brought in by early spring."

"And Bright Moon?" Wilson saw the worry in his eyes. "Heavy as she is with child, are you taking her?"

"Got no choice." Jed sipped on his coffee. "I wish there was a woman here, but there ain't."

"You could ride into Baxter Springs and bring Ellie Zeke back." Wilson shrugged. "That's a thought."

"I could do that." Jed nodded quietly. "But no, I was figuring on taking her with me, trade my furs, then take her on to her brother He Dog's village to have her baby."

"You reckon she can make it that far in her condition?" Wilson asked. "Riding horseback is hard on a body, especially a woman heavy with child."

Jed shrugged. "I know, Pa, but Bright Moon says she can make it, and swears she can have the baby by herself with no help."

"Most times women probably can, but sometimes they have complications. By her looks, I don't figure she's got over a month to go." Wilson pointed out. "But, with any female, you can never know for sure about anything."

"That's what she says." Jed replied. "Maybe a month, give or take."

"If you ride hard, there's time enough for you to reach Baxter Springs, ride back with Ellie and still get your furs to Bridger." Wilson suggested.

"No, I'll not leave you alone here with two women unprotected." Jed shook his head and frowned. He hated the thought. He had lost a good friend leaving him alone at the cabin and he wouldn't do it again.

Lately, there hadn't been any trouble in the valley or trespassers since he had killed Bear Claw two summers ago. Since Ed Wilson's arrival, they had enjoyed the peace and serenity of the mountains and the beautiful flower-covered meadows. Hunting, trapping, and just sitting around the cabin smoking their pipes and talking had been happy times for Jed. Walking Horse, Little Antelope, and a few warriors from the Arapaho had come during the warm months. On their last visit, Walking Horse had even talked Red Hawk, the Crow, to come with them. At first, the warrior had declined, saying jokingly that riding with the Arapaho was beneath a Crow's dignity. However, Walking Horse insisted he wanted to hear Red Hawk tell of the great Crow Killer's fight with the mighty Blackfoot Chief Bear Claw. The Arapaho had wanted to hear the story first hand as only Red Hawk could tell it.

The first night after their arrival, Walking Horse and his listening warriors hadn't been disappointed. For over three hours, Red Hawk had given a phenomenal account of the story. Jed could only shake his head as the handsome, charismatic Crow kept the Arapaho warriors transfixed and awestruck with the telling. Other than actually defeating Bear Claw, Jed couldn't remember doing any of the great deeds of valor the warrior spoke of in the oration. Nevertheless, Walking Horse and his warriors were held completely spellbound. They loved the story, hollering for more every time Red Hawk paused. No, he wasn't about to call Red Hawk out about the story.

"You bit the Blackfoot's ear off?" Little Antelope shook her head at some of the outlandish things the warrior told. "Your friend, Red Hawk, still likes to tell tall stories other than the more subtle truth."

Jed grinned. "Surely you don't think he would make up a story like that, do you?"

Throwing back her head, making her long black hair fly, Little Antelope smiled at Bright Moon. "If that Crow's mouth is moving, beware, it is probably a lie."

"I owe that one my life many times." Jed chided her. "Many times, and so do you."

"Yes, I do, but he is still very loose with the truth." The woman smiled. "You would not have bitten off Bear Claw's ear nor scalped him."

"And just why not?"

"Because, Husband, you respected him as a warrior." Bright Moon interrupted. "You may be an Arapaho Lance Bearer, but you are still a civilized man."

"Who says I am civilized, you?" Jed smiled at Bright Moon.

Jed didn't know about being civilized, but Bright Moon was right, he did respect the Blackfoot Bear Claw. The warrior could have taken Jed's life back in the Arapaho village when Jed lay helpless in his sleeping robes, but he hadn't. The night passed in a festive mood as everyone enjoyed the evening. Gathered with his best friends and the ones he loved, around a large fire, the great bear killer was happy and at peace.

"You are not that kind of a man." Bright Moon added, leaning against Jed at the log table. "Not my warrior."

"Well, it's been an entertaining story for our people."

"It is that, alright." Little Antelope smiled. "I do not understand why one such as Red Hawk is not married."

Jed looked to where his friend sat. "Because, his heart is just too wild and his blood lusts for the joy of battle. He still wants to sow more wild oats before he settles down."

"What are wild oats, Husband?" Bright Moon didn't understand Jed's words.

"It's just a white man's saying." Jed laughed. "Red Hawk is as free as the wind and he wants to stay that way. At least for a while yet."

"Wild oats!" Little Antelope frowned. "One day, that one may sow too many of these wild oats."

Jed smiled. Yes, gathered with his friends in his beloved mountains had been a wonderful time in his life. He remembered looking around the table at the laughing warriors and hoped peace would remain in his remote valley.

Bridling the paint horse, Jed took his rifle and rode south, toward the far pass. He needed time alone to think. He had to figure out what would be best for Bright Moon. The days were getting warmer, and to get the best prices for his pelts, he had to travel to Bridger soon, but what should he do with Bright Moon in her condition. He thought of Bate Baker, the fur buyer in Baxter Springs. The settlement was closer where he could trade his furs to the trader there, and Bright Moon would have Ellie and her grandfather to look after her. The thought of doing business with Baker soured his stomach. The man had been partly to blame for Lem Roden's death at the hands of the trapper Rufus Cross and his men. Baker hadn't done the shooting, but he could have given Jed and Roden a warning.

About to kick the paint horse into a lope, Jed reined in as the grey wolf appeared high above him on a ridge. Alone, far out in the valley, their eyes locked momentarily, then the wolf turned and disappeared as suddenly as he had appeared. Jed smiled, since the wolf didn't seem anxious, assuring him there were no enemies, bear or man, nearby. Many times over the last few years, the great wolf was like a sentinel, warning him of imminent danger. Never once had he been wrong. He owed the big grey his life many times over and he would never be harmed in Jed's valley.

Sitting the paint horse alone, far from the cabin, Jed thought back on his days in the high meadows. His mind wandered to the many battles he had fought and the many men he had killed to hold onto his land. He knew the valley had come at a terrible price, but he would kill again if he was ever challenged. White trappers like Abe and Vern, Wet Otter the Pawnee, Small Mountain the Blackfoot, and many others had challenged him and died. It had been their choice to die in these

mountains. Jed had never sought out any of them to do them harm. All
had come to this valley, his valley, to kill the great bear killer. They all
had wanted his power. Now, most of them rested on the tall scaffolds
sitting on the high ridge above that held their bones. The enemy
warriors thought by killing him, they would acquire his powerful medicine of the grizzly. Jed knew the Arapaho's beliefs, but he still couldn't
understand the wild tribe's way of thinking.

Starting to knee the paint forward, his eyes locked onto the fresh
tracks of a grizzly that had passed in the night. Not nearly as large as the
man-hunters had been, but it was still a grizzly. Normally a night stalker,
Jed knew if the opportunity arose for a fresh kill, the grizzly would take
it. Several times, since living in the valley, Jed had found where a bear
had ambushed and taken down a full-grown elk with one mighty swipe
of his paw. He would have to warn his pa of the bear's presence. Old
Beauty, the cow, would be mighty easy pickings if she ventured too far
from the cabin. He wondered, for her safety, perhaps it would be better
to start staking her closer to the cabin and keep her in the corral at night.

The south pass leading over the mountain was free of any sign of
riders. Only the wild horses that roamed the valley had left their tracks
on the ground. Turning back toward the cabin, Jed let the paint set his
own pace as his mind studied on the problem of Bright Moon and his
furs. There were pros and cons between going to Baxter Springs or on
to Fort Bridger where he would receive the best price for the pelts. Bate
Baker was a scoundrel and a thief, and Jed didn't trust the trader nor did
he like the man. If Baker thought Jed had to bring his furs to Baxter
Springs, the wily old trader would give little or nothing for his beaver
pelts. Bridger was tough, but at least he was honest. However, he
wondered if Bright Moon, in her condition, could travel all the way to
Bridger on horseback and then on to her brother's village. He knew her
time was near, but for the terrible winter and late thaw, they would have
already departed to the Cheyenne village.

Bright Moon and the little one were his main concern. They came
first and the furs were secondary. He shook his head as he remembered
the way she argued with him over her strength and ability to ride so far.
He knew his young wife was a full-blooded Cheyenne, a strong and hardy
race of people, but he still worried for her and the unborn child's welfare.

"I am Cheyenne. The little one will be fine." The black eyes had snapped with pride. "Cheyenne!" Those were her final words as she chided him for thinking her weak and unable to make the long ride.

Kicking the paint into a slow lope, Jed had made up his mind. He would take the pelts to Bridger, then ride on with Bright Moon to the Cheyenne village. He hoped his decision was the right one, but even if she got into trouble, Jed knew there would be women at Bridger to help her. Jed knew his step-dad would refuse to go and stay behind to look after the valley and his prized cow. Jed didn't like leaving the farmer at the cabin alone, but there hadn't been any trouble for two summers. He should be safe enough, alone in the valley. Besides, there was no use in arguing with him. The old Irishman was hardheaded and wouldn't change his mind.

After turning the paint loose on the pasture, Jed hung his bridle on a barn peg and sat down at the log table. Thanking Bright Moon for a cup of coffee, he studied the grazing horses, then looked over at the two people who were eagerly awaiting his decision.

"Tomorrow, I will prepare the furs in bundles." Jed toyed with his coffee. "We will leave in two sleeps."

Bright Moon smiled. "Where do we take the furs, my husband?"

"Fort Bridger, then we will ride on to your brother's village." Jed pulled her down beside him. "Are you sure you are up to such a long ride?"

"Yes, I am sure. I still have not forgotten when you would not let me go on the hunt with you after the shaggies last fall because of the little one." Bright Moon turned her beautiful accusing dark eyes on him. "Yes, Husband, both of us will be fine."

"You remember what happened two winters ago?" Jed looked at Wilson. "We got caught in a bad storm and almost didn't make it out of the mountains."

"But, we did make it back to our lodge safely and we will this time." Bright Moon argued. "And, I would also have made it just fine to Turner's Hole last fall, my husband."

"You did your part." Jed smiled. "You made five beautiful coats to take to Bridger this season."

"Perhaps it would have been more if someone hadn't been so hard-headed."

Wilson raised his hand and stopped the bickering. "How many pack animals you gonna need this year, Jed?"

"Probably only four animals this trip, Pa." Jed sipped his coffee. "I'll leave the little mule behind."

"She may not like that." Wilson laughed.

"You'll be alone here so watch her and listen to her and the grey wolf's warnings." Jed didn't like leaving his stepfather behind, but arguing with him was useless. The farmer was determined to stay behind and watch over the valley. "If trouble was to come to the valley, do not fight, hide out in the cave. There are plenty of supplies, powder, and shot cached there."

"It would take an army to dig me out of there."

"It would, providing you get inside behind the rocks." Jed nodded. "You be careful. You hear me? Don't fight for this place."

"I'll be careful, boy." Wilson shrugged. "We've had no trouble since I've been here."

"No, we haven't, but trouble is like a bad dream, it comes when you sleep." Jed cautioned him.

"Then I won't sleep." Wilson laughed.

"And keep a barrel of freshwater in the cave."

"I will, I will." Wilson smiled. "You worry too much, Jed."

"Pa, I don't like leaving you behind." Jed looked around the valley floor. "This is a dangerous land, full of killer animals and warlike tribes. Either of which will attack a defenseless quarry."

"I'll be fine, and I ain't defenseless." Wilson assured him.

Seeing he wasn't going to talk Wilson into coming with them, Jed changed the subject. He told of seeing the tracks of the grizzly further down the valley. "He's not a huge grizzly, but he's big enough to take down the cow."

"I'll stay alert for anything, man or beast." Wilson nodded.

"One last time, you sure you won't change your mind?"

Wilson looked along the tall ridges that lined the flat meadows of the valley and shook his head. "These old eyes are gonna have all this majestic beauty to themselves, and they're gonna enjoy every minute of it."

"Okay, but you sleep with one eye open." Jed admonished him. "Never let your guard down for a minute. Not one minute."

"How long you figure to be gone?"

Jed looked over at Bright Moon and shrugged. "At least a month, maybe two. I just don't know this time."

"Don't you worry none." Wilson smiled. "I'll be just fine, boy."

"Remember, keep freshwater stored in the cave." Jed looked across the table. "Just in case you have to hole up in there a while."

"Quit worrying, Jed." Wilson laughed. "I'll have the mule and the wolf to watch over me."

"I've lost good friends here, Pa. A lot of blood spilled and many bad fights in this valley." Jed nodded thoughtfully. "I can't help but worry."

"Well, you just take care of Bright Moon and the little one. I'll be fine." Wilson assured him. "And when you get back, if old Beauty cooperates, we'll have all the fresh milk the young one can drink."

"Remember, keep your eye out for that young grizzly." Jed warned. "Old Beauty would be a mighty tempting meal for him."

"It'll be over my dead body and probably the mule's too… the way they've taken to each other." Wilson looked to where the Jersey cow and little mule were side by side grazing contentedly.

Dawn broke over the eastern summit of the high peaks as Jed examined the cinches of the pack animals with their heavy bundles of furs. Softening Bright Moon's saddle with two extra blankets, he averted his eyes as she looked daggers at him.

"That ought to keep you comfortable." Wilson straightened out the soft trade blankets. "Yes, ma'am, just like riding in a rocking chair."

"I am not a child." Bright Moon glared at the farmer then grinned as she hugged him. "You be careful, my father. This is a dangerous land."

"I'll keep my eyes peeled."

"And remember the call of the grey one." She urged Wilson. Bright Moon had come to think of him as she would her own father. "He will always warn you if anyone comes into the valley."

Wilson nodded. "I believe you. Jed said the wolf and the mule make a good team."

"You ready?" Jed lifted the woman easily into the saddle.

"We're ready, my husband." Bright Moon shifted in the saddle to get comfortable.

Seeing Jed shake his head, Wilson asked. "What's the matter, son?"

"She's heavy." Looking up at the woman, Jed smiled. "I believe she's getting fat."

Frowning down from the Appaloosa, Bright Moon pointed to the paint. "Husband, you are not funny. Let's go if we are going."

"We're going." Jed shook hands with Wilson and looked across the valley. "Stay safe, Pa. I'll get back as soon as I can."

Swinging up on the paint, Jed gripped the lead rope and started the pack train toward the north pass. Leaving the cabin always made him sad. The beautiful valley was his home, and Jed would never leave this land. The mountains and valley had laid claim to him, and he was part of it now. He had shed his blood and even killed men to protect the valley and if forced, he would kill again to hold onto it. Reining in, before passing out of sight of the cabin, Jed and Bright Moon turned and waved back at Wilson.

The morning was beautiful. The fresh new grass had already greened up the meadows and the warm weather had budded the hardwood trees. The freezing weather had left a scar along the mountainside with a string of downed trees and broken limbs from the cold. As always, time would eventually erase the wounds with the coming new life. Even a few new flowers had sprung up already across the meadows.

"Will he be alright, my husband?" Bright Moon asked as they rode away from the cabin. "He will be alone and he seems sad."

"I think he'll be okay." Jed looked back to where Wilson stood in front of the cabin. "But, with the young one coming, we have no choice. We have to get you to your brother's village."

"This is true, Husband." Bright Moon smiled. "And if we sit here talking, we will never get there."

"Yes, ma'am, you are right." Jed nudged the paint. "Let's ride."

Topping out over the north pass, Jed reined in long enough to let the horses blow. Having done nothing all winter, the horses were soft. Carrying two bundles of heavy furs up the steep pass, each weighing a hundred pounds, had the horses blowing. The animals had come out of the terrible winter a little thin, but they were still in good flesh. With only hay to eat, they had grown grass bellies. Hay alone would keep their bodies filled out, but the hay had little strength in it. Jed only wished he had corn to feed them to slick them off. Wilson was right about the corn for the cow. The dry grass of the valley would keep her from starving, but she needed grain to help her give rich milk. Looking down at the valley from high up, Jed could see the cow and mule with several other horses grazing peacefully far below. At this great distance, the grazing animals appeared tiny. For now, everything seemed peaceful, and he hoped it would stay that way in his absence.

The trip into Fort Bridger had taken two days longer than usual. With Bright Moon's condition, Jed had kept the days short, not wanting to tire the woman. Only her dark eyes spoke as he reined in and lifted her from the spotted horse.

"The way you are riding, it will take us all summer to reach the trader's post."

Jed looked at the small stream and motioned. "Sit down over there while I unpack the horses."

"I will build a fire." Bright Moon started gathering dead limbs.

"I will do that." Jed tried to take the wood from her.

Jerking away, Bright Moon frowned at him. "A warrior does not do woman's work."

"But." He looked down at her bulging stomach.

Smiling, she placed her hand on his arm. "I am okay, Husband. I told you, Cheyenne women are strong."

"Okay, hard head, I'll unsaddle and hobble the animals."

She rolled her eyes. "Yes, you unsaddle the horses."

Fort Bridger hadn't changed as Jed and Bright Moon passed through the lodges that dotted the outskirts of the post, and then through the log gate. Reining in at the tie rail, Jed dismounted and lifted Bright Moon from the spotted horse.

A lone hunter had already alerted the trading post of the arrival of the great Arapaho Lance Bearer. Out hunting, he had spotted them earlier and raced back to the stockade with the news. Crow Killer had always been both a spectacle and a curiosity wherever he showed up. Waiting outside to greet the warrior known as Crow Killer throughout the tribes, Alex Caldwell blinked in shock, then smiled as he took in the tall Cheyenne woman.

"Jed Bracket, it's good to see you and Bright Moon." The trader smiled. "Well now, it looks like we'll be greeting a new little one before the month is out."

"Mister Caldwell." Jed shook the extended hand and looked over at Bright Moon. "Yes, I expect we will."

Caldwell looked over at the four horses and the heavy packs. "I'm surprised your trapping was so good, with the bad winter we had."

"Yes, sir, the winter was a real tomcat for a fact." Jed agreed, as he helped Bright Moon onto the porch. "Not quite as many furs as we took last season, but we managed to snare a few good ones."

"I'm afraid the other trappers hereabout weren't near as fortunate as you were." Caldwell shook his head. "It was a mighty mean winter."

"It was a bad couple months for a fact." Jed agreed. "Does that mean my plews will fetch a little more this season?"

"Yes, I imagine we'll have to pay a little more for them." Caldwell laughed. "We definitely won't have near as many bundles to take back east to St. Louis this season."

"Well, your misfortune seems to be my good fortune."

"May I take Bright Moon in and make her comfortable?" Caldwell held out his hand. "I know she's had a long trip in her condition. You and my clerks can see to the sorting of your pelts."

"Thank you, Mister Caldwell." Jed nodded. "I'd appreciate that."

Caldwell smiled at Bright Moon. "You're even prettier than you were last year, little lady."

"No, Mister Caldwell, I am the same woman." Bright Moon looked at the storeman, then back at Jed. "Just fatter as some say."

"Prettier." Caldwell laughed. "Don't argue with an old man."

"The beaver… same price as last year?" Jed interrupted the argument.

"Same price this year, but we'll talk about next year's prices when we get through dickering over these." Caldwell spoke over his shoulder as he led Bright Moon into the store. "But, for now, I'm gonna get our guest of honor a comfortable chair and a good meal."

"Thank you, sir." Jed smiled. The post trader had always had a softness when it came to Bright Moon. Several times, he had told of knowing her and Little Antelope since they were in a cradleboard on their mother's back.

Helping the clerks inside with the heavy bundles, Jed watched as the two young men sorted and graded the pelts. Stepping through a side door into the living quarters, Jed found Bright Moon sitting in a hide chair, eating happily on a bowl of peaches and cream. Returning to the clerks as they finished their tally of his pelts, Jed took the offered paper.

Caldwell walked over and studied the paper, then nodded his head. "Suits me, if it does you, Jed? I paid a little extra like I said."

"I'll settle for your offer." The dark eyes looked at the trader. "I'm thanking you, Mister Caldwell."

"Good, good." Caldwell smiled happily. Each season, Jed always brought in prime furs. They were softer and better cured than any others coming into the trading post. Bridger always snapped and growled at what he called a ridiculous price given for the pelts, but he knew they were prime furs that would bring him a good profit in the east. "Now, Jed, you'll be needing supplies I reckon?"

"That we will." Jed acknowledged. "My usual order, plus I'll be needing five new rifles, and extra powder and shot for the Cheyenne."

"And the Arapaho?"

"Yes, sir, and the Arapaho."

"I guess you've heard Chief Slow Wolf passed this last fall?" Caldwell looked to see Jed's reaction.

"Yes, Walking Horse sent word by Big Owl and several others before the bad weather hit the high passes." The dark head nodded sadly. "Slow Wolf was a great chief. I owe him my life."

"I met him a couple times, and yes, he was a proud and honorable warrior." Caldwell agreed.

"He was at that." Jed nodded. "I wish I could have seen him one last time before he went to be with his ancestors."

"Who is the chief of the Arapaho now?"

"Walking Horse." Jed thought of his friend. "He's the hereditary chief of the Arapaho now."

"Oh yes, a great warrior himself." Caldwell piled flour, sugar, coffee, cans of peaches, lead and powder on the plank counter. "I've met him a few times. The last time being when you and Jean Leblew tied into each other, two summers ago."

"He will be as great a chief as he is a warrior." Jed thought of the warrior. "He is my brother and my friend."

"I believe you." Caldwell remembered the looks Walking Horse had given him as they brought the wounded Jed into the trading post. He knew the hard look the warrior gave him meant nothing had better happen to Crow Killer. "Yes, sir. I'll bet he can be a rough one."

"Has any Cheyenne come in yet this spring?"

"No, sir, haven't seen hide nor hair of them so far." Caldwell shook his head. "You headed there when you leave here?"

"I'll be taking Bright Moon to her brother's village where the women can see after her."

"Good idea." Caldwell agreed. "I've heard of them giving birth alone, but I don't cotton to that idea. That is, was I you."

"Neither would I." Jed looked through the door where Bright Moon had fallen asleep in the chair. "At first, I thought to take her to Baxter Springs so Ellie and her grandfather could look after her."

Caldwell snapped his fingers. "Doggone, Jed, I plumb forgot to tell you. There's a young man over at McGraws waiting for you to show up."

"Another one? Is he looking for a fight like Leblew was?"

"No, he says Elizabeth Zeke sent him. Says he has a message for you."

Jed looked again to where Bright Moon was sleeping peacefully. "You say he's over at the blacksmith shop?"

"Yes, sir, that's where he's been camped out, waiting for you to come in." Caldwell nodded. "Been here pert near a week now."

"Tally my supplies. I'll be back and we'll settle up." Jed trusted Caldwell. The trader had always treated him fairly. "And don't forget, toss in five more fifty-caliber rifles."

"I haven't forgotten, I'll add them in." Caldwell was uncomfortable as he looked over at Jed. "One other thing, Jed."

"Yes, sir."

"This year I'm giving you full price as we agreed to last year for your beaver plews, but next year it will probably be only half." Caldwell shook his head. "There's not many buyers hankering for beaver skins these days."

"That all?"

"The other furs will still be practically the same." Caldwell nodded, as he stroked the soft furs. "Especially these prime buffalo coats, they are beautiful."

"Alright, that seems fair enough to me." Jed agreed. "I'll be back after I see this fella that's looking for me."

"I'll get a good hot meal in her when she wakes up."

Nodding, Jed turned toward the blacksmith shop across the post's grounds. The loss of the beaver prices would be hurtful, but he would survive. Every trapping season, he had swapped out what his beaver plews brought in to buy the supplies he needed to carry him over the long winter and throughout the year. The gold and silver coins he had received from his other furs were hidden back in the cave behind his cabin. He had never touched a single coin from his cache. He wasn't worried about money, since living in the valley didn't take spending money, just a store of supplies. His meat came from the elk, buffalo, and smaller animals that roamed the valley and mountains. There was plenty of fresh meat. Only flour, salt, sugar, powder, and other staples had to be procured from the trading post. No, even without the money from the beaver, they would be just fine.

Busy shoeing a horse, Otis McGraw looked up to find Jed standing only a few feet away, watching him. Dropping the horse's foreleg, the old hostler reached out his hand.

"Goodness gracious, Jed. You gave me a start." McGraw grinned as he pumped away at Jed's powerful hand. "You're a sight for sore eyes, boy."

"Sorry, Otis, didn't mean to startle your old ticker." Jed smiled. "It's good to see you too."

"Dang it, lad, you tiptoe around like an Injun." McGraw looked around. "Shucks, you are an Injun. Where's my mule?"

"I didn't bring her this time."

"Why not, she crippled or something?"

"No, sir. She's baby-sitting."

"Baby-sitting what? I know she can't have a foal." McGraw laid down the hoof rasp he had been using.

Jed grinned. "She's baby-sitting a jersey cow back in the valley."

"A cow?" McGraw scratched his chin. "Now, ain't that a waste of a good mule?"

Jed changed the subject. He knew the old hostler would talk about the little mule all day. Why McGraw was so taken with the animal, was a curiosity to him. "Mister Caldwell says there's a man waiting around here to see me."

"Man no, but there's a young'un waiting. He's asleep in there." McGraw pointed his thumb toward a stall. "He's been staked out waiting on you to show yourself for pert near a week."

"Asleep this time of day?"

"This ones an odd critter for sure." The shoulders of the old one shrugged. "He roams the place most of the night like a stalking cat. Sleeps mostly in the daylight hours."

"Is this one trouble for me, Otis?" Jed looked around. "Like Leblew?"

The big head shook. "Nah, I don't think so. He's just a big kid."

Jed looked over at the stall. "Roust him out, Otis. Let's take a look at this young man."

CHAPTER 2

Jed watched as the slender youngster extricated himself from the stall, kicking blankets away from his entangled feet. The boy was indeed young, probably still in his late teens. The dirty and wrinkled store-bought clothes, covering his stocky frame, showed he was a town dweller. The brown hair of the man had grown long, but there was no sign of any facial hair. Rubbing his eyes clear as he quietly followed McGraw toward Jed, the youngster stopped a few feet from where the buckskin-clad figure stood.

"You awake, young fellow?" Jed studied the sleepy figure. "Understand you've been waiting for me. Why?"

"Yes, sir. I am, if you're Jed Bracket that is." The youngster looked Jed up and down closely. "I've been waiting for you nigh on a week or more."

"Why?" Jed repeated. "What do you need me for?"

"Miss Elizabeth Zeke sent me here to fetch you."

"Miss Ellie?" Jed looked at the youngster. "What's your name?"

"Dibbs Bacon."

"And Ellie wants me to come into Baxter Springs?" Jed studied the youngster. "Is that it?"

"Yes, sir. She said for you to come as soon as you can." Dibbs nodded. "She sent me here, figuring you'd be bringing your furs to Bridger about this time of year."

"Well, tell me, Dibbs, do you know what she wants me for?"

"No, sir, Mister Bracket. I didn't ask." Dibbs shook his head. "She didn't say a word about nothing."

"I'm running late this year." Jed studied the youngster. "Tell me, what if I'd passed on through the post and headed for the Cheyenne villages?"

"Well, sir, then I reckon I would have tracked you down there."

"You're awfully young to be out there on your own, ain't you?" Jed was curious about the young lad.

"I'd say that was one man's opinion." The voice hardened. "One opinion I don't hold with."

Jed looked over at the trader's store, trying to hide his smile, then turned his attention back to the youth. "You ride on back and tell her I'll come into Baxter Springs just as quick as I can."

"I'll have to tell her something." Dibbs shrugged. "Any idea how long you'll be?"

"Just tell her I'll come as quick as I can get there." Jed assured him. "But, I've got pressing business to take care of first."

"I'll tell her." Shrugging, Dibbs turned. "Reckon, I'll get my horse and head back."

"How old are you, Dibbs?"

"Seventeen, I think." The youngster replied. "My age, it's kinda like my name."

"What do you mean?" Jed was curious.

"My folks were killed by the Blackfoot." Dibbs explained. "John Bacon, an old Indian scout, found me squalling under my folks burnt out wagon."

"Sounds like you were lucky."

"I was, only got me a few burn scars to show for the ordeal." Dibbs frowned. "Papa John raised me until his death last year."

"Sorry."

"It's okay, he went the way he wanted." Dibbs continued. "He always said he wanted to escape this old earth while he could still get around on his own."

"You saying he did?"

"Yep, he did." The youngster nodded. "His old ticker gave out one day without any warning."

"And the name?"

"He told me I got the name when he and Rollie Long flipped a coin." Dibbs laughed. "He said he didn't know who my folks were, so I was up for dibs on the flip of a coin. So, that's what he called me."

"Why would this Long fellow want a baby still in swaddling clothes?"

"Rollie Long was a free trapper. He had a Cheyenne woman with him who mended my burns and wet-nursed me while I was still a babe. Well, she up and took a shine to me."

"You know anything about the Cheyenne woman?"

Dibbs shook his head. "No, just her name, Wyonette."

"Wyonette? They still looking after you?" Jed asked.

"Yes, sir, that was her name." Dibbs nodded. "But nope, they're both dead. Killed by the Metis and Cree down from the north."

"Same time your pa was done for?"

"No, sir, a little earlier, I reckon."

"My name's Jed, not sir." Jed looked over at McGraw. "You're pretty young to be riding so far alone."

"Don't let these clothes fool you, mister. I'm old enough." The slate grey eyes narrowed. "After Papa John passed, I drifted into Baxter Springs and went to work for Miss Ellie. She dressed me in these store-bought clothes. Said buckskins weren't civilized."

"Sounds like Ellie alright."

"I was filthy, and she was being nice without embarrassing me, I reckon." Dibbs shrugged. "I found you, didn't I?"

"Yes, you did. Tell Ellie that I'll be along quick as I can."

"I'll tell her." Dibbs turned to a nearby stall. "I'll be seeing you."

Jed took a second look at the young man as he led his horse from the corral. Perhaps he had been too quick to pronounce judgment on the lad. At first glance, he had overlooked the strong muscular frame and the easy stride Dibbs had when he walked. He didn't know anything about the youngster, except he wasn't a town kid. The easy way he mounted the horse, the Hawken rifle resting across his saddle, the long skinning knife, and the cold hard look. No, Dibbs Bacon may dress like a store clerk, but except for his youth, he moved, rode, and spoke like a true mountain man. Jed had been around Lige Hatcher and men like him many times. Dibbs was young, but he already had the stamp of a hard man with cold, sharp grey eyes. Jed knew the youngster was still young, but Dibbs Bacon could be a dangerous man.

Returning to where Bright Moon was resting in a rope-back chair, Jed looked down into her pretty face. Caldwell brought her out a cool glass of water and smiled at Jed.

"You hungry, Jed?"

"No, Mister Caldwell, we need to be moving on as soon as we get the horses packed."

"The youngster bring bad news?"

Jed shrugged. "I don't know, but it seemed urgent."

Looking over at Bright Moon and her condition, Caldwell shook his head. "What will you do with Bright Moon?"

"My plans haven't changed. I'll take her on to the Cheyenne village where she will have help with the baby."

"It's still a far piece to the south. Can she ride that far?" Caldwell asked.

"She'll make it okay." Jed looked down at her. "Leastways, that's what she says."

"I'll make it husband if you don't talk Mister Caldwell to death before we get going."

"Yes, ma'am, we're leaving."

Jed loaded the horses as the supplies were carried from the post. Five new, freshly oiled Hawken rifles were wrapped in canvas to keep the night dew from rusting them. Caldwell handed Jed a heavy bag of coins that he dropped into his side pouch.

"Over the last few seasons, you've done well, Jed." The trader smiled. "I hope you continue to do so, and I hope to see you next spring."

"We'll be back." Jed nodded. "You can count on it."

"You take care of the little lady." Caldwell looked at Bright Moon. "She's very special."

"That I will."

"And remember, about the beaver plews."

"I'll remember."

"It's a shame the shining times are finished." Caldwell wagged his head. "Those were the golden times, a real mountain man's times."

"The shining times aren't finished, Mister Caldwell, just the beaver trade is all." Jed smiled. "We've still got plenty of good times ahead."

"Not to hear Jim Bridger tell it." Caldwell laughed. "To him, life ended back a few years."

"Maybe so, I reckon the rest of us will have to make out the best we can."

"The mountains were untamed back then. We were as free as the wind to ride and hunt wherever we wanted." Caldwell nodded. "Now, look at me, trapped in this post like a caged bird."

"You can still hunt."

"Nope, I've had my wings clipped. These old bones are too old now to go riding around these mountains."

"Well, you take care of them bones, Mister Caldwell."

"Good luck to you, Jed, and to you, little lady." Caldwell smiled at Bright Moon.

"And you, sir."

Lifting Bright Moon gently onto the spotted horse's back, Jed swung up on the paint. Looking down where Caldwell and McGraw stood outside the trading post, Jed nodded, then turned the horses toward the gate. Without being laden with the heavy fur bales the horses stepped out smartly. All four of the horses Jed led were loaded with supplies they'd need for the coming year. The heavy pouch of gold coins, payment for the year's take of furs, rested in a leather pouch hanging from Jed's shoulder. Passing back through the gates, Jed reined in as an older squaw stepped in front of the paint.

"Does not Crow Killer remember me?"

"I remember you, Elk Woman. One does not forget the mother of the Silent One."

The Assiniboine squaw pretended to be looking at Bright Moon's swollen stomach. "Your woman is heavy with child, Crow Killer."

"What does Elk Woman wish?" Jed asked her.

"Leave your Cheyenne squaw here at the post. She will be safe with Bridger." The squaw looked nervously about as other women and warriors started to gather. "She is too heavy with child to ride far."

"Speak plainly, woman." Jed looked down at the old woman.

Lowering her voice, Elk Woman whispered. "Danger awaits Crow Killer before he reaches the land of the Cheyenne. I tell you this because you were a good friend of my son, the Silent One."

"Tell me."

"Even a Cheyenne in her condition cannot ride a horse fast enough to escape your enemies."

Jed stared down at the squaw. "What enemies?"

"Two bad white men and several warriors rode from the village last night, after dark came over the land."

"Assiniboine?"

"No, these are Pawnee dogs who live many sleeps south of here."

"Pawnee!" The word leaped out of Jed's mouth unexpectedly. "What are Pawnee doing this far north at Bridger?"

"Two whites brought them here from the south to attack you." Elk Woman warned. "They bragged about taking your scalp all over the village."

"Who were the whites?"

"Hunters is all I know, Crow Killer, and now they hunt you."

"How many warriors?"

"Maybe eight, maybe more." The old squaw shrugged. "I saw eight is all."

"Thank you, Elk Woman. Do they know where I ride to?" Jed asked.

"Yes, they know. One of the white hunters overheard you speaking with the trader Caldwell." The old squaw continued. "He followed you inside the post and listened to your words."

"Hunters from the south." Jed was curious. He thought there had been a peace pact made with the Pawnee Nation.

"I cannot speak more." Elk Woman patted Bright Moon's knee. "Leave her, Crow Killer. You cannot fight these dogs and protect this child at the same time."

Shaking his head, Jed thanked the woman. "Go to Bridger if you need anything. Tell him to put it on my bill."

"He will not believe me. I am just an Assiniboine squaw."

"Here, take these." Jed reached into the coin sack and handed her two double eagles. "He'll believe them. If you need more, tell him."

"Thank you, Crow Killer." Elk Woman dropped her eyes. "May the great spirits protect my son's friend."

"No, Elk Woman, it is I who thank you."

"Ride with caution and look to the woman." Elk Woman smiled as she stepped back. No one had seen the exchange of the coins. "She is a beautiful girl, for a Cheyenne, and she carries the blood of Crow Killer, the greatest of the Lance Bearers."

Again, Jed had to worry about the trail ahead. In Bright Moon's condition, he didn't dare push the horses hard. Heavy jolting in the saddle would not be good for her or the baby. Nor could he run the horses to escape in the event of an attack. He had to keep a close lookout for ambush and hoped to see his enemies before they could get close enough to shoot. At the first clear creek they crossed, Jed slid from the paint and helped Bright Moon from the Appaloosa. Wrapped up, on the packsaddles, were five new Hawken rifles he had bought for Walking Horse, He Dog, and Crazy Cat. Unwrapping the weapons, Jed checked their flints, then loaded each rifle except for the priming pan. Bright Moon's smaller thirty caliber Hawken rifle, fully loaded and primed, hung from her saddle.

"Why do you load the rifles, Husband?"

"We may have trouble ahead of us." Jed studied the trail ahead as far as he could see. "See to your rifle, Bright Moon."

Bright Moon looked to where he was working. "The Assiniboine squaw at the trading post warned you of this?"

"Yes, she says Pawnee warriors rode from the post late last night."

"The Pawnee is a tribe south of Cheyenne lands." Bright Moon looked out across the near valley. "How many?"

"Seven or eight." Jed rehung the weapons. "And two white men."

"Only eight? Then we will kill them if they attack."

Jed laughed. "It'll be two against ten."

"No, Husband, three against ten." Bright Moon patted her stomach. "The Pawnee are women, not warriors."

"Hopefully, they'll just ride back to their country, but I doubt it." Jed thought of the whites.

"What did the man at the stable come to see you about?"

Jed wasn't aware Bright Moon knew of the rider who had been sent for him. "Medicine Thunder has asked that I come to Baxter Springs."

"My sister sends for you?"

"Yes."

"Then you must go. Perhaps she has much trouble." Bright Moon looked behind her. "We could ride to the white village of Baxter Springs."

"No, it is farther away now and we don't know yet if the Pawnee wait for us or not."

"If you rode there you would know what my sister wants."

"Not until you have had the baby, then I will go there." Jed shook his head.

"The baby could still be a month away from coming." Bright Moon argued. "She might need you now. She would not have sent a rider all the way here if it were not so."

"Maybe so, woman, but first you will have the baby. We will speak no more of this."

Jed remembered the big Pawnee that had killed Bow Legs back on the Blue River and Wet Otter, the Pawnee who had led his warriors to Jed's valley to attack him. Bright Moon was wrong about them being women. The warriors from the south may not be as mighty in battle as the Arapaho or Cheyenne, but they were still dangerous enemies. Alone, Jed knew he could outrun or outfight them, but with Bright Moon heavy with child, flight wasn't an option. He was worried, and right now, his only choice was to push forward toward He Dog's village with caution and hope for the best. If the Pawnee planned to attack them, they would know where he was headed and would let them get far away from Bridger before attacking. They would not incur the old trapper's wrath by breaking his law.

The afternoon passed quickly as the sun sank slowly in the west. Jed reined into the same small canyon where he had camped in his first trip through these lands three years before. The difference was, this time he didn't have the small black mule with him for a watchdog. After she had led them home safely in the heavy storm from their buffalo hunt in Turner's Hole, he had sworn never to take a trip away from the canyon without her. He regretted leaving her but had intentionally left her to stay behind with his stepfather for his protection. The little mule was a caution for sure, nothing slipped by her without being seen or heard.

Piling his packs and packsaddles behind a large boulder, protruding from the canyon wall, Jed hobbled the horses on the lush valley grass behind him out of harm's way. No enemy would be able to slip in to steal the horses or stampede them into flight without being spotted. Gathering dead limbs to start a fire, Jed pushed last winter's dead grass away from his old campfire. As the fire lit up and started to burn, Jed looked toward the entrance of the canyon. From this vantage point, he had a good field of fire, if he and Bright Moon were attacked in the dark. He knew from the mouth of the canyon, his fire could be spotted, but it couldn't be helped. Bright Moon needed a hot meal and the fire for warmth.

The cloaking darkness and silence engulfed them as they finished their food and settled in for the night. After getting Bright Moon in her robes and warmed, Jed put out the campfire. He wanted his eyes adjusted to the dark. The glow of the fire would diminish his night vision, and his eyes wouldn't be as sharp if he looked into the flames, even for a second. He knew it was a human weakness to stare into the welcoming blaze of a fire. Priming the rifles, Jed stood them with Bright Moon's rifle against the boulder that sheltered them from the canyon entrance.

"The Pawnee will not attack in the dark of night." Bright Moon pulled her blanket over her as she watched Jed preparing. "They fear the dark spirits."

Jed nodded solemnly. "No, but they could be here with the coming of daybreak when the spirits depart the land."

"That would be very foolish, Husband." Bright Moon smiled. "The cowards would not dare ride against the great Crow Killer in full daylight."

"Doesn't anything bother you?" Jed shook his head in exasperation. The woman didn't know the meaning of fear.

"Only of losing you, my husband." She laughed lightly. "That is all this one worries about."

"And not the Pawnee?"

"They are no different from the Paiute back at the big river." Bright Moon shrugged. "Against an Arapaho Lance Bearer, they are nothing."

"I'm so glad you're not overconfident." Jed set the last rifle against the boulder, then poured himself a cup of coffee. "If they attack, you can tell them they should fear me."

"I am Cheyenne, you are Arapaho." Bright Moon touched her stomach. "This one will be the mightiest of warriors. None will be his equal, Spotted Panther has seen it in the stars."

Jed grinned at the woman. "You seem sure it will be a boy."

"I am sure. The elders of our lodges said it would be so, and it will."

"You haven't even been to your village in a year. How could they tell you anything?" Jed questioned her.

"Long before you came into my life, I was told this by Spotted Panther, the greatest of our medicine men." Bright Moon explained. "He has never read the stones or the smoke wrong."

"Oh really!" Jed remembered his own, prophecy. The old medicine man White Swan had told him of his future and most had come true. Somehow, these old ones were wise men with telepathic vision who could somehow foretell the future.

"Yes, he said the boy's name would be Eagle's Wing."

Jed had seen it rain on a hot summer day exactly as the Arapaho Medicine Man had predicted. Looking at the woman curiously, he wondered at the many times, he had seen things predicted by the old ones of the tribes that didn't seem possible, but their prophecies had come true.

"Go to sleep, Bright Moon. Tomorrow will be a long day for you and the little one." Jed took his rifle and slipped around the boulder. "You will need your strength."

The night passed quietly. Only the sounds of night birds or the far-off call of the wily coyotes were heard from where Jed sat and watched throughout the night. Staring up at the huge starlit heavens, he watched the fiery path of a burning meteor as it plummeted toward the earth. Even in his youth, he had always been comfortable with the night cloaking him in darkness. The brilliant stars as they covered the sky above him and lit up the night were majestic. He remembered when he was young, his mother pointed out the different stars and constellations, telling him their names. Her death, back on the western trail, had been a great loss to Jed. A shock that still weighed heavily on his heart during the nighttime when the stars, she had told him about, sent out their glimmering lights.

Only the occasional snort of a horse as it cleared its nose came from the grazing animals. Jed had never scouted out the small canyon, but He Dog had told him the walls of the canyon were impassable. The entrance he had come through was the only way in or out of the small canyon.

Daybreak found Jed kneeling down cooking a hot breakfast before starting for He Dog's village. Bright Moon was now eating for two and needed a hot meal before they rode out of the canyon. If the village hadn't been moved, it would be a hard two day's ride before they reached it. Jed tried to remember the trail leading south and west toward the Cheyenne Camp. If confronted, ten to one odds would be hard to overcome, but he swore she would not be harmed. There weren't enough Pawnee out there to get past him while he lived.

Walking cumbersomely to where he knelt over the fire, she looked down at him. "It is not warrior's work to cook our meals."

"Just this once." Jed handed her a plate of fried bread and side meat. "You will need all your strength today."

"You think they are out there?"

"I don't know." Jed chewed on his food. "It doesn't matter. If they are they are. If not, we'll have a pleasant ride to your brother's village."

"Maybe they just left the trading post and are not after us at all." Bright Moon took the cup of steaming coffee from Jed. "Perhaps, the Assiniboine woman was wrong."

"Perhaps, let's hope it is so." Jed felt it and knew the Pawnee and whites would be waiting, but he didn't see the need to worry her.

Bright Moon knew she had false hope before the words left her mouth. The Pawnee knew Crow Killer would be a great coup if they could defeat him in battle. Plus, they had probably watched as he carried the rifles and supplies from the trader's post. She knew they would have spotted their horses. The paint horse, the Appaloosa, and even the Pawnee horse, that once belonged to Wet Otter, were in the string of horses Jed had brought to carry his furs. These were some of the most beautiful horses in the land. To steal them from Crow Killer and ride them for all to see would be a great honor and bring much glory to any warrior. Their hate for the Arapaho Lance Bearer was great. He had killed Wet Otter and humiliated the ones that followed the Pawnee Chief to the great valley in the mountains. Now, he was almost in their grasp, leading Wet Otter's horse would be a slap in their face. Bright Moon knew they would have instantly recognized the bay horse of Wet Otter as they entered Bridger's Post. They would be filled with hatred for Crow Killer. Now, they would come for the horse, their pride, and revenge.

Far from his valley lair and closer to the Pawnee villages would give them the encouragement to attack and kill the great bear killer. Bright Moon knew once the Pawnee saw he was encumbered by a pregnant woman, they would think the signs favored them. They would have the Arapaho warrior alone, without help, and now, would be the time to attack.

The horses were caught, saddled, and loaded with their precious cargo of food and supplies for the coming year. Jed lifted Bright Moon onto the spotted one, then handed her the Hawken rifle. Strapping another rifle across his back with his bow and lance, he held his own rifle on his lap as he swung on the paint. The other four rifles hung on the packsaddle of a near horse, in an easily reached place. Kneeing the paint horse, Jed led the small caravan out onto the trail and continued to the southwest. All morning, Jed kept the horses at an easy walk as he scanned the trail closely for any sign of ambush. If he could spot the Pawnee before they came close, maybe he could even the odds some. Along the trails, the valley grasses were still short from the harsh winter, making it hard for an enemy to conceal themselves.

Nearing another small creek, as the sun stood almost overhead, Jed reined in and studied the nearby trees and brush before helping Bright Moon from the horse. None of the horses alerted or showed any sign of another animal as they swigged deeply of the cold water. Jed shook his head as he stood waiting within reach of the horse carrying the rifles. He trusted the paint's natural instincts, but he still wished the mule was with them. The mule was like a bloodhound and could smell out anything on the trail ahead. Jed had never seen her keen sense of hearing and smell equaled in any horse. Silent One had sworn the mule could smell the breath of a mosquito before it bit her.

The Cheyenne village of He Dog lay clustered along the banks of a large tree-covered valley. Brightly painted lodges lay scattered, dotting the flat valley. The Cheyenne called this place the flint land, a place they came to make their flint arrowheads. Heavy walls of flint, granite, and other rocks lined the valley. Smoke floated high above the village, drifting with the prevailing wind. Warriors, women, and children moved through the village. The children busy at play while the women were busy with their chores. The hunts had been highly successful for the village as the meat racks were heavily laden with deer and elk carcasses. Strips of fresh meat hung drying, curing in the sun. Dried meat that would be needed badly with the coming days until the time for hunting the shaggies came again.

Several warriors rode their horses through the village, patrolling and watching closely over the people. Since Yellow Dog's death, at the hands of the hated Arickaree, He Dog had become chief, and the village had become closely guarded. Not even a fox could move anywhere near the village without being detected. He Dog was still very young, but since attacking the Ree and returning to the village, he had quickly matured, becoming a disciplined and well-respected leader of his people.

After watching him dispatch the huge Ree, no warrior disputed his word when he gave an order. The yellow horse, He Dog had taken from the Ree, still carried the dried scalp of the dead warrior braided into its mane. All who looked at the face of He Dog knew he had become hardened, a great warrior and killer of his enemies. When an order was given, the young chief meant to be obeyed. Sentries were posted every minute of the day and night far from the village. No enemy could ride against them without being spotted before they could get close. The threat of an Arickaree retaliation for the raid on their village was foremost in He Dog's mind.

Several warriors sat in a circle laughing with the young chief when two horses raced through the camp, reining in hard beside the group. Two young warriors slid from their blowing horses and walked to where He Dog had risen from his backrest.

"Our chief, as you have ordered, we watched the trails north of our village. We have followed eight warriors of the Pawnee and two white hunters to the trader's post of Bridger." The taller scout motioned quickly with his hands as he spoke. "Then we watched as they left the post with the two whites and started back to their lands to the south."

"We followed them, but the Pawnee never looked for tracks on the trail, they seemed to be intent on something else." The other scout spoke up. "They were concerned about something and several times, they sent a rider back to watch the trail."

"Did you see Crow Killer and my sister Bright Moon?"

"No, my chief. We rode as close as we dared to the trader's post, but we did not see them from where we watched." The taller warrior Grey Fox shrugged. "Your orders, my chief, we were not to be discovered near the post."

"You have done well, Grey Fox." He Dog nodded. "How far are these Pawnee away from here?"

"They move slowly, maybe a day's ride to the east."

"You have done well. Go eat and rest."

"Yes, my chief." The two young warriors nodded and walked away.

"I am curious." Crazy Cat watched as the two men retreated. "The Pawnee rarely go to Bridger to trade."

"Their villages are far to the south." Another warrior spoke up. "Do you think they go to find Crow Killer?"

"Why would they do this?" Crazy Cat shook his head, then looked at He Dog for an answer. "Why would they seek out Crow Killer?"

In council, the young chief always thought out any problem before giving his opinion and this time was no different. He sat silent as he listened to his best and most loyal warriors talk. He had heard his father say many times it was best for a leader to keep his thoughts to himself and not speak foolishly.

"These warriors act suspicious. They must be planning to ambush someone... it could be Crow Killer." Ice Walker spoke up.

Crazy Cat shook his head. "The Pawnee will ambush and kill anyone weaker than they are. I do not think they would attack Crow Killer after the way he killed their chief, Wet Otter, two seasons past."

"That is exactly why they would dare attack, for revenge" Ice Walker argued. "The young ones say there are eight Pawnee warriors on the trail."

"Eight Pawnee against Crow Killer." Crazy Cat laughed. "Bah!"

"Do not forget the whites that ride with them, my brother."

He Dog looked around at the warriors. "It is at least a day's ride on the trail to where Grey Fox and Black Panther last saw the Pawnee."

"This is so. What does He Dog wish?"

"If the Pawnee were waiting to ambush Crow Killer, we are too far away to help." He Dog looked around the group. "We must know for sure who they hunt. Do any of you wish to go find out what has happened?"

"I will go at once." Crazy Cat stood up. "Any who wish to ride with me retrieve your weapons."

"Do not attack these Pawnee dogs unless they have harmed Crow Killer and my sister, or unless they attack you." He Dog nodded at Crazy Cat. "We do not need trouble with them."

"A Pawnee attacking a Cheyenne." Crazy Cat spit. "That will be the day."

"Do not underestimate your enemy, my friend." He Dog nodded. Since the loss of Yellow Dog, the young chief rarely smiled as he once did as a youngster. The loss of his brother had an extreme settling effect on the once-fun-loving young man. Now, he was Chief of the Cheyenne with the heavy responsibility to care for his people. "Ride with caution."

"They are Pawnee. How could you overestimate a Pawnee? We go."

He Dog shook his head slowly as he watched Crazy Cat walk away. The warrior was proud and brave in battle, maybe too brave. Crazy Cat had been Yellow Dog's best friend and advisor who he had much faith in. The warrior feared nothing, no odds were too great and He Dog knew this could be his one weakness. Underestimating an enemy was always dangerous and someday could be Crazy Cat's undoing.

After drinking their fill, Jed again helped Bright Moon onto the Appaloosa and nudged the horses across the small stream. Their pace had been slow and easy. The horses were fresh and strong, even after several days of travel from the valley. Still, Jed held the horses to an easy walk so he could check out every spot on the trail ahead.

"How far do you figure your brother's village is from here?"

"If he has not moved from the flint canyon, we will be there by dark time with the new sun."

"Tomorrow evening you think?"

Bright Moon smiled. "Tomorrow evening, I know."

"How do you feel?"

"Like a melon fixing to pop." She laughed again. "How do I look, Husband?"

"Like a melon fixing to pop." Both started to laugh uncontrollably.

"Should we not be quieter?"

"Why be quiet, if they're out there and wanting to fight?" Jed shrugged his shoulders. "They will surely know where we are."

"If they are going to attack us, they cannot let us ride much closer to my brother's village."

"You are right, woman." Jed agreed. "We've come far enough now from Bridger to make them feel safe from the old hunter himself."

"I do not think they fear Bridger as the other tribes do." Bright Moon frowned. "They trade at a post far south of this place."

"Maybe not, but you're right, they ain't gonna let us get much closer to the Cheyenne village if they plan to attack."

"No, they won't, because they are right there." Bright Moon nodded. "There, see them? They hide behind the cedar trees like cowards."

Jed reined the horses in hard and looked to where she pointed. Eight warriors sat their horses quietly, watching as they rode from the little creek bottom. Quickly reining around, Jed led the horses and Bright Moon back to the small creek and quickly pulled her from the Appaloosa. Pushing her down behind the sandy bank, he quickly grabbed the extra rifles and checked their priming. Laying out powder horns and shot beside her, Jed had Bright Moon watch the trail as he tied the horses back in the safety of the trees.

"They have not moved toward us, Husband." Bright Moon watched the strung-out line of riders as they rode from the trees. "They toy with us like a fox plays with a field mouse. I do not see the whites."

Jed studied the creek bank closely. He knew if the whites had circled to their rear, they would have little cover. Moving Bright Moon into a low hollow, Jed quickly stacked the packsaddles around her.

"Tell me when they start forward."

"Husband."

"What Bright Moon?"

"Tell the Pawnee they better hurry. I fear the little one will get here first."

Jed hovered over her sweat-stained face. Gathering blankets, Jed quickly placed her atop the bed. "You'll be alright."

"The little one is who is important, not me, Husband." Bright Moon smiled. "You fight, and I will bring Eagle's Wing into his new world."

"Alone?"

"Women have had babies alone for many, many moons." She smiled. "And right now, I do not think you have time to help me."

Jed looked up over the small embankment to where the Pawnee waited. All still sat there, none had moved forward. Standing up, Jed walked forward to where the Pawnee could see him plainly. Raising his hand, he stepped forward a few more feet. Only an arrow's flight separated them as he spoke.

"What do the Pawnee people want?" Jed raised his voice to cover the one hundred yard separation.

A lone rider rode forth from the line of warriors and raised his fist. Jed nodded as he recognized this one as one of the warriors who had taken Wet Otter's dead body from his valley. Now, he knew why the Pawnee had come here, revenge!"

"What does the Pawnee want?" Jed repeated.

"We have come for you, bear killer." The warrior raised his rifle. "You, Crow Killer, will die for the killing of our brother Wet Otter."

"Do not be as foolish as Wet Otter was." Jed warned. "You do not have to die here in this place."

"Does the Arapaho dog think he is invincible?" The warrior laughed. "You are alone except for the big-bellied woman."

"I bleed, Pawnee, but I do not die." Jed shrugged easily. "If you force this fight, you and many of your warriors will die."

"Even the great Crow Killer cannot kill us all with one shot." The Pawnee smiled. "I, Pony's Tail will take your scalp, Arapaho. Then your woman who is heavy with child will live in my lodge."

"Tell me, Pony's Tail." Jed stalled for time. He knew he could kill this one and maybe one other, but then he would have to race back to where Bright Moon was probably having her baby for the other rifles. Still, he didn't want to draw fire toward her and endanger her or the baby. "Tell me, how did you know I would be at Bridger?"

"I will answer your question. It will be your last." The warrior was sure of himself. "All the tribes know you trade your furs every year at Bridger with the thawing of the snows."

"So you waited until I came to the post?" Jed looked around for the whites. "Where are your white friends?"

"Yes, we waited, but not many days. We were lucky you came quickly. And the whites are near you." Pony's Tail grinned. "We were finally rewarded when you and your woman rode into Bridger."

"My woman is Cheyenne, sister of He Dog, Chief of the Cheyenne." Because of Bright Moon, Jed wanted to avoid this fight if he could. "Do you want the Cheyenne for an enemy?"

"We do not fear the Cheyenne or He Dog." Pony's Tail laughed. "The lowly Arickaree killed his brother Yellow Dog."

"Yes, they killed our great chief, but like cowards from ambush, the same as you do now."

Pony's Tail frowned. "We are already enemies of the Cheyenne. And your woman has much beauty."

Jed knew a fight was inevitable. The Pawnee had the advantage and they wanted his supplies, horses, and Bright Moon. To bring the scalp of the great bear killer to their village would bring them much glory. Jed knew he was only seconds from confrontation with the warriors. Cocking the rifle, he was about to kill the warrior called Pony's Tail when the repercussion of a rifle went off to his right, causing the warrior's head to explode. Firing quickly, Jed dropped another warrior from his horse, then watched as a third Pawnee was knocked to the ground. He had no idea who was hiding behind the heavy tree foliage. Pulling the extra rifle from his back, Jed fired again, but missed as another Pawnee dodged sideways.

Too far from his extra rifles, Jed quickly strung his bow and waited as the last five charged their horses straight at him. His one shot from the bow missed its running target. Ramming his lance into the soft ground, Jed pulled his war club as he dodged the screaming warriors as they tried to get a shot at him. Again, the unknown shooter fired, bringing another Pawnee from his horse. Seeing the warrior fall, the Pawnee reined in their horses, demoralized. Someone else was firing at them, not the lone Lance Bearer before them. Trying to figure out where the rifle fire was coming from, the four remaining warriors hesitated, then turned their horses in panic and raced back to the southwest. Jed's war club came down powerfully as he lunged forward and managed to pull the fifth Pawnee from his horse and bash his head in.

From the corner of his eye, Jed noticed the two white men, slipping through the heavy brush, trying to flank him. Quickly reloading his rifle, Jed knelt and waited. Suddenly both of the white men broke from their cover and charged directly toward him.

Again, the heavy discharge of a rifle brought the lead hunter to his knees, screaming and holding his leg. The second hunter fired too quick and missed Jed, then started to run for his horse. Cutting the rawhide string that held him to the lance, Jed quickly raced after the man. Fast of foot, Jed was on the slower, terrified hunter before he had run far.

Turning, the man dropped his rifle and raised his hands. The hunter was young, too young to be dangerous. "Don't kill me, please. I was just following my brother."

Jed was about to answer the frightened man when the rifle spoke again blowing a huge hole in the man's chest. Turning, Jed blinked in amazement as Bright Moon appeared from behind a large tree. Holding two rifles in her hands, she walked toward him. He couldn't believe his eyes as the woman, heavy with child, moved clumsily up to him.

"It's you!" Jed was so relieved she was safe that he could barely retain his emotions. "I thought you were having the baby."

"You would not leave me to fight unless I lied about the baby." Bright Moon walked to where one of the Pawnee stared up at her. "I put water on my face to make you think the baby was coming."

"You kinda storied to me, woman?"

"I said what I must, to keep you alive, my husband." Bright Moon looked down at the wounded warrior.

"You killed three warriors, Bright Moon, and one of the whites." Jed was almost in shock. He couldn't believe she killed these warriors all by herself. Standing before him, she appeared as calm as a summer day.

"You kept their attention, giving me time to get close to them. I couldn't miss from this distance."

"And the baby?" Jed looked at her stomach.

"The baby is fine. Now, he is a bloodied warrior." Bright Moon touched her stomach. "He has felt death and war. He will be a mighty warrior."

"He will be if he takes after his mother." Jed couldn't believe his young bride could have the courage to fight as she had. "That's for sure."

Bright Moon discharged the rifle again, finishing the wounded Pawnee. "I will kill anyone that tries to take you or my son from me, Husband."

"I believe you, woman." For the first time, Jed understood the depth of her love for him and her unborn son. He knew the Cheyenne were brave and fearless warriors, but he had no idea their women were.

The dark eyes turned from him, then she walked toward the other white who was holding his bleeding knee and whimpering. "The Pawnee and these white dogs came to kill you, steal me and my child. They deserved what they got."

Jed watched as Bright Moon pulled his lance from the ground, then dipped it in the blood of the warrior she had just killed. Touching it to her stomach, she raised the lance to the skies and whispered something Jed could not understand. Seeing her step toward the wounded white, he moved to stop her. Before he could reach her, she had pushed the sharp lance through the soft stomach of the pleading white.

"Bright Moon… enough." Jed took the bloody lance from her.

"He came for your blood, Husband. Anyone who aims to harm you will die." Bright Moon looked down at the dying man without emotion. "Now, he soon will be dead. Now, it is enough."

CHAPTER 3

After hearing the far-off gunfire, Crazy Cat and his warriors rode hard, knowing Crow Killer and Bright Moon could be under attack. Reining his horse to a stop, Crazy Cat moved forward to where Jed stood beside Bright Moon, near a small creek. The other Cheyenne warriors walked their horses around the meadow to where the dead bodies lay strewn about in disarray. In disbelief that Crow Killer had killed so many alone, the warriors mumbled softly among themselves.

"I am sorry, Crow Killer, that we did not get here sooner to help." Crazy Cat dismounted and looked back across the field.

"How are you here, my friend?" Jed couldn't believe the Cheyenne were there, so far from their village.

"He Dog sent us to find you and Bright Moon."

"We're fine, thanks to Bright Moon." Jed shook hands with the warrior. "She killed three Pawnee and both white men."

Crazy Cat was shocked as he looked at her stomach. "This one killed five enemy warriors in her condition?"

"She did for a fact."

"In her condition?" Crazy Cat repeated.

Jed smiled, looking over at Bright Moon. "Yes, in her condition."

"We must hear more of this when we return to the village." Crazy Cat let out a shrill war-whoop which was taken up by the other warriors.

"You will hear of nothing, Crazy Cat." Bright Moon winced. "Now, we must hurry to the village."

Jed looked at her strained face. "The baby?"

"I was not lying, my husband. The little one wants to come into this world and meet his father, and I fear he will not wait long." The woman winced again.

Crazy Cat had the warriors gather the horses and weapons from the dead men before they turned and headed for He Dog's village. The bodies were left in the meadow. Jed didn't like to leave the dead ones for the vultures and night animals, but he had no choice, Bright Moon was in much pain. The baby wanted to come into the world.

The drums of the village beat steadily through the night as Bright Moon lay in the woman's lodge, giving birth. Jed hadn't figured she'd wait to have the baby until they reached the village, but she had and now the pains of birth racked her slender body. Waiting nervously, Jed, at He Dog and Crazy Cat's insistence, told of the short fight with the Pawnee. Astonished, they could only shake their heads as he told how the fight had developed and Bright Moon's heroic and accurate shooting had saved their lives.

He Dog laughed. "We should have asked more horses for her."

"She, shot three Pawnee warriors?" Ice Walker was astounded.

"Don't forget both whites." Crazy Cat added.

"I believe your words. I saw the bigger white, Bright Moon stuck Crow Killer's lance through his stomach." Grey Fox continued. "He still lived when I found him. He told me what the squaw had done to him."

He Dog shook his head. "We should have asked many more horses for her."

Suddenly, the whole village became quiet. Jed stared at the woman's lodge, near the edge of the village where the mothers were taken to give birth. Crazy Cat's woman and another walked toward the chief's lodge carrying a small bundle. Stopping, as Jed stood up, they placed the bundle in his trembling hands.

"Take it, Crow Killer." The older of the women pushed the bundle in his hands. "You have a beautiful daughter."

Pulling back the soft blanket of rabbit fur and deerskin, Jed looked at the pile of coal black hair and chuckled. "I don't think your mother can call you Eagle's Wing, little one."

"No, I don't think that would be a good name for a girl." Crazy Cat laughed as the warriors pushed closer to see the baby. "Why do you say that?"

"Before the fight, Bright Moon predicted a boy. She told me that your medicine man, Spotted Panther, said it would be so." Jed touched the rosy cheek tenderly. "Reckon he was wrong this one time."

The older squaw, Pine Woman, pointed to the far lodge. "Bright Moon wishes for you to come to her. Take the little one and go."

Grinning, as Jed walked away, Pretty Feather, the woman of Crazy Cat, smiled at the warriors, then turned for her lodge.

"What is it, woman?"

"Crazy Cat will find out soon enough." Pretty Feather laughed lightly. "But, I think you should gather the people for a feast and dancing tonight."

Crazy Cat and He Dog watched as Jed stooped through the forbidden squaw lodge door, then back to where Pretty Feather and Pine Woman disappeared inside a lodge. "Perhaps we have missed something, my chief."

"Maybe so." He Dog returned to his backrest and sat down. "I will never understand women."

Ice Walker laughed. "Wait until you are married, it will get much worse."

"How can this be so?"

"You will see, my chief." Crazy Cat grinned. "Yes, someday soon you will find out for yourself."

Stepping into the dim lodge, Jed moved to Bright Moon's side quietly. The tired dark eyes and sweaty face told him she had been through an ordeal giving birth. Kneeling beside her, he took her extended hand. Bright Moon looked at the small bundle he held so gingerly.

"You have met your daughter, my husband?"

"She is beautiful." Jed pulled back the covering exposing the small wrinkled face. "She looks like her mother."

Bright Moon ran her fingers down the baby's face. "I would like to call her Ellie Thunder."

"If that is what you wish."

"Does it please you, my husband?"

"Yes, she will be named after a beautiful Arapaho woman."

"And my sister." Bright Moon added.

"Do you need anything?"

"Not yet." The tired woman smiled. "Are you disappointed?"

"I'm the happiest man in the tribes this day." Jed smiled. "Thank you for her."

"We couldn't name her Eagle's Wing."

Jed laughed lightly and shook his head. "No, I reckon we couldn't at that."

"You liked the name Eagle's Wing?"

"Well, yes I did." Jed nodded. "Maybe next time."

"I do not want to wait." Bright Moon smiled.

"I don't understand." Jed blinked in shock as she pulled the blanket back, revealing the small naked form next to her.

"This is your son, Eagle's Wing." She looked down at the baby boy lying quietly beside her. "Spotted Panther is never wrong."

"Twins!" Jed shook his head as he looked back and forth at the dark-headed babies. "A boy and a girl."

Pine Woman stepped through the lodge opening frowning, then ordered Jed out. Kissing Bright Moon lightly and touching the two babies, Jed exited the lodge and walked to where He Dog and the other warriors sat gathered, waiting for him. Looking back at the lodge, Jed shook his head in shock.

"Did you not tell Crow Killer of the mark on the little warrior's back?" Pine Woman asked curiously.

"No, Mother, I thought one shock was all he could stand in one day." Bright Moon looked down at the birthmark on Eagle Wing's shoulder. "He carries the same lance mark my husband wears."

"Spotted Panther predicted this." Pine Woman nodded, as she stared at the mark and smacked her lips. "This one will be a great warrior of the people."

"Yes, Spotted Panther said he will be a great war leader when he has grown to manhood." Bright Moon touched the little face. "Like his father."

"What is wrong, Crow Killer?" He Dog watched the expression on Jed's face. "Have you seen a spirit person?"

"Twins." The word was barely a whisper. "Bright Moon had twins. A warrior and a maiden."

A yell went up from the gathered warriors as Jed was slapped on the back and congratulated. Several of the warriors went screaming through the village yelling at the people.

"Pretty Feather was right." He Dog laughed. "Tonight, we will celebrate long into the night."

Jed motioned to where a young warrior stood listening. "Gather the Pawnee horses and weapons and bring them here."

"Yes, Crow Killer."

Reaching into a buckskin pouch, Jed pulled out several cigars that he had bought at Bridger for the occasion. Passing the strange things out to He Dog and his warriors, he grinned as they smelled and tasted of them.

"This is the tobacco the white men smoke when a new papoose is born." Jed pulled an ember from the fire and lit his cigar. Watching him blow smoke to the four winds, the warriors quickly lit theirs. Smiles sprang to their faces as they tasted the flavor of the barley.

"These are far better than our pipe smoke." Crazy Cat nodded. "Much better."

"Where is the lodge of Spotted Panther?" Jed stood up as the seven horses were led up.

"You gonna kill him for giving you so many mouths to feed?" Grey Fox blew smoke and joked with Jed.

"These horses are for him." Jed took the lead ropes. "I will take them to him. The rest of the weapons and supplies the Pawnee and whites carried will be divided between Crazy Cat and his warriors."

Nodding, the warriors smiled as Crazy Cat stood up. "Thank you, my brother, for the gifts."

"It is I who thank you and your warriors for coming to help us."

Grey Fox shook his head. "With Bright Moon, you did not need our help."

"No, this time I was lucky." Jed replied. "She is indeed quite a woman."

Leading the captured horses, Jed stopped before the large lodge that had been pointed out to him. Before he could call out, a tall thin elderly man stepped from the lodge. A single eagle feather protruded from the grey head. The eyes of the medicine man were sharp and bright, shimmering like the rays of a bright sun. The man was tall and straight as an arrow as he stood proudly before Jed.

"Crow Killer, it is good to finally meet the husband of my grand-niece."

"It is good to meet Spotted Panther, the great Medicine Man of the Cheyenne."

"You arrived in the night."

"Yes, just in time, I think." Jed replied. "Bright Moon's time was near."

"You have also been in a fight with the Pawnee." The old medicine man looked at the horses. "I saw the fight in the smoke of my fire."

Jed noticed Spotted Panther didn't ask questions. He seemed to already know what had happened. "Yes, we had a fight. I bring these horses to Spotted Panther as a gift."

"A gift because of the fight?"

"No, they are a gift for the safe delivery of my children and my wife, Bright Moon." Jed smiled.

"They are healthy, and in time, they will grow strong." Spotted Panther nodded. "The spirit people blessed you, Crow Killer, with a fine woman and two strong children. The little one, Eagle's Wing, will kill many whites in the battles to the north. And the little maiden will be the mother of many leaders of the Arapaho."

"Whites?" Jed was curious. "How can this be, Uncle?"

"Times are changing, Crow Killer. You cannot stop the flood of whites coming into our lands." The old one nodded sadly. "One day, there will be a great war with the whites. Your son, Eagle's Wing, will earn many coups riding beside another great warrior."

Jed had seen the immigrant trains, but so far none had stopped in the lands of the Arapaho. "These are sad words for my ears, Spotted Panther."

"It is written." The old medicine man looked sadly at Jed. "What is seen in the fire cannot be changed, my son."

"To fight against the strength of the whites is a bad thing." Jed warned. "They are more numerous than the stars in the sky."

"No, we cannot win, but our people will fight for their land." Spotted Panther continued. "There will be much loss of lives on both sides, much sadness in our lodges."

"I hope you are wrong this time, Spotted Panther."

"I hope it will be so, but my smoke is never wrong." The old face hardened. "Never!"

"This is bad news for my ears."

"Go now, my son. Enjoy your children, raise them strong." The medicine man nodded.

"If there is ever anything you need."

"I have everything an old man could need." The old one smiled. "Ride with caution, Crow Killer. The trail you take soon, to the west, will be dangerous, my son."

"Trail ahead?" Jed was curious and wondered how the medicine man knew of any troubles.

"You will soon ride to the west to the white man's village." Spotted Panther stroked the neck of one of the horses. "Leave my niece and the children here, until you return, for their protection."

"Am I riding into danger, old one?"

"My vision only says you must be careful in the days ahead." Spotted Panther frowned. "Your enemies are many. They will even follow you back to your lodge in the great valley."

"My enemies?"

"Go now, visit with Bright Moon and the little ones before you depart." The old one raised his hand. "Look to the skies, Crow Killer. In time, all your questions will be answered."

"Thank you, Uncle."

Jed handed the lead ropes to a young lad, then returned to where He Dog and Crazy Cat sat looking at the Pawnee rifles they had been given. Seeing the seriousness of Jed's face, they laid the weapons aside as he sat down.

Looking back at the medicine man's lodge, Jed shook his head. "How does he know what will happen in the days ahead?"

"He is Spotted Panther. He speaks with the spirit people." He Dog looked closely at Jed. "Tell us, what has the medicine man seen in his fires?"

"I have to ride to see Medicine Thunder with the new sun." Jed looked into the small fire. "Spotted Panther says it will be a dangerous trail."

"I will ride with Crow Killer." Crazy Cat drew his skinning knife.

"No, my friend, I do not know what the trail ahead will be." Jed sighed. "Where I ride, you would be in danger from many whites."

"I have never known Spotted Panther to reveal anything that does not come true." Ice Walker puffed on his cigar.

"I would ask my brothers, He Dog and Crazy Cat, for a favor."

"Ask Crow Killer, anything." He Dog spoke up.

"I need to leave Bright Moon and my children in your care while I am away." Jed looked at the warriors. "They will be safe here."

"This will be as you ask." He Dog nodded. "We did not know you would be leaving us so quickly. I sent a runner to Walking Horse, telling him and Little Antelope to ride here to our village."

"I will not be able to wait for them." Jed frowned. "Medicine Thunder awaits me, to come to her as we speak. I feel her summons is urgent."

"We understand." He Dog nodded. "Tonight, there will be a celebration by the village in your children's honor, but you stay with Bright Moon tonight."

"I will leave out before the new sun comes."

"With my chief's permission, I and several warriors will ride with Crow Killer until he is safely past Bridger's Post, then we will turn back." Crazy Cat looked at He Dog.

"It will be so."

"Thank you, my friends." Jed smiled. "I have powder and shot for your rifles in my pouches."

"I had the young men put your supplies in my lodge." Crazy Cat pointed at the youngsters carrying Jed's bundles into a lodge.

"Thank you, my friend." Jed pulled the bag of gold coins from his leather pouch and handed it to the warrior. "Place this with the rest."

"We will be ready with the new sun." Taking the pouch, Crazy Cat, watched as Jed looked to the lodge where Bright Moon and the babies were moved to.

Jed looked at his friends and brothers sadly. "Spotted Panther says there will be a great war with the whites in the coming years."

"If the old one says such a thing will happen, it will be so." Grey Fox nodded his head.

Crazy Cat looked into the fire. "The Sioux have already seen the oncoming whites. Their wagons are like long worms crossing their best hunting grounds."

"He says my son, Eagle's Wing, will fight the whites in a great battle."

"Whose side will Crow Killer be on?"

"I will return to my valley, but I will not fight against you, my brothers." Jed shrugged. "Nor will I fight against the whites, unless I am attacked."

"When I was young my father spoke of a war with the whites. I fear troubles are coming to our lands." He Dog warned.

As Jed held both babies in his arms, he couldn't believe his good fortune. Both were perfectly made with dark eyes and a shock of black hair covering their little heads. Pine Woman moved about the lodge, watching over the proceedings and bringing in food for them. Clucking her tongue as Jed played with the babies, she frowned, waving a gnarled finger at him.

"What is wrong?" Jed looked up at the old squaw. "What is she looking at?"

"A Cheyenne father does not hover over his children as you are doing."

"So?"

"She believes you will spoil them." Bright Moon laughed. "Make them soft."

"I aim to, every day of their lives, and you too, woman." Jed smiled.

Bright Moon smiled. "We are lucky to have one such as you, my husband."

"And I am blessed for my family."

"You will leave in the morning?"

"Yes, Crazy Cat and a few warriors will ride with me to Bridger."

"Did you see Spotted Panther?"

"I did." Jed nodded. "He's a peculiar one, but a great man."

"Why do you say that?"

Jed shrugged. "He seems to know what you are thinking before you speak."

"I told you he was a great medicine man."

"I believe you." Jed nodded. "He knew about the children before I took him the horses."

"The Pawnee horses?"

"I gave them to him."

"Good." Bright Moon held Eagle's Wing to her breast. "What else did he say?"

"Nothing." Jed didn't mention what they had talked about. Nothing of the coming battles against the whites that would be Eagle's Wing future if the old medicine man's predictions came true. There was no need to worry her now of something that would happen many years in the future.

For two days, Jed pushed the bay horse of Wet Otter as he rode at a pretty good pace until they neared Bridger's Post. Reining the horses down to a walk, he looked over at Crazy Cat and his warriors.

"Will you go in and trade at Bridger?" Jed turned to Crazy Cat.

"No, when we pass the post, we will leave you and return to the village." The warrior shook his head. "But first, we will watch to be sure no one from Bridger follows you."

"Can I bring you anything from the white village of Baxter Springs?"

"You have already given us powder and shot for our new rifles. That is enough." Crazy Cat nodded. "Just come back to us safely, my brother."

"I will be back soon. There's so much waiting for me back here."

"This is good." Crazy Cat smiled. "We will hunt the shaggies together when you return."

"Be careful, my brothers. The Pawnee could attack you on your return." Jed warned. "The bodies of the dead Pawnee have been removed. The ones that rode with the whites and lived may have reached their village by now with their dead warriors."

Ice Walker shook his head. "The whites were left where they lay."

"We will ride and watch at the same time, but they are just Pawnee." Grey Fox laughed.

Detouring around and out of sight of the post, Jed reined in and shook hands with the warriors. "Tell my brother, Walking Horse, he is not to come after me or tell Red Hawk anything."

"We will do as you ask." Crazy Cat agreed. "But, Walking Horse is very hardheaded."

"Danger lurks near the white village for you, my brothers." Jed nodded solemnly. "Do not follow me, just take care of my family."

"As if they were my own."

Waving farewell, Jed kicked the bay horse into an easy lope toward Baxter Springs. He didn't know the youngster, Dibbs Bacon, so he wasn't even sure Ellie had sent the boy for him. Perhaps it was a trap to lure him back along the trail to Baxter Springs, where he could be ambushed. Every hunter would know he carried much gold from the sale of his furs. Jed had ridden so many trails of danger in the last few years, it made him suspicious of anyone he didn't know. Although, Dibbs Bacon seemed like an honest young man, but he was a complete stranger to him.

The cold nights on the trail and the wet crossings of the rivers had become second nature to Jed. He knew Ellie needed him, but now he wished more than anything to be with Bright Moon and the children. He swore, as the bay horse plodded along, that this would be the last trail he would ride.

Jed didn't want to explain his presence in Baxter Springs so he gave the Carter farm a wide birth as he passed. He wanted to speak with Ellie before letting anyone else know he was back in the settlement. If she did send for him, then it must be serious. On this trail, he had decided to ride the long-legged bay horse of Wet Otter. The paint was too loudly colored and his markings were one of a kind. The black and white overo markings were a dead giveaway and anyone spotting the horse would know Crow Killer was near Baxter Springs. He was curious and wondered what could be so important for Ellie to send for him. Still, he knew the woman the Indians called Medicine Thunder was levelheaded so to send for him this way, whatever she needed must be urgent.

Slowing his pace so he would reach the town after the sun went down, Jed studied every movement along the small road. He had ridden hard with little rest, and now, the slow plodding of the bay almost rocked him to sleep. Entering the town at dusk, he turned into the alley behind Doc Zeke's office. Slipping from the horse, Jed tied him to an oak tree and tapped lightly on the side door.

Several seconds passed before the old doctor opened the door slightly. "Jed Bracket."

"It's me alright, Doc Zeke."

"Come in, come in, lad." The little man looked up at Jed smiling. "Ellie said you'd be coming soon."

"As quick as I could." Jed looked into the room. "Is she here?"

"Yes, she's in her room." The doctor ushered Jed into the front room. "Wait here, I'll go get her."

The young woman, Medicine Thunder, hadn't changed a bit as she appeared in the doorway. Tall and willowy with long black hair and dark eyes, Jed could see the relief in her face. Rushing to him she hugged him, then stepped back and looked deeply into his eyes.

"Oh, Jed, you have come."

"I'm here, Ellie." Jed looked down into her worried face. "What's wrong?"

"First, let me fix you something to eat, then we can talk." Protesting he wasn't hungry, Jed was pulled into the kitchen and pushed down into a kitchen chair. "You'll eat first. You must be as hungry as you are tired."

Pots and pans rattled as she placed the wood in the stove. "What is wrong, Ellie?"

Looking at him, she tried to smile. "Tell me, Jed, how are Bright Moon and your father doing?"

Jed smiled, he knew he would have to placate her until she was ready to talk. "I started here with Bright Moon, but I changed my mind. I didn't want Bate Baker to get my pelts."

"You were bringing Bright Moon here?" Ellie placed a hot cup of coffee in front of him and her grandfather. "Why?"

"She was heavy with child and I was worried for her."

"Bright Moon is having a baby? I can imagine you were worried. Two men alone so far from a woman's help."

"I was scared for sure, but Bright Moon just laughed at us."

"Where is she now?" Ellie placed a plate of potatoes and fried pork in front of him. "The Bacon boy said you were at Bridger's Post, but he didn't mention seeing Bright Moon."

"That's why I was so long coming. I took her to He Dog's village." Jed sipped his coffee. "We barely made it before she started having bad pains."

"And the baby?"

"They're both fine."

"They?" Doc Zeke looked at Jed. "She had twins?"

"She did, and they are as healthy as any newborn could be."

"Oh, Jed." Ellie smiled. "Tell us, are they boys, girls?"

"One of each." Jed pushed his plate back. "Bright Moon named the girl Little Ellie Medicine Thunder after you, Ellie."

"And the boy?"

"Eagle's Wing is what the old medicine man, Spotted Panther, named him years ago."

"Years ago?" Doc Zeke was curious. "Did you say years ago?"

"I did. He predicted the firstborn would be a boy and he was." Jed bit into the meat. "I don't know how, but he sure did for a fact."

"Thank you, Jed." Ellie smiled. "Ellie Thunder, that was thoughtful of you and Bright Moon."

"Enough of this. Now, why have you sent for me?" Jed stared at her. "No more stalling."

Toying with a sugar spoon, Ellie was quiet for several seconds, then looked up at Jed. "I have bad news, Jed."

Jed's heart tightened in his chest. He knew it was Lige. During the heavy storms that had descended on his valley, his mind had returned time and again with thoughts of the old scout. He worried about the wagon train making it safely through the deep passes of the Gallatins.

"Lige?"

"Yes, he was killed somewhere along the Gallatin River west of here."

"Who told you this, Ellie?"

Handing him a well-worn envelope, Jed quickly read the enclosed piece of paper. "The Gallatin is west of here. Red Hawk told me about this land. He had passed through these lands after stealing the spotted stallion from the Nez Perce many seasons ago."

Ellie nodded. "Yes, that is what I was told."

"This letter is from Chalk Briggs." Jed turned the letter in curiosity. "How did you get it?"

"He sent it by some trappers he met that were headed this way." Ellie teared up. "They, in turn, gave the letter to Dibbs and that's how I got it. Mister Briggs said my father had been killed, but the letter didn't say how."

Jed remembered the terrible past winter. Crossing the frozen rivers, trying to get the train through the snowed-in passes to safety might have been the old scout's undoing. "What do you want of me, Ellie?"

"I have no right to ask you now, Jed, not with the babies and all." Ellie dropped her eyes. "I can't ask you."

"Are you not the one that rode with me to save my brother Walking Horse's life?" Jed frowned at her. "I am indebted to you. You have every right."

"But, the babies." Ellie dropped her eyes. "And Walking Horse is my brother too, Jed."

"They are safe with He Dog in his village." Jed put his hand on hers. "They'll be there when I get back."

"The trappers I have questioned say the Gallatin Range is to the west and north, a very dangerous place for people traveling alone."

"Then you want me to take you there?"

"I have no right to put your life in danger." Ellie shook her head. "Those men said hostile Indians, rogue Metis, and white trappers from Canada frequent that range."

"It is just a range of mountains like any others." Jed shook his head. "They are just men, Ellie."

"I would like to see my father's grave and leave a headstone of some kind to mark it." Ellie looked down at the table. "Then we would know where he is buried, if we should ever want to go there."

"It will be a long, hard ride."

"I know, but could you take me there?"

"Do you know where we would find his grave?"

Ellie pointed at the letter. "On the back, Mister Briggs drew a map for us to follow."

"You approve of this, Dr. Zeke?" Jed looked at the doctor. "She'll be in danger anywhere west of here."

"No, I don't approve, but Ellie insisted." The grey head shook. "And as you well know, she's a strong-willed young lady."

Jed turned the paper and studied the roughly drawn map that pinpointed what was an encircled X on the back page. Jed was not familiar with the country northwest of Baxter Springs. He had been no farther west than his stepfather's farm along Pennington Creek. The X pinpointing the grave was in the Gallatin Range of Mountains near a river crossing that followed the immigrant trail to Oregon. He didn't see any reason they would have trouble following the map west and locating the grave. He knew the most danger, would be crossing the dangerous lands often inhabited by hostile Indians and white renegades.

"Alright, Ellie, if you're dead set on seeing Lige's grave. I see no problem with us following this map."

"Thank you, Jed." Ellie nodded. "It would be a comfort to see Papa's grave and know where he is buried."

"I'll see to my horse, then I'll bed down in your barn."

"There's no need for that, the nights are still chilly outside." The doctor spoke up. "You will stay in the living room tonight."

"The barn will be fine." Jed thanked them for the dinner and walked to the side door. "We'll get supplies in the morning when Mister Woods opens."

"How far off do you think this place is?" Dr. Zeke asked as Jed slipped through the doorway.

"I have no idea, Doc." Jed shook his head. "I'll do some checking before I turn in."

The saloon in Baxter Springs hadn't changed any. Everything was the same as it was the day Jed and his stepdad had killed Rufus Cross and some of his men. Even the bloodstained floor where Constable O'Rourke had bled out after taking Cross' knife to the stomach hadn't been cleaned or covered. Even the stoop-shouldered saloonkeeper standing behind the bar was the same man that had been tending the bar the day of the killings. The slender saloon man recognized Jed immediately as he moved lightly across the room. He paled slightly as he well-remembered the tall, dark-headed man with the hard eyes walking toward him. He had seen death in the man back then, and today, he was seeing the same thing.

Several trappers, buffalo hunters, and locals sat about the tables, swigging down mugs of beer and whiskey chasers. The trapping season was over for a few months. Now, all the men had to do was spend their hard-earned hide money getting drunk, playing cards, and fighting. Easing up to the nervous barkeep, Jed nodded and laid a coin on the bar.

"Been a while, Jed Bracket, or do you prefer Crow Killer?" The saloon man greeted Jed.

"If I had my way, not long enough, Simon." Jed looked around the room, ignoring the question. "Not near long enough."

"What'll you have?"

"Information." Jed looked down at the twenty-dollar gold piece in his hand. "That much worth."

"Right now, I may be kinda short on information." Simon Buck looked greedily down at the coin. "What do you want to know?"

"I'm looking for some trappers that came in from the west, two or three weeks back." Jed studied the room. "You see 'em in here, just point them out."

"Now see here, Jed." Buck swallowed hard. "I don't want any more trouble in here."

Jed smiled. "No trouble, Mister Buck. I just need some information they might have."

"Well, alright then." Buck nodded at a table where three trappers were playing monte. "You might ask them three, but you mind your manners."

"Thank you, Simon."

"No trouble, Jed." The worried saloonkeeper begged. "Please, be peaceable, no trouble or killing."

"Well, now, Simon, you know I am a peaceful citizen."

The stoop-shouldered barkeep shook his head and frowned at the words. This one, everyone called Crow Killer, was anything but peaceful. He had proved it many times in the past in Baxter Springs. There were fights with the Shoshone and with the Wilsons. No, this one wasn't peaceable when riled.

Approaching the table, Jed sensed the three trappers had already spotted him moving their way. Standing quietly, waiting for the hand to play itself out, Jed studied the trappers. All three looked friendly enough. He figured, by the men making sure Ellie received the letter from Chalk Briggs, they should be decent men.

"What'll it be, Injun?" The smaller of the men turned his eyes up at Jed. "You wanna play?"

"No money." Jed shrugged.

"Then what do you want?"

"I'm looking for some information is all."

"Information costs money, boy." A larger man laughed.

"You ain't full Injun, young man, but you could be mistaken for one." The older of the group laid down his cards. "Now, what do you want to know?"

"Some have mistaken me for an Indian alright." Jed smiled easily. "I was wondering how far it is to the Gallatin Range?"

"Why, you headed out there?"

"Thought I would. Heard there's good hunting in that range."

"Depends on who's doing the hunting, mister." The older man pointed at the deck. "Deal the cards, Dexter."

"You gonna tell me?"

"Riding into the Gallatins right now is a very dangerous thing to do, young man."

"Indians?"

"Not Injuns, mister." The older man looked up at Jed again and scoffed. "You've heard, there's some kind of maniac running loose in the Gallatins, ain't you?"

"No, can't say that I have. Just rode into town from the east." Jed replied.

"There's a cold-blooded killer on the loose in those mountains. Even the local Injuns are scared to ride alone at night." The man looked down at his cards. "This one kills for the sheer fun of it. Leastways, that's what we've heard. Ain't experienced it ourselves though."

"White man?"

The man shrugged as he studied his cards. "Who knows? All we know for sure is he favors a sharp knife to do his killing."

"Indian mean, that's what he is." The man called Dexter sipped on his whiskey. "I tell you t'was an Indian, a white man don't kill that way. Carves up his victims something awful, he does."

"How far?"

"You fixing to take Doc Zeke's girl to find her pa's grave, ain't you?" The bigger man grinned. "That'd be a pretty dangerous and stupid thing to do."

"Maybe, I am." Jed was surprised the men knew why he was in town.

"The name's George Masters, in case you're wondering. The young one, Dibbs Bacon, spilt the beans and told us you was coming here and why."

"You must be Jedidiah Bracket or as some call you, the great bear killer, Crow Killer." The bigger man looked Jed up and down. "We've heard about you."

"I'm a thanking you for bringing word of her father."

"Actually, we didn't." Masters shook his head. "We passed the letter to young Bacon. We were still running our traps and for some reason, he was headed this way in a hurry so we gave it to him."

"Well, I thank you anyway."

"We knew Lige Hatcher. Hunted with him some, back in the day." Masters looked at his cards. "Good man... sure was a shame he went under."

"What happened?" Jed was curious. "How'd he die?"

Masters tossed his cards in. "An early bad storm hit the Gallatins. It were sure bad, icy trails, winds, and snow hit there all at once. All Chalk Briggs told us was that Old Lige was trying to get them, pilgrims, across the river when his horse stumbled, throwing him onto some rocks."

"Hit his head. Kilt him deader than last year's turkey." Dexter shook his head. "Leastways, that's the way we heard it from Briggs."

"You boys see the grave?"

"We seen it alright. Almost lost our hair doing it."

"What happened?"

"The Gros Ventre claim that road and those mountains." Masters shook his head. "With the killings and all, they've taken a dim view to anyone coming into their country without asking."

"They let the wagon train pass."

"That they did, but old Lige was on good terms with them folks." The bigger trapper laughed as he laid out his cards. "He married one of their women back in the shining times. He's a member of the Gros Ventre Tribe."

"Gros Ventre?" Jed hadn't heard that about Hatcher.

"Yep, Christian Indians when they want to be."

"They might be Christians, but they can be plenty mean when they're riled." Dexter shuffled the dirty cards. "Take my word on it and stay outta them mountains, boy."

"How long you figure it'll take me to reach there?"

"It's easy enough, just follow the wagon ruts west of town for about two weeks to the west. You'll find the grave alright." Masters continued. "Sits a quarter mile back on the east side of the river. You can't miss it."

"It's got a busted wagon wheel for a headstone." The smaller trapper added. "Can't say who put it up. Maybe those Christian Injuns."

"If you can keep your head, it's easy to find." Dexter laughed at his own joke.

Motioning at the bartender, Jed ordered a quart of whiskey for the trappers. "Thank you, gentlemen, for the letter. It was kind of you."

"Told you it were the Bacon kid, what brought it." Dexter eyed the whiskey bottle hungrily. "Not us."

"I'm giving you some good free advice, Crow Killer." Masters took the whiskey bottle. "Don't take her back into them mountains."

"I'd sure take your advice, Mister Masters, but she won't."

Dexter laid down his cards and looked up at Jed. "We had us a killing a couple weeks back, right here."

"You think it was the killer?"

"Who else would it be?" The smaller hunter shook his head. "Man can't even get drunk and pass out in safety around these parts."

"Squires and his bunch of hide-hunters had just ridden in from the west when it happened." Dexter shuddered. "Sure gives a man the creeps."

"So, you think it was the killer from the Gallatins?"

"I do." Dexter looked down. "He carved that hunter's head clean off and stuck it on a picket fence out back."

"Yeah." Masters agreed solemnly. "We figure whoever it was, followed Squires and his men back here from the Gallatins."

Jed looked down at the table. "How long did you say Squires and his bunch been back?"

"Got here a while before we rode in."

"And you're figuring this knife killer followed them?" Jed asked.

"I do. I figure he's got a big hate on for someone." Masters replied.

"He's a crazed, bloodthirsty killer, mister." The smaller hunter muttered as Jed turned. "That's what he is. You best watch your back if'n your crazy enough to head out to those parts."

"Good luck to you then, Jedidiah Bracket." Masters nodded. "You watch out for that killer. They say you won't even see him coming until your throat is cut."

"He killed many?" Jed turned back around.

"Enough." Dexter replied. "According to some of the Gros Ventre warriors, we spoke with, he's killed over twenty Cree and Metis in the last year."

"Twenty!"

"It's like we were telling you, Mister Bracket. Don't take the girl into the Gallatins." Masters warned.

"I'll speak with her."

"You do that." Masters looked up at Jed. "If'n you don't have any luck with her, then keep your powder dry and good luck to you."

"Thank you for the information, Mister Masters."

"Keep your eyes on the skyline, Injun." Dexter laughed drunkenly.

"I'll do that."

Jed hardly turned around when he noticed a buckskin-clad figure, blocking the door. The man was tall, heavier than Jed, with arms that seemed to reach below his knees. Not a word was spoken yet, but somehow, his instincts told him trouble stood in the doorway before him. Cradling his rifle in his left arm, Jed started for the door as the tall man reached out his long arm and blocked his path.

"I heard those boys back there call you, Bracket." The voice was high pitched, funny-sounding coming from such a huge man. The tall man was pencil-necked with a huge Adams apple that bobbed up and down when he spoke. The eyes were whitish colored, making the man seem a little crazed.

"I'm Bracket."

"Well, now, tell me what you're doing here, Mister Bracket?"

"Let me pass, mister."

"Nope, you'll have to answer my question or move me." The tall one laughed crazily. "You killed a friend of mine. Matter of fact, two friends of mine."

Jed now had no doubt. He knew trouble faced him and the man wouldn't be talked out of it. "Now, just who were your friends I killed?"

"Luke Grisham for one."

"Luke Grisham." With the suddenness of an eye blink, Jed's rifle cracked into the man's stomach, sending him retching through the door onto the porch floor. "You sure keep company with sorry friends, mister. Next time you block my path, I'll kill you."

Masters smiled and nodded his head slowly as the tall straight back of Jed Bracket disappeared from the room. "Reckon old skinny Squires there got away pretty lucky tonight."

"He's rough alright." Dexter laughed as he listened to Squires retching on the walkway. "He may just get the girl to her pappy's grave and back."

"You're right, boys, he's a wildcat for meanness." Simon Buck pointed at the bloodstains on the floor. "He's the cause of most of them."

"He's still up against the killer and the Gros Ventre." The smaller hunter spoke up. "Reckon which one will get him first. I'll wager on the killer."

Masters shook his head. "I don't figure the Gros Ventre will be the trouble, but the killer sure could."

"Even here in civilization, that killer gives me the shakes." Dexter admitted. "I ain't going back into them mountains again until that animal is done for."

"The Gros Ventres will get the killer sooner or later, I figure." Masters picked up the cards. "Sides, I don't figure he's after us."

Dexter poured himself another drink, then set the bottle down hard. "Then who?"

"Well, I figure it was someone who did him some meanness."

Masters took the cards. "Remember, it was Squire's man that got his throat cut, not one of us. Let's play."

The stoop-shouldered bartender, Buck, sighed after Jed had disappeared through the door. "I knew Jed couldn't come in here without causing some kind of trouble."

Masters laughed. "I don't figure he started anything, Simon, but he sure finished it quick."

A set of piercing eyes watched from the darkness as Jed dropped the tall man with the blow from his Hawken. Slender hands gripped the bone handle of his skinning knife as hate glared from the watcher's hardened eyes. Stopping the urge to step forward and use the knife on the downed man, the eyes disappeared back into the darkness of the alley. There would be another day for him to kill this one and the four hunters that rode with the man. Now, was not the time, with the lights of the saloon, he could be spotted easily.

Jed led two horses and a packhorse to the front of Wood's Mercantile and started to enter when Dibbs Bacon met him on the porch. A few inches shorter than Jed, the youngster was dressed this time in new buckskins, a hunter's attire.

"Good morning, Mister Bracket." The face was friendly, something Jed wasn't used to in Baxter Springs.

"Mister Bacon."

"Ellie sent me to find you." Bacon smiled. "She said I should ask you."

"Ask me what?"

"If you'll allow me, I'll ride with you and help you find her pa's grave."

"I've been told that's dangerous country, Mister Bacon." Jed studied the buckskin-clad figure. The lad was still young, in age, but there was something Jed had seen in his eyes. "Why would you want to go?"

"I've been there before. Thought I'd lend Miss Ellie a hand. Make sure she's protected."

Jed grinned, the youngster had a feeling for Ellie. "Well, Mister Bacon, it's your neck, I reckon. If Ellie don't mind, grab your pony."

"We pulling out today?"

"Just as soon as I round up supplies and get Ellie."

"I'll fetch my horse."

"You say you've been to the Gallatins before?"

"That's where my pa was killed." The young face hardened. "I've been back a few times."

"You said before that his ticker played out on him."

"You might say that." The face hardened. "Anyway, he's dead now. Don't matter how, does it?"

"No, I don't reckon it does."

"You know dead's a permanent condition, Mister Bracket." Bacon could feel the huge razor-sharp hunting knife poked into the side flap of his moccasins.

"How many days will it take us to reach the pass where the grave is?" Something about the youngster's actions troubled Jed. Looking down at the large, bone-handled skinning knife, he remembered the hunter's saying how the killer liked a knife to do his killings. To take a man's head off quickly, would take a big knife and a sharp one. Exactly the kind of blade Bacon carried.

"Depends on our pace, trouble, weather, many things can slow us down. I figure, though with no trouble, maybe ten, twelve days, pushing at a steady pace." Dibbs looked across the street.

"Okay, Mister Bacon. I'll meet you behind the doctor's office." Jed looked at the youngster. "Do you know where the grave is?"

"I should, I buried the man that's in it."

"Those trappers inside said they buried Hatcher."

"They lied to you." Bacon shrugged. "They had the note from Chalk Briggs alright. They probably passed the grave on their way back, but I'm the one that buried the man that's in it."

Jed nodded, maybe it was a good thing for the youngster to ride with them. Apparently, he knew the layout of the mountains and the grave's location. It would save Jed time looking for the grave and give them an extra rifle to help protect Ellie if needed. He had lied to Bacon. The hunters hadn't mentioned anything about burying Lige Hatcher. All they spoke of was how the grave was marked.

Neither Jed nor the youngster noticed the tall figure watching them from the saloon door. Walter Squires, the skinny trapper, who Jed had floored and two other hard-looking men, studied Jed and Dibbs from their vantage point, out of sight behind the door. A cruel grin broke out across the thin face as Squires turned back inside the saloon.

"We'll let them get out of town a ways before we start out." The big Adam's apple bobbed up and down as the skinny man cackled. "Sugar, you and Pete go get us some supplies, then find the other boys."

"With what, Walt?" The short one called Sugar looked up at the tall man, shrugging his shoulders. "We done drunk up what little you gave us of our hide money."

Handing over a gold coin, Squires nodded. "Now git!"

"What we gonna follow after that one for?" The one called Pete spoke up. "We just got ourselves here. I'm wanting to drink and kick up my heels a bit."

"You can't drink without money and I'm holding onto that for you." Squires frowned. "Remember the last three seasons, you two were broke after a week in town."

"He ain't worth it, Walter." Sugar spoke up. "Besides, I've heard he's bad medicine. You kinda found that out yourself last night."

"Yeah, and that killer, roaming the Gallatins, is out there some-place." Pete added. "I ain't hankering to tangle with either one of them."

"We'll pick up some help along the way." Squires shrugged. "Sides, the killer ain't after us."

"Someone cut off poor old Riley's head." Pete seemed to pale. "You could be wrong. It might just be us he's after."

"What for, we haven't done anything."

Both of the other hunters shook their heads. What hadn't they done? Killing, robbing traps, stealing. "We don't like it, Walter."

The hard slap of the bony hand sounded as the smaller hunter, Sugar, landed on his back inside the saloon. "He killed my brother. Now, he's gonna die."

Helping the downed hunter back to his feet, the two trappers sauntered off to the mercantile store as Squires returned inside the saloon. "He's gonna get us killed, Pete."

"He's the boss, Sugar. Where would we be without him?"

"Alive, maybe." Sugar rubbed his face. "I've heard bad things about that one. The one they call Crow Killer."

"Personally, I'm more scared of the killer out there."

"You figuring it's us he's a hunting?"

"Someone followed us all the way in here from the Gallatins with our plews." Pete looked around the streets. "Then the very next day after we got here, someone cut off poor old Riley's head."

"It were probably just an irate hunter that followed us." Sugar shook his head.

"And you're figuring this hunter rode all the way to Baxter Springs just to kill Riley?" Pete argued with the short hunter. "You know what, Sugar, you're stupider than Squires."

"We've done a lot of folk's mischief, Pete." Sugar looked up and down the boardwalk. "He just might be related to someone we killed."

"Could be, we've put a lot of men under alright." Pete agreed. "A lot of men. I ain't proud of it either."

"Then why in tarnation is Squires so anxious to lead us back out there where that killer is?"

"He may be figuring on killing Crow Killer before we get anywhere near the Gallatins. Pete rubbed his jaw. "That would be my guess."

"You know what I'm thinking?"

"What would that be?" Pete was curious.

"I'll tell you." Sugar grinned slyly. "I've got it figured. It's the woman he wants. I've seen him eyeing her ever since we've been in this pigsty. He didn't say a word about riding out until he heard them trappers say this Crow Killer was taking her back to the Gallatins."

"No." Pete grinned. "You mean he ain't after that Injun because of his brother?"

"Luke Grisham wasn't his brother stupid."

"That's what he said."

Pushing through the mercantile door, Sugar shoved Pete ahead of him. "If I were you, old friend, I wouldn't believe everything old Walter said."

"You mean he's crazy enough to go after a white woman?"

Sugar nodded slowly. "She's a pretty filly and you know Squires is half crazy."

"He'd have to be all crazy to steal a white woman. They'd skin us alive if we get caught even thinking of such a thing." Pete grumbled.

"We've been trading with Bate Baker for many a year now." Sugar scratched his scrubby jaw. "Ain't you seen the way Squires has watched that girl ever since she's been back here from the east?"

"No, can't say I ever noticed." Pete shook his head.

"Well, he has. Come on."

CHAPTER 4

For five days, they had let the horses pick their own speed along the well-rutted immigrant trail that traveled over mountains, then dipped down into the lower valleys before starting another long climb up again. The trail west would be a fast trip so Jed bought only enough supplies, plus lead and shot, to get them to the Gallatins and back. They were traveling light and there would be no time for hunting on this trip.

As immigrants traveled west, they discarded furniture and baggage alongside the mountain trails to lighten their load as the hard pull up the rocky terrain became harder. With every mile, the tough mountain road became steeper, putting a heavier strain on the oxen and horses pulling the heavy Conestoga Wagons. During a hard snowstorm, the ice beneath the work team's feet would be treacherous as they leaned into their collars and yokes straining against the heavy loads they were pulling. Every mile along these rough mountain trails was extremely difficult and hard work for the teams, even in good weather.

Although, he was eager to get back to Bright Moon and the twins, the slower pace suited Jed. The trip would take a couple of days longer at this speed, but he was able to carefully study the trail for any signs of trouble. Many times in the past, Jed had ridden long, dangerous trails similar to the remote trail they were now traveling on. These were dangerous, unsettled lands, and travelers passing along the western road knew to be on their guard. To lose one's way, fall behind, or forget to be vigilant had caused the death of many a pilgrim in these heathen lands.

As they started their climb, higher into the mountains, Jed could feel the air cooling, especially at night as they huddled around their campfire. Normally, covered in beautiful aromatic wild flowers during the summer months, it was too early for them to be in bloom at the higher elevation. The mountain air was sweet and clean, carrying the smell of cedar and mountain pines, and the higher peaks, looming above them, were still covered in snow. Jed could just imagine the plight Chalk Briggs had found himself in when the heavy sleet and snow started falling so early last season.

Lige Hatcher was considered an old man in his profession, but no wagon scout knew these mountains and the dangers they held better than he. If anyone could guide a huge train filled with green immigrants through these passes safely, it would be Hatcher. Jed knew, since the old scout was killed, it must have been a freak occurrence. Lige Hatcher was too smart and trail wise to get himself in a bad predicament unless it had been by pure accident.

"Tell me about the babies, Jed." Ellie pushed her horse up close to Jed, taking his mind from his thoughts. "You haven't spoken much of them."

Smiling, he shrugged. "They look exactly alike. Like my mother always said, they are like two peas in a pod. You can't tell them apart by looking at their faces."

"I bet they're beautiful." Ellie grinned. "They would have to be."

"I think they are, but then I'm probably prejudiced."

"Has Little Antelope and Walking Horse seen them?"

"They probably have by now. When I left He Dog's village, he had sent for them."

"Little Antelope will be so happy." Ellie smiled. "My sister wants children of her own."

"Yes." Jed thought of the little woman. "She does."

"Where is Red Hawk?" Ellie looked at Jed. "I figured he'd be with you."

"There was no time to send for him." Jed thought of his Crow brother. "Now, I wish he were here."

"You two are close."

"Yes, we are." Jed nodded. "He is a great warrior and friend."

"He's something alright. A real specimen of manhood." Ellie remembered the handsome warrior.

"I worry for him sometimes."

"You worry for Red Hawk?" She smiled. "Why?"

"He leads his warriors deep into Comanche lands to steal horses and raid." Jed frowned. "I fear for his safety."

"Why does he do the things he does?"

"He's just got a wild spirit that can't be tamed, I reckon." Jed smiled as he thought about the half-wild Crow warrior.

"He is that for a fact." Ellie agreed. "Perhaps, he'll get married one day and settle down."

"He might get himself married alright. Plenty Coups wants grandchildren, but I doubt he'll ever settle down." Jed smiled.

"Only time will tell." Ellie smiled to herself. "He'll meet someone one of these days."

Dibbs, riding several yards in front of the small caravan, held up his hand to halt the procession. Waving Jed forward, he motioned to a densely thicketed pass a few hundred yards down the trail.

"Ahead, there's a good place to set an ambush if we've been spotted."

"I will ride forward and check it out." Jed looked back to where Ellie and the packhorse waited. "Watch over Ellie."

"No, I will look it over." Dibbs studied the dense underbrush. "You take care of the woman and watch for my signal. Move forward slowly, where anyone hiding in there can watch you."

Before Jed could protest, the youngster dismounted and slipped silently forward, disappearing inside the jumble of thickets along the trail. Watching as Dibbs moved away, Jed felt the hair on his neck rise. This one wasn't the normal city youngster. He moved light like a mountain cat and was swift like an antelope out on the Kansas plains. Something about the boy made him curious and uneasy. He hadn't given Jed time to argue before he handed him the horse's reins and moved forward as if he was expecting danger ahead.

Several minutes passed before Dibbs appeared on the trail ahead and motioned them forward. Noticing blood on the youngster's hand as he mounted, Jed waited for Dibbs to speak first.

"They were there alright, two of them." Dibbs saw Jed looking at the blood and quickly wiped it on his horse's neck.

"Sentries?"

"Probably. They were Cree Indians down from Canada." Dibbs smiled. "They were young and careless."

"You kill them?"

"I killed them before they could carry word to their friends camped out in the bottoms below us somewhere."

"Their horses?"

"They weren't much count." Dibbs shrugged. "I killed them too."

Jed looked over at the calm young man. For the first time, he was seeing this one in a completely new light. No matter his age or whatever else he was, Dibbs Bacon was a dangerous person to have as an enemy. He had just killed two men and there had been no sound of a struggle, plus he showed no sign of emotion. The youngster was a mask of calmness that most men who had just killed couldn't muster. Jed was impressed, not good, but he was impressed with the youngster's callousness. Dibbs was already a killer and the boy wasn't even out of his teens yet. He knew it took a different kind of man, a cold-blooded man, to kill a horse, even an injured one. Yes, Dibbs Bacon was a dangerous one for sure. Jed wondered if Dibbs could be the crazed killer everyone was talking about. Probably not, he was still just a youngster.

"Canada's a long way from here." Jed looked at Dibbs as Ellie rode up. "Don't the Cree live across the border to the north?"

"Most of the time they do." Dibbs mounted his horse. "They had us spotted, Jed. If I hadn't killed them, by morning, they'd have all their warriors up here on our necks."

"Is that the only reason you killed them?"

"Yep, that's the only reason." The voice came out hard but then a smile broke out on his face as he greeted Ellie. "False alarm, Miss Ellie."

Jed couldn't figure out Dibbs. One thing, he wasn't a braggart and he wanted to keep Ellie safe. "We'll camp pretty soon, Ellie."

"I'll fry us up some hot pan biscuits."

"No, ma'am, no fire tonight this close to the pass." Dibbs kicked his horse, back in the lead. "There's a nice little mountain stream a couple miles ahead. We'll camp there tonight."

Jed was curious, Dibbs had admitted he had been to the Gallatins, but now he described the trails like he was very familiar with them. Yes, this one was a strange one alright. He just couldn't figure the young man out. Who was he, or better yet, what was he?

The horses were hobbled on the short tender grass that had just started to sprout from the cold mountainous ground. Doing as Dibbs asked, Ellie looked into the packs and brought forth cold bread and side meat. She also produced a fresh can of peaches that made Dibbs' mouth water as he stared at it. Finishing his cold supper, Jed picked up his rifle and walked out on the road where he could study the surrounding mountains.

"They'll be down lower, where it's a mite warmer." Dibbs had slipped up behind Jed as silent as a stalking cat. "We're safe enough for now."

"For now?" Jed was curious at the words. "Do you believe they're looking for us?"

"The Cree sometimes ride with the Metis from Canada and sometimes with the rogue white hunters that prey on the weak." Dibbs knelt down and touched the rocky trail. "They're all a bunch of thieves and murderers. Yes, I believe for some reason they are following us."

"They won't miss the two you killed?"

"They'll miss them alright, but it'll be daylight before they ride out looking for them."

"Then what?"

"Depends."

"On what?"

"On how many they send." Dibbs tossed a rock into the brush. "If they send one or two, I'll kill them, more than that, we'll kill them."

"I don't want Ellie in any danger if we can avoid it." Jed studied the face before him. The youngster seemed so calm talking about more killing. "I just want her to see the grave, then we're headed back."

"I feel the same." Dibbs agreed. "But, out here in these mountains, some things can't be avoided, like killing."

"What about the wagon trains?" Jed was curious. "How do they get through without trouble?"

"Too many folks on the wagons, and these killers don't dare take on so many." Dibbs voice hardened. "They just pick off trappers and smaller outfits. Especially, smaller hunting parties."

"You seem to know them pretty well?"

"I do." Only a nod came from the young one. "I know them very well."

Jed didn't know much about Dibbs Bacon, but he did know the youngster was an experienced mountain man, experienced far beyond his years. Whoever had taught him the ways of the mountains had instilled the wiliness of an animal. Jed watched the lad, and nothing moved or made a sound that he didn't notice. Jed didn't know whether he, himself was as versed and alert in these mountains as Dibbs Bacon was. The youngster's keen senses were uncanny.

"You said you'd been here several times since your step-pa was killed."

"I have been."

"You didn't say how he was killed."

Seeing Ellie walking toward them, Dibbs smiled. "She is such a lady."

"Yes, Dibbs, she is." Jed knew the youngster wasn't going to answer his question.

"What are you two talking about so secretly?" Ellie smiled. "What are you plotting?"

"Just tomorrow's ride."

"How much longer is it to the grave?"

"Well, Miss Ellie, we've been on the trail a little over five days now." Dibbs calculated. "I figure from the looks of where we are, another four days at least."

"Then we're making good time?" Jed asked.

"Yes, sir, we are. Now, let's go back and get a little rest."

"Sounds good to me." Jed watched as the young hunter followed Ellie as they walked back to the camp. Something bothered him, and he couldn't put his finger on what it was. He noticed Dibbs was never without his rifle. Even while he was eating, the rifle rested across his lap. He also carried two long skinning knives, one in each of his high-topped moccasins. Jed had watched him with the knives as he honed them sharp enough to shave with, then Dibbs killed a squirrel sitting on a limb with one of the knives. The knife found its target unerringly dead center. Jed knew if this youngster had been born an Arapaho, he would be welcomed into the Lance Bearer Society and the same with the Cheyenne Dog Soldiers. Remembering their first meeting at Bridgers, he knew he had completely misjudged Dibbs as just a young inexperienced city lad. He had learned a good lesson, and in the future, he would never try to judge another man by his looks.

Dark was coming on as Jed led the horses to water, then hobbled them again on fresh grazing. Returning to the camp, he found Ellie alone, repacking the grub sack. Dibbs had disappeared and was nowhere to be seen.

"Where's Dibbs?"

She looked around the camp. "I thought he went with you."

"No, he's not been with me." Jed looked at the darkening shadows.

"I'm sure he'll return soon." Ellie looked at Jed. "Tell me more about Bright Moon and the babies."

"Well, they're about this long and this big around." Jed laughed, holding his hands spread. "I can almost hold both of them in the palm of one hand."

"They could have been ours." Ellie seemed wistful.

"Things weren't meant to be that way, I reckon." Jed shrugged. "You had your way of life and mine was different."

"Was it so different, Jed?"

"Yes, Ellie, you were born a lady, and me, I'm just a natural loner, living by my wits, back in the mountains."

"I guess so." She agreed. "Anyway, I'm so glad you're happy, and I can't wait to see them."

"When we return, you'll have to come to the valley and spend some time with Bright Moon and the little ones."

"Perhaps, Little Antelope and Walking Horse will come for a visit too." Ellie smiled. "We can all have a good visit."

"Walking Horse is Chief of the Arapaho now. He can no longer ride as he wishes."

"You mean he has to stay close to the village and his people?"

"Yes, but I will get word to my brother and hopefully he will be able to come." Jed smiled at the pretty woman. "Perhaps, Red Hawk will come too."

"That would be nice, but how would I get there without you to guide me?" Ellie questioned him.

"Maybe, Dibbs will bring you."

"Dibbs?" Ellie looked at Jed. "You think he could find your valley?"

Jed nodded. "I think we have misjudged our Mister Bacon. I believe he could do about anything he puts his mind too back in these mountains."

"But, he's just a boy, Jed."

"Yes, in years he's still young." Jed agreed. "But he's an experienced hunter. You sent him to Bridgers alone to find me."

"Yes, I did, but there's an established road leading right to the post." Ellie shook her head. "Your valley has nothing but a trail, and it's completely hidden and far from civilization."

"There's something about him." Jed frowned. "I can't get a handle on him."

"You don't trust him?"

"It's not exactly that. I just don't think he's telling us everything about himself."

"I see."

"How long have you known him?"

"Not long. Maybe two weeks before I sent him to find you."

"And you know nothing more about him?"

"He came into Baxter Springs with a bloody knife wound and completely exhausted." Ellie explained. "Grandpa fixed him up and got him a job at the livery stable. I bought him some store-bought clothes. The buckskins he wore were torn, bloody, and filthy."

"And?"

"His wound healed up, then he earned enough to outfit himself with a horse and rifle." Ellie thought back. "Then he vanished again for three weeks. When he returned to town again with his clothes covered in blood, he had the letter Mister Masters had given him. After reading the letter, I bought him some more clean clothes and I asked him if he could ride to Bridgers to find you."

"Bloody?"

"Yes, bloody, said it was from a deer he killed."

"Well, he sure didn't have any problems finding me."

"I'm glad you are here, except for the babies." Ellie smiled. "Your place is with them, not here in these strange lands."

"You asked for help, Ellie." Jed shook his head. "Here I am."

"Thank you." Ellie reached out and touched his sleeve. "You've always been there for me, Jed."

"You get some sleep." Jed watched until she drifted off into a sound sleep, then taking his rifle, he slipped out into the night. He needed to find out what Dibbs was up to. Sitting silently, in the dark of the night, Jed listened for the youngster's return. The moon was far past its zenith when he spotted Dibbs' figure slipping as silent as a stalking cougar through the dark as he returned to camp. The soft leather moccasins covering his feet made no sound as he walked past where Jed sat in the shadows.

Jed followed Dibbs as he slipped into the dark camp and looked about for him. The gun barrel silently touched the lad's leather hunting shirt making him whirl in a crouch. Jed noticed the skinning knife that had appeared as if by magic in Dibbs' hand.

"You startled me, Jed."

Lowering the rifle, Jed watched as the knife was sheathed. "Where you been, Dibbs?"

"Back up the trail." Dibbs tried to make out Jed's face. "We've got company coming. We've got to move now."

"Who's coming, the Cree?"

"No, you remember the tall hunter you slugged back in the saloon?"

Jed thought of the tall skinny man. "I remember him."

"It's him, and he's brought four other whites with him." Dibbs quickly told Jed how he had scouted back up the trail and discovered their camp. "They're fools... had themselves a campfire big enough to roast a full bear on."

"You think they're following us?"

"They're not exactly after me or you, Jed."

"Then who?"

"The big skinny one, Walter Squires, is after her." Dibbs nodded over to where Ellie slept.

"What?"

"I heard him brag about it several times while he sat by that fire."
Dibbs swore. "He's crazy or something. He seems to be obsessed with
Ellie. He aims to steal her from us."

"He does, huh?" Jed frowned. "How does he know Ellie?"

"From Baxter Springs, I reckon. She's not exactly unknown back
there you know." Dibbs replied. "Squires and his bunch have always
stayed around the settlement during the summer months. Drinking,
cards, and meanness was always their long suit."

"Yeah, she's known for sure." Jed knew Ellie was well known in the
settlement since her return from the east. She was also the most beautiful
woman in the settlement and surrounding lands.

"Ellie is a very handsome woman."

"That she is."

"Squires followed us here to take her." Dibbs explained. "When he
speaks of her, his voice and eyes are crazed. His mouth waters like a
coyote after a rabbit."

Jed knew Dibbs could be right. Early summer was here, and there
would be no trapping for several months to come. There was no other
reason for Squires and his men to come back into the dangerous
Gallatins so early in the spring. "You could be right."

"I know I'm right. We must ride on, now." Dibbs looked out in the
dark. "I passed several Metis riding toward Squires' camp as I slipped
away. They've probably joined him by now."

"We could stay here and confront them here when they ride in."

"There won't be any confronting, Jed." Dibbs paced back and forth.
"We'll have to kill 'em, every son of them."

"You said there's just five." Jed stood up. "We'll surprise them and
take their weapons."

"Five not counting the Metis is what I said." Dibbs shook his head.
"No, many Cree are camped just over the mountain to the south. One
shot would bring them up here on us."

"You have any better ideas?"

"Hopefully, I've delayed Mister Squires for a while." Dibbs smiled
coldly. "When the Cree find their dead ones, maybe they'll think the
skinny one and his men are the killers."

"You think so?"

"I made sure to fix the tracks to look so." Dibbs grinned wider. "It'll be a good joke on that killer. Won't it?"

"You fixed the tracks?" Jed couldn't believe one so young thought as this one did. "You aimed to get those five whites killed."

"Hopefully, it could happen alright. Oh well, some live some die." Dibbs responded coldly. "Maybe, they'll kill them filthy Metis as well."

Jed looked at the cool youngster as he loaded his horse. Never had he seen such a cold-hearted one as this lad. "And?"

"All we have to do is stay ahead of old Squires and the Metis until the Cree catch up to them." Dibbs grinned. "Then, someone is bound to die. With any luck, they'll lose a few of their own men as well."

"For one so young, you're kinda bloodthirsty ain't you?"

"Not as bloodthirsty as some." Jed could hear the cold words, but what he didn't see in the dark was the hardness that came over the youngster's face. "I just wish I had the time to put them all under myself."

"Why do you hate Squires and his men so?"

"That's for me to know... only me."

"Ain't the Cree and Metis on friendly terms?" Jed was curious.

"They have been." Dibbs snickered. "But, when they find what's left of their dead warriors, they might just get a little angry and start a fight without asking."

"I'll wake Ellie and gather our pouches." Jed knew there was no sense pushing Dibbs for the answer. In time, further down the trail, the youngster might tell him.

"I know a place a few miles west where we can look back down the trail. Maybe, we can see and hear what's happening to poor old Squires." Dibbs turned for the horses. "With any luck, they'll all kill one another."

Jed didn't understand the youngster's hardness, but he knew they had to ride on. There was no time to discuss the matter, even if Dibbs would talk about it. He knew he couldn't save the whites without putting Ellie in danger. The chain of events Dibbs had started would just have to play itself out. Arousing Ellie, Jed carried the packs down to the stream and helped Dibbs saddle her horse and packhorse. Swinging up on the bay horse, Jed motioned Ellie to follow him as Dibbs hung back to cover their rear. If Dibbs was right, Squires and his men wouldn't hit the trail until daylight. If the Cree found their dead warriors and took up the trail of the unsuspecting white hunters there could be a fight before midday. Jed didn't want the white hunters killed, but he didn't mind them being slowed down a bit. Dibbs had said the skinny one wanted Ellie, for this foolishness he might die, but it would be by the hand of the Cree, not his.

Just before midday, Dibbs caught up to them as they crossed the peak of the rutted mountain trail. From their vantage point, they could see almost three miles down into the valley they had just climbed out of. They heard no sound of a fight yet.

"We will wait. From here, we'll be able to see anyone coming up the mountain road." Dibbs smiled cruelly. "Any rifle reports will carry an echo throughout these canyons and passes."

"You say there's five hunters?"

"Yes, there are five counting the big hunter Squires." Dibbs nodded. "And maybe ten Metis."

"Wonder how many Cree?"

"Maybe twenty now." Dibbs shrugged. "Maybe less."

"How do you know?"

The grey eyes locked on Jed. "Because, I have been in their camp many times over the last eight months."

"You're friends with them?"

"Hardly." Dibbs pulled one of his long knives from the scabbard sewn in his moccasin. "Hardly."

"Why are these people from Canada down here in these mountains?"

"I told you, they hunt for stragglers along the immigrant trail." Dibbs checked the priming of his rifle. "For many years, they've roamed these mountains from here, north to Canada."

"Renegades?" Jed studied the lower trail.

"They're renegades alright." Dibbs added. "They kill and rob from anybody they find."

"Do they know we're here?"

"I don't think so, not yet. For now, all they're looking for is the ones that killed their friends." Dibbs turned his head as he listened intently for any sounds of gunfire. "But, Squires knows we're here for sure."

Jed couldn't understand the youngster. His words and actions were cold, calculating, calling out his hatred for Squires, the Metis, and Cree.

The one standing before him was still young to carry such deep hatred. Watching the young one's movements and listening to him talk, Jed knew Dibbs Bacon was a very dangerous person when angered. Still, Dibbs seemed to have Ellie's safety foremost in his actions. Jed knew the youngster had a fondness for Ellie, and wondered if that was enough for him to ride with them into this dangerous country.

"Tell me, Dibbs, I'm curious."

"About what?" The young face turned toward Jed with a straight face.

"Your voice and words seem to say you hate the Metis and Cree."

"Hate?" The head shook in denial. "I kill them. It's far beyond hate I feel for these animals."

"But, you are so young."

"I've been told you were young when you took up the lance." Dibbs smiled. "Around Baxter Springs folks speak of you like a demon."

"Yes, I was young." Jed nodded. "The difference is, I don't hate. I have only killed when challenged."

"Killing is killing, my friend." Dibbs dismounted. "Tell me, Jed, what is the difference?"

Jed looked at the youngster and shook his head. "Dibbs, every animal kills to eat or protect their young, but not because of hate."

"Every dog kills, my friend. Either way, you find yourself dead one day."

Suddenly, both men turned their heads to the east. They could hear the sound of gunfire coming from the canyons below. Several shots were fired quickly, then only silence came from the lower trail.

"Sounds like a standoff down there."

"I reckon that'll keep Mister Squires and his bunch busy for a while." Dibbs grinned. "I think we can go on about our business."

Jed looked down the canyon where there was nothing but silence. "Maybe, they'll turn and ride back to Baxter Springs."

"I'd say that'll be kinda hard for him to do."

"What do you mean?"

"I cut their horses loose last night and scattered them." The youngster smiled. "I'd say they're like a pig in a mud hole, stuck."

"Why'd you do that?" Jed stared hard at the lad. "I reckon you do want them dead."

"Squires and his men followed us here to kill you and me, and take Miss Ellie." Dibbs listened for more gunfire. "Squires has somehow made a deal with the Metis to help him get her."

"That's what you figure?"

"That's it." Dibbs kept his attention down the trail. "The Metis and Cree roam these mountains and watch this road to kill any unfortunate traveler. They normally don't fight with each other."

"But, now you've fixed it so they will?"

"I hope it worked out that way." Dibbs grinned. "But now, I fear somehow old Squires talked himself out of his mess."

"What do you mean?"

"You hear that?"

Jed shook his head. He didn't hear a sound from back down the mountain. "I don't hear anything."

"That's what I mean." Dibbs cussed under his breath. "I fear Squires has somehow made a truce with the Cree. Now, he's recruited them to help him. Now, we've got more fighters to contend with."

"Could be you're right. There's sure no fighting back there."

"If we're going to see the grave, let's get."

"Does Squires know these mountains?"

"He and his companions hunt and trap these valleys every year." Dibbs continued. "He knows them alright, like the back of his hand. And he knows the Metis and Cree."

"These are Gros Ventre lands aren't they?"

"They are, but the Gros Ventre are friendly to most hunters." Dibbs replied. "They don't look for trouble, even with the Metis and Cree."

"Scared of them?"

"No, I wouldn't exactly say that."

"Then why do they let them hunt and kill in their lands?"

"These are big mountains with plenty of game for all." Dibbs pointed across the huge range. "As long as you don't attack their villages or hunters, they'll trade with you peacefully."

"And the Cree and Metis don't bother the Gros Ventre, is that it?"

"I said they are killers and thieves, not stupid." Dibbs turned his horse. "They ain't about to rile the Gros Ventre into a fight and lose their easy money along these trails."

"So each side makes a profit off of leaving the other alone?"

"Exactly." Dibbs smiled. "Now, you're getting the idea. This is just a killing field out here."

"Killing field?"

"Yeah, the big dog eats the little dog."

Jed listened for several minutes, then swung up on the bay horse. He hated to ride off and leave Squires and his men without knowing if they were coming after them, but he had no choice. Ellie could be in danger and she was their main concern. If Dibbs wasn't lying, the white hunters were coming after them and now they had reinforcements. There was no doubt, Squires had followed them into these mountains to steal Ellie, and there was no other reason. No matter how this worked out, the white hunters deserved the fate that befell them.

For three days, they traveled the well-marked wagon road that ran straight through the Gallatin Mountains. Dibbs had ridden out several times along the trail, leaving Jed and Ellie to follow. Nearing dark, Jed made camp beside a large water hole protected on two sides by a large rock outcropping. From his vantage position, Jed watched and listened for the young man to return. Jed's only concern was to get Ellie to the grave, then safely back to Baxter Springs. He believed Dibbs about Squires being after the girl so he wasn't about to let her out of his sight.

"He's very good at slipping around isn't he?" Ellie was slicing side meat for their supper. "He's starting to make me nervous with the wildness in his eyes and the way he talks."

"I know." Jed sat with his rifle, watching the far mountain. "I feel the same way. I just can't figure him out."

"Something's happened to him and made him that way." Ellie looked at Jed. "Do you think he's the killer everyone in Baxter Springs speaks about?"

Jed jerked his head at her words. "You heard about that?"

"Yes, but I had no reason to think it could be Dibbs."

"Maybe, someday he'll tell us." Jed nodded. "But, there's one thing for sure, he hates the ones following us."

"And us?" Ellie looked at Jed.

"No, we have nothing to worry about from him." Jed shook his head. "I believe he'd give his life to protect you."

"Is there something you're not telling me, Jed?"

Jed wondered if he should tell her. "Dibbs says the big trapper, Squires, has come here to abduct you."

"Abduct me?" The dark eyes blinked. "Is he crazy or something?"

"He must be crazy." Jed replied. "I don't mean to worry you, Ellie, but I thought you should know."

"Thank you for telling me, Jed."

Jed knew the Indian culture of warfare and killing was their way of life, but the way Dibbs acted was different. The youngster would come alive before heading out to scout the surrounding canyons. Most young men his age would have been terrified to go out into the dark alone, but not Dibbs Bacon. He appeared to relish the darkness and the danger it held. He would slip away for hours on end during the dark hours, then reappeared at daylight as they were breaking their night camp. The youngster seemed to thrive without sleep or rest.

"Dibbs said tomorrow we would reach the Gallatin River and the grave." Ellie smiled at Jed. "I'm sorry I got you into this. I should have just let Pa be dead and rest in peace."

"He also said we were in Gros Ventre country, now. Red Hawk told me they were a very hostile and private tribe who sometimes frowns on strangers coming into their lands."

"But, they let the wagon trains pass through from the east."

"Dibbs says your pa was friends with them." Jed didn't see fit to mention Hatcher's Indian wife. "Anyway, I doubt there's much they can do against a whole train full of people armed to the teeth."

Hearing something on the trail, Jed slipped beside a large rock, pulling Ellie behind him. Suddenly, Dibbs appeared several yards in front of them bent over and running fast. Panting and out of breath, he knelt beside them.

After catching his wind, the youngster rose and walked to the horses. "We go, now."

"What is it?"

"The whites somehow survived the Cree and made allies with

them." Dibbs regained his air. "Worse still, for some reason, many Gros Ventre warriors have Squires and his men following them here."

"Is Squires friendly with these Gros Ventre?"

"Not that I'm aware of." The light-haired youngster shook his head. "But, I think our friends back there have told them of us and her."

"To save their hair."

"Squires is a coward. He'd sell his own mother to save himself."

"Can we still reach the grave?"

"There is nothing ahead on the trail." The grey eyes flashed. "We can reach it alright, but getting out of here might be tricky."

"We could turn around now." Ellie stared at the two men. "It is up to you, Jed."

"Are you scared, Ellie?" Jed looked at her.

Ellie hesitated, then answered. "Yes, I'm scared, but we've come this far, I would like to see his grave."

"It doesn't matter whether we go back or forward, we have no choice now. The trail back is blocked by Squires, his men, and the Gros Ventre." Dibbs nodded. "I don't know what's become of the Metis or the Cree warriors. Hurry, let's ride."

The wagon trail was easy to follow, lit up by a full moon. Dibbs, knowing the road, led the way while Jed rode behind the procession, watching their back trail. With the coming of the new sun, daylight broke out in the east, showing them the lands they were passing through. The tall mountains were beautiful, laying shrouded in the early morning fog and low clouds. Passing down a long sloping part of the trail, Dibbs reined in and pointed to a strange wagon wheel standing alone fifty paces from the road. The makeshift headstone was nestled in a small, tree-lined cove. Farther down the trail, almost a half-mile, Jed could see the shimmer of the water reflecting off the Gallatin River.

"There's your father's grave, Miss Ellie."

"Are you sure, Dibbs?" Ellie shuddered as she looked at the grave.

"I am sure." Dibbs nodded toward the wheel.

Kicking her horse, Ellie rode to the grave and looked down at it for several minutes before dismounting.

Jed looked around the site… articles of discarded furniture, broken wagon parts, even one abandoned wagon sat alongside the road near the grave. All the debris was the result of overloading the wagons and teams, and entering a mountain range of high passes and rough roads over the years. Not to mention the heavy snows and ice that had come early, causing more misery for the immigrants. From the signs, the heavy winter storms that had raged unexpectedly across his valley, had hit there the same way. Terrible havoc and damage had been caused when the storms caught the wagons in its savage path, high in the mountains.

Looking across the river, Jed wondered if Chalk Briggs and his wagons had been able to get across the western mountains safely. There was a possibility the immigrant train could be ahead somewhere, broken down and waiting for help. The hunter, Masters, had said Briggs had given him the note for Ellie as they were making the crossing here on the Gallatin. Sliding from his horse, Jed stood beside Ellie at the grave. Holding her trembling arm he walked with her nearer to the grave.

"I will ride back and watch our back trail." Dibbs turned his horse. "We cannot remain here long."

"We won't."

CHAPTER 5

Walking Horse, with Little Antelope and several Arapaho warriors trailing him, rode into the Cheyenne village of He Dog. They waited for the young chief's invitation to dismount, according to protocol, the age-old custom that most tribes honored. Stopping only long enough to greet her brother and Crazy Cat, Little Antelope rushed to the lodge where Crazy Cat pointed to. Pushing through the hide flap, she stopped and looked to where Bright Moon was holding the two babies.

Kneeling, as Bright Moon held one of the babies out to her, she smiled as she took the little one into her arms. For several minutes no words were spoken between the sisters as Little Antelope fawned over each baby.

"They are beautiful, Sister." Little Antelope held them close. "A little princess and a warrior."

"They look like their father." Bright Moon smiled softly as Little Antelope kissed her.

"They look like both of you."

"You have ridden hard to come here so quickly." Bright Moon could see Little Antelope was tired. "I am glad you are here."

"The trail was longer this time. The horses seemed to walk so slowly over the mountains."

"You must be tired and hungry. Would you like to rest?" Bright Moon asked as she smiled at her sister with the babies.

"No, I want to enjoy this moment forever with my nephew and niece."

"You will have many moments with them, Sister." Bright Moon replied. "They will be with us many, many seasons to come."

Little Antelope gently touched Little Ellie's smooth skin. "Do you remember when you said you would not have children?"

"I remember, Sister. How foolish I was to say such a thing." Bright Moon laughed lightly.

"Not foolish, just young." Little Antelope crooned to the babies. "Now, you have two."

Bright Moon could read the unspoken words as she watched her sister make a fuss over the babies. "Soon, you will have your own."

"We will see. I long for that day." Little Antelope held Little Ellie close to her. "My lovely princess."

"And what of Eagle's Wing, Sister?"

"He is handsome, with such penetrating eyes for one so young."

"He will be a Lance Bearer one day." Bright Moon pointed to the baby's back. "Look at the mark on his shoulder."

"I see it." Little Antelope ran her finger over the birthmark of an Arapaho Lance. "The blood that runs through his veins will make him a great warrior for the people."

"Let's take them outside to meet their uncle and show them off."

Walking Horse, Big Owl, and several other warriors closed in around Bright Moon and Little Antelope, wanting to get their first view of the children of Crow Killer. Each warrior leaned over the small heads, laughing as they admired the babies.

"At this rate, Bright Moon and Crow Killer will have their own village soon." Big Owl laughed, making his huge stomach bounce up and down. "Already, they have a good start."

"They are so small and beautiful." Walking Horse shook his head.

Little Antelope placed Eagle's Wing in the warrior's huge hands. "Don't you dare drop him, Husband."

He Dog smiled as Walking Horse sat down and stared wonderingly at the baby. He knew what Walking Horse was thinking. He also had the same feelings when he held the babies for the first time.

"I predict he will be a great warrior one day." Big Owl laughed. "I Big Owl will teach him all he needs to know."

"What will my brother, Big Owl, teach him... how to eat?" Crazy

Cat slapped the three hundred pound warrior on the back and laughed.

"Big Owl speaks the truth. This is what our medicine man, Spotted Panther, has seen in his smoke." Bright Moon smiled proudly. "Yesterday, he said Eagle's Wing will fight one day with the greatest Sioux warrior of all. He will be victorious against his enemies and count many coups."

"What chief was that, Bright Moon?" Crazy Cat asked. "The Sioux are our brothers and allies, but we do not normally fight with them against our enemies."

"He did not say what warrior or what fight, but he has never been wrong." Bright Moon smiled as she looked at her son.

"Talk of war tires me, my friends." He Dog pulled out his medicine pipe and looked at the group of warriors. "We will leave the women with the little ones and go smoke the pipe and talk of other matters."

Bright Moon took He Dog by the arm and led him a few feet away. "I will speak with you and Walking Horse after you have your smoke."

"About what, Sister?"

"Later, Brother." Bright Moon looked to where Walking Horse was playing with the baby. "I must rescue my son."

"We will speak." He Dog motioned for the men to follow him.

With reluctance, Walking Horse released the baby. "You will let me hold him later?"

Bright Moon smiled. "You will have many years ahead to be with him, to teach him the ways of his ancestors, the ways of the Arapaho Lance Bearer."

Little Antelope looked at He Dog as he sauntered away with the warriors. "What is wrong with my brother, He Dog, he seems tired."

"Since he has become chief, he has many worries for his people." Bright Moon shook her head. "He is no longer the young playful warrior you knew, Sister."

"This I can see."

As the evening turned into night, He Dog and Walking Horse sought out Bright Moon where she sat with Little Antelope and the babies. Leaving the little ones in Little Antelope's care, Bright Moon joined them outside the lodge.

"We are here, Sister. You wish to speak with us?" He Dog asked curiously.

"My husband has ridden west." Bright Moon took the seat He Dog motioned her to. "Spotted Panther says there will be much danger for him."

"Are you asking that we follow him and help him on this trail?"

"No, you know he forbids any warrior to follow. He does not wish any of you to follow him into danger."

Walking Horse looked over at her. "Do you want us to ask Red Hawk to follow him to the west?"

"No, this is not what I want to speak of."

"Then what is it, Sister?"

Bright Moon looked to the lodge opening where the crying of a baby sounded. "My husband's father is alone in the far valley where our lodge is. I wish for you and Walking Horse to go there or send warriors to make sure he is safe."

"You know I cannot leave the village. I am the chief of my people." He Dog shook his head. "I do not think Walking Horse could leave his village for very long either."

"I know this." Bright Moon looked hard at her brother. "But, we must see to his safety."

"I will speak with my warriors." He Dog nodded. "We will discuss this matter around my fire tonight."

"Thank you, my brother." Bright Moon smiled.

"Your babies cry." He Dog looked over at the lodge. "See to them, I will walk with Walking Horse. We will speak of this."

"Thank you, He Dog." Bright Moon turned toward the lodge where Little Antelope was crooning to the little ones.

"Tell me, Sister." He Dog stopped her. "Has there been trouble at Crow Killer's valley for you to be worried about the one called Wilson?"

Looking back at the young chief, she shook her head. "No, it has been peaceful there for two summers now."

"But, you still think the white needs our protection?"

"He is my husband's father. I do not want anything to happen to him." Bright Moon replied. "He is from the east and not used to the ways of the mountains."

He Dog nodded his head, then turned for his own lodge. As principal chief and leader of the Dog Soldiers, it would be impossible for him to be away from the village for any extended time. Every village expected their chief to keep them safe and free from danger. Many tribes were their allies, but there were always hostile tribes lurking about, waiting to strike any undefended village. Walking Horse had brought Little Antelope to be with her sister, but being head chief of the Arapaho, he would have to return to his village within a few days. To ride to Crow Killer's mountain valley would take several days, and even then, warriors would have to remain in the valley if they wanted to be sure the white was safe.

He Dog took a seat beside his lodge with Walking Horse, where Crazy Cat and several other warriors sat in a semi-circle smoking their pipes. The gathered warriors were all experienced and older men who belonged to the dreaded Dog Soldiers of the Cheyenne and the deadly Lance Bearers of the Arapaho. Scars marking their bravery in battle showed on every warrior. These men were the bravest of the brave, and great and fearless fighters in the face of the enemy. They had watched as Bright Moon had spoken with her brother, and now, they were curious. They could read the concern in her face as she talked. Smoke, rising from the small fire, drifted high into the air as they sat waiting for their chief to speak.

"You have seen me speak with Bright Moon?" Every head nodded. "My sister wishes that we send warriors to Crow Killer's valley to see to the safety of his white father."

"Is he in danger?"

"She does not know this, but he is alone and she fears for him." He Dog looked around the circle of dark faces. "Each of you know we killed many Arickaree people when we attacked them for killing our chief."

"Does He Dog think the Rics might attack Crow Killer's valley?" Crazy Cat asked.

"This I do not know, but Bright Moon is worried." He Dog shook his head. "You know the bravery of my sister. If she worries, then perhaps there is need."

"We have all met this white man, father of my brother Crow Killer. He is a good man, but he is old and unprotected. I think we should do as Bright Moon asks." Walking Horse suggested.

"With my chief's permission, I will take four warriors and ride to the lodge of Crow Killer." Big Owl spoke up.

"Take only single men." Walking Horse nodded at the big warrior. "You will stay with the white one until Crow Killer returns from the west."

"And Bright Moon?" Crazy Cat looked over at He Dog. "Will she stay here or go with Walking Horse to his village."

"It was Crow Killer's wish before he rode to the west that Bright Moon and the children would stay here with the Cheyenne people." The young chief looked around the circle. "It will be so."

"I will take my people back to our village with the new sun." Walking Horse nodded solemnly. "My warriors will ride to the valley when we return."

"I am sad we did not get to visit longer, my brother." He Dog stood up and shook hands with the warrior. "But you will return soon."

Bright Moon and Little Antelope watched from their lodge as the men spoke. They could tell by the hand signs that warriors would be riding back to the valley. Bright Moon knew there hadn't been any trouble for several moons, but the white one was old and far from the white village of Baxter Springs. He would be an easy victim if an enemy did ride in secret against the valley. She was happy Walking Horse would send his warriors. She would have them take the trade goods Crow Killer had traded for at Bridger's Post with them.

"You and the little ones will come with me and Walking Horse to our village." Little Antelope held Little Ellie in her arms.

"I told my husband I would remain here with the Cheyenne and my brother He Dog."

"Crow Killer will not mind as long as you are safe." Little Antelope suggested. "And you know you and the little ones will be safe with the Arapaho."

"I know, Sister. We would be safe and welcome in your lodge." Bright Moon smiled. "I will think on it during the dark hours."

"Come with us, Bright Moon." Little Antelope pleaded as she looked down on the sleeping babies. "They are old enough now to travel in their backboards."

Kneeling beside the babies, Bright Moon smiled. She knew the valley of Crow Killer lay closer to Arapaho lands than the Cheyenne village. She could see no reason not to journey with Walking Horse and his men to their village. The journey would be safe enough as no one would dare attack the Arapaho Lance Bearers. She would enjoy her time with Little Antelope, and she knew her sister didn't want to part so soon with the children.

"I will speak with He Dog."

Ellie sadly stared down at the grave as Jed poked around the ruins and the littered discarded remains of many passing wagons. He could see where varmints had dug under the debris, looking for a warm place out of the cold. Jed studied the heavily ridged mountains, then looked down where the Gallatin River flowed slowly through the valley. Today, the air was warm and pleasant but earlier in the year, Jed knew this same tranquil scene would have been totally different. The train had been caught unaware of the approaching storm, and the ice, snow, and blowing winds, would have made the passage on the slippery mountain trails and across the river extremely treacherous. Only experienced, strong men, like Chalk Briggs and Lige Hatcher, would have been able to lead the greenhorn pilgrims across the Gallatins safely. Jed looked to where Ellie stood over the grave. It was still hard to believe the old scout had succumbed to a mere storm and gone under.

Walking back to where Ellie stood, Jed looked up to see Dibbs riding in fast.

Reining the blowing horse to a sliding stop, he pointed back up the mountain. "We've got ourselves a problem, Jed."

"Problem?"

"There, coming down the crest of the trail." The youngster smiled coldly.

A party of armed warriors with five whites, rode their small horses, slipping and sliding down the steep embankment, reining in less than fifty yards from where they waited. None of the warriors were painted for battle and most had only old trade rifles and bows. Five of the warriors carried in their hands the rifles they had taken from their prisoners.

"If I holler, Miss Ellie, you get yourself behind that wagon quick."

"Hold on, Ellie, they haven't made an unfriendly move yet, and none of them braves are wearing paint." Jed held out his hand.

"Paint?" Dibbs frowned. "Paint or no paint means nothing in these lands."

"Dibbs, you act like you want them to start something." Jed frowned. "What tribe are they?"

"Gros Ventre."

"Wait until they start something… you hear?"

"I wouldn't mind doing a little killing, especially those dogged whites." His face had grown as hard as a rock. "No, sir. I wouldn't mind it a bit."

"Can you count, boy? There's twenty-five against us two." Jed couldn't believe the change in the youngster.

"Only twenty, Jed. Those whites are their prisoners or so it seems."

"That's still mighty big odds." Jed frowned at the youngster. "You just keep still."

"I'll kill three or four before they reach us." Dibbs spat.

"We've got Ellie to see after, boy." Jed frowned again at Dibbs. "I'll handle this. We'll only fight as a last resort."

"Yes, sir, Mister Crow Killer." Dibbs looked over at Ellie. "Just the same, Ellie, you get behind that pile of rubble quick if the shooting starts."

One of the warriors kicked his horse forward slowly with his hand held high. Jed nodded and kicked his own horse. The warrior was a magnificent looking man, a warrior in his full prime. Muscles bulged from his huge chest and arms, making his legs seem undersized. Plainly clad, the warrior wore only a breechcloth and a leather hunting shirt. Jed studied the strong face, which seemed friendly enough as no hostility of any kind showed.

"That one is the brother of their chief." Dibbs nodded at the approaching warrior as Jed started away. "His name is War Bonnet, and he is a bad one."

"You seem to know these Gros Ventres pretty well." Jed threw back over his shoulder.

"I do, you be careful out there." Dibbs cocked the rifle. "They can take your hair and you won't know it until you go to comb it."

"Well, thank you, Mister Bacon." Jed looked back at the youngster. "You keep the rifle lowered and stay quiet, you hear?"

Looking over at Ellie, the young hunter nodded. "Old War Bonnet there is a bad man. He used to be one of the worst killers out here."

"So is Jed." Ellie looked at Jed's broad back. "I thought you said the Gros Ventres were friendly."

"Only when it suits them, Miss Ellie." Dibbs smiled. "Kinda like Jed there, ain't that right?"

"Jed can be dangerous, but only when he has to."

"Yeah, I heard that around Bridger and Baxter Springs from several people." Dibbs watched as the two men reined in their horses, just feet apart facing each other. "I believe you, Ellie. He looks like he could get mean."

"You better believe me, Dibbs."

Several seconds passed as the two men studied each other without speaking. Jed knew an Indian could smell fear in a man from just watching him. A sweaty brow, a slight twitch, a blink, or a nervous hand would speak the truth.

"What do you want here?" War Bonnet finally spoke as his eyes studied Jed without blinking. "These are Gros Ventre lands."

"You are War Bonnet?"

"I am War Bonnet." The deep-set black eyes took in the long black hair, then the bow and lance on Jed's back. "What is your name?"

"I am Crow Killer of the Arapaho, your friends who live east of here."

"My people have heard of a warrior named Crow Killer that lives with the Arapaho." The dark hands of the warrior moved quickly as he spoke. "Speak, what does Crow Killer want here in Gros Ventre lands?"

"I have brought my sister to the grave of her father." Jed looked back at Ellie. "With your permission, we will stay the night. Come morning, we will leave Gros Ventre country. You have my word, this is all we want."

"Your sister? That one is a white squaw." War Bonnet looked doubtfully at Ellie, taking in her lighter complexion and white clothing, then back at Jed. "She is not Arapaho."

"Her skin is whiter than most Arapaho, but she is an Arapaho woman." Jed looked into the dark eyes. "She has come to see the grave of Lige Hatcher, Rolling Thunder to some."

Curiosity seemed to cross the broad face. "I know Rolling Thunder. He lived with my people two seasons when I was a boy. He took as his woman, my mother's sister, Spotted Fawn. When she was killed by the Cree, he left us and returned to the east. Even though Lige Hatcher was white, we adopted him because he was a courageous fighter and mighty hunter."

"Yes, Rolling Thunder is white, but this woman's mother was Arapaho. Honor Rolling Thunder and let her grieve at her father's burial site." Jed requested.

"And the white one that rides with you?"

"He is just our guide. He says he buried Rolling Thunder here." Jed looked back at Dibbs. "He led us here."

"That one lies."

"What does War Bonnet say?"

War Bonnet studied Ellie for a long time. "To visit Rolling Thunder, she will have to ride with us to the north."

"What?" Jed looked closely at the warrior. "Is that not his grave?"

"No, the one you look for has not gone to be with his ancestors, yet." War Bonnet shook his head curiously. "Perhaps, he has gone to be with them now, but he still lived when I saw him last."

"I don't understand War Bonnet's words?"

"Rolling Thunder had been hurt badly in the head when our women found him." War Bonnet continued. "Even now, he still does not know who he is, but we recognized Rolling Thunder. The Gros Ventre women take care of him as we speak."

Turning to where Dibbs sat his horse, Jed looked curiously at the youngster. "Come out here, Dibbs."

Frowning, Dibbs reined in beside Jed. "Now what?"

"War Bonnet says this is not the grave of Lige Hatcher."

"All I know is I buried a white hunter right here on this spot." Dibbs stuck out his chin. "Right under that wheel."

"This one lies." War Bonnet pointed his rifle at Dibbs. "This one is the wolf pup of the hunter, Bacon."

"Wolf pup?" Jed was curious. "What does he mean, boy?"

"Let old War Bonnet tell it, he knows everything."

"This one knows what I speak. He has killed many in these mountains." The warrior pointed his finger at Dibbs and screamed. "Him kill whites, Metis, Cree, and many others! He hunts alone like a lobo wolf. He is young, but he is a devil. Many think he is crazy in his head. He is the Bloody Hand."

"Has he killed any of your people, the Gros Ventres?"

"No, that is only reason he still lives and rides these lands." War Bonnet calmed down. "My brother, Elk's Head, Chief of the Gros Ventre says we will not harm him as long as he does not kill any of our people."

Jed shrugged in disbelief. "Surely War Bonnet does not believe one as young as this one could be such a killer against experienced warriors?"

"Young?" War Bonnet scowled. "Did he not tell you of killing the Cree and Metis back on the trail?"

"He told me he killed two warriors trying to ambush us."

"Do not be fooled by his looks, Crow Killer. Yes, he is still young, but he has killed many warriors and taken their hair. His heart is like the dark spirits, it has turned black. His face has turned away from any people since his father was killed six moons ago by white hunters from the east."

Jed turned his eyes on the five captives, then back at Dibbs. "This true, boy… what he says?"

"He slinks through the night like a coyote." War Bonnet continued shaking his rifle barrel at Dibbs. "He is like a wisp of smoke in the wind. He vanishes whenever we follow him… another reason we have not driven him from our lands."

Shrugging, Dibbs looked up the trail to where Squires and his men sat with the Gros Ventres warriors. "It's true enough."

"Tell me now, so War Bonnet can hear your words." Jed insisted. "Why do you kill?"

"They killed my pa and took his scalp." Dibbs shook his head. "Those five whites up there and their Cree and Metis friends. They also killed Rollie Long and his Cheyenne woman Wyonette."

"Why did they kill your pa and the others?"

"Ambushed is the word… murdered." Dibbs spat and glared up at the white men. "Never gave them a chance."

"Why, Dibbs?" Jed stared at the youngster. "Why would white hunters kill another white man?"

"For their horses, pelts, and out of pure cussedness." Dibbs looked down at the ground. "Maybe, they just didn't want us hunting in these mountains. The Metis and Cree that ride with Squires, those renegades don't need a reason to kill and rob."

"They killed Long and his woman before they killed your pa?"

"Less than a week before." Dibbs continued. "They skinned poor Wyonette alive. We found what was left of them after the varmints had finished."

"Him speak with a false tongue. It was old wolf Bacon and the other one, Long, stealing furs from traps and robbing camps." War Bonnet pointed at Dibbs. "We watch. We know this one's father is a thief… steal horses, furs, anything to sell for white man's gold. He teach his young wolf pup many bad things before he die."

"They didn't steal from the Gros Ventres?"

"No, they very cunning like the wolf. They no steal from my people." War Bonnet shook his head, then pointed back to where Squires sat his horse with the other four whites. "They only steal from other whites. That is why my chief allows them to hunt here and trade with our people."

"Your people wanted their trade goods, so you put up with their stealing from others?"

"It was not our concern as long as they only rob and kill each other." War Bonnet shrugged. "My people need the trade goods they bring into our mountains."

"So, what has changed?"

"Several sleeps ago while you stay at fire with woman, this one kill two Cree who watch the trail. Then he sneaks to their camp and kills the horse guard, a Metis, before turning their horses loose."

"So, this changed your mind about this youngster?"

"Some maybe, but one of my people was injured very bad the same night."

"And you think this one done it?"

War Bonnet looked hard at Dibbs. "Tracks all covered with other tracks. If we knew for sure this one would be dead as we speak."

"This true, Dibbs?" Jed hadn't even known the Gros Ventres were near his camp.

"I told you already." The face hardened. "Yeah, I killed the Cree and Metis, but I didn't harm any Gros Ventre. I ain't that stupid to harm one of them deep in their country."

"Well, tell me again." Jed glared at the youngster. "Why do you kill?"

"Revenge, Crow Killer, revenge." Dibbs smiled. "And before Mister Squires and his four friends reach the safety of Baxter Springs, they'll be dead along with their Metis and Cree killers. I already killed one of the dogs back at Baxter Springs."

"So, you're the killer of the Gallatins that everyone fears?"

"That I am. I want them dead… all of them."

"You have a powerful hate inside you for one so young." Jed moved his horse closer to Dibbs. "Tell me again, why do you kill as you do?"

"That's my pa lying there under that wheel." Dibbs snarled. "Squires, his men, and a few Metis and Cree from the North Country ambushed him while he slept. They killed him in his sleep, like cowards."

"What about Lige Hatcher?" Jed looked back at Ellie. "What happened to him?"

"He was hurt bad, blood covered his face." Dibbs looked at the grave. "I owed him plenty. I owed him for saving my life two summers back. He pulled me out of this river as I was going under."

"Where is he?"

"Mister Hatcher took a bullet to the head. It seemed to have addled him or something. He was talking crazy. I stopped the blood and patched him up best I could, then toted him closer to the Gros Ventre village where he would be found. Then I had to ride hard after Squires and his men."

"How bad was he hurt?"

"Pretty bad I think. I don't know why he was in our camp. Him and Pa weren't exactly on speaking terms. He was probably talking with Pa about the trail ahead over the Gallatins when Squires and the Metis attacked." Dibbs shrugged. "He was hit hard. I figured him for a goner so I left him near the Gros Ventre village."

"You were the only survivor?" Jed was curious. "How come they let you live?"

"They didn't let me do nothing." Dibbs glared at the whites. "I was out hunting when they put on my pa, old Bailey, and Lige. If I had of been there, things might have turned out different."

"Tell me, Dibbs, why would Squires and his partners ride with the Metis and Cree from Canada?"

Dibbs looked up at the group of riders. "The Metis and Cree are from north of the border, and nobody in these parts would ever tie Squires in with these cutthroats. He uses them to rob and kill, then they split their plunder and return north across the border. Squires and his bunch ride back to Baxter Springs to sell their loot."

"So, your pa steals from Squires, then Squires steals his pelts back from him." Jed shook his head. "Is that what happened?"

"My pa might have robbed a few traps, but he never killed."

"Alright, then what happened?" Jed looked at Dibbs. "Where were Chalk Briggs and the immigrants?"

"I figure about then, they were across the river and heading up the mountain." Dibbs shrugged. "The weather had turned fierce overnight. I tell you that norther blew in with a vengeance, never seen anything like it. That's why I couldn't make it back to camp that night. That day, the ice and snow was terribly bad, it was bone-chilling cold. I figure Mister Briggs knew he had to keep his people moving or the animals would freeze where they stood in their traces. With the wind howling like a banshee, they probably never heard the shooting."

"And this hunter, Squires and his men, just came out of nowhere and attacked your camp with the wagon train people so close?" Jed questioned the youngster.

"The signs they left in the snow showed they rode straight into our camp, killed Pa and Bailey outright. Wounded Hatcher real bad, then took everything we had. Horses, mules, guns, pelts, everything." Dibbs nodded at the whites. "I already told you, the tall one up there is the one you knocked down back in the saloon in Baxter Springs. His name is Squires. See, one of the warriors holds my father's Hawken. It'll have a B carved in its stock."

"And you followed them back to the settlement?"

"I did for a fact."

"And you killed the man back in Baxter Springs?"

"I already told you I did." Dibbs grinned his lopsided grin. "Yeah, then I stuck his ugly head on that post."

"What about the train?"

"Couldn't see a thing, it was snowing something awful." Dibbs tried to recall. "The wagons had disappeared into the mountains when I returned from my hunt and found Pa."

"Do you think it was possible they were able to cross the mountains?"

"All I know is they rolled away from here and crossed the river. I don't know what happened after they crossed the first mountain." Dibbs continued. "Like I said, I toted Hatcher through the storm to the Gros Venture village, then I took in after Squires and his men. Didn't have time to go looking for the pilgrims."

"What then, Dibbs?" Jed looked at the youngster. "Did you catch up with Squires?"

"No, but a good many Metis and Crees met their maker." Dibbs shrugged. "I followed the wrong dat burn trail. Squires and his men fooled me... left me following the Metis trail north, while they turned east, back to Baxter Springs."

"This time he speaks truth. We followed his trail where he killed many Metis and Cree warriors." War Bonnet looked at Dibbs. "He did bring Rolling Thunder to us, and this is why he still lives."

"Yeah, I killed plenty of Metis and Cree." Dibbs shrugged. "But, I've never killed one of your people. Only the Gros Ventres' enemies."

"These hunters are not the enemy of the Gros Ventre." War Bonnet pointed at Squires.

"The Metis and Cree are my enemies." Dibbs responded. "That is why I kill them."

"Many moons ago the Cree killed our Gros Ventre brothers and many women." War Bonnet frowned.

"I tell you this, War Bonnet, I have never killed any Gros Ventre. Not one." Dibbs looked at the big warrior.

"This is why my brother still lets you ride in our country." War Bonnet stared hard at Dibbs. "But, now, War Bonnet says you must leave our country and never return, or you will die."

"It figures, I do your killing for you." Dibbs sneered. "The great Gros Ventres don't kill. They are a weak people. Their great warriors are cowards."

"Shut up, Dibbs, before he cuts your throat." Jed warned.

"Don't you know, Jed, the mighty Gros Ventre are religious now. They have become Christian Indians."

"We do not kill unless attacked." War Bonnet glared at Dibbs. "It is true, my brother and Father Abraham forbid us to kill. That, Bloody Hand, is another reason you still walk this land."

"Don't worry, War Bonnet." Dibbs spat. "I'll do your killing for you."

"No more, Bloody Hand. If you are seen in our lands again, we will kill you as we would a lobo wolf."

Jed studied the warrior's face as it turned dark. He already guessed why War Bonnet and the Gros Ventres hadn't killed Dibbs Bacon. Most Indian tribes were superstitious about anyone acting strangely. They thought he could be touched in his mind and feared to kill one such as him, as it could bring bad luck down on the whole tribe. Jed knew if Dibbs had killed one Gros Ventre, they would have killed him.

"Why do you call him Bloody Hand?"

"When he kills, he dips his hands in his victim's blood and smears his face." War Bonnet held up his hand. "He drinks their blood like a rabid dog."

Shrugging, the youngster grinned insolently. "I guess I accidentally fell into their blood a few times."

"Where did you get the note from Chalk Briggs about Lige Hatcher being dead."

"From Masters. I met up with him and his men west of the river." Dibbs continued. "For some reason, Mister Briggs had figured Lige Hatcher dead and had given him the note to take to Miss Ellie. Masters and his men were still running their traps. When I told them I was riding east, they asked me to bring it to her."

"Why didn't you tell me of the letter back at Bridger?"

"I can't read, Jed." Dibbs confessed. "I'm just an ignorant mountain runner."

"Did you fix it so Squires would follow the girl back into these mountains where you could get to him?"

"That's a lie." Dibbs face turned hard. "I would never put that girl's life in danger. Coming here was her idea, not mine."

"Why would Chalk think Lige was dead?"

"Can't say about that for sure, but I reckon when Hatcher didn't rejoin the train, they figured him dead." Dibbs explained. "When I told Masters I was headed for Baxter Springs, they asked me to bring the note to Miss Ellie. I can't read so I had no way of knowing what it said."

"Who drew the map on the back with the wagon wheel cross on it?"

"Reckon that was me." Dibbs admitted. "After Masters gave me the note, I drew the map on the back."

"You knew back at Baxter Springs that Hatcher may still be above ground?" Jed stared hard at the young man.

"I knew he was alive the last I seen him." Dibbs looked at Ellie. "I figured I'd help her find her pa and bring him back, providing he still lived."

"But you were actually after Squires and his men?" Jed's face grew dark. "I say you used her to lure Squires and his men into these mountains."

"I knew he'd follow the woman." Dibbs admitted. "Figured, I'd have him dead before she was in any danger."

"Then you knew all along Squires was after Ellie?"

"Squires wanted the woman. I heard him bragging about it back in Baxter Springs. I figured he would be following us." The grey eyes went cold. "I never could get them alone back in town. This seemed like my best chance of getting them."

"Will you take us to the woman's father?" Jed could see the anger in the older warrior's face as he listened to Dibbs brag of his killings.

"I will do this only for Crow Killer and Rolling Thunder." War Bonnet looked at Dibbs. "But, this crazy one will no longer ride our mountains again."

"What is War Bonnet gonna do with the whites?" Dibbs looked up at Squires, unconcerned that War Bonnet might kill him.

War Bonnet followed the hateful gaze of the youngster. "Them same as you. They are no longer free to hunt our mountains."

"You gonna turn them loose?" Dibbs smiled. "Or kill them?"

"All of you will leave these mountains and return to the east." War Bonnet's face hardened. "None will ever return to our mountains."

"Now, that suits me just fine." The voice was hard and cold. "I can almost guarantee you they won't be coming back."

"You will wait here." War Bonnet turned his horse toward his warriors.

"He's giving them back their rifles." Dibbs smiled coldly, then laughed as he watched Squires take his pa's Hawken. "He's releasing them. They can run for home and hide in these mountains, but they can't hide their tracks."

"You going after them, I reckon?"

The laugh was almost demonic, pure evil. "I'll have my pa's rifle back in a few days… count on it."

"Dibbs, Miss Ellie likes you and put her faith in you." Jed knew what the young man had his mind set on. "Ride back to Baxter Springs and leave these men in peace. She'll find you plenty of honest work."

"I'm a hunter, Jed, that's all I know, and I've still got game to hunt." Dibbs watched as the five whites disappeared over the high ridge.

"You're young, you can learn anything you want." Jed watched the hard eyes. "Ride back to my valley with me. There you can hunt all you want."

"I know what I want and it sure ain't peace or a job. And it won't be animals I'll be hunting until those men pay." Dibbs gripped the reins so hard his hands seemed to swell.

"You're dead set on killing Squires and his men?"

"Set in stone… dead. Their dying will come hard. You can count on it." Dibbs looked hard at Jed. "Stay out of it, Crow Killer. Do not make an enemy of me."

"War Bonnet said your pa was stealing their furs." Jed tried to reason with the youngster. "Said he was robbing their traps."

"That we were, but Squires did his fair share of robbing too." Dibbs watched as War Bonnet turned his horse, back to where they waited. "There was no need for them to kill Pa the way they did. They cut his hands off."

"Is that why you cut their heads off?"

Nodding slowly, Dibbs looked coldly straight at Jed. "I was taught to always do your enemies one better. A head for two hands seems about right to me."

Reining in next to Dibbs, the warrior looked at the two men. "The white hunters are leaving our lands and will never return."

Picking up his reins, Dibbs nodded. "Then, I will leave your lands too."

"No, Bloody Hand. I gave my word." War Bonnet held up his powerful arm. "You will camp with us until the new sun comes again."

"I reckon you're protecting those killers again." Dibbs spat with hate rolling from his tongue.

"I give them one sleep to get far away." The warrior nodded. "You try to leave this place, my warriors will kill you."

"You can't kill me, War Bonnet, your brother forbids it." Dibbs laughed. "But, it don't matter none in the long run. I've got my whole life, plenty of time to run them down. They can't ride far or fast enough to shake me from their trail."

War Bonnet shook his head as he looked at Dibbs. Jed knew he wanted to kill the young hunter, but his brother Elk's Head had forbidden it. War Bonnet had said the village elders and the shaman had spoken against it in council. The elders of the tribe and their chief, Elk's Head, feared the death of the crazy one would bring a curse down on the tribe. War Bonnet wasn't fooled. He knew the youngster wasn't crazy in the mind, only in his actions. He was crazy alright, kill-crazy, filled with hate.

Riding out of hearing distance of Dibbs, the warrior looked at Jed. "I should kill this bloodthirsty one, but I will not disobey my brother or my people's wishes."

"Because you think he is touched by the spirit people?"

The dark head shook in denial. "This one not touched by anything but his hatred. He kills like a crazy person, but he is not crazy."

"Then why can't he be killed?"

"My people think he is crazy, I do not." War Bonnet shook his head. "They have seen the way he kills and mutilates his victims."

"I will return him to the white village after we ride to your village." Jed nodded. "But first, we must find out if Rolling Thunder still lives."

"No, with the new sun, my warriors will ride with him to the far corners of our hunting grounds, there he will be released unharmed. If he returns, he will die." War Bonnet declared.

"War Bonnet has spoken. It is not for me to interfere with another tribe's wishes." Jed was relieved Dibbs was being allowed to ride safely from Gros Ventre lands. Hopefully, he would be smart enough to keep riding. The youngster hated deep in his heart, but Jed had to admit Dibbs Bacon was a brave man. One who didn't fear death.

"I did not speak of this, but your people in the long wagons crossed safely over the mountains." War Bonnet assured Jed. "My warriors rode with them and helped them get through the storms until they cleared the deep passes."

"War Bonnet, why did your people help the whites of the train?"

"It is the teachings of our teacher, Father Abraham. He told us to do this thing." The warrior explained. "But, mostly for our brother and friend Rolling Thunder."

"For this, I thank you, War Bonnet." Jed held out his hand. "For this, you will always have my thanks and friendship."

"It was my warriors who told the wagon leader of the death of Rolling Thunder." War Bonnet looked over at Ellie. "They looked at him before they rode to the whites. To them, he looked like he had gone to his ancestors already."

"I imagine he did."

"She is a comely squaw." War Bonnet looked at Ellie. "She does not look Indian."

"Yes, she is." Jed was studying on the letter, not War Bonnet's words. He figured after the Gros Ventre warriors had told of Lige's death, Chalk Briggs had run into Masters and his men headed east and had given them the letter which they then gave to Dibbs.

"She is not taken by anyone?"

"No, she lives with her grandfather, a white medicine man." Jed replied.

"Why do they call her Medicine Thunder?" War Bonnet stared at Ellie.

"She has the white man's magic in her hands to cure the sick." Jed smiled. "She has great medicine."

"That is good."

Jed nodded. "Yes, it is."

"Come, we go from this place."

CHAPTER 6

Jed reined in beside Ellie and quickly told her that Lige may still be alive, but omitted all he had learned about Dibbs Bacon. He couldn't see any reason to worry her about the youngster. Motioning to them, War Bonnet led his warriors across the Gallatin River, then found a small clearing to make camp. Two warriors stood guard over Dibbs as a fire was built and meat set to cooking. Jed was curious why War Bonnet had left Dibbs holding his rifle. Maybe they wanted the youngster to try and flee. He knew some of the warriors feared the youngster, not because of his bloodlust, but because they thought he could be touched in the head.

Ellie took charge of the cooking as the warriors expected she would. In the Indian villages of the west, warriors did all the fighting, and protected the women and children. The women did almost all the physical work which was beneath the status of the warriors. Even young boys, still in their adolescence, were not expected to work. Outside of watching over the vast herds of the tribe's horses, most boys were free to swim, hunt, fish or whatever they chose, but soon enough, they would bare the responsibility of protecting the villages. Many times, in the wild of these great mountains, the responsibility of protecting the village could end their lives while still in their youth.

The eastern sun showed its brilliant face over the tall mountain peaks of the Gallatins. War Bonnet was true to his word and Dibbs Bacon was escorted back to the east with a full contingent of warriors. War Bonnet informed him this was his last warning and he better not let his face be seen in Gros Ventre lands again. Jed and Ellie watched as the youngster rode down the rocky trail that led to the east. Dibbs never looked back as he slowly disappeared from their sight.

"Will he be safe out there or will those warriors kill him?" Ellie raised her hand to wave.

"They won't kill him. I figure he'll be safe enough, Ellie." Jed looked up at the snowcapped mountains. "I don't know about the ones he'll be hunting though."

"I know, these last two days I've seen Dibbs in a different light." Ellie stared down the trail. "He's so filled with hate."

"You're right, he is filled with hate." Jed agreed. "I doubt he'll ever get his fill of killing, even after Squires is dead."

"Do you really believe he aims to kill all those men?"

"Dibbs thirsts for blood, so yes, I believe he does." Jed nodded. "Providing he catches up to them, but I figure he will."

War Bonnet rode his horse to where they stood looking down the trail. "Come, we go to village."

Late in the afternoon of the second day, Jed spotted the far-off smoke from many fires, curling into the air as they wound their way through the narrow mountain trails. The mountains were beautiful but they would be more magnificent with the coming of new fresh grass and flowers, growing in abundance along the trail. It was too early in the spring for flowers to be seen on the tree-lined slopes, but soon they would fill the air with wonderful fragrances. Jed wished he could enjoy these mountains with their majestic beauty, but there was no time. Hopefully, they would find Lige Hatcher alive, he wanted to return to Baxter Springs quickly so he could journey back to his valley to be with Bright Moon and the little ones.

War Bonnet held up his hand and halted the procession as several mounted warriors rode forward and surrounded them. Every one of the Gros Ventre warriors was a prime example of strength and courage. Jed could see there was no way these warriors were weak or cowardly. Kicking his horse forward, War Bonnet led the column of warriors, along with Jed and Ellie, into the throng of curious villagers. A huge warrior, even larger than War Bonnet, stepped from a large painted lodge and studied the mounted riders.

"You have returned, my brother." Elk's Head, the head Chief of the Gros Ventre, looked up at Ellie and Jed. "And you have brought guests."

"Yes, my chief." War Bonnet motioned Jed and Ellie down from their horses. "This is the great Arapaho Lance Bearer, Crow Killer, and the woman is Medicine Thunder. They are friends."

"Then they are welcome in our village."

"The woman is the daughter of Rolling Thunder." War Bonnet looked at Ellie. "She is a medicine woman."

Elk's Head nodded sadly. "You are the daughter of my brother Lige Hatcher?"

"Yes, my chief. How is my father?" Ellie inquired.

The chief looked at Ellie, surprised that she had understood his words. "He lives. His body has not mended fully. I fear his mind has been lost."

"His mind?" Ellie looked up at the chief. "What do you mean?"

Elk's Head pointed to his forehead. "His wound was here. The scar is bad. He remembers nothing."

"Where is he?"

"He waits there, but prepare yourself." Elk's Head pointed to a near lodge. "He stays with my sister, Small Crane. I think he believes her to be his dead wife."

Following Ellie to the lodge, Jed took her by the arm. "Be careful, Ellie, we don't know how bad he's hurt."

"Yes, be prepared. He may not know you, Medicine Thunder." Elk's Head stopped before the lodge.

Stepping inside the warm lodge, Ellie's eyes focused on the form sitting before the fire. Lige Hatcher rested against a buffalo robe backrest. The blue eyes that stared into the small fire were sunken deep into their sockets, unseeing. No sign of recognition showed on his face as Ellie moved closer to him. Smiling brightly, she stopped as he pulled back in fear. Nodding at the old squaw, Ellie crooned softly as she knelt beside the wounded man.

"It's alright, father… it's me, Ellie, your daughter." Ellie sat down before him, trying to get a closer look at his covered wound. "I came to visit with you."

She could see the reddish, purple coloring on his face. Small Crane or perhaps the Gros Ventre medicine man had the wound covered with ermine skins and salve. Touching his hand, she talked to him softly as Small Crane moved beside her. Slowly, Hatcher started to relax but only stared blankly across the lodge.

"I need to remove the bandage." Ellie spoke quietly to the woman. "I need to see the wound."

"You are a healer of the whites?" The voice was soft, almost a whisper. "I heard the warriors talking outside."

"Yes."

Nodding, Small Crane moved beside Hatcher. "Sometimes, he lets me change his bandages, but at times, he refuses to be touched. I will try to remove the covering."

"You have been very kind to my father." Ellie smiled. "Thank you, Small Crane."

"You told him you were his daughter." The older woman studied Ellie. "Is this true? Are you Rolling Thunder's daughter?"

"Yes, my mother was Arapaho." Ellie nodded. "Rolling Thunder is my father."

The woman eased her hands slowly toward the bandages. "Rolling Thunder was the husband of my aunt Spotted Fawn."

"Such a beautiful name." Ellie watched intently as the ermine skin was unwrapped from the nasty wound.

"Yes, my sister was a beautiful woman." Small Crane replied sadly. "We will speak no more of her."

Wiping away the grease from the ugly gash, Small Crane patted Hatcher softly and moved back. The bullet had torn the scalp away from his forehead as it had passed, leaving the white skull gleaming from beneath the ragged tear. Studying the wound, without touching his face, Ellie could see the wound was clean, but it still seeped blood from the unclosed wound.

"How many days has he been here, Small Crane?"

"Many sleeps, maybe this many." She tried to count, holding up her fingers several times. "The wound should have scabbed over by now. I think the evil spirits live in it."

"Yes, it should have." Rising, Ellie slipped quietly back outside to where Jed and War Bonnet waited. "Jed, will you get my medicine bag from my horse, please?"

"How is he?"

"The wound is ragged, but not too terribly dangerous physically. Mentally, I don't know." Ellie looked back at the lodge. "But, I need to stitch the wound together so it can heal properly."

Jed stopped and turned around. "How are you gonna do that?"

"I'll try to kill the pain with laudanum." Ellie replied. "Then, we'll just have to hold him down while I stitch the skin back together."

"What is this laudanum? Will it kill Rolling Thunder?" War Bonnet misunderstood her meaning.

"It is a white man's medicine, actually a Chinese medicine." Ellie explained. "It will not kill, it will only make my father sleep."

"Rolling Thunder is strong. You try to hold him, I think him fight hard. Maybe hurt himself." The warrior cautioned.

"The medicine will help."

"Is he himself?" Jed turned to where Ellie stood, waiting beside the lodge entrance.

"No, he just sits there with a blank stare."

Retrieving the doctor bag, Jed handed it to her. "I'm glad you brought this with you, Ellie."

"I don't know why I brought it with me this time." Staring down at the black bag, she admitted. "It's become a habit, I guess."

"What do you want me to do?"

"Wait outside until I call you." Ellie touched Jed's arm. "Have War Bonnet bring a couple more strong warriors inside."

Spooning two ladles of the awful tasting stuff down Hatcher was a job in itself. After the first taste of the bitter medicine, Hatcher turned his head, making a horrible face, refusing more. After several attempts, Small Crane finally managed to get one more spoonful down his throat. Sitting back, Ellie threaded her sewing needle and waited for the laudanum to take effect. She hated to forcibly hold him, but she knew that was the only way she would be able to stitch up the ragged wound.

From behind her, she heard someone step through the door, then the warning sound of the medicine man's rattle shaking told of his presence. Standing over Ellie, the old man frowned and shook the rattle several times in her face. The voice was low and menacing as he gyrated around the lodge.

"Our medicine man, Crooked Leg, does not want you to do this." Small Crane retreated from the menacing old man. "He forbids it."

Several times, since returning to the west, Ellie had come up against the Indian medicine men, refusing to let her use her white man's skills on the sick. She remembered Plenty Coops of the Crow and his medicine man's refusal to let her help the ailing Crow Chief until Red Hawk intervened. "Tell Crooked Leg if I do not treat Rolling Thunder, he will die from the infection."

"He say you lie." Small Crane looked fearfully at the wrinkled face and buffalo horn headpiece.

"I understood what he said."

"Crooked Leg say no, he forbids it!"

"I don't care what the old devil says." Ellie stood up to face the medicine man. "Tell him to leave, this is a white man. He is my father and I'm going to doctor him in the white man's way."

"Rolling Thunder is Gros Ventre!" The rattle shook fiercely again as the medicine man stared at Ellie.

"Get out!"

Retreating outside, Crooked Leg stopped in front of Jed and War Bonnet. "White squaw has bad temper. I go... the spirits say Rolling Thunder will die."

Jed grinned slightly as the old man walked proudly away. "Well, she does have a bad temper."

"I think all women have bad tempers. Maybe, daughter of Rolling Thunder has worse temper than most." Elk's Head watched the medicine man walk away. "Maybe, Crooked Leg smart, he leave."

"She knows Rolling Thunder needs the white man's medicine to live. She would not harm her father." Jed assured the chief.

Two young warriors walked up and stood quietly beside War Bonnet. Jed couldn't help but notice the proud straight form of the taller young brave. Handsome and heavily muscled, the warrior already wore a lone eagle feather in his topknot. In most Indian cultures, only a warrior who had killed an enemy or counted coup on a live foe was permitted to wear the honor of an eagle feather in his hair. Jed figured this warrior to be in his early twenties. He was curious since he remembered War Bonnet had said the Gros Ventre were a Christian people who did not kill.

"This one is Wanicantha or Little Wound." War Bonnet nodded at the taller warrior. "And this one is Two Badger. They will help."

"I thank you for helping."

Neither warrior spoke or acknowledged Jed's words. "This one is the great Crow Killer of the Arapaho people. He lives far from our lands to the east."

"You do not need to thank us." Little Wound looked at the lance protruding from Jed's arrow quiver hanging on his back. "I have heard of the Lance Bearers of the Arapaho."

The voice was strong, Jed couldn't tell if the young warrior was hostile or friendly as he spoke. Something about the warrior made Jed curious… his face, the slope of his eyes and cheekbones reminded him of someone. From outside, Jed could hear Ellie as she called them inside. Blinking, he looked strangely at Little Wound before entering the lodge. His eyes told their story… the young warrior had the same eyes as Ellie.

Entering the lodge, the men looked down at the body that lay before them. War Bonnet stepped back from Hatcher. "Does he live?"

"He lives. It is just the medicine I gave him, making him sleepy." Ellie answered the warrior. "I need you to hold him tight. I'll be stitching very close to his eyes."

With all the laudanum in him, Ellie knew Hatcher would feel no pain, but she did not want him thrashing about as she cleaned and stitched the nasty tear. Hatcher's blue eyes blinked open slowly as the men took hold of him. Muscles bunched under the doeskin shirt as Hatcher tried to pull free before passing out. Quickly, after thoroughly cleaning the wound, Ellie closely examined the gouge in the forehead. The rifle ball had gouged a deep furrow into the skull of the old scout's forehead.

With deft hands, she checked for any more bone fragments before administering a mixture of ointment and liquid antiseptics. The slender hands quickly worked the needle and thread around the ugly wound, pulling the gash back together tightly. Smearing more salve over the wound, she bound it with a clean bandage. Leaning back, she nodded slowly, then stood up.

"How is he, Ellie?" Jed had never seen a head wound so serious as this one that hadn't killed its victim outright.

"The bullet cut a furrow in his skull, but it did not penetrate or breakthrough." Ellie looked sadly at Hatcher. "It won't kill him, but it's gonna leave a very nasty scar across his face."

"I'll bet he has a wicked headache for a few days." Jed added.

"He'll have that for sure."

War Bonnet looked at the handy work of Ellie's stitching and grinned. "Squaw does pretty work. If I get cut, I will send for her."

Turning, Ellie stared up into the face of a tall, handsome warrior who was looking down at her curiously. For several seconds their eyes locked before Ellie knelt and closed her medical bag. Hatcher had passed out from straining against the strong men and the laudanum. Now, he lay asleep, resting in a deep slumber.

"Thank you, everyone. We'll let him rest now." Ellie ushered the men from the lodge.

"Will Rolling Thunder regain his mind?" Small Crane asked as the lodge emptied of men.

"He will live, but I don't know about his mind." Ellie shook her head. "No doctor or medicine man can tell about a man's mind."

"I have seen warriors with head wounds who lose their minds like this." Small Crane looked down at Hatcher. "Some regained their thoughts, others never."

"The white medicine men call it amnesia when one cannot remember anything."

"Can this ever be healed by the white man medicine?"

"Sometimes." Ellie looked at the lodge's flap. The young warrior bothered her. "Small Crane, who was the young warrior that looked at me so strangely?"

"His name is Little Wound." The squaw replied. "He is the son of Rolling Thunder."

"What?"

"If you are the daughter of this one, then he is of your blood." Small Crane pointed down at Hatcher and smiled. "My nephew is already a great warrior... brave and honored by his people."

"My brother?" Ellie looked down at Hatcher. "Does Rolling Thunder know of him?"

"Yes, Rolling Thunder brings gifts to Wanicantha every year when he passes near here with the wagon lodges."

"Wanicantha?"

"It is the Gros Ventre name for Little Wound." Small Crane added. "Your brother is very easy to look upon, is he not?"

"Yes, he is indeed a very handsome young man."

"All the young maidens try to catch his eye."

"He's not married?"

"No, not this one. He is too busy making war on the Cree and others to take a squaw."

Ellie smiled as she thought of Red Hawk. "Sounds like another warrior I know."

"Is he handsome and wild too?"

"Yes, very." Ellie thought of the Crow warrior. "Pretty as a butterfly, but wild and elusive as the fleet-footed antelope."

"And you have not married this warrior?" Small Crane grinned toothlessly. "Is he too fast for you to catch?"

"Me? Of course not." Ellie was embarrassed. "Why would you say this thing?"

"I am an old woman, Medicine Thunder, but I hear your voice and look into your heart." Small Crane laughed. "I think you have feelings for that warrior you spoke of."

"You're being silly, Small Crane." Ellie blushed and turned from the lodge. "I do have feelings for Red Hawk, but only as a friend."

"I don't think so." Small Crane cackled as she watched Ellie's face turn red. "No, I don't think so."

Exiting the lodge, Ellie found Jed and Little Wound sitting under a large tree engaged in conversation. Walking to where they sat, she motioned them back to their seats as she sat down tiredly. Looking at Jed, she smiled and knew what was on his mind. He wanted to get back to Bright Moon and the babies.

"How long before your father can travel, Ellie?" Jed asked her.

"It will be a few days at least." Ellie looked at the warrior. "That is, providing we can get him to go back with us."

"Then his wound is not dangerous?"

"Not physically, I don't think, but mentally, I don't know." Ellie shrugged. "We'll just have to watch him a few days."

"Okay."

"If you want to return, Jed, go ahead. I'll be safe here until he can travel."

"You know I ain't about to leave you here alone." Jed seemed to get vexed at the thought. "Squires is still out there somewhere."

"I don't think we'll see any more of Mister Squires out here." Ellie looked at Little Wound. "Besides, I wouldn't be alone, Jed."

"What do you mean?"

"Has he not told you yet?"

"If you are speaking of this one, he don't talk much." Jed looked at the warrior. "Anyway, what has he to tell me?"

"What would you say if I told you he's my brother?"

"I already deducted that, but I wasn't sure." Jed smiled. "You two sure do favor."

"And just how, Mister Bracket, did you deduct that?"

"The eyes, Ellie. You both have Hatcher's eyes." Jed looked at Little Wound. "It seems you have a new sister here, Wanicantha."

The dark head nodded. "My father spoke of her many times over the years when he passed through. I never thought I would meet her in this way."

"Well, what do you think?"

"She is a handsome squaw for an Arapaho, and she is truly a good medicine person." Little Wound smiled. "She pleases me, but with one problem."

"And what's that?" Ellie was curious. "What problem do you have with me?"

"The warriors are already gathering their ponies to buy you." Little Wound was serious, causing Ellie to frown.

Jed laughed out loud, surprising Ellie, who seldom heard him laugh. "I don't see anything funny, Jed Bracket."

"How many horses will Little Wound ask for her?"

"Many."

"Well, I get half for bringing her here."

"Done." The young warrior grinned, then stood to his feet. "I will return later to check on Rolling Thunder." The young warrior looked at Jed and grinned. "Don't let the warriors run off with her."

As the warrior strolled away, Ellie nodded as she studied the powerful back and arms. Little Wound carried himself with the typical swagger of a proud and arrogant warrior of the tribes. Straight as a lodgepole, the warrior had confidence in his abilities as a fighting man.

"He's something alright." Jed had read her mind. "Were you surprised?"

"Yes, I was." Ellie nodded. "And you're right, he is something."

"What about Lige?"

"Let me have a week with him here, then we'll return home." Ellie apologized. "Thank you, Jed. I know you want to get back to Bright Moon and the babies."

"I do, but a few days won't matter." Jed nodded. "Take as long as you need with him."

"You know, my first love will always be you, but we both know it wasn't meant to be." Ellie smiled.

"I know."

"The babies could have been mine." Ellie dropped her eyes. "If I hadn't been so righteous."

"It just wasn't meant for us, Ellie. I'm sorry."

"Don't be, Jed, you're a very lucky man."

"How's that?"

"You've had four women that love you, and I think each one of them still does."

"Four?" Jed blinked in shock at her words. He knew she spoke of Sally Ann, Bright Moon and herself. Was the fourth woman she spoke of Little Antelope?

"Don't play coy with me, Mister Bracket." Ellie stood up and started for the lodge. "And now you've been blessed with two beautiful children that will love you."

"You haven't seen them yet." Jed smiled. "How do you know they are beautiful? They could be ugly."

This time Ellie turned and smiled. "I don't have to see them, they're beautiful alright."

Jed watched the slender woman walk away. Her straight shoulders and aristocratic carriage showed the same pride as that of Little Wound. He thought of the four women she spoke of. He couldn't figure how everyone thought they knew his mind. Many times, Red Hawk had implied and spoken the same words.

Meat was placed on spits over the large fire as warriors gathered in a large circle, watching the women of the tribe cook deer and buffalo steaks. The celebration was being held in Rolling Thunder's honor since he was leaving the Gros Ventres' village with the coming of the new sun. The old scout was up, walking about and talking a little. His words were mostly slurred and he still had no idea what he was saying or what had happened to him. His memory seemed to have evaporated like the fog of an early morning.

Later, Jed watched as Hatcher sat in the circle with the others, not speaking, only studying the sizzling meat. It had been a full week since Ellie had sewn the wound shut. Physically, he seemed fine, it was just his mind. He couldn't converse with the others and he didn't know Jed, Ellie, or any of the Gros Venture. Jed had questioned Ellie several times if he would ever recall his past, but she couldn't answer. Only time would tell.

The dancing went on with the young women pretending they were indifferent to the glances of the young men. Secretly, each wanted a particular, special one of them to ask for a dance. Several warriors had asked Ellie to dance and she had accepted. She had a natural way of making everyone like her. Laughing as she shuffled her feet around the huge fire, she was the center of attention for most of the young men. Jed was amazed that she had learned the Indian dances so quickly. No dancer himself, he remained sitting, content to talk with the elders.

One of the middle-aged warriors, who had danced with Ellie several times, stood in front of Little Wound and motioned to the outside circle. Several haltered horses were led forward by a youngster to where the warrior proudly stood with his arms folded. Looking over at Jed, then back at Ellie, Little Wound nodded slowly.

"This is Beaver Tail. He is one of the greatest warriors of the Gros Ventre." Little Wound introduced the warrior. "He has offered these ten horses for my sister in marriage."

Jed stiffened, he knew that horses were normally offered for the bride price for a new wife among the tribes. The warrior, Beaver Tail, had offered the horses with a deep respect for Ellie and Hatcher. Jed knew

Ellie would not accept, still, it was a ticklish situation. Little Wound had to somehow turn down the bride price without causing the warrior to lose face or be offended. The ten horses were an honest bid for Ellie. Little Wound had to be diplomatic with his words since he didn't want to shame the warrior in front of the whole village.

War Bonnet stood up and nodded at the warrior. "Beaver Tail's offer of these good horses is a great honor to the daughter of Rolling Thunder. She is proud he thinks so highly of her, that he would offer so much, but she cannot marry at this time. Her first responsibility is to her sick father, Rolling Thunder. When he has recovered, then she will consider Beaver Tail's offer."

Nodding slightly, the warrior smiled at Ellie and moved back to where he was seated. Jed let out a breath of relief. He didn't know how Little Wound would have retrieved himself from the proposal without hurting the warrior's pride. War Bonnet, knowing Little Wound wasn't sure of himself in this situation, had stepped in and replied for him.

"Thank you, Uncle, I didn't know of a good way to turn down the offer." Little Wound eased himself down beside War Bonnet and looked over at Jed. "My joke last night about the young men offering horses for my sister was in bad taste."

"No harm done, Nephew." War Bonnet chuckled. "Next time, you will think before you speak."

Little Wound smiled. "I will never speak of this again."

Jed looked at Ellie, then at War Bonnet. "My friend, it grows late and tomorrow's new sun comes quick. We must retire to our sleeping robes."

"With the new sun, I will ride to the east with you, Crow Killer." Little Wound spoke up.

"You will ride with us to the lands of the whites?" Jed was shocked. "It is a far and dangerous journey, my friend."

"I will make this journey if my uncle gives his permission."

War Bonnet nodded slowly. "Perhaps, this is a good thing, Nephew. You will help your father Rolling Thunder and your sister home safely."

"Thank you, Uncle."

"It will take two men to keep Rolling Thunder and Medicine Thunder safe on such a long journey."

"Do you see trouble on the trail?"

"I see one woman and a senseless one as trouble, yes." War Bonnet looked into the fire. "These are dangerous lands you will travel through."

"This is so, Uncle."

"With only one warrior to watch over them, it would be very hard if you were attacked."

"That is also how I see it." Little Wound agreed. "I will return when they are safe."

As the sun busted out brightly over the eastern mountains, Jed had the horses saddled and ready with provisions provided by the Gros Ventre. The tribe was as most other tribes. If they were treated with respect and dignity, they would repay in kind. Jed's only worry was if Hatcher would leave the tribe he felt so at home with. His worries were groundless as the old scout mounted a saddled horse without complaint. He smiled as he patted the little horse on the neck. Ellie hugged Small Crane and nodded to War Bonnet and Elk's Head, then turned to her horse and smiled as Jed helped her mount. Keeping her horse close to Hatcher to assure him he wasn't being left alone, Ellie waved once more as they turned north for the Gallatin River. There they would turn back east and home.

Jed studied Little Wound as they left the village behind. Armed with the typical bow and quiver of arrows, he also carried a war axe and a skinning knife in his belt. The young warrior rode relaxed, but Jed could tell his sharp eyes took in every bend of the trail as they followed the narrow passage away from the village. They could be attacked anywhere in these mountains, but it would be difficult to surprise them. Jed knew the young warrior was a trusted ally, and he was thankful the warrior had decided to ride with them to the east.

After an uneventful day of riding, the oncoming night found them camped on the bank of a fast running stream which Little Wound said would empty into the Gallatin a day's ride ahead. Jed remembered the terrain markings from the passage they had made days prior on their way to the Gros Ventre village. Unsaddling and hobbling the horses to graze on the short grass alongside the stream, Jed and Little Wound studied the clear stream before turning back to the fire Ellie had burning brightly.

"We will keep watch closely on this trip." The Gros Ventre spoke up. "A very close watch, Crow Killer."

"You expect trouble?"

"There is always trouble in these mountains." The dark head nodded. "Many renegades and killers roam these mountains."

"What renegades?"

"Mostly thieves from the north, but we have some bad Indians of our own, looking to steal or kill." The shoulders shrugged. "With my sister's beauty, there are many that would dare attack us."

"We have bad actors in our country as well." Jed added. "I thank you for coming to help protect her."

"I came to protect her and my father, Rolling Thunder, who now cannot defend himself." Little Wound looked at Hatcher. "Will he recover his mind?"

"This I don't know, but your sister's grandfather is a medicine man as well. Perhaps, he can answer your question when we get back to the white man's town."

"Tell me, Crow Killer, my sister calls you Jed. Are you a white man or an Indian?" Little Wound stared hard at Jed. He looked at the long dark hair, black eyes, and dark complexion. "You look Indian."

"My people are Arapaho and my heart is Arapaho." Jed smiled. "But, I reckon I am a little of both worlds."

"Around the Gros Ventre fires, they say you have killed many enemies." Little Wound could see some of Jed's scars but the long fringed hunting shirt hid the worst. "They also say you are protected by the great bear's medicine."

"I have killed, and some believe I have the power of the grizzly." Jed thought back on the killer bears and his beloved valley. "Maybe I do."

"Most of the stories come from my father."

Jed laughed. "Rolling Thunder can sure tell some whoppers for sure."

The warrior shook his head. "No, this time I can tell he did not make-up stories."

"And you Wanicantha?"

"Yes, I have killed." Little Wound admitted. "I wear this eagle feather for killing a chief of the mighty Cree."

"What did he do?"

"Many years ago, he raided our village and killed my mother." The dark face turned darker with the memory. "I was young then, but I remembered his ugly face. When I became a full-grown warrior, I rode with War Bonnet and challenged this mighty warrior to fight."

"I understand, this was a good thing for you to do."

"Father Abraham said I should not kill or wear the eagle feather, the sign of counting coup." Little Wound explained. "I was still a young warrior. The Cree was in his prime as a warrior. I was not ashamed to kill him or wear the feather. He killed my mother and many others before Father Abraham came among my people."

"Sometimes a man must kill if he is a man."

"Father Abraham does not smile on me as he once did." Little Wound continued. "He wants me to remove the feather."

"And what do you wish to do?"

"I will wear the feather in honor of my mother." Little Wound looked at Jed. "I will not remove it."

"There is no shame in what you did." Jed shook his head. "To do less would have been far worse."

"My brother, Crow Killer, thinks like a warrior." Little Wound nodded. "Do you have a woman?"

"Yes, a wife and two babies."

"I have seen my sister look at you. Why do you not take her for your squaw?"

"The white part of me teaches a man can only have one wife."

These words caused Little Wound to nod slowly. "So you are part white?"

"Yes, I am part white. Tell me, Little Wound, do you have a woman?"

"I had a wife and a boy child." The warrior nodded sadly. "Both died of the face rotting sickness the whites brought among my people."

"I'm sorry, my friend."

"Come, let us see if my sister is a good cook."

Daylight found the procession traveling east along the bank of the stream that led to the Gallatin River. Hatcher was in good spirits, speaking occasionally with Ellie and Little Wound. Jed rode far ahead, scouting out the lands they were passing through. Midafternoon found them sitting their horses at the Gallatin crossing. Everything seemed peaceful enough as the horses hadn't alerted to anything near the riverbank. Across the river, Jed could see the broken and discarded items the immigrants had been forced to leave behind. The peaceful river flowed slowly with only small ripples breaking the surface of the water.

"I will cross first, Crow Killer." Little Wound kicked his horse into the river's cold water. "This is a bad place. It is filled with bad spirits."

Jed knew the Indian tribes were much more superstitious of the spirit world than the whites. At night, anything could turn them back from a trail or hunt like an owl hooting or the hissing call of a wildcat from the shadows.

The Gallatin had gone down with the winter's snowmelt passing, but it still ran belly deep on the horse at midstream. Jed watched the warrior ride out on the far side then siding Hatcher with Ellie behind him, Jed pushed his horse into the river. Scanning the far bank, Jed kept the horses moving slowly across the Gallatin without stopping. Their horses dripped water as Jed rode out of the river and reined in beside the warrior.

"The water of the Gallatin is always cold." Jed and Ellie were both shocked when Hatcher blurted out the short sentence. "Always hated crossing that old river."

"I'll be danged, he must have recognized the river." Ellie smiled brightly. "That is a good sign."

"He'll get his mind back then?"

"Maybe, we'll just have to wait and see."

"You know that track?" Jed asked as he rode to where Little Wound had dismounted and was studying the ground closely.

The warrior pointed to several tracks, then circled one set with his finger. "I know the track. The young white, Bloody Hand, rides the horse that leaves this mark on the ground."

"I too recognize the crooked print."

"He is a young fool." The warrior frowned. "When we turned him loose, we followed this same horse track many miles."

Jed dismounted and studied the tracks closer. "These tracks are only two or three days old."

"Bloody Hand follows the whites who killed the one buried there." The warrior pointed at the iron cross, then to where the trail of two parties split. "The Metis rode the trail north to their own country. The Bloody Hand follows the whites to the east."

Jed noticed Hatcher looking over the piles of discarded furniture and boxes like he was confused. The old scout kept turning in his saddle as if he was looking for answers. His eyes went back several times to the iron wheel cross where Dibbs had said he was buried.

"Hopefully, he won't catch them." Jed turned his attention back to the tracks. "Five to one odds aren't very good."

"The Bloody Hand, the one you call Dibbs, is young, but he is a man hunter, a killer." Little Wound shook his head. "I think he will kill these whites. He is across the river now. Soon, he will be out of our country. Over here, War Bonnet doesn't care who he kills, providing they are not Gros Ventre."

"We've still got a couple hours till dark, let's ride." Jed swung up onto his horse. "We'll make camp east of here."

"It would be best for all, if the Bloody Hand dies." Little Wound thought on the tracks as they rode. "I think these whites set a trap for him. They are in no hurry."

"Appears that way alright." Jed agreed.

"I think perhaps the young white rides into an ambush." Little Wound smiled. "There were no tracks of the Cree warriors along the river."

"Or they're riding slow, waiting for us to catch up." Jed added. "Either way, there is nothing we can do about it now."

Jed counted the days he and Ellie had been at the Gros Ventre village. Squires and his men should have been more than halfway back to Baxter Springs by now. Instead, they were hardly two days hard ride ahead of them. Why would they delay, they weren't hunting or pleasure riding. It made Jed extra cautious, thinking Squires could be foolish enough to try to take the woman from them. Dibbs had warned Jed several times, that Squires was crazed and thought only of having Ellie. The hunter had hung around Baxter Springs, then followed them west to the Gallatins to try to take her. Ellie was indeed a beautiful woman, but would any man be so foolish as to get himself killed trying to steal her? Abducting a white woman was taboo in the west. When the foul act was found out, every white hunter in the mountains would be searching to get her back. Jed knew Ellie wasn't a full-blood white, but most people out here didn't know about her Indian blood. She was Doc Zeke's granddaughter and that would be enough to have the whole countryside up in arms, out looking for her, providing Squires could get her away from Jed and Little Wound.

All during the dark night, Jed and Little Wound took turns standing watch over the small camp. The fire was extinguished early to darken the place where they lay under their warm buffalo robes. Jed couldn't sleep, as he sensed the horses were restless, fidgeting while they grazed and moved about on the short grass. Several times, they lifted their heads and their ears pricked up, looking up the trail, always in the same location. As the full moon showed itself over their campsite, Little Wound slipped silently beside Jed and whispered softly in the dark.

"Something or someone is out there." The dark head was barely visible in the dark. "I will go see what is there."

"No, wait until the new light comes." Jed grabbed the warrior's arm. "It could be a trap."

"I think it could be the Metis."

"Tell me of these Metis, that Dibbs spoke so much hatred about?"

"Half French renegades that run with the white hunters sometimes." Little Wound nodded. "They are very dangerous killers from the north. I think they watched as we passed, back where the trail split at the river, then followed us here."

"What do they want?"

"I think my sister." The warrior growled lowly. "Maybe, the white hunter, Squires, has offered to pay them much in furs and horses for her."

"Would they be so foolish?" Jed looked into the dark stillness, worrying for Ellie. "Why would Squires get them to do his dirty work?"

"If she is stolen by Indians, the white hunter wouldn't be blamed for such a deed."

"That makes sense alright."

"If the Cree have joined the Metis, we are outnumbered. They may have many warriors riding with them now." Little Wound suggested. "I know these Cree and Metis dogs, they would never chance getting killed over a mere woman, but they would fight for horses and furs."

"Then you think Squires has bribed them to steal her?" Jed asked.

"Yes, the one called Dibbs, the Bloody Hand, told me to warn you of this before we released him." Little Wound continued. "This is why I ride back to the white village with you."

"Thank you, my brother."

"Even if my sister has much beauty, the white hunter must be crazy to come this far to steal her." The warrior looked at Ellie.

"Yes, he is." Jed agreed and looked to where Ellie lay. "Well, we'll just wait and see."

"I think whoever it is, they will show themselves with the new sun."

"Why didn't Squires come for her himself?" Jed couldn't figure Squires letting Ellie fall into the Metis' hands. "He's got four hunters with him, it don't figure."

"This white might be crazy, but crazy like a fox. I told you, he believes if he were found out, he would be hunted by every white man in this country." Little Wound explained. "A white man stealing a white woman is a bad thing, and he would be hunted as a renegade. That is what I think."

"But if the Metis from Canada took her?"

"They are not white." The warrior explained. "Whites think Indians are animals, and few would hunt for a woman taken by Indians. They know it would be hopeless to ride after her into the northlands."

"You're right." Jed agreed.

The first peek of the early morning sun showed the trail back west and up the Gallatins clear and bright. Jed and Little Wound's eyes finally found what they had been watching so closely for, throughout the night. Six riders sat their small horses in plain sight across the narrow trail. Standing up, Jed walked out into plain view. He wanted these warriors to know they had been spotted. Sometimes, a show of strength would dissuade and stop an all-out fight. Most Indians didn't like to face a deadly set-to if they could help it. They knew most white hunters were deadly with the Hawken rifles they carried.

"It is as I thought, they are Metis." Little Wound nodded. "The big one in front is their leader. They call this one Batiste. Many times, he has ridden into our lands with the whites for plunder."

"You know him then?"

"I have fought against the Metis many times." Little Wound replied. "Yes, I know him."

Jed watched the big Metis carefully. "I thought your father Abraham frowned upon the Gros Ventre fighting."

"Sometimes, what Father Abraham doesn't know is a good thing." Little Wound grinned. "We are still heathens, we never tell him everything."

"Where are the Cree warriors?" Jed looked the rocky road over but could see nothing.

"If only these few can take the woman, the white hunter won't have to pay so many horses." Little Wound nodded up the trail. "The big hunter probably kept the Cree and the rest of the Metis with him in case Batiste fails to get my sister."

"Makes sense." Jed nodded slowly. "He was smart, cause our Metis friend up there is going to fail."

"I hope Crow Killer's medicine is strong today."

Jed could see the man was big, dwarfing the small horse he rode. But that was all he could see as the face was hidden by a fur hat that shadowed the face from this distance. Seeing they had been spotted, the heavyset rider rode forward and circled his horse two times, then raised his rifle.

"I reckon he wants to talk." Jed raised his rifle.

Little Wound nodded. "Yes, he will talk first, then fight."

"Well, let me go see what our friend wants."

"You watch this one very close. He lies, cheats, steals, and kills." Little Wound frowned. "This one no good. Do not trust him."

"I'll watch him alright, but the trick is, he better be watching me." Jed kicked the bay horse forward.

Little Wound made sure Ellie and Hatcher stayed out of sight as Jed rode up the trail toward the Metis. Stopping halfway between the two parties, Jed waited as the one called Batiste approached. The man wasn't so tall, but the closer he rode, the bigger he seemed. The Metis leader was broad, huge through the shoulders with arms like coiled steel. Jed knew this one could have incredible strength if he ever got his powerful hands on a man. Weapons protruded from all over the man. A beautiful Hawken rifle, two short pistols, and two long knives were visible. Jed was curious, few mountain men had use for the one-shot, short-range pistols out here.

Jed waited as the man reined in and studied him closely. He knew the Metis was measuring him and looking behind him where Little Wound stood. Ellie and Lige were out of his sight, hidden by the trees and underbrush that lined the trail.

"So, you have the Gros Ventre dog, Little Wound, with you." The voice was deep, guttural coming out in a hoarse whisper. "This one has killed many of my people."

"What does Batiste do in this place?" Jed's voice was hard and cold. "What do you want?"

The hard black eyes settled on the rifle Jed held, then shifted to the bow and quiver of arrows. Grinning slightly, the broad mouth opened in an evil sneer. Jed knew the man had sized them up and was thinking he had the advantage if a battle erupted. The Metis could see Little Wound was armed only with a bow and quiver of arrows.

"I will tell you what we want in time." Batiste spat. "But first, you tell me what kind of Indian are you?"

"Arapaho."

"Arapaho, you are far west from your lands." The thick lips drew back.

"I aim to get closer."

"Perhaps, my friend, you will, then again, perhaps not."

"Spit it out, what are you here for?"

"First, tell me how do you know I am Batiste?"

"I've got ears. They say you are a coward and a backstabbing killer just like all French half-breeds." Jed nodded up the trail at the other Metis. "A dog who needs help to do his fighting."

"Batiste a coward?" The big man shook his head sadly. "Who says this bad thing about Batiste?"

"What do you want?" Jed repeated.

"Monsieur, a man only has his good name." The big man shrugged. "Now, you have taken even that from me."

"Cut the bull, Batiste."

"Alright, Arapaho, I will tell you what I want. We will take your horses, that rifle, and mainly the woman who rides with you." Batiste studied Jed's eyes. "Why does the pretty one hide from my eyes?"

"What pretty one, Batiste?"

"Mon ami, do you think Batiste a fool? We have watched you. We have seen the woman with much beauty who rides with you, the old scout, and the Gros Ventre."

"Yes, she rides with us." Jed admitted. "Tell me, Metis, is she worth dying for?"

"Maybe, she will bring many horses and furs from the crazy white." Batiste laughed. "But, I will not die this day, my friend, you will, if you do not do as I say and turn her over now. Then, perhaps, I will let you live another day."

"Ain't happening, Frenchy." Jed flattened his hand. "Ride on and live. Move that rifle an inch, and I'll kill you where you sit. Your choice."

"Many times, I have heard of the courage of the Arapaho Lance Bearers." Batiste eyed the lance on Jed's back. "Are you one of these? "

"I am."

"You know my name." Batiste ginned. "What do they call you?"

"I am called Crow Killer."

"Aiyee." The big Metis howled. "I have heard of you also. Many times you have been spoken about around our fires."

"This is good. Leave this place Metis and live to rob another day." Jed's voice hardened. "Or die here today."

"Tell me, Arapaho, have you killed the mighty grizzly with only your knife as they tell?"

"I have and I will kill you the same way."

"The woman is very beautiful, but she isn't worth dying for, my friend." The strong brown hand edged closer to one of the pistols. "Is she your woman, Arapaho?"

"My sister and I sure ain't your friend." Jed frowned.

"Your sister?" Batiste shrugged. "Then you lose nothing if you give her to me."

"You're wrong there, mister." Jed turned the rifle as the big man moved his hand closer to his pistol. "Move that hand one more inch, and I'll blow you clean into next year."

"We are six." Batiste stayed his hand. "You are two, with one old one to help you."

"I wouldn't underestimate the old one if I were you."

"That one is supposed to be dead." Batiste laughed lightly. "I know Hatcher. We have met and even fought against each other in the past."

"He looks alive enough to shoot a rifle and he is a crack shot." Jed nodded coldly. "Someone must have lied to you about him being dead."

"Yes, I know this one called Hatcher." Batiste smiled. "He is a brave man. I am glad to see he still lives."

"Since I am a dead man according to you, why do you want the woman so bad? You know trying to take her could get you killed. You have plenty of maidens in your own village." Jed eyed the big man.

"Yes, we do, but no woman of our village matches her beauty." Batiste looked to where Little Wound stood.

"Is she worth dying for?"

"Maybe she is." Batiste laughed. "We will give her to the white hunter Squires perhaps, when we are tired of her company."

"Then why do you wish to die for a mere squaw?"

"Since you are already a dead man, Arapaho, I Batiste will tell you." The big Metis sneered. "The big hunter, Squires, promises many horses and much money for her. Many horses."

"Where is he gonna get so many horses?"

"The white says he has many horses in your white village." Batiste fidgeted in his saddle. "It is said he is a big chief in your white man's town."

"He lies through his teeth. Where is this brave hunter? Why does he not try to take the woman himself?" Jed questioned.

"He waits ahead, we are to bring him the squaw." Batiste smiled. "Look up the trail, Arapaho, you will see there are six of us."

"That ain't near enough, mister." Jed shook his head. "With the head bird dead, I figure the rest of the buzzards will scatter to the winds."

"I know the one who rides with you." Batiste looked at Little Wound. "This day, I will eat his heart."

"You may have to kill him first, and I don't think you have the nerve to face a real warrior alone while he's facing you."

"Today, I will face this one. He is Little Wound, a dog of the Gros Ventre Wolf Society." Batiste spat. "He killed my uncle, a great Cree chief."

Jed hadn't heard of the Wolf Society, but he figured it was a tribal society as the Arapaho Lance Bearers were. "I wouldn't know about that."

"You ride with him, you lie." Batiste frowned. "He brags about his black deed to all who will listen."

Jed remembered Little Wound telling of killing a Cree chief. "He has never spoken of killing your uncle."

The big Metis studied Jed's hunting shirt closely. The dark eyes took in everything, trying to appraise how strong or dangerous the Arapaho could be. Over his campfires, the whites and other Indians had spoken many times of the Lance Bearers and how courageous they were in a fight. Batiste had killed many a white trapper and Indian warrior in single combat. He wasn't a coward, but he was no fool either. He always made certain his foe wasn't as dangerous or as strong as he was. He wouldn't dare challenge a man to personal combat unless he was sure he would win. No, the Metis was not a coward, but he knew death was a permanent arrangement, and he wasn't ready to die so young. Kicking his horse closer to Jed, he smiled wickedly. Many times, he had fought hand to hand to the death. So far, he had always guessed right and won his battles.

"Perhaps, I have a solution to our problem."

"And just what would that be?"

"I see no reason my men or your Gros Ventre friend should fight and maybe be killed." The strong white teeth showed from behind thick lips. "In one hour, you will send the woman and your horses to me, or meet me here in single combat."

"One hour?" Jed figured the man thought he could win without endangering his men or himself.

The dark face grinned widely. "One hour."

"You know, Frenchy, I wouldn't put off for an hour something I could do right now." Jed spread his hand dismissing the man's words. "Let's get to it, right here and right now."

"The knife and the war club." Batiste raised his arm. "These are my weapons."

"Now, that sounds like a fine choice to me." Jed pointed to a small flat piece of ground just below the trail and midway between the two groups. "I will speak with my friend so he will not interfere in the fight."

"And I will speak with mine."

Little Wound and Ellie watched as Jed rode back to where they stood waiting. Handing his rifle and shot pouch to the warrior, Jed started removing his buckskin coat and leather hunting shirt.

"It is as I thought, you are to fight Batiste." Little Wound took the weapon. "The Metis must think he can defeat you. That is the way he kills. When you are dead, then he will come for me."

"Are you saying Batiste is a coward?"

"No, I do not say he is a coward. He just likes to fight when he thinks he has the advantage."

"Do you know how to use the rifle?"

"I know very little. I have never wished for the white man's weapon." The Gros Ventre touched his bow. "I prefer this weapon, it is silent but deadly."

Jed nodded solemnly. "If this turns out bad, don't let them take your sister."

"They will have to kill me first."

"Don't let them take her, Little Wound, not alive!" Jed looked over at Ellie. "Promise me."

"I give Crow Killer my word."

"If this goes bad for me, try to kill Batiste with the rifle." Jed pulled his war club. "Maybe the others will leave without a fight."

"I do not think so." Little Wound shook his head. "These Metis are half white. Their fathers are French trappers and their mothers are Ojibway or Cree squaws. Very mean people, very bloodthirsty. No, they will fight to take my sister."

"Don't let her be taken prisoner by this scum."

"I told you, Crow Killer, you have my word." The warrior reached out his hand. "Good luck, my friend."

Ellie walked up beside Jed. "How many times will you have to fight other people's fights, Jed?"

"This is my fight, Ellie."

"No, you fight for me as you did the last time." Ellie touched his bare arm. "This time, I understand. Be careful and come back unharmed."

CHAPTER 7

Swinging up on the bay, Jed rode to where Batiste was waiting, already stripped down to his bare skin except for his leather pants and moccasins. He had to admit, the Metis was more powerful-looking without his shirt, quite a fearsome sight. The muscles in the man's forearms were awesome and the huge chest was immense with broad rippling coils of muscle, wound like bands of steel. The chest and torso were covered in thick, curly, black hair that reminded Jed of the deadly grizzly.

Batiste laughed and flexed his biceps into a steel mound of muscle. "I am a voyager of the north country. These came from portaging heavy boats on my back, up and down the great rivers of the north, since I was a lad."

"Well, Frenchy, you should have stayed north 'cause you sure ain't carrying boats now." Jed tapped his scarred chest. "And these came from fighting and killing big mouths like you."

The smile left Batiste's face as he took in the many scars that crisscrossed Jed's chest and stomach. Jed's words had done what he had hoped as it took a little steam out of the mixed blood's confidence. Both men stepped forward with their weapons reaching out in front of them. Their sharp blades looked like the flicking deadly tongue of a serpent.

"He has done this many times?" Little Wound asked as he watched the beginning of the fight.

Ellie nodded. "Many times, and I hated every time he's fought."

"I hope he is the great warrior they say he is." Little Wound pulled several arrows from his quiver. "Sister, do you hate the killing or the danger he is in?"

"I hate both. Look at that monster, he's so dangerous looking. I don't think he's ever faced such a formidable foe as this one. I fear for him this time." Ellie admitted.

"What about the great bears he killed?"

"They were animals."

"So Batiste may be worse than an animal." The warrior shook his head.

Ellie tried to avert her eyes but couldn't. "I'm scared this time."

"I fear for him too." Little Wound added. "I know this Metis, and I have seen him fight. Around our fires, the name of Batiste is greatly feared. The old ones speak of his power. Yes, this one is a very dangerous enemy."

Picking up the rifle, Ellie checked the priming, then gathered the shot and powder pouch. Looking to where the two combatants cautiously circled each other, she braced the heavy rifle over a low limb.

"I thought you did not like killing?"

"I can't let him die because of me." Ellie stiffened. "I won't let him be killed. I won't."

"You must not do this. You cannot kill the Metis." Little Wound stepped beside her and laid his hand on the rifle's barrel. "It would dishonor Crow Killer. For a man with his pride, it would be a thing far worse than dying."

"I cannot let him die."

"You have feelings for this one?"

"Yes, and I always will."

"We will wait and see how this fight goes." Little Wound strung his ash bow and notched an arrow to it. "If the fight goes badly... only then will we interfere."

Watching from where Ellie left him, Hatcher looked up and laughed. "They gonna tussle ain't they?"

Ellie looked at the old scout. "Yes, Pa, they're going to fight."

"Well, young un, I'm betting my biscuits on Crow Killer."

"I am too." Tears welled in Ellie's eyes, then hardness covered her face as she tightened her grip on the rifle.

The powerful Metis was the strongest warrior Jed had ever encountered. His grip was like a steel vise as he grabbed Jed's wrist. Wrenching free before Batiste could snap his wrist like a twig, Jed knew he couldn't let the Metis get a grasp on him again. One thing was in his favor, Jed was quicker as his blade had already left several small rivulets of blood running down the half breed's chest and arms. Grinning, the powerful fighter stalked slowly forward, his huge arms reaching out for the elusive smaller man.

"I will catch you soon, Arapaho." The yellow teeth showed. "Then, I will crush you like a bug."

"I'm right here, Frenchy... start crushing." Jed circled to his left, away from the deadly war axe.

Suddenly, with a quick rush that surprised Jed, the Metis charged forward, intent on grappling with him. Falling backward under the sheer weight of the heavier Metis, Jed kicked out with both feet, catching Batiste in the stomach and sending him flying over his head. Rolling to his feet with the speed of a cat, Jed rushed forward and ripped an ugly slash across the man's hairy back as he tried to rise.

Enraged, Batiste whirled and rushed again at Jed. "Aiyee that hurt a little, monsieur."

"I bet it did." Jed nodded and pointed the skinning knife toward the maddened Metis. "I've got some more hurt for you right here."

"I'm coming." Batiste started forward, but then stopped in shock as an arrow stuck in the fatty part of Jed's leg. Whirling, he looked to where his men were waiting. "Ah, the dogs, they were not to interfere in this fight."

"I bet." Jed jerked the bloody arrow from his leg. "Let's get on with it."

"No! You have been fouled." Batiste started to throw down his weapons when the Hawken discharged, staggering him forward with a shocked look on his face. "I'm afraid we have both been fouled, monsieur."

Grabbing the falling man's body, Jed eased him to the ground as the other Metis raced forward. Looking to where Ellie was reloading the rifle, Jed blinked in surprise. Little Wound was rushing forward, sending arrows at the charging half breeds. Again, the rifle roared as another

Metis was thrown from his horse. With a shrill yell of defiance, the others turned and raced back up the mountain trail. Seeing the remaining four riders disappear, Jed looked down at the dying man.

"You were a good adversary, monsieur." The Metis coughed as his dark eyes stared at Jed. "I think you would have defeated Batiste this day if the others hadn't interfered."

Jed shook his head. "You are the strongest and bravest man I ever faced. It could have gone either way."

The bloody hand reached up handing Jed a beautiful stiletto knife, the kind favored by most Frenchmen. "This is yours, Crow Killer. A gift from Batiste Montaugre, the Metis."

Taking the stiletto, Jed nodded. "Thank you."

"Sometimes when you hold the knife, remember Batiste. In another time, Jed, we might have been friends."

"How do you know my white name?"

"The young one, Bloody Hand." Batiste coughed up blood. "The one you call Dibbs."

"What about Dibbs?"

"The big hunter Squires, his men, and many Cree caught Bloody Hand and tortured him with fire. They forced him to speak of you."

"He's dead?"

"For one so young, he was a brave man." Batiste blinked his eyes slowly. "Even with the fire burning him, the young one cursed and spit at Squires."

Jed looked down into the dying man's face. "Then he is dead?"

"Yes, but before he was captured, he killed many Cree warriors." Batiste barely could raise his arm to point. "His body lies up there."

"Did he kill any of the whites?"

The big head turned slightly. "The white hunters are cowards. They let the Cree get killed first, then they moved in on Bloody Hand."

"You are sure?"

"I am dying, this is no time to lie." Batiste coughed again. "Beware, Crow Killer, the one called Squires wants your woman. He has looked at the squaw, and now, he is crazed to possess her."

"Well, he won't have her." Jed's jaw snapped into a hard knot. "Where did he go?"

"His plans were for us to bring her to the white settlement to the east." Batiste grabbed Jed's arm in pain. "There, outside your village, he would have our horses and money waiting."

Jed knew, by the labored breathing, the Metis was almost finished. "Well, I reckon we'll go see Mister Squires."

Batiste spit up blood. "If we do not come to him, he will know we failed to get her."

"Will he come back here for her?"

"No, I think he will wait in the settlement for you to ride in with her." Batiste coughed again. "He doesn't know you found out he wants her. He thinks taking her from you will be easy."

"Thanks to you it won't be." Jed looked down into the bearded face. "Thank you, Batiste."

"Beware of him, Crow Killer." Batiste stiffened. "He has some of my men and many Cree following him."

"I will keep my eyes to the skyline until we get her home safely."

"He is no good. I thought about killing him long ago." Batiste's eyes started to close as his voice faded. "I think we would have been friends."

Jed nodded as the big head rolled sideways. "In another time and place, I believe we might have been."

"Is he dead?" Ellie stood beside Jed.

"He's dead." Jed nodded. "Thank you for saving my life."

"I fired before I saw him drop his weapons." Ellie tried to hold back the tears. "But, I have no regrets for killing him."

Jed held her in his arms as she started to sob. "You had no way of knowing."

"I killed two men, Jed." Ellie seemed to shake. "Something I've condemned you for so many times."

"Today, you saved all our lives, Ellie."

"I never would have believed it; she shot two men clean through their gizzards." Hatcher shook his head as he looked at Ellie.

"Yes, Lige, your daughter is quite a woman."

Ellie turned back for the horses as Little Wound stepped beside Jed. "Batiste said Bloody Hand is dead?"

"That's what he said." Jed nodded.

"Do you wish to look for his body?"

"No, there's no time. It's too dangerous for Ellie if we turn back to search for him. We'll let him and Batiste rest where they lay." Jed put his shirt on and gathered his rifle and pouches where Ellie had dropped them. "We have to return her and your pa to Baxter Springs quickly."

"There could still be danger along the trail."

"Hopefully, the white hunters that killed Dibbs won't find out we killed Batiste and his men. They'll be back in Baxter Springs waiting and drinking." Jed started to where Ellie waited. "I believe we'll be safe enough on our ride back."

"I think the Metis that fled today will circle us and ride to your village to tell the whites what happened." Little Wound frowned. "They still want the rifles and horses offered."

Ellie studied the blood covering Jed's leg as he limped toward the horses. "Let me take a look at that leg."

"No need, the arrow barely penetrated my leg." Jed looked down at the blood. "It bled a little when I pulled it out is all."

"There is a need, Jed." Ellie shook her head. "It's called infection."

Jed's face turned beet red as she wrapped a blanket around him, and ordered him to remove his leather britches. "I don't think it's that important, Ellie."

"Off!" Ellie stood to her full height. "Sit down and drop them now."

"Ellie."

"Honestly, Jed, I've seen your bare legs before in case you have forgotten the swimming hole?"

Embarrassed, Jed looked over at Lige and the young warrior. "Alright, alright."

"That's better." Ellie cleaned the blood from the wound. "You're right for once, it isn't serious."

"Told you weren't no need for a fuss."

"It'll be a little tender for a few days." Ellie applied salve to the wound and wrapped the leg tightly, tying the bandage off. "Besides, I got to see your bare legs again."

"Ellie, I can't believe you said what you did in front of your brother and father." Jed looked to where Little Wound was getting the horses ready. "It's downright embarrassing."

"What did I say?"

"About seeing my legs."

"Well, it was the truth, wasn't it?" Ellie grinned innocently.

"Yes, but you could have told him I had a breechcloth on." Jed frowned hard at her. "And that we were swimming."

"Men." Ellie laughed. "I swear, Jed, I'll never figure you out."

"Men, what about you women?"

"You had him whipped, boy, before the girl plugged him dead center." Hatcher grinned from ear to ear. "Yep, old Batiste was a dead man for certain."

Ellie looked around as Hatcher spoke. "You knew the dead man, Pa?"

"As well as I know myself, girl." Hatcher laughed. "Trapped some with him back in the shining times. Fought against the thieving rascal many a day."

The ride back to Baxter Springs had been quiet as Jed expected. Either he or Little Wound took the lead, always keeping Ellie and Hatcher to the rear. Jed wanted them out of harm's way in case of an ambush. Keeping in a steady dog trot along the rock path, which passed for a road, Jed pushed the horses hard. He wanted to cover the distance back to Baxter Springs as quickly as he could without crippling the animals.

Jed had told Dibbs about his hidden valley, hoping the youngster would return there with him one day, leaving the Gallatins and the hate he held in his heart far behind. As tortured as Batiste said Dibbs had been, Jed worried if he told Squires and his killers about the valley, possibly putting his stepfather in danger. He knew Dibbs didn't know the exact location of his valley, but still, he worried. Squires and his men were experienced mountain men, and they knew their way around the mountains. If they asked questions in Baxter Springs and rode back into the high mountains, they might follow the trails and stumble onto his valley. With a little riding and searching, they could find it.

Jed had no way of knowing what Squires would do if Batiste didn't bring Ellie to him. He new logically the easiest way to kidnap Ellie would be to wait until she returned to the settlement. No one in Baxter Springs would be able to track them into the mountains to try to rescue her. He nodded and thanked heaven Batiste had warned him of Squires, otherwise he would have left Ellie behind in the settlement defenseless. He was hoping Squires would give up his craziness about Ellie.

The streets of Baxter Springs were shrouded in darkness as Jed reined in behind the doctor's office and slid lightly from his tired horse. Taping quietly on the door, Jed ushered Ellie into the room as the passageway opened. Ellie's grandfather opened his eyes in surprise as Jed pushed Ellie and Hatcher before him into the well-lit room.

"Ellie, my granddaughter." The old doctor smiled brightly and took her in his arms. "You're home safe, girl. Thank goodness you've brought Lige back alive."

"He's alive, Grandfather, but just barely." Ellie turned her attention to Hatcher. "Pa has lost his memory."

"His memory?" Doc Zeke took a closer look at the old scout.

"A rifle ball gouged a deep furrow in his forehead." Ellie held her hand on Hatcher's shoulder. "Any closer and it would have killed him."

Jed watched as the old doctor examined Hatcher's scabbed-over wound. "Have you seen the trapper Squires or his men here in town?"

"Yes, they came in four or five days back." Zeke was absorbed in examining the scar. "But, I haven't seen Squires in a couple days. That little squirt called Sugar has been keeping an eye on my office all day."

"Sugar?"

"Yep, I can't figure the why of it though." Zeke looked over at Jed. "He just sits in front of the saloon drinking and watching this place like a hungry buzzard looking over a dead skunk."

"But, you haven't seen Squires or the one called Pete?"

"No, not since Bate Baker was found dead in his store."

"Bate Baker's dead?" Jed turned his head in surprise.

"Yes, it was Squires and two other fellers with him, named Pete and Nobles, that found old Bate." The doctor looked at Jed. "I haven't seen hide nor hair of any of them since."

"How did he die?"

"Everyone thinks his heart gave out on him." Zeke grunted. "That's the thinking alright."

"And you, Doc?"

"I didn't mention it, but it looked to me like he was strangled."

"Strangled?"

"Yep, his windpipe was crushed." Zeke explained. "Took a strong man to do that and Squires is a very big man."

"That he is, but why would Squires want Baker dead?"

"I found this under Bate when I examined him." Zeke handed Jed what looked like a tuft of hair. "Squires wears a greasy hunting shirt covered with pieces of hair like this."

"You think the trader ripped the hair from Squires' shirt in the struggle?"

"I figure so, but that isn't Injun hair in your hand, boy." The old doctor pointed at Jed's hand. "That came from a white."

"I know, it's Dibbs Bacon's hair." Jed frowned. "I recognize the reddish strands mixed with the brown."

"That's a shame, he seemed like a likable enough young feller."

"Well, Batiste spoke the truth. This hair proves for sure Squires killed Baker, same as he killed Dibbs."

"But why would he kill our fur buyer? He was the only hide buyer in these parts closer than Bridger. Every spring, Squires and his drunken partners brought their pelts in to trade with him." Zeke questioned him.

"I don't know why, but he did for old Baker, this proves it." Jed held up the tuft of hair.

"Why did they kill the young fella Dibbs?"

"Dibbs Bacon was the mysterious Bloody Hand, the killer from the Gallatins and Squires knew he was hunting him."

"Could be he was protecting himself, but killing Bate don't make sense."

"Fur traders can be replaced." Jed studied the piece of scalp closely before handing it back to Zeke. "I figure he wanted him shut up so he couldn't talk."

"Talk about what?" The old doctor took the hair.

"I don't know for sure." Jed nodded at the tuft of hair. "Keep that, we may need it for evidence if Squires gets away from me."

"I'll do that."

Pulling Ellie close, Jed whispered to her. "Put some things together, we're riding on come daylight."

"Where are we going, Jed?"

"We're heading to my valley. You'll be safe there until I run Squires and his renegades to the ground."

"Why did he kill Mister Baker?"

"It's just a guess, mind you, but I figure he made Baker tell where my valley's located."

"And he didn't want Mister Baker telling you?"

"Exactly." Jed nodded. "It's only a guess, but why else would he cut his nose off to spite his face. Bate Baker was the one who bought his furs and kept him in drinking money."

"Why would he scalp Dibbs?"

"The youngster's hair was a trophy to him, Ellie, only a trophy." Jed frowned. "By the looks of his hunting shirt, he's killed many a man."

"And Grandfather?"

"He'll be safe enough." Jed looked down into her dark eyes. "It's you Squires wants. Besides, if I'm right, we'll find him and the others waiting somewhere between here and the valley."

"Where are you going?" Ellie took hold of Jed's arm as he turned.

"I'm gonna take a quick look around the settlement for Squires or any of his men." Jed looked at Hatcher. "I don't figure they're still in Baxter Springs, but maybe the one named Sugar can tell us something."

"Be careful, Jed."

"Feed him real good and be ready to ride at first light." Jed looked to where Hatcher was being examined by Doc Zeke. "Stay inside, Ellie, and keep that rifle close."

"Should father go with us?"

"He'll be safer with us." Jed continued. "If I'm wrong and Squires is still in town, he could kill Lige or try to make him lead him to my valley."

"If you think it's for the best." Ellie finally learned to rely on Jed's judgment. So many times in the past, she had argued with him, but not anymore. "We'll be ready."

"I don't like dragging you into the mountains." Jed apologized. "But understand, Ellie, I've got to get you where I can protect you."

"You need me to look at that leg, Jed?" Doc Zeke motioned to the bloody leggings. "Peers you've been fighting again."

"No need, Doc. Ellie fixed it up." Jed looked over at Ellie and smiled. "You know she's seen my legs before."

"Jed Bracket, I swear." Ellie blushed.

Doc Zeke nodded and laughed. "In her profession, I'll bet she'll see a lot of men's legs before she's done."

"Remember now, lock the doors and keep your rifle close by."

Slipping out into the back alley, Jed moved to where Little Wound was waiting beside the tied horses. "We'll feed and water the animals first, then we'll take a walk around town."

Putting the horses in the corral with Doctor Zeke's buggy horse, Jed looked at Little Wound in the dark. "Come, we go. Walk softly and stay in the shadows."

"We go after the bad ones?"

"Providing Squires and his killers are still in town." Jed eased across the darkened street slowly. "Hopefully, we can end this tonight."

"And if they are not in this place?"

"All of them may not be, but at least we know one of them is still here."

Doc Zeke had been right, the hunter called Sugar sat lounging in a chair outside on the saloon porch, holding a bottle of whiskey in one hand and his smoking pipe in the other. The hunter was well on his way to getting drunk, without a care in the world. The filthy bloodstained man seemed to smile as he pulled on the jug. Jed noticed the short hunter's eyes were riveted on the doctor's office. Peeking inside a side window of the busy saloon, he didn't see any sign of Squires or the one they called Pete. Masters and his men were the only customers inside, sitting at the same table where Jed had last seen them. Even with a slight limp, the moccasins on Jed's feet made no sound as he circled the building and came up on Sugar from behind. As the cold steel blade of the skinning knife touched the hunter's throat, Sugar dropped his whiskey jug, becoming frozen with fear.

"You've got one chance, little man, to get out of this alive."

"Tell it, mister." The frightened hunter swallowed hard. "I'm a good listener."

"Stand up." Jed pressed the knife against the man's throat as Little Wound took his rifle and pipe. "Now, walk quietly to the alley."

The three men moved silently into the darkened alley. Only the dim light from the street's night lamp cast a faint glow as the men turned behind the saloon into the cluttered alley. Removing Sugar's dangerous skinning knife, Jed turned the man to face him.

"Your name's Sugar ain't it?"

"Yeah, what of it?"

The blade pressed a little harder, causing Sugar to swallow hard again as a thin line of blood oozed down his neck. "One more smart remark and I'll guarantee it'll be your last."

Only a nod came from the hunter as he looked into the dark face of death. "I ain't done nothing."

"Where's Squires and the other one?"

"I don't know."

"Wrong answer." The knife pressed harder. "Last chance, mister. Where's your boss Squires and his men?"

"He and the others rode out to Bridger yesterday."

"Who are the others?"

"Nobles, Scarface, Pete, and Harve."

"Anyone else with them?"

"A few Metis and Cree." Sugar tried to swallow.

"Some of Batiste's men?"

"Yeah, they got here yesterday. Said you killed poor old Batiste." Sugar whined. "They're plenty mad about it, swearing revenge on you, Crow Killer."

"Is Squires still planning on taking the woman?"

"He's gone completely loco now. You bet, he ain't forgot about that one." Sugar was blinking his eyes like a bee in a hailstorm.

"What's Squires' plans?" Jed pressed harder. "And, mister, you better not lie."

"He wants the woman. He figures you'll take her with you back into your mountains and he'll be waiting for you." Sugar trembled. "He's filled his pack animals' bags with whiskey and he's already given the Injuns with him, money... my money."

"Why?"

"Ever since he first seen her, he's been nuttier than a woodpecker after a pecan. He's gone crazy, fascinated by her." Sugar tried to move his head. "She's all he talks about, can't get his mind off her."

"No, I mean, why the whiskey?"

"He'll keep them Cree and Metis liquored up enough so they'll stay with him. That's why."

"Why would he think I'll take her with me into the mountains?"

"You can thank that killer Bacon for that. The kid told him that was your plan." Sugar swallowed in fear as the knife cut deeper. "He told Squires about your valley and how you intended to take her there with you."

Now, Jed understood. Dibbs was going to have his revenge from the grave. With the hate that drove the youngster, he had convinced Squires before he died that Jed was taking the girl back into the deep mountains. Dibbs had no way of knowing Jed's plans for Ellie, but he had somehow, even in his tortured pain convinced Squires with his story. He had purposely lied to Squires about the girl so the hunter would follow Jed into the mountains and hopefully to his death. If Batiste hadn't told him of Squires' plans for Ellie, he would never have suspected she was still in danger from the hunter. Dibbs had warned him, but he hadn't taken the youngster seriously. Only a crazed man would go to this much trouble over a woman. Especially a woman that didn't want him. Even being tortured like he was, Dibbs Bacon had planned the death of Squires and his men. Jed had to admit, even in his last minutes the boy had sand. If only he could have turned his hatred in a better direction.

"The boy, why did you kill him?"

"Boy? Shucks, mister, that kid was a killer in his own right. He made us look like amateurs." Sugar tried to pull back from the knife. "He's killed plenty of us over the last year or so. The Cree finally caught him."

"Did Squires kill his pa?"

"Yeah, we killed that old wolf."

"Does Squires know where my valley lies?"

"Not exactly, but the fur man gave him a rough map some Nez Perce warrior had given him." Sugar tried to swallow. "Said it laid out the trail straight to your valley."

"Squirrel Tooth," Jed spoke the name softly, it had to be the Nez Perce. Somewhere ahead, between Baxter Springs and his valley, the five trappers and their allies could be waiting. Should he take Ellie with him or leave her in the settlement? Either way was a dangerous gamble. If he took her, they could be ambushed somewhere along the mountainous trails. If he left her in town, Squires could double back and find her alone and defenseless. "Why did you kill the fur man?"

"The old doctor told you, huh?" Sugar moaned slightly. "I told Squires the doc would know right off, he strangled the fat man."

"You like killing don't you, Mister Sugar?"

"It was Squires." The man was frantic, but he couldn't move. "He killed the boy and the fur man, it weren't me."

"But, you stood there and watched."

"I had no choice. Squires has gone kill crazy, I tell you." Sugar eyes were bugged almost from his head. "I didn't want him killing me."

"Why does he want the woman so badly?"

"Shucks, mister, ain't you looked at her sideways yourself?" Sugar tried to smile. "She's the prettiest thing this side of the divide."

"He wants her bad enough to die for?"

"I done told you, mister, he's crazy and aims to have her." Sugar tried to move away from the knife. "He'll kill any man that stands in his way. He's paying them cutthroats everything he owns to help bring her in. Promised them many horses, furs, and gold to get her."

"How many does he have riding with him?"

"Enough to get the job done, I reckon." Sugar calmed down. "If you're planning on killing me, you dang heathen, do it. I ain't begging or saying another word."

"Well, Mister Sugar, be careful you don't get what you wish for." The blade cut deep. Sugar's eyes blinked slowly as his lifeless body gurgled in blood, then slipped to the ground. "Come, we go."

Little Wound looked at Jed, then down at the body and shook his head. He had underestimated the Arapaho. This one was a deadly warrior, not to be challenged. Following Jed back to the doctor's house, they tapped quietly on the back door, waiting for Doc Zeke to let them in. Ellie met them as they entered the kitchen. Placing plates of food on the table where Hatcher sat eating, she ignored the fresh blood on Jed's hunting shirt.

"You boys find the feed for the horses alright?"

"We did, Doc. Thanks."

"Did you find out anything?" Ellie sat down at the table beside Hatcher.

"Nothing has changed. We'll leave at daybreak." Jed picked up a fork. "I'll pick up fresh supplies before we pull out."

"We'll be ready."

"Wear the buckskins that Little Antelope made for you." Jed wolfed down his food. "You'll look more like a man."

"Okay, Jed. I'll wear one of Pa's old hats to cover my hair." Ellie added.

"Good." Jed nodded. "Probably won't matter none, but we'll try to make anyone watching think you're a man as long as we can."

"How are you doing, Lige?" Jed looked to where the old scout was eating heartily. "You getting enough to eat, old pard?"

"Sitting on top of the log pile, boy. A man can't do much better." Hatcher spoke slowly, then smiled. "Good food, a pretty woman for a cook, and a warm lodge."

"That's fine." Jed smiled. "You ready to go for another ride?"

"We going hunting?" The old scout was talking fine. His words weren't slurred in the least. Looking at the old hunter, he appeared normal, but Jed knew he still didn't remember some things.

"You might say that."

Laying his fork down, Hatcher leaned forward and looked closer at Jed and Little Wound. "Don't I know you two young fellers?"

"My name's Jedidiah Bracket." Jed looked curiously at Doc Zeke. "And this is your son, Little Wound."

Scratching his head like he was puzzled, Hatcher studied Jed's face. "No, I remember you being called something else. Crow Killer, that's it."

"You remember right, Lige." Jed smiled. "I am Crow Killer."

Ellie smiled as she patted Hatcher's hand lightly. "He may be slowly regaining his memory."

Doc Zeke nodded slightly. "You could leave Lige here with me."

"No thank you, Doc. You couldn't handle him if he decided to ride off alone."

"I didn't think of that." The old grey head nodded. "You're right, of course."

"Maybe being in the mountains and seeing things familiar to him will revive his memory quicker." Ellie looked at Hatcher. "Let's hope so."

"I hope so too." Jed added. "And, we might just need his rifle before this is finished."

"He has a strong constitution physically." Doc Zeke looked at Hatcher. "But the mind is fragile… a completely different thing altogether. With luck, it could return quickly, then again, it may not ever fully return."

"Let's hope for a quick recovery, shall we?" Ellie smiled at Hatcher.

"If you folks are talking about me, ain't nary a thing wrong with my thinking." Hatcher looked around the table.

"No, Lige, we were speaking of one of my patients." Zeke winked at Ellie. "We sure couldn't put nothing over on you, old friend."

"Darn right, you couldn't."

"Alright, let's all turn in." Jed finished eating and stood up. "We've got a long day tomorrow."

"How long will my granddaughter be gone this time, Jed?" Doc Zeke looked sadly at Ellie.

"I couldn't say for sure, Doc. However long it takes to sort out this mess, I reckon."

"Take care of her." The old doctor pleaded. "I know her going is for the best. She might not be safe here with me."

Across the street, from the dark, a cry went up and sounds of several men running across the board sidewalk came to them. A lone voice was hollering something about a dead body. A fist beat hard against Doc Zeke's door, yelling he was needed. Opening the door, the old doctor looked outside where men were standing at the entrance of the alley. Jed pulled Little Wound back into the kitchen and watched as Doc Zeke walked out the door. Ellie looked back at Jed, then down at his shirt.

Returning to the house a few minutes later, Zeke closed the door quietly and looked at Jed. "Someone killed the one called Sugar. Cut his throat."

"Reckon that's one less we'll have to worry about." Jed nodded.

"Well, he's dead for sure." Zeke looked curiously at Jed. "I sure couldn't help him none."

"That's too bad." Jed shook his head.

"Baxter Springs has sure had its fair share of killings these last weeks." The doctor continued. "The gravediggers are going to get mighty rich digging in the dirt if this keeps up."

Little Wound looked at Ellie, who was staring hard at Jed. "This one called Sugar, him good bad man now."

"The hunters over there think it's the killer from the Gallatins who probably followed Squires and his men back to Baxter Springs." Zeke sat down heavily at the table. "Several heard Squires talking about someone following him and this is the second of his men killed in our settlement."

"This dead one helped the Metis kill Bloody Hand and fur man. He say other white would kill again to steal my sister." Little Wound spoke up again. "It is good he is dead."

"Sister?" Doc Zeke looked curiously at the warrior. "What does he mean, Ellie?"

"Yes, Grandfather. Little Wound is my father's son by a Gros Ventre woman." Ellie smiled at the warrior. "He's my half brother."

"I see." The old man looked at them. "Yes, I see the resemblance now. You seem to have brothers and sisters all over these mountains."

"You said Squires had some Indians with him, did you see them yourself?" Jed questioned the old man.

"There were some outside Baker's place when I went over there to see the body."

"How many were there?"

"Six is all I seen." The old doctor replied. "But, there could have been more, I reckon."

Pulling Jed to the side as he started for the back door, Ellie looked up at him. "A few days ago, I killed two men, Jed. I can't judge you or my brother."

Taking her shoulders, Jed smiled down at her. "He's just one less killer we'll have to worry about waiting to ambush us now, and he is one white that deserved killing."

"But how many more will die before this is over?"

"Squires and his men don't have to follow us into the mountains." Jed's face grew hard. "I'll kill every mother's son of them if they try to take you. Count on it, Ellie."

Little Wound stood by the stove, listening. "These bad men, my sister. They deserve to die if they follow."

"I reckon it's up to Squires, his Cree, and Metis warriors." Jed stared down at her. "This is not your fault, Ellie. They're bringing this down on themselves. They don't have to follow Squires."

"Metis?" Ellie's face paled. She hadn't heard her grandfather speaking to Jed. "What Metis?"

"Sugar said some of Batiste's men came here and joined Squires, his hunters, and the Cree warriors."

"Why? Why would the Cree and Metis come here?" Ellie questioned him. "Surely they are not after me too."

"I reckon the Metis came here after me to get revenge for Batiste and collect the horses they were promised. Squires is still after you, Ellie." Jed warned her. "The one called Sugar says he's gone loco. He'll do anything to get you."

"I don't even know the man."

"Well, he knows you, girl. I can't protect you here, Ellie. We've got to go where I can get some help."

"You mean Walking Horse?"

"Maybe and Red Hawk if we can get back to the valley and send word to them." Jed released her. "Now, you get Lige to bed and try to rest. We'll be riding hard tomorrow."

At daylight, Jed had the horses saddled and supplied from the general store. He had sent Little Wound on ahead to scout out the immigrant road before daylight. With the settlement being in a fever over Sugar's killing, Jed didn't want anyone to see the Gros Ventre in town. As worked up as the town was right now, anyone of the men might take a shot at him without asking questions. Lifting Ellie on her horse, Jed turned to help Hatcher but stopped as the old scout held up his arm.

"I can get on a horse by myself, Crow Killer." Hatcher pulled himself into the saddle. "Where's my rifle and shot pouch?"

"You want your rifle?" Ellie asked in surprise.

"Well, woman, I ain't going hunting with my bare hands, am I?"

Grinning, Jed handed a rifle to Hatcher. "Thank you kindly, Crow Killer."

"You're welcome, Lige." Jed swung up on the bay.

"Where's the Indian, ain't he coming?" Hatcher looked around for Little Wound and cussed. "They're never on time for nothing."

Both Ellie and Jed were shocked as they looked at the scout. The bright blue eyes of the old hunter came alive as he looked down at the rifle and hung the shot pouch around his neck.

"You know where my valley lies, across the mountains, Lige?" Jed was testing the hunter.

"Sure, I know, boy. You think I've lost my touch, is that it?"

"Well, lead out, scout." Jed nodded. "Take us home."

"Thought this was to be a hunting foray?"

"It is, Lige. You just keep a sharp lookout for anything moving in front of us. You hear?"

"I hear you, boy." Hatcher clucked to his horse. "Well, come on, we're burning daylight sitting here."

Both Ellie and Jed couldn't believe it when Hatcher kneed his horse and pointed him east, away from Baxter Springs, onto the well-traveled immigrant trail. Waving farewell to Doc Zeke, they fell in behind the scout. Ellie didn't know what to think about her father's memory. So far, he hadn't acted like he knew her or Doc Zeke. Out of sight of Baxter Springs, Jed let Hatcher lead the procession as he studied the heavy foliage and brush along the trail. The old scout was doing fine, holding the horses in a slow trot, heading east toward the Carter homestead. The broad shoulders of the older man were squared and straight, showing a cocky tilt to his head as he proudly led the small caravan along the sandy road to Bridger. The old scout's head, except for the scabbed over scar, wasn't giving him any trouble. Jed purposely hadn't loaded Hatcher's rifle and the scout hadn't checked. Somewhere ahead, Little Wound would rejoin them and Jed didn't want Hatcher to mistake him for a hostile and shoot. Jed didn't know how Hatcher's aim was now, but before getting his head wound, the old scout was deadly at any distance with a rifle. He hardly ever missed and Jed sure didn't want Little Wound shot by accident.

"You think he'll remember the cutoff that leads to the river?" Ellie looked back at Jed. "That'll be the first test."

"We'll see pretty soon." Jed was curious himself. "Carters is just over the next small rise."

Suddenly, Hatcher reined in as Little Wound appeared off to their right. Motioning with his rifle at the warrior, Hatcher nodded, then kicked his horse on down the road. Little Wound looked curiously at Jed as he reined in behind the column.

"Rolling Thunder seems to know me." The young warrior looked at Jed. "At least he didn't try to shoot me."

Jed laughed lightly. "That would be hard to do with an empty rifle."

"Maybe his mind returns."

"He's got me puzzled for sure." Jed shook his head. "We'll see if he turns south just ahead."

Carter's hounds heard the horses on the road and raced out from the cabin, bellowing their lungs out with their deep bawl mouths. Scarred from many battles with wolves, coyotes, and bobcats, all five dogs were ugly as sin. Standing sideways, they were skinny enough to read a newspaper through. Rail thin, the dogs looked to be all teeth and head. Carter stood on his front porch cussing at the dogs to shut up and get away from the fidgeting horses.

"I'm sorry, Lige, about the commotion and racket." The skinny farmer waved at Hatcher, smiling up at him. "Those crazy pot-lickers of mine don't miss nary a thing that moves around here."

"That's alright, Jake." Hatcher recognized the farmer. "They're just doing their job, that's good."

"Why don't you folks light and have a cup of coffee and maybe a hoe cake."

"Sorry, Jake, but we're headed hunting and kinda in a hurry."

"Well, maybe next time, old hoss." Looking at the old scout, Carter nodded his head. "Looks like some varmint tried to take your scalp, Lige."

"They tried." Hatcher automatically touched the healing wound. "Pert near got her done too."

Both Ellie and Jed looked curiously at Hatcher as he spoke with Carter. "He knows Mister Carter."

"He seems to, alright."

"And how is your beautiful daughter, Ellie?" Carter spoke as Hatcher kicked his horse.

"Beautiful as ever, even dressed like a man in all them buckskins."

"I'm fine, Mister Carter." Ellie watched her father closely as he reined in his horse and turned to face her. "How is your wife, Mister Carter?"

"She's feeling a little poorly today, Ellie." The farmer nodded his head toward the cabin behind him. "She's still laid up, resting this morning."

"Anything I can do for her?" Ellie studied the cabin. "You want me to look in on her."

"No need, she's just feeling a little poorly this morning is all."

"She with child again, Mister Carter?"

"Yes, ma'am, I believe she may be."

"How many does this make, Jake?" Hatcher looked down at the scarecrow of a man.

"Seven living, Lige. We lost two on the way west." Carter looked away. "You remember?"

"I remember, Jake." Hatcher nodded. "I helped put them in the ground."

"I'll always be beholden to you, Lige. Always."

"Well, you best take her into town and let Doc Zeke check her over."

"I'll do that, Ellie, first chance I get." Carter looked at Jed. "I didn't even know you were in the area, Jed."

"Reckon I slipped by while you slept, Mister Carter."

"Speaking of slipping by, some other riders passed my place a few nights back, heading east."

"You see them, Jake?" Jed asked as Little Wound rode up and reined in his horse. "Could you recognize any of them?"

"No, I didn't. They seemed to be on the sneak in the dark. Dang scum, they shot one of my dogs with this." Carter walked back to the porch and returned with a bloody arrow. "Old Buck was my best dog."

Handing the arrow to Jed, the farmer waited as he examined the bloody shaft, then handed it to Little Wound. The warrior only glanced at the arrow before nodding.

"Cree." The warrior pointed at the dark paint on the feathers. "A warrior called Black Moose."

"Black Moose?" Jed thought it a strange name. "He must be here with Squires."

"Him as mean and crazy as Batiste." Little Wound handed Carter back the arrow. "He has many warriors that follow him."

"How many?"

"I will cut their trail and find tracks." The Gros Ventre kicked his horse forward. "Then we will know how many we will have to fight."

"Well, Jake, like I said, we've got a few miles to cover." Hatcher kicked his horse and started down the road. "Be seeing you on my next trip west."

The turn off from the main road was covered in weeds and over-grown from little to no use except for the wild animals. Jed was baffled as Hatcher turned his horse without hesitation onto the trail. Looking at Ellie he shrugged, then called for Hatcher to rein in.

"What we stopping for, Crow Killer." The old scout reined his horse around. "Figured we'd make camp at the river and that's still a far piece to cover yet."

"I know, Lige, but we need to wait until Little Wound scouts the trail ahead."

"What for, there sure ain't no buffalo down here in these parts." Hatcher shrugged. "But, if that's what you wish, so be it."

"Thank you, Lige."

Several minutes passed as they sat their horses silently before they spotted the warrior loping his horse toward them.

"Maybe this many come out on the trail ahead." The warrior held up his open fists twice.

Jed nodded slowly. "You're saying twenty or more riders?"

"Maybe, maybe a few more." The warrior replied. "I think five whites, the rest are Metis and Cree warriors."

"You sure?"

"I am sure. Men dismount and rest their horses. I see tracks very plain in soft ground." The warrior slid from his horse. "White man wear heavy hunting moccasin. Metis and Cree wear different type moccasin."

"Did he say Metis and Cree?" Hatcher had been listening.

"He did, Lige."

"What are they doing this far east and south?" Hatcher rubbed his scraggly face. "The Cree and Metis don't normally run together."

"Looking for us." Jed knew there was no sense not telling the old scout.

"Them French half-breeds must be up to some kind of deviltry."

"That's about the size of it, Lige."

"We got problems, boy?"

"Plenty, I think."

Hatcher looked over at Ellie. "They're after the girl aren't they?"

"Why do you say that?"

"Because, Crow Killer, as far as I know, there's nothing else around here this time of year to lure them this far into white man country." Hatcher checked the priming on his rifle. "And the Metis and Cree aren't ones to waste their time just riding the countryside. Sometimes, they even fight, but only for money."

"Yeah, I heard. A young fella told me back in the Gallatins that they fought each other on occasions." Jed remembered Dibbs' words. "I reckon they've made up for this hunt."

"Why my rifle ain't even loaded. I swear, this old coon is sure slipping in my old age." Hatcher had looked down at the rifle's empty priming pan. "Reckon, I best fix that here and now."

"No, you ain't losing your mind, Lige. I reckon I forgot and gave it to you unloaded."

The scout might have lost some of his memory but his natural instincts as a hunter and Indian fighter hadn't been lost. Jed watched as Hatcher quickly loaded and primed the rifle, then held it out for him to see.

"This ain't my gun, Crow Killer."

"No, Lige, it ain't. I'm sorry."

"Where's my Hawken?" The voice seemed confused. "You know the one with the brass tacks decorating the stock."

"We don't know, Lige. Maybe the ones ahead have it." Jed wasn't lying. Squires or one of his hunters, who had shot the scout probably had his prized rifle. The Hawken that Hatcher was so proud of had an extra two-inch long barrel and was trimmed out with brass tacks. For distance and accuracy, no other rifle around these parts could match it.

"Well, when we meet up with them fellers, I reckon I'll know her." Hatcher nodded. "Maybe they'll give it back."

"Maybe they will, Lige." Jed looked at Ellie. "I'll take the point, Lige. You bring Ellie along slow."

"I'll do it, boy." The old scout agreed. "I'll keep my eye on her."

Nodding at Little Wound, who had taken up a position in the rear, Jed kicked the bay horse and headed down the trail. The tracks of many horses were plain to see in the soft sand. Jed's dark eyes were as sharp as a hawk. It would be hard for any of the riders to drop off to the side of the trail without spotting their tracks. Still, he was riding slow and cautious, taking no chances of riding unaware into an ambush.

He knew Squires had to be loco, crazed with the thought of the girl to bring his cutthroat Metis and Cree this far east to steal her. It was a natural way of life for hunting and raiding parties to bring back captive women and children to their villages from far-off tribes. However, he had never known of a white man trying to steal a white woman. Every man's hand would be turned against anyone trying to take a white woman captive against her will. It would be a death warrant for Squires and his men if they were found out. Ellie was the only reason the hunter would be in these lands with so many Cree and Metis fighters. Squires must have offered the Metis and Cree warriors riding with him many horses and furs to lure them this far from the safety of their lands. Jed just didn't know where the hunter expected to get the plunder he had promised. But, he knew the Metis would be expecting many horses if they're able to take Ellie. They hadn't come this far from their hunting grounds just to steal a woman for a white man.

The dampness of the river came up to Jed as he reined in and looked down at the slow-moving river that was bordered by huge sycamore, oak, and elm trees. Light shimmered off the calm river as it quietly rolled downstream. It was this crossing that he remembered the fight with the trappers Abe and Vern years before. He never camped at their old campsite. Still, the darkened stones of their fire remained a reminder of the fight as he passed by.

Riding slowly and cautiously down to the river, Jed studied where the tracks of the riders he followed had entered the water. Waving Little Wound forward, Jed slid from the bay and waited as the warrior dismounted.

"We will camp here tonight." Jed looked to where Ellie and Hatcher sat their horses. "I will cross the river and follow their tracks."

"Be careful, my brother." Little Wound studied the moving water. "These are dangerous men we follow, and they are great warriors."

"I know they are, Little Wound."

"Black Moose is out there somewhere." The dark eyes of the young Gros Ventre looked across the broad river. "He is a mighty warrior."

"This would be a perfect place for an ambush." Jed studied the far bank curiously. "You're right, they could be across the river, waiting for us to cross."

The young one shook his head. "What could the white man have offered the Metis and Cree to ride with him this far?"

"I don't know." Jed looked back at Ellie. "It is a curiosity. One day, maybe we'll find out."

"The Cree and Metis are raiders, but to come this far for just a few horses." Little Wound shook his head. "There must be more offered."

"I'm going across. If things go bad get her and your pa back to the safety of Baxter Springs fast."

"Keep your eyes open and your nose to the wind, my brother." Little Wound studied the wide river. "Watch out for Black Moose."

"You do the same, Little Wound." Jed waved to Ellie and Hatcher, then kicked the bay horse into the peaceful slow-flowing river.

Dripping water as he swung back onto the wet animal, Jed studied the tracks, then followed the trail to the east. Nothing appeared out of place as he rode. The animals, birds and squirrels, were quiet, but that was expected when humans were near. For two hours, he pushed the bay in an easy trot as he followed the tracks of at least twenty or more horses. In the deep sand, it was difficult to count just how many horses rode ahead of him. None moved away from the trail as they all followed the path to the east. Reining in, Jed slid from the bay and looked down at the tracks while he studied on his problem. It was almost dark and he needed to return to the river to cross with Ellie and Hatcher before the moon rose over the river. If he decided to ride on south, following Squires and his raiders, he must go quickly. Maybe, with so many of the enemy in front of him, he needed to return with Ellie to Baxter Springs. Jed knew without a doubt for him to turn back to the settlements would leave his stepfather undefended and likely to be killed. Squires was a killer and he knew to get Ellie, he had to lure Crow Killer back into the mountains away from Baxter Springs. Finally deciding, Jed turned the bay back toward the river.

Little Wound stood waiting as Jed led the horse from the river. "Have you found them, my brother?"

"No, they continue further south."

"What will we do?" The young warrior could see the worry in Jed's face. "To follow them farther will be very dangerous for my sister and father."

"I have no choice, we must ride on to my valley if we are to save my father."

"The moon will be full tonight, it will be a good night to ride."

"I will let the horse rest a couple hours, then we'll follow Mister Squires." Jed led the tired bay horse and hobbled him on the deep grass alongside the river. "I figure they're camped a few miles ahead."

"This is a dangerous trail we follow, my brother."

"It is, Little Wound." Jed agreed. "Either Squires or me will die before this trail is finished. This I promise you, my brother."

Little Wound had looked into the worried eyes of Crow Killer as he came out of the river. He knew the warrior spoke the truth. Hatred for Squires seemed to leap out of the man's face and words.

Daylight found them safely across the river and many miles from the crossing. Jed scouted out the trail and the plain tracks in the soft sandy trail while Little Wound stayed to the rear, guarding Ellie and Hatcher. Two rifles hung from Ellie's saddle and two more were tied to the packsaddle of the led horse. Jed had taken all the precautions he could, but he knew they were still outnumbered at least twenty or more to four.

Long odds, but he had to ride on and try to reach his valley. Hopefully, Squires would get lazy and let them get ahead of him and his men somewhere before they reached the crossing of the Snake. He thought of sending Ellie and Hatcher back to Baxter Springs with Little Wound while he continued to the valley, but it would be safer for her with him where he could see after her.

Jed thought out the trail ahead in his mind. If they were lucky and if Squires did slow down there were several places ahead where they could pass the larger party without being seen. The only problem was, once they passed Squires and his killers, their tracks on the soft trail would give away their presence. The raiders would know they were ahead and charge after them, and then it would be a horse race to his valley and the protection of the cabin. They were outnumbered badly. However, if they could reach the cabin first, Ed Wilson and the solid log walls of the cabin could possibly make the difference. Jed didn't know how much further the Metis and Cree would be willing to ride into these unknown lands to catch up with the girl. There was another possibility... if he could reach the cabin, they would catch fresh horses and be able to outdistance Squires riding south to Crow lands. Jed hated the thought of running, but he had Ellie and Hatcher to think of.

Jed studied the fresh tracks on the trail. He had closed the distance between the two parties, but Squires hadn't given him any chance to flank them along the narrow pathway. The man might be crazed, but he was a mountain man alert for any danger. He had kept the Metis and Cree on alert, watching for any enemy. Finally, after pushing the horses hard for a whole day and night, he knew he had closed in on his quarry. The Snake was only a few miles ahead from where Jed lay bellied down on the trail, looking down at the camp Squires and his men had set up. Jed couldn't believe his good luck. The ones below were actually making camp for the night. He couldn't understand why they had stopped short of the river to make camp other than they didn't know these mountains.

The Hawken tickled his finger as he looked down to where the big white trapper lay sprawled across his saddle. He could feel the heavy grained stock, and his finger itched to kill the big hunter. It was indeed a tempting shot, but for now, Jed couldn't chance it. Even if he got lucky and killed Squires, the others would be riled up like a hornet's nest and there was no natural protection back along the small trail. Slipping back to the bay, Jed quickly returned to where Little Wound was making his way slowly along the trail.

"We're in luck." Jed looked to where Ellie and Hatcher had stopped their horses. "They're going into camp less than three miles ahead. When they sleep, we will try to pass them in the darkness."

"Is the trail wide enough to pass unseen?" Little Wound questioned Jed. "And after we pass, you know with the coming of daylight, they will see our tracks on the trail."

"Only when the new sun comes. Hopefully, by then, we'll be across the Snake River and many miles ahead of them."

The warrior shook his head. "Our horses have been ridden hard, they are tired."

"We have no choice, this is our one chance." Jed realized what the Gros Ventre spoke was true.

"How far is the cabin, Jed?" Ellie tiredly asked.

"One day's hard ride from the river ahead." Jed smiled. "Can you two make it a few more miles?"

"We'll make it, Crow Killer." Hatcher grinned. "Don't you worry yourself none about me and Medicine Thunder."

Jed was shocked, Hatcher was almost back to his old self. He had called Ellie by her Indian name. "I know you will, Lige."

Little Wound listened to the soft words as Jed looked at Ellie. He knew there were great feelings between them. He was curious why Crow Killer hadn't taken her for his woman. In his village, a warrior could have all the squaws he could afford.

"I could have killed Squires." Jed looked at the thoughtful warrior. "Maybe, I should have and this would be over."

"You are wrong, Crow Killer." The warrior shrugged. "If you had, one of the others would have taken his place."

"I know, it would have been too chancy."

"I think soon you will have another chance."

Squires and his men had settled in around two fires. Most sat smoking pipes and talking quietly while others patrolled the camp and grazing horses. Lying on his back with his hat covering his face, Squires seemed to be already asleep. Jed and Little Wound studied the camp from their higher vantage point.

"We will wrap the horse's feet in cut-up blankets, then we will move down the trail and pass them." Jed spoke softly to the warrior. "We must keep the horses quiet as we pass. Don't let them snort or nicker."

"I think soon they will all be asleep." The warrior showed his white teeth in the dimming darkness. "He is foolish. The big hunter has given them some white man's whiskey."

"I reckon that's one way of holding them. Maybe that's why they follow him." Jed could see the whiskey bottles being handed around. "I reckon that's what the pack animals of his are toting."

"Like most Indians, the Metis and Cree have a great weakness for the white man's firewater." Little Wound grinned. "It gives us the advantage."

"They don't even know we follow." Jed shook his head. "They haven't put out any scouts."

"Even in our country these whites and Cree were very foolish." Little Wound shrugged. "If my uncle War Bonnet had permitted, we would have rid our hunting grounds of these dogs."

"Let's get the blankets cut up."

"What about the two Cree who watch the horses near the trail?"

"I will take care of them when we get close."

Little Wound raised his hand. "It is my turn, Brother. You stay with my sister."

"You just be careful." Jed warned.

"I am always careful."

As Little Wound had predicted, the whiskey bottles lay empty and most of the drunken but contented warriors were already fast asleep from the effects of the liquor. Jed smiled, knowing Squires had made his first mistake. Leading the horses, Jed moved quietly down the trail toward the sleeping camp. The sound of the muffled feet of the horses barely broke the quiet of the night. Little Wound had disappeared into the night as Jed, Hatcher, and Ellie led the horses past the camp. He could hear the men's loud snoring and was amazed at their carelessness. In their drunken condition, Squires would have trouble getting them back on their horses even after the coming of the new sun.

Almost an hour passed before Little Wound appeared from behind them afoot and stopped beside Jed. "Four of our enemies went to meet their ancestors in the dark of the moon."

"Four?"

The dark head nodded. "My knife found two of our enemies and my arrows found the bodies of two more as they slept. Black Moose will bother us no more."

"The odds are getting better." Jed realized the Gros Ventre was indeed a dangerous one. "Maybe we should go back and finish them while they are drunk."

"The odds are not good enough yet, my friend." Little Wound shrugged. "Hopefully, maybe one of my arrows found one of the whites."

Ellie had heard the words between the two warriors. "No, Jed, that would be murder to kill them in their sleep.

"Do you realize what they intend for you, Ellie?"

"My life is not worth twenty men's lives." Ellie replied. "If we ride hard, we'll be safe at the cabin in a day."

"Alright, Ellie, let's ride."

Little Wound helped Ellie into the saddle. "It was a good idea, Sister."

The Snake appeared before them in the gloom of the night as Jed led them down to the crossing. This river wasn't as wide as the big river, but its current was faster and the water was deep enough for several yards to swim a horse.

Smiling at Ellie in the dark, Jed asked. "You ready for another wetting, Ellie?"

"I'm ready."

"You can remove your buckskins and keep them dry if you like."

"Jed Bracket, I swear!"

Jed laughed lightly. "Ellie, it's dark and we promise not to look. It sure beats riding all night with wet leather on."

Shaking her head, she turned beet red. "Is it Jed Bracket, the civilized white man talking or Crow Killer the heathen?"

"Suit yourself, ma'am. I'm just trying to be of help is all." Jed smiled.

"Do both of you promise to keep your eyes straight ahead."

"Yes, ma'am, you have our word on it."

Quickly replacing her clothes as she waded from the river, Ellie looked worriedly to where Jed, Hatcher, and Little Wound waited ahead. She knew even if they had looked, they couldn't see her clearly with the darkness of the night. Still, the thought of being seen standing stark naked even in the gloom of the night was embarrassing.

"Pretty good view wasn't it, Little Wound?"

"Pretty good."

"Did you two look?" Ellie's face was turning redder.

"We had to look down the river to see what was coming." Even with the danger they were in, Jed couldn't resist the chance to tease her.

"Oh!"

"You need help on your horse, Miss Ellie?"

"You keep your distance, Mister Bracket."

Laughing, Jed swung up on the bay, then turned serious. "These horses are tired, and it's still a long pull, over the mountains to the cabin."

"Will they make it, Jed?"

"They'll have to." Jed replied. "When Squires finds our fresh horse sign, come daylight, he'll know we're ahead of him and he'll be after us. And that's not counting the dead bodies of his fighters."

"What dead bodies?" Hatcher asked.

"Your son had to kill a couple of Squires' sentries so we could get past their camp in the dark."

Jed could feel the horse under him stumble and knew the animals were almost finished. They had been ridden a long way from the Gallatins. Now, being pushed over the mountains and across the rivers to his valley without rest had finally taken its toll. Rested, they were all strong animals, the best, but even the strongest of horses could travel only so many miles without rest and feed. Reining in, he slid from the bay and motioned for the others to dismount.

"We'll walk awhile." Jed looked over the tired horses. All of them stood with their heads down and slightly spraddle legged. They were exhausted and without a little rest, they weren't going much further. He needed the horses. There was no way Ellie could cross the last few miles of mountains that still lay ahead on foot.

"I will wait up there to see if I can catch sight of the enemy coming behind us." Little Wound pointed at the highest part of the trail where it leveled off again. "Take my horse and go."

"Don't wait too long."

"I will catch up." The warrior nodded. "Take her and my father and hurry from this place."

All morning, Jed led the horses along the mountain trail, occasionally letting the fatigued horses rest and nibble at the lush grass along the rocky trail. A couple of the horses were so exhausted; they wouldn't even sniff the grass.

"I hope he will be coming soon." Ellie kept looking behind her, trying to spot her brother.

"He'll be along, Ellie. Don't worry." Jed tried to assure her.

Wearily she shook her head. "Soon, I hope."

Lifting her bodily onto the bay packhorse, Jed pointed his finger and smiled as she started to protest. "The pack animal hasn't carried much of a load. You ride a while and rest."

"How are you, Pa?"

Hatcher waved his hand. "I'm fine, lass, just fine."

"How far is it to your cabin now, Jed?"

"Only a few miles now, girl." Hatcher spoke up as he started afoot up the trail.

"We'll make it then?"

"Sure we will." Jed started the horse forward. "Tonight, you'll sleep in a bed and have a hot supper."

"That sounds wonderful."

The sun started to set when Ellie let out a sigh of relief as Little Wound came trotting into view as he turned a bend in the trail. Pulling Ellie from the bay, Jed set her on a rock and waited for the warrior to catch up.

Huffing, his chest blowing like a bellows, Little Wound trotted up and knelt beside Ellie. Several seconds passed as he caught his breath. Standing slowly, he looked back down the long trail.

"They come." The brown finger pointed. "They are very close. We must hurry."

Jed looked at the tired horses. "Ain't much hurry left in these animals."

"They will be here soon." The warrior motioned with his hand. "Their horses are much stronger than ours."

"What will we do, Jed?" Ellie looked at her father and she could see he gave out. "Pa can't go much further."

"We'll make this last climb to that hogback, Ellie, then you'll be able to see the cabin."

"Then let's go. I do remember it's all downhill to the cabin from there."

Ellie was right, it was all downhill from where they stood at the flat hogback that overlooked the broad valley, but they would have to be afoot. The horses were finished after the last climb and they refused to go further. Even if they were forced forward, they would just slow the party down.

"We'll have to walk from here." Jed turned to Ellie and Hatcher. "Can you two make it?"

"We'll have to."

"We'll leave the horses here. They'll find their way down to the valley if Squires and his men don't steal them."

"They cannot steal, horses too tired to go further." Little Wound shook his head. "Cree and Metis cannot take horses from here until they rest."

"This time, I will wait on the summit for them to show themselves." Jed patted the rifle. "The Hawken will slow them up a little on the narrow pass below, or it will kill them."

"Be careful, Jed, please." Ellie touched his sleeve. "And don't you dare stay here too long."

"I'll be along. Now, hurry as fast as you can." Jed tried to run the tired horses down the trail to no avail. Following the three down the rough path a few yards, Jed glanced across the deep canyon for his inspiring light that always glimmered in the sunlight. Today, there was no sign of the shimmering light. He wondered if this was a good sign or a bad sign. Little Wound stood waiting on the trail for Hatcher to follow.

"I'll wait here with you, lad." Hatcher looked at Jed. "It'll give Little Wound time to get her to the cabin safely."

"No, Lige, but thanks anyway. If you can get Ellie to the cabin, you and your son will have your hands full holding off Squires and his men." Jed was surprised to see Hatcher was almost back to his normal thinking.

"You will be along soon?" Ellie looked hard at Jed. She didn't like the sound of his words. "Promise me, Jed."

"I'll stay ahead of them." Jed smiled calmly and nodded at Little Wound. "Now, go quickly."

CHAPTER 8

Walking Horse grasped He Dog's extended arm, then swung up on his sorrel horse. Behind him, on their fleet buffalo runners, sat Crazy Cat and four Cheyenne plus the Arapaho warriors that had ridden with him to the Cheyenne village. With Bright Moon's urgings, He Dog and Walking Horse had agreed to send Cheyenne warriors to Crow Killer's valley to check on the white father of her husband. Bright Moon and Little Antelope each carried one of the babies in their grass and leather papoose cradleboards secured to the squaw saddles on their horses. After much arguing from Bright Moon, they decided that she and the children would return as far as the Arapaho village with the warriors. From the village, Crazy Cat and Big Owl with their mixture of Cheyenne and Arapaho warriors would continue to Crow Killer's valley.

The morning was peaceful and serene. The sun had appeared on the trail making it a warm, enjoyable day as they rode leisurely southwest to the Arapaho village. Fresh budded flowers graced the trail, enlightening the path with their beautiful colors. Birds sang from the high limbs and squirrels barked furiously, scolding the passing column from their lofty perches in the tall trees.

As Bright Moon rode closer to her sister's village, she looked down into the dark face of Eagle's Wing and smiled happily. The babies dangled from their papoose boards content and happy, neither uttering a sound. The thick unkempt black hair stood straight out from their little heads. Several times, different warriors would pass by smiling as they studied the small bundles. They were beautiful babies, as beautiful as the morning itself. Most of the warriors were young unmarried men, and each looked upon the children, hoping someday, they would be blessed with such a family.

Three days of pleasant riding found the small caravan nearing the Arapaho village. The village scouts spotted the coming warriors and rode into the camp proclaiming their chief was approaching. The entire village eagerly awaited the arrival of their beloved warriors. Walking Horse with his straight back and carriage like a returning king, proudly led the warriors into the throng of cheering villagers. They were home once again. Squaws and children gathered around Little Antelope and Bright Moon, pushing close for a look at the babies. Finally, after greeting their chief and satisfying their curiosity about the children of the great Crow Killer, most of the people dispersed to their lodges.

Holding Ellie in her arms, Little Antelope looked at Walking Horse's broad back and wondered if she would ever hold a child of her own. Smiling, she looked down at the dark, bright eyes of the baby and kissed her softly. The little face with her pretty smile and her baby smell made Little Antelope happy. For now, she would have to be content holding the babies of her sister and her warrior.

Kneeling beside the cooking fire, Bright Moon glanced over to where Walking Horse, Crazy Cat, and Big Owl sat smoking their pipes and talking. She knew the warriors would be riding out with the new sun, headed for the far-off valley of Crow Killer. Bright Moon knew she and the children would be safer if she stayed behind in the Arapaho village as she had promised Walking Horse and He Dog. Still, something urged her to go home to her valley and she couldn't shake the feeling. Looking to where the babies lay on a buffalo robe before the lodge she smiled. She would speak with Walking Horse after they ate. He could deny her wishes to return to the valley, but she knew in her heart she had to go. The Arapaho and Cheyenne lodges no longer satisfied her as they once did. Bright Moon wanted to be in her own lodge, surrounded by her own things. She made up her mind, she and the children would return home to the lodge of Crow Killer.

Little Antelope knelt beside Bright Moon as she ladled spoonfuls of thick deer meat, wild onions, and greens into bowls for the men.

Studying her sister's face, Little Antelope looked over at the children, then back at Bright Moon.

"Something troubles, my sister. You have something on your mind?"

Smiling, Bright Moon nodded. "Little Antelope, you know me well."

"We are sisters. We both carry the same blood and same feelings." Little Antelope looked at Bright Moon. "Tell me, what do you think of?"

"I must return to my lodge with the warriors when they ride with the new sun." The younger woman shared her thoughts. "I know it is foolish and dangerous for the children, but my heart says I must go to my own lodge."

"Walking Horse will not permit this." Little Antelope picked up the food. "And you are right, Sister, it is a foolish thing to do."

"I will ride with Crazy Cat and Big Owl, or I will ride alone." Bring Moon declared. "I must return to my husband."

"And the babies?"

"They will return with me to their father."

"Bright Moon, you know there is much danger beyond the village."

Looking at the babies, Bright Moon continued. "They are my babies, Sister, and Crow Killer is my husband. Something speaks to me, and I must go to him."

"His wishes were for you and the babies to stay here where it is safe." Little Antelope argued. "He will look for you here or with our brother He Dog."

"I am going, Little Antelope. No words will stop me." Bright Moon shook her head.

Nodding sadly, Little Antelope stood up with the filled bowls. "We will speak with Walking Horse after he eats."

"Thank you, my sister."

"I think you are being foolish." The beautiful woman smiled down at Bright Moon and thought of Jed. "But, I understand your thoughts."

Looking up at her sister, Bright Moon nodded. "I know you do, Sister."

"No!" The word was harsh and final as Little Antelope finished telling Walking Horse of her sister's wishes. "That is impossible. She will stay here in the village where she and the children will be safe."

"I will not do this, Brother." Bright Moon looked up at the chief's dark face.

"You, woman, will do as I say." Walking Horse towered over the tall woman. "It is my brother Crow Killer's wish for you to remain here with the children."

"I am going." Bright Moon held her ground. "I will ride with the warriors or alone."

"You lied to us back at He Dog's village. You said you only wanted to ride as far as the Arapaho village. I could have you guarded and prevent you from leaving." Walking Horse threatened.

"Walking Horse cannot keep watch over me constantly." Bright Moon argued. "And I am not a prisoner."

"You would endanger Crow Killer's children?"

"With Crazy Cat and Big Owl, there is little danger."

"Of course not, Bright Moon, only deep rivers, wild animals, and hostile tribes that you must pass through all the way to Crow Killer's valley." Walking Horse looked around at Little Antelope for help. "Speak with your sister, wife. Tell her how foolish this idea is."

"I have spoken with her, my husband." Little Antelope shook her head. "She will not listen to my words."

"I'm going." Bright Moon smiled up at him. "And you can't stop me, my brother."

"We could ride with her and the warriors as far as the big river." Little Antelope suggested. "From there they could ride safely on to the valley of Crow Killer."

"I cannot be sure." Walking Horse waved his hand. "I say no. I am chief, Bright Moon. You will not go on this foolish and dangerous trail."

"You are my sister's husband, and I respect you, my brother." The woman smiled. "But Crow Killer is my chief, Walking Horse, not you, and I am going."

Shrugging as he looked at the set face of the woman, Walking Horse finally nodded. "Crow Killer will be angry with me for being soft."

"No, he will thank you as I do, Brother." Bright Moon smiled.

"We will ride with you to the big river, but I cannot go further." Walking Horse gave in. "With Big Owl away, someone must be here to lead the village in case of danger."

"We will be safe." Bright Moon smiled. "There has been no trouble has there?"

"Yes, there has been some trouble." Walking Horse frowned. "The Rics ride our hunting grounds as do the Pawnee and Comanche."

"Comanche this far north?" Little Antelope looked up at Walking Horse. "Why would they be here in our lands?"

"They raid to the north because of Red Hawk the Crow." Walking Horse shook his head. "He has them stirred up like a hornet's nest."

"What has the braggart done now?" Little Antelope thought of the handsome warrior. The Crow was an enemy warrior to the Arapaho, but he had saved her life twice and she finally warmed to him. If he was Arapaho, she would have welcomed him as her brother.

"Not much… just stole some prize buffalo runners and women from the Comanche people this past winter."

"Winter?" Little Antelope was curious. "But, it's late spring now."

"It was last winter." Walking Horse explained. "The Comanche didn't think there would be any horse raiding with the severe cold winter, so they didn't place guards on their herds. Red Hawk slipped in and stole over a hundred of their prized buffalo runners while they huddled under buffalo robes in their lodges like women. He also stole some young squaws who were out gathering wood for their fires. He was almost back to his lands when the Comanche finally caught up with him."

"What happened?" Bright Moon looked at the warrior. She too had come to like Red Hawk. Next to Walking Horse, he was the best friend and brother of Crow Killer, and he had a charming personality that couldn't be denied. The Crow warrior was headstrong, wild as a deer, strong as a buffalo, but none could deny his rugged appeal to the opposite sex.

"Luckily for Red Hawk… Big Owl, me, and some of our warriors were across the river hunting the flatlands when the Crow and his men came racing across the meadows with the Comanche in pursuit. You should have seen it, horses strung out, running with their manes and tails flying in the wind. Several Crow warriors rode with Comanche squaws held in front of them, screaming for their warriors to free them. War cries and enraged howls from the oncoming Comanche ripped the air. And there was Red Hawk, brandishing his bow and turning flips on the back of his great spotted stallion, taunting the maddened Comanche." Walking Horse laughed. "What a show he put on, even for a Crow. From where we sat watching, the earth shook with the pounding of so many hooves running hard, like the wind blowing across the flatlands. Yes, it was something to behold."

"And, I guess you helped the Crow, my husband?"

"Yes, we did. The chase made our blood boil for battle so we had to." Walking Horse thought back on the short battle. "It was great sport even if they were only lowly Comanche. But now, we must be on watch for more of their raiding parties as well."

"Did Red Hawk even thank you?" Little Antelope frowned.

"That one owes me no thanks, woman. Red Hawk saved my life and yours many times." Walking Horse nodded. "But, yes, he did give us several good buffalo runners."

"He almost killed you once many suns ago."

"Yes, he did, but now he is our friend, and you know that better than any of us." Walking Horse added.

"So that's why the Comanche come into our lands now, because of Red Hawk and his wild ways?" Little Antelope frowned.

"Yes, they come looking for their women and horses." Walking Horse looked at Bright Moon. "Or some of ours."

Little Antelope now knew why Walking Horse did not want Bright Moon and the children to leave the safety of the village. The Comanche and Pawnee were warlike people, not as strong as the Arapaho or Cheyenne, but still, they were a dangerous enemy. She studied the far western horizon, if only Jed was here to see to the safety of his family. Looking over to where Bright Moon stood, she wanted to say something to stop her from leaving the village. This trail would be dangerous, but she knew it would be futile to speak more of it. Bright Moon was young and headstrong. She was going to her husband, and no words could stop her.

"I will prepare our packs for the journey to the big river." Little Antelope turned to her lodge.

"Is your decision final?" Walking Horse looked down at the wiggling babies. "This could be a dangerous trail, my sister."

"Perhaps, but I will be closer to my husband." The woman nodded solemnly. "Something tells me I must return to my lodge."

"Crazy Cat and Big Owl have planned to leave with the new sun."

"We will be ready." Bright Moon nodded. "Thank you, Walking Horse."

The tall chief looked down again at the little ones and smiled. "They do look like my brother Crow Killer."

Bright Moon smiled. "Yes, they do. I will pack our supplies on my husband's paint horse."

Looking to where Little Antelope waited, he smiled. Someday, he hoped for children of their own that he could hold and teach the traditional ways of the Arapaho. Until that day, he would have to be content with taking care of his people.

Several Crow warriors watched from the heights as Walking Horse swam the small group of warriors and squaws across the broad Yellowstone River. Riding down the steep riverbank, they waited as the Arapaho rode dripping wet from the river. Most were young warriors, just coming-of-age, riding the hunting grounds of the great Crow Nation. Long Leaper sat proudly, several feet in front of the Crow, and waited as Walking Horse led his people to where they waited.

"Is Walking Horse headed to the big river?"

"It is good to see, Long Leaper." Walking Horse nodded as he studied the cold face of the young warrior. "Yes, my warriors ride to the valley of my friend Crow Killer."

"Crow Killer bah, this is one Crow he has not killed yet, Arapaho." Long Leaper spat. "And neither have you."

Walking Horse smiled easily. "Do you not remember our last meeting, Crow?"

"I remember." Long Leaper knew the warrior spoke of the time the Arapaho Chief had almost strangled him for looking so long at Little Antelope. It had taken him almost a month to regain his speech after Walking Horse's strong grip had lifted him bodily from the ground, nearly squeezing the life from him, bruising his windpipe.

"Let us pass in peace then." Walking Horse nodded to the northwest. "Today is no time for arguing foolishly."

"We let you pass, Arapaho, only because my chief says it is to be so." Long Leaper moved his horse aside. "Perhaps, Walking Horse, one day soon it will be different."

"Tell Red Hawk we ride to the north." The Arapaho Chief nodded. "We ride to the lodge of Crow Killer."

The Crow didn't answer as he followed the party of Arapaho and Cheyenne up the steep bank to the plateau overlooking the river. Only a scowl crossed his face as Walking Horse led his people across a flat meadow and disappeared from his view.

"Crow Killer, bah!" Long Leaper spat again. "One day…"

"One day, what Long Leaper?" The warrior, Hide's His Face, had been listening to the conversation. He knew Long Leaper hated Crow Killer because the Arapaho had killed his father, Wild Wind, years before. He also hated Walking Horse for embarrassing him in this same place two years prior in front of the warriors and the Arapaho woman.

"Why did you not tell the Arapaho of the Comanche raiders that we watched pass to the north two sleeps ago?" A young warrior questioned Long Leaper. "Now, Walking Horse leads his people in that direction."

A sour grin came across the dark face. "No, I said nothing. Perhaps with luck, Walking Horse and the Comanche will find each other somewhere ahead on the trail."

"Red Hawk would not like that, Long Leaper." Iron Oak shook his head. "It would be a bad thing if anything should happen to the women and babies of Crow Killer."

"Who will tell him?"

"I say this, my friend, if any harm comes to Crow Killer's woman because of this, Red Hawk will cut your heart out and feed it to the buzzards."

"I did not see her." Long Leaper stared at the warrior. "Who is to say different?"

"I will, Long Leaper. Yes, you saw her." The younger warrior frowned. "One does not miss such a woman with her beauty."

"Perhaps, if you are so worried about the woman, Iron Oak, you should go to the village and tell Red Hawk." Long Leaper pointed to the south. "Go!"

"You do not scare me, and maybe I will go." The warrior scowled. "My friend, your hatred for Crow Killer and the Arapaho will one day get you killed."

It was a two-day ride to the big river and another day's hard ride to Crow Killer's valley. Walking Horse kept the horses in an easy walk so the children wouldn't be bounced around in their cradleboards. The days were warm and peaceful as they passed to the north and west. Crazy Cat and Big Owl kept riders out in front and on their flanks to sound the warning if danger approached. Several herds of elk and deer sprang to their feet in the tall waving grass as they slowly passed by. A huge grizzly with her two cubs stood on her hind legs and sniffed the air. Bad eyesight prevented her from seeing the riders clearly, but she knew they were there. Moving back, away from the danger, she whirled and led her babies into the near thickets.

"Look, Bright Moon." Little Antelope pointed and laughed. "She has two babies just like you."

"Perhaps one day, Eagle's Wing will do battle with them as his father did."

Little Antelope smiled, flashing her snow-white teeth in the sunlight. "I fear they will have to wait a few years yet."

Later in the day, one of the younger Cheyenne, riding far out on the flanks of the moving riders, got lucky with a long shot from his bow. He brought down a small doe that now lay draped across his horse's back. They were all in good spirits. Tonight, they would camp beside the big river, where they would feast before Walking Horse and Little Antelope returned to the Arapaho village.

Moving along the trail, they waded through the new spring grass that was almost knee-high on a horse. Wild flowers showed their pretty colors as their horses pushed them aside, stomping them down as they passed. The wonderful aroma from the smashed flowers filled the riders' noses with sweet lilacs and sunflowers. Everyone was in a festive mood, enjoying the late afternoon's warmth and beauty of the valley. Lulled into a false feeling of peace, no one had any idea they were being watched by several pairs of dark eyes, hidden behind the far scrub oak and blackjack trees.

The Comanche raiding party had accidentally came upon the small caravan of warriors and two squaws as they were heading back south to their hunting grounds. Several fresh scalps and ten horses had been their bounty so far on this war trail. A squat warrior, his face painted completely in black, stared with cruel eyes as Walking Horse led the riders past where they sat concealed.

"They are Arapaho and Cheyenne, my chief." An older warrior covered with blue colors spoke to the squat one. "These are not the ones who attacked our village and took your woman."

"Did you not see the two squaws who ride with them?" The black face grinned hideously. "They were very comely women."

"I am not blind. Both are Arapaho women, very beautiful."

"They will replace my woman who was taken from me." The warrior nodded. "And the children will be raised as Comanche."

"Look, Spotted Bull, look at the ones riding with the women, my chief." The older warrior pointed out. "These warriors with them are the dreaded Lance Bearers and Dog Soldiers. They will not give up their women without a fight."

"Then we will fight."

"Many of our warriors could die this day." Ten Bears argued as he knew the warrior was speaking foolishly. "Let them pass without a fight."

The cruel dark eyes turned on the older warrior. "Does Ten Bears fear death?"

"No, not when there is a reason to die." Ten Bears declared. "There are nine fighters with the women. All have the long shooting rifles. My chief, are two squaws worth one Comanche's life?"

"We have twenty warriors." Spotted Bull studied the riders as they passed. They were the dreaded Lance Bearers of the Arapaho and the Dog Soldiers of the Cheyenne, but most were young, no match for his experienced warriors. "We will follow them to the river. Yes, these women are worth a fight and their horses are prime animals. Look, Ten Bears, look at the spotted horse the squaw rides and the magnificent paint horse she leads."

"Their scouts watch closely." Ten Bears watched as the flank riders passed. "They will see us when we leave the trees."

"I wish to fight with these dogs." Spotted Bull argued. "My blood calls out for their death. My stolen woman and horses call for their blood."

"Your woman and horses were not taken by these warriors."

"I need more to show for this trail than a handful of scalps." The Comanche Chief shook his head. "The woman, the Appaloosa horse she rides, the children will be payment for my losses."

"It will be suicide for many of us, my chief." Ten Bears argued. "Maybe we will win, but at what cost?"

"Let them pass, then we will follow." Spotted Bull scowled at the older warrior. "Be careful, old one, your fighting blood cools as it ages."

"No, my chief, it becomes smarter as it ages." Ten Bears replied.

Noticing several bunches of wild onions, one of the outriders for the Cheyenne, Ice Walker, reined in and slid from his horse. The onions would be a tasty welcome to add to the flavor of the deer he had laying across his horse's withers. Busy picking the onions, Ice Walker looked up as his horse alerted and turned sideways. The young warrior's sharp eyes quickly picked up the body of riders coming out from the cover of the trees and were now following far behind the warriors of Walking Horse. Ice Walker knew the caravan had not yet discovered the oncoming riders, as they were keeping far back out of sight. Forgetting the onions, the young warrior flung himself on his fleet horse. Bending low over the flying mane, he hurried after the riders ahead. The warriors behind him might see him, but Walking Horse had to be warned in time to get ready to defend the women and babies.

Reining to a sliding stop beside the startled riders, Ice Walker pointed to their rear. "Riders are following us."

"How many?"

"Maybe twenty and they are painted for war. We must find shelter." Ice Walker warned.

"What tribe follows us?" Walking Horse followed the warrior's gaze. "Did they see you?"

"This I do not know, my chief. They were too far away to tell." Ice Walker replied.

"We will take shelter at the river." Walking Horse looked over the flatlands. "Grey Fox, ride out and bring in the other scouts."

"I go."

"Tell me, Ice Walker." Walking Horse stopped the young warrior. "Do they have the white man's rifles?"

"I had no time to see if they carried rifles. I am sorry, my chief." The young warrior apologized.

Kicking his horse into a hard trot, Walking Horse led his small band to the big river. Visiting Crow Killer in the past, he remembered at the great river crossing there was a large pile of fallen logs, thrown together by the raging currents. The logs would make the perfect shelter to fight the oncoming warriors, but the barricade was on the north side of the river.

As they reached the river, Crazy Cat quickly organized four warriors for a rear guard. Big Owl and two others swam their horses across the wide river to check for any enemies on the other side. Seeing nothing wrong, he motioned for Walking Horse to start the women and children across. A single warrior swam beside the horses, carrying the backboards that held the children. No matter what happened, Crow Killer's children would be protected. The warriors would forfeit their own lives to save the children. Walking Horse was already cursing himself for letting Bright Moon talk him into foolishly letting her return to Crow Killer's valley. If anything was to happen to the children or Bright Moon, he would never be able to face his friend again.

Splashing from the river, Walking Horse quickly herded everyone inside the small natural barricade the floodwaters had formed of the downed logs. Big Owl and his warriors were already busy stacking more dead drift logs in place to repel the enemy.

Riding into the enclosure, Crazy Cat slid from his horse and moved beside Walking Horse. "Would it not be wiser to ride on to Crow Killer's valley?"

"If it were just us and the women, I would say yes." Walking Horse looked to where Bright Moon was wrapping the children in dry blankets. "But a long, hard-running fight would be too dangerous for the little ones. It could do them harm."

"Walking Horse is right." Crazy Cat acknowledged. "But we will be trapped in this place."

"You could be right, my friend. There will be no help coming from Crow Killer that we know of." Walking Horse looked out across the river. "Maybe we should send a warrior back to Red Hawk for help."

"It would take two sleeps of hard riding for a rider to reach the Crow lands and return." Crazy Cat speculated. "Providing they could get past these oncoming enemies."

"And it would leave us with one less warrior." Big Owl spoke up.

"You must decide quickly, Walking Horse, before the ones that follow reach the river." Crazy Cat looked anxiously toward the river. "We must send for help or leave this place now."

"The young one who warned us, Ice Walker, perhaps we will send him." Walking Horse watched as the young warrior, Grey Fox, crossed the river with the outriders. "First, let us see if these warriors will cross the river in pursuit of us."

"They will cross. They do not follow us to share our deer." Big Owl laughed.

"Ice Walker needs to ride for Red Hawk now before he is spotted." Crazy Cat insisted. "Now!"

"We will wait."

Spotted Bull, Ten Bears, and twenty Comanche raiders sat their horses, strung out along the riverbank, staring at the pile of logs where they could see the heads of many horses above the log wall. Motioning at two warriors, Spotted Bull sent them upstream to cross the river and circle the barricade to see what the Arapaho were up to. They had failed to spot Ice Walker earlier as he raced away across the grasslands to warn Walking Horse. Spotted Bull showed his contempt for the ones behind the barricade by sitting in plain sight, showing himself and his men plainly. He knew he had the advantage in numbers. The Comanche knew the ones inside the fallen timbers could plainly see them where they sat their horses so there was no use for stealth now.

"To cross here would make us good targets for their rifles, my chief." Ten Bears shook his head in disgust. Spotted Bull was a great warrior, fearless in battle, but the older warrior thought him to be too rash and foolish. Many a warrior could lose his life crossing the river.

"I will wait for Half Moon and Little Hog to return, then we will see." Spotted Bull was plainly aggravated. He knew better than to charge straight at the fallen timbers, it could cost him many warriors. His chance at a surprise attack was gone. Now, he had to attack these warriors in a frontal attack if he wanted the women and horses.

"There is nothing to see, Spotted Bull." Ten Bears argued. "It will be foolish to attack such a strong place."

"I, Spotted Bull, am Chief of the Niyaka Comanche." The squat warrior glared at the older man. "Hold your tongue or leave us."

Ten Bears didn't back down. "To steal horses and take scalps is good, my chief, but if we lose many men, we will all lose face."

Walking Horse watched from behind the log jam as the warriors sat their horses quietly, staring across the great river. He knew the tribe and recognized a couple of the warriors as the same ones chasing after Red Hawk in late winter. The big warrior covered in black paint, sitting in the middle of the warriors, was the same one who had run his horse hard, trying to catch up with the fleeing Crow.

"The black-faced one and the warrior beside him seem to be arguing." Crazy Cat nodded toward the river.

"They are Comanche." Walking Horse looked at Crazy Cat. "The same ones we fought during the cold times, many sleeps ago."

"Why are they this far from their own lands?"

"They come here to raid and take revenge against Red Hawk the Crow." Walking Horse shook his head. "And we are the ones unlucky enough to be found by them."

"We are not Crow." Crazy Cat frowned.

Big Owl laughed. "I will ride over there and tell him your words, my friend."

"No, me and my warriors will ride over there and tell him."

"We cannot do this thing, Crazy Cat. We have the women and children of Crow Killer to protect." Walking Horse held up his hand. "Now is not the time for bravery."

The Cheyenne warrior nodded slowly. "I know we cannot take a chance, but I believe the nine of us can defeat these twenty Comanche dogs in battle."

Big Owl laughed. "We could maybe, but how many would we lose, then who would protect the children? No, my friend, let them come here and ride into our rifles and arrows."

"I will do as you say, Walking Horse." Crazy Cat's blood was hot, wanting to fight. "But, if they charge this place, we will kill some of them. Then, my friends, we will attack."

"We will send Ice Walker for help. Only one is needed to ride back to Red Hawk." Walking Horse looked at the gathered warriors. "We have water and deer meat to eat for a few sleeps."

"Ride to who for help, Walking Horse?" Ice Walker had just led his horse into the enclosure and hadn't heard his leaders talking about Red Hawk.

"Someone must ride hard to the Yellowstone and bring Red Hawk and his warriors back to help us." Walking Horse looked at the young warrior. "Crazy Cat and I have chosen you to do this thing, Ice Walker."

"I will do as you ask and go for the Crow." Ice Walker agreed. "But, I do not like it to be so. Where is the pride for a Cheyenne asking a Crow for help, like a woman?"

"Would there be pride in our lodges if we permitted Crow Killer's children to be lost?" Crazy Cat knew the warrior's feelings, and he felt much the same. "This is not the time for pride."

"I said I would go for help."

"No, I am younger and not as experienced in fighting." The young Cheyenne called Grey Fox spoke up. "Ice Walker may be needed here. I will ride for Red Hawk."

"Every Cheyenne warrior is free as the eagle, and each one can follow his own path." Crazy Cat looked closely at the young warrior. "If you wish to take this dangerous trail, then go quickly."

Grey Fox nodded. "I will bring Red Hawk or I will not return."

"You will return my brother and you will bring the Crow, Red Hawk." Ice Walker grasped the shoulder of the young warrior. "Ride with the wind and set your eyes to watch everything that moves."

"Circle far behind the barricade, then cross the river downstream." Crazy Cat instructed the youngster. "They may have warriors watching us."

Racing his fleet horse from the barricade, Grey Fox did not see the two Comanche warriors, Half Moon and Little Hog, sitting their horses, watching him from a grove of trees behind the enclosure. Riding right at them only the hiss of two arrows made a sound as he was knocked backward from his horse.

Only a sigh came from the barricade as Big Owl raced his horse out of the enclosure. Again, the arrows sung out as the big black horse of the huge Arapaho raced right at them across the open banks. Mounting, Crazy Cat and two warriors followed Big Owl from the enclosure in a hard run. The arrows hadn't missed their mark as the big Arapaho reeled from the two shafts that penetrated his huge body. Still, with the strength of three men, Big Owl charged into the surprised Comanche and buried his war axe in one of the warrior's chest. Crazy Cat finished the other Comanche as Big Owl sank slowly from his horse.

"Go quickly, Ice Walker, circle the Comanche and ride for Red Hawk." Crazy Cat and the other warrior tried to raise the wounded Arapaho from the ground. "Ride fast… bring help quick as you can."

Ice Walker looked down momentarily at his friend Grey Fox, then whipped his horse hard, racing downriver. "I will return."

"Big Owl is hurt badly, Crazy Cat." Another Cheyenne called Tall Tree looked into the eyes of the big warrior.

"Quick, we must get him on a horse and return quickly to the barricade." Crazy Cat looked to the crossing where he watched as the Comanche riders started entering the water.

"Big Owl will not go with us, Crazy Cat." Tall Tree lowered the heavy body back to the ground. "Today, our brother has gone to meet his ancestors."

Looking down at the unseeing eyes, Crazy Cat shook his head slowly, wondering how a small arrow could kill such a mighty warrior. "I will not leave Big Owl to be scalped by the Comanche dogs. Hurry, help me get him on his horse."

"We must hurry or we may meet our ancestors this day too." Tall Tree looked at the swimming horses in the river.

"Big Owl will go with us. I will not leave one such as this warrior to be butchered by these dogs." Crazy Cat reached down for Big Owl. "I will die here first."

Bearing the body of the great Arapaho Lance Bearer, the two Cheyenne barely returned to the safety of the fallen trees when the Comanche rode up from the river. Only the loud wails of Bright Moon and Little Antelope could be heard as they cried for Big Owl. Looking down to where Crazy Cat lowered the great body, Walking Horse could only shake his head in sorrow for his fallen friend. So many times since childhood, they had hunted or ridden the war trail. To lose such a warrior and friend was beyond grief. No longer would he hear the booming laughing voice of his friend.

"We have ridden many war trails together." The words were spoken softly, barely discernable. "Now, you will fight no more. Go to our ancestors and ride the great prairies in the sky. Rest in peace Big Owl, my brother."

"Walking Horse, the Comanche are preparing to charge." Tall Tree pulled the warrior from his thoughts. "We must be ready."

"Everyone check your rifles and each pick an enemy." Walking Horse looked out across the barricade of trees. "Do not miss or we may all perish this day."

"We will avenge our dead brothers." Crazy Cat cocked his rifle. "We will not miss these dogs."

"I fear one of the warriors has gone for help." Ten Bears looked down at the two dead Comanches, Half Moon and Little Hog. "Now, we are two less, my chief."

"As they are, Ten Bears." Spotted Bull looked down at the bloody body of Grey Fox. "I watched as they carried another one inside the log place they hide behind."

Looking at the log wall, Ten Bears shrugged. "We cannot attack such a place as they are protected by."

"We must attack before the one who has escaped returns with more warriors." Spotted Bull turned toward the trees. "Now, there are only a handful of warriors with the women."

"A handful of warriors with rifles, my chief." Ten Bears knew the warriors behind the log wall. They were the greatest and the most feared fighters on the plains. The dreaded Lance Bearers of the Arapaho and the Cheyenne Dog Soldiers. Many times over the years, he had been in skirmishes with these same warrior societies. Ten Bears knew they would never run. All would die protecting the women. To run would be shameful, worse than any death.

"We will kill these warriors, then we will return home with many scalps, horses, and great honors… and their women!" Spotted Bull raised his arm and yelled.

Ten Bears looked into the set face of his chief. He knew death looked out at them from behind the logs. "If some of us are to die here this day, so be it. Let us do this thing quickly so the ones who survive can return to our lodges."

Spotted Bull motioned his warriors to stop before the barricade, just out of range of the long shooting rifles. Riding a few steps forward, the Comanche sat several seconds, then raised his long spear.

"Come out from your hiding place, Cheyenne and Arapaho dogs, and fight us hand-to-hand like warriors!" The black painted chief yelled out. "Are the great Cheyenne and Arapaho cowardly women?"

"We like it here, Comanche." Walking Horse answered. "Our friends will be here soon to help us."

"We watched as your warrior rode for help." Spotted Bull laughed. "It will take him many days to return. By then, I will have your scalp and your women."

"Come and take them, Comanche dog!" Crazy Cat yelled out. "Or meet me in single combat. The winner gets the women."

"No, all of you come out, then we will fight like men."

"We will remain here until help comes." Walking Horse shook his head. "Our warriors are coming."

"You are women, scared to meet us in battle."

"Perhaps, but we will not come out." Walking Horse laughed. "But, you can come in."

"Cowards!" Spotted Bull screamed and motioned his warriors forward.

Leaving Little Antelope to watch over the children, Bright Moon took her rifle and shot pouch, then joined the warriors, waiting behind the log barricade. She could plainly see the Comanche as they circled the enclosure in a slow walk, gradually moving their horses into rifle range.

"They will charge this place, then try to climb over the logs." Walking Horse looked around at the warriors. "We must kill as many as we can before they reach us."

"If I were the Comanche, I would sit outside and wait for us to starve." Tall Tree laughed. "To ride against the wooden wall is death."

"They know we have sent for help." Crazy Cat growled. "They must attack and kill us quick, then retreat from the Crow hunting grounds and return to their own lands before Red Hawk comes."

"They come." Walking Horse lined his sights on the leading Comanche. "Do not miss, my friends."

"I won't, but my rifle might." Another young warrior laughed. "But, I've still got my bow and lance."

No fright showed in any of the faces behind the barricade, only a stubborn set to their jaws, showing disdain for the oncoming warriors. Walking Horse knew if he gave the word, the warriors would race forward to fight the Comanche in hand-to-hand combat. He knew they were too outnumbered to fight up close until they had evened the odds a little with their rifles. With Grey Fox and Big Owl dead and Ice Walker riding for help, there were only six warriors left to protect the women. The Cheyenne and Arapaho were valiant warriors, but the three to one odds against them was too much to gamble the women and children's lives on.

Fire and smoke belched out from the barricade as fingers touched off the powerful shooting Hawken buffalo rifles. Bright Moon hadn't missed her shot as she casually reloaded her rifle and looked through the smoke for another target. She could see at least three of the enemy down outside the log walls as she looked for an upright figure. Smoke, completely obscured the enclosure as again and again the rifles belched smoke as the attackers started over the log barricade with their axes and bows. Retreating to where Little Antelope covered the children with her body, Bright Moon reloaded and waited for the first enemy warrior to come over the logs into her sights.

The smoke cleared as most of the rifles were silenced. The fight turned into personal combat between the warriors. Only the screams of the fighting and dying warriors and the clashing of their steel blades sounded as they fought to the death. The Comanche were shorter in stature than the Cheyenne and Arapaho, but they were powerful, skilled fighters and they still outnumbered Walking Horse and his warriors. Lances were buried in the ground as the Lance Bearers refused to retreat or give an inch in the face of the fierce battle. Crazy Cat was everywhere, his war axe brandishing terrible blows down on the enemy warriors.

Bright Moon's Hawken spoke again as she killed another Comanche about to stab Walking Horse in the back. The heavy smoke and screaming war cries of the fighters turned the small enclosure into complete bedlam. Reloading, as she stood over Little Antelope and the children, Bright Moon waited, barely able to tell the warriors apart in the haze. Whirling to her right, as an older warrior materialized from the smoke, Bright Moon touched off the rifle. Ten Bears grimaced in pain and surprise as the thirty caliber ball found his stomach and knocked him backward.

The heavy war axe of the warrior fell from his bloody hands as he looked in disdain at the small woman who had shot him. "Killed by a mere woman, I told Spotted Bull this place was evil."

The words were barely discernable to Bright Moon as the warrior spoke in Comanche. She didn't know the language, but she knew what he was thinking by the way the older warrior looked at her in disbelief.

Bright Moon started to reload her rifle when another warrior sprang through the smoke and raised his long spear. Painted all over in black paint, she knew this one was the leader of the Comanche that Walking Horse had spoken of. The Comanche was so close, she had no time to reload before he would be on her. Drawing the rifle back, Bright Moon waited as the warrior stepped forward with his spear raised. Suddenly, from the ground, Little Antelope launched herself against Spotted Bull and grabbed at the heavy spear. Trying to wrench his weapon away from the screaming woman, the Comanche didn't see Bright Moon as she stepped forward. He only felt the sharp pain as she slashed at him with her skinning knife.

Kicking and screaming, Little Antelope let loose of the long spear. Spotted Bull lunged after her as she rolled away from him. Blood ran down across his stomach, from the wound where the sharp knife had sliced him open. Again, the knife cut deep as Bright Moon sprang on the warrior's back and plunged her knife into him. Grabbing the fighting woman by the hair, Spotted Bull slung her to the ground and raised his long spear. Glaring with hatred, the warrior plunged the sharp weapon straight down as he fell atop the small body of the fighting woman.

Walking Horse and Crazy Cat both watched the final moments of the fight as the black painted Comanche collapsed on top of Bright

Moon. Seeing their leader fall, the remaining Comanche warriors quickly retreated over the logs. Rushing forward, Walking Horse lifted the dying Spotted Bull's body and rolled it away from Bright Moon. Blood completely covered Bright Moon's body as they looked down on the woman in despair.

"She is dead?" Little Antelope wailed. "She died fighting to protect me and the children."

"She gave her life for them." Walking Horse shook his head.

"Don't send me to my ancestors yet, Sister." The weight of the heavy Comanche had momentarily knocked the breath from Bright Moon. "Help me up."

"Bright Moon, my sister, you are not dead, but the spear did find your side." Little Antelope knelt down, examining Bright Moon.

"It is nothing." Bright Moon stood unsteadily to her feet as Little Antelope examined the wound where the spear had penetrated her skin slightly. "It bleeds heavy, but I will not die."

The smoke cleared inside the log jam showing several bodies lying about. Eight warriors lay dead on the ground inside the enclosure. Two Arapaho, one Cheyenne, and five Comanche warriors would fight no more. The young warrior, Tall Tree, lay dead across a Comanche. Four more Comanche bodies lay outside the enclosure.

"Tall Tree was a great warrior." Crazy Cat shook his head slowly. "We will bury our dead, then we must leave this place quickly, if Bright Moon can ride."

"I can ride." Bright Moon checked on the children, then started toward the river to wash off the blood. "The wound is a slight thing."

"Thank the great spirit." Walking Horse followed the slim figure with his eyes as she walked away, then down at Little Antelope. "Your sister is quite a woman, and so are you, little one."

"She killed three enemy warriors today, my husband." Little Antelope smiled. "The Comanche Chief was one and she saved your life also."

"A woman protecting her children is as dangerous as any wild thing." Walking Horse smiled down at the babies. "She would have made a great lance bearer."

"Bright Moon has killed before." Crazy Cat nodded. "Protecting Crow Killer, but today she was protecting the children of Crow Killer."

"Let us build places for our fallen to lie, then we must leave this place."

Red Hawk, Ice Walker, and ten Crow warriors sat their horses in front of the log barricade and looked down at the dead bodies of the nine Comanche. Pointing back from the river into the trees, Ice Walker rode to where the bodies of the fallen Arapaho and Cheyenne rested on their wooden burial scaffolds. Dead horses lay under the scaffolds.

"The great Arapaho Warrior Big Owl has gone to meet his ancestors." Red Hawk looked at the huge dead bay horse, the only animal large enough to carry the big warrior. "He was a great Lance Bearer."

"And Tall Tree, Grey Fox, and Little Elk have also gone to meet their ancestors." Ice Walker rode his skittish horse around his friend's burial scaffolds. "You will be missed, my friends."

"Come, we must catch up with the others." Red Hawk turned the great spotted stallion to the north, following the trail leading to Jed's valley. Studying the tracks in the soft dirt, he kicked the stallion into a slow lope. "The Comanche have been beaten, but Walking Horse now has few warriors left to defend Crow Killer's children and the women."

"Does Red Hawk think more enemies may be waiting ahead for them?"

"In these lands, there are many enemies." The handsome Crow shook his head. "This I do not know, but we must hurry."

"It was bad luck for us to run into the Comanche. We lost many friends." Ice Walker shook his head as he took one final look at the scaffolds.

Staring hard to where Long Leaper sat his horse, Red Hawk frowned. "Walking Horse should have been warned the Comanche were seen in our lands."

Turning from Red Hawk's hard stare, Long Leaper looked at Ice Walker then back at Red Hawk. "What does Red Hawk say?"

"Come, we go." Red Hawk nudged the spotted horse. "We will speak of this later when the ones ahead are safe."

CHAPTER 9

*J*ed studied the rocky mountain trail that led back to the west and north toward the Snake River. Looking down from a high vantage point, at the lower valley, he could see Little Wound, Hatcher, and Ellie almost halfway down the north pass as they hurried down the trail leading to his cabin. From where he stood, he was too far to see the cabin plainly through the high trees. The only chance for Little Wound and the others to reach the cabin safely was for him to hold the pass. His lone rifle would have to hold back Squires and his men as long as he could while the others raced downhill. His timing had to be perfect. At the right moment, he had to leave the high knoll and race down to the cabin as fast as his legs could carry him. To stay too long, guarding the trail, would make him an easy target for Squires and his sharpshooting hunters when he started across the flat valley toward the cabin. The white hunters were horseback and excellent marksmen with their far-reaching Hawken rifles. Jed was afoot, so the run to the cabin would be a desperate race for his life

The clatter of a dislodged rock, rolling on the lower trail, turned Jed's eyes back downhill. Squires and his men were rounding the last bend in the trail that could effectively hide them. Now, the distance between them was only a short, hard run for a horse before they would be on him. Drawing a fine bead on the first rider, Jed touched off the Hawken. He didn't miss. The rider was flung backward from his spooked horse. Squires quickly reined his horse behind the curve in the trail. Reloading the rifle, Jed touched off another round that ricocheted off the rocky pass wall. The trail along this part of the mountain was narrow. One side of the trail fell off into a deep ravine, and the other side was a steep upward climb. Jed knew if they charged him in mass, he could get a couple providing he didn't miss, then the others would be on him.

Quickly glancing down the trail, he could see Little Wound hurrying Ellie and Hatcher before him. They were a little more than halfway to the safety of the cabin. He wondered if he could hold off the hunters and the many Metis and Cree fighters, and reach the cabin alive. Suddenly, Jed saw the figure of his stepfather, Ed Wilson, running from the cabin to help Ellie and Hatcher. Relief engulfed him as they reached safety and seeing Wilson alive and well. Now, if he could reach the cabin, he would have Little Wound, Hatcher, and Wilson to defend the cabin against twenty or more enemy fighters. Big odds, but the thick cabin walls would even the coming fight. Now, all he had to do was outrun Squires and his oncoming warriors to the cabin. Even as fleet afoot as Jed was it would be a close race against horses in the rough terrain.

Firing one last shot at Squires position, Jed sprang from his hiding place and raced pell-mell down the mountain trail, springing in long leaps as he covered the ground. His strong lungs were working like ballasts as they sucked in the life-giving oxygen that let him run so hard. Running at high speed on the treacherous trail, he had to be careful not to lose his footing on the loose rock. A quarter ways down the path, Jed heard the first rifle speak from behind him, then the whining of a heavy slug as it tore up the ground many feet in front of him. Shooting downhill, Squires men needed a lucky shot to find their racing target. Jed's strong legs pumped faster as he pushed himself harder, weaving back and forth across the trail. This was a race of life and death not only for him, but for the ones below.

At the pace he was running, Jed was afraid to take his eyes from the rough trail for fear of falling. Behind him, he could hear the exultation of several yelling war cries as the Metis and Cree whipped their horses in a dangerous lunging run down the mountain. His rifle was empty from his last shot and in his hurried race downhill, he hadn't had time to reload the weapon. Several rifles discharged behind him, but from the lunging backs of the running horses, the warriors couldn't get a good bead on Jed's fleeting form. All he could do was run as fast as his powerful legs could move. Once off the downward trail and on the flat meadow, he still had a hard run to the cabin. He knew at the start of the flats, the advantage would be with the horses and their riders.

Jed thought of the killer grizzly and the pursuit she had given him over the mountains three seasons ago. The she-bear had never given up the pursuit of her enemy, the same as the ones chasing him now. She only had her claws and teeth, but these warriors had the far-shooting Hawken rifles. This time, it wasn't just his life hanging in the balance, but the lives of the ones in the cabin. The long hard days of riding with little sleep were beginning to take their toll as Jed's lungs began to burn from the great effort they were putting out in keeping his legs pumping.

Turning as he stepped onto the flat valley floor, Jed quickly took in the warriors scrambling down the steep grade in pursuit of their quarry. The riders were less than a hundred yards up the trail and gaining on him fast. Drawing in two deep breaths, Jed took off as fast as his legs could carry him toward the cabin. There was almost a mile to the safety of the cabin, a long run against men on horses. Weaving and dodging through the maple and mountain cedars, trying to dodge any rifle balls coming his way, Jed knew he wouldn't make it. A man is fast, but compared to a hard-running horse, he was slow. Halfway to the cabin, Jed stopped and reloaded the Hawken. Today, he might die, but he would take a few of the ones following with him.

The heavy buffalo rifle roared fire and death as Jed squeezed the trigger and watched another of Squires' Cree warriors fall before he turned and hurried for the cabin. Several of the Metis and Cree were closing fast, some trying to race their tired horses alongside Jed. Reaching for his lance, Jed was about to plunge the Arapaho medicine lance into the ground when several rifles went off behind him. Knocked sideways, Jed felt the hot sear of a lead ball as it grazed his side. Staggering forward, toward the voices of Hatcher and Wilson as they hollered at him from the cabin door, Jed knew he would never make it. Blinking the haze from his eyes, he screamed at Ellie as she raced from the cabin toward him.

"Go back, Ellie." Jed whirled as several warriors closed in on him. "Get her back, Pa."

Spotting the woman, running from the safety of the cabin straight at them, Squires and his other four white hunters whipped their horses after Ellie as she ran toward Jed. Yelling out in rage, Hatcher took a fine bead on Pete and squeezed off a shot. Flung backward from the horse, as if he'd been hit with a sledgehammer, the hunter was dead before he hit the ground. Intersecting Ellie as she ran toward Jed with her rifle, Squires pulled her fighting and kicking in front of him on his plunging horse. Reining in hard, Squires ducked his excited horse behind a tree and looked back to where Pete lay.

"You've got her, Squires. Now, let's get out of here." One of the whites screamed as another shot rang out from the cabin. "I don't know who's in that cabin, but they can sure shoot."

"They'll pick us all off if we keep sitting here like a bunch of ducks." A hunter named Nobles reined in his horse and watched as Jed limped to the cabin. Several Metis tried to race after him only to be driven back from the hail of gunfire coming from the defenders. "You got what you wanted. Now, let's go!"

"At least we got some lead in one of them." Nobles watched as the wounded Jed collapsed in the welcoming arms of Hatcher, Wilson, and Little Wound. "They're dead shots, Squires. We've done lost two more Cree."

"We've got them outnumbered. We'll just hem them up in their cabin." Squires looked about at the sullen Metis.

"You've got the girl." Nobles shook his head. "What more do you want?"

"Yeah, I got her, alright." Squires pushed the fighting girl down hard across his horse's withers. "But, we've got to get some trophies for the Metis and Cree."

"I'm telling you, Squires, you rush that cabin and all we're gonna get is dead."

"The scalps and rifles inside that cabin will keep the Metis from taking ours." Squires studied the cabin from behind a large cedar tree. "We've got to get them something for this trail to keep them pacified, they've lost too many warriors."

"How you planning on getting them out of there without getting our heads blown off?" Nobles looked up the trail at the strongly built cabin. "They've probably got enough food and water in that place to fort up for a year."

"I'm smarter than that, Mister Nobles." Squires watched as the ones ahead stood in the cabin, firing through the doorway. "One thing they ain't got."

"Oh yeah, what's that?"

"Water."

"Water for what?" Nobles shook his head.

"I aim to burn them out, that's what." Squires laughed hysterically. "When their tails catch on fire, they'll leave that cabin quick enough."

"What?" Nobles scratched at his coarse beard. "Now, that's real smart thinking. You burn that cabin and there goes your scalps, rifles, and plunder."

"Be sensible, Squires." Another hunter spoke up. "Let the Metis and Cree have those horses out there and let's ride. That's plenty of plunder for the red devils."

"What, you don't want any plunder yourself, Harve?"

"Whoever's in there is a fine marksman." The one called Harve studied the cabin. "That Cree lying over there must have been at least a hundred yards away and he was a moving."

"So?" Squires growled. "You scared?"

"Dang right I am." Harve swallowed hard. "To charge that cabin is gonna get plenty more of us killed."

"So you boys are running without any plunder?"

"I'll have my skin in one piece and that's better than loot to me." Nobles argued. "I'll get my plunder another day."

Squires looked up at the cabin. He had the girl he wanted so badly, but the one called Crow Killer was still alive. He had heard too many stories about the Arapaho Lance Bearer back in Baxter Springs. Here, he and his men had the advantage. He had to kill Crow Killer now or the Arapaho would be on their trail before they cleared the first mountain. He had the girl, but as long as the Arapaho lived, Squires knew he would know no peace. He would be a hunted man, even in the far north.

"Are we closing in on the cabin or we gonna sit here and palaver all day?" Nobles questioned him.

"We're closing in, but you men stay hidden." Squires warned his riders. "I don't want to lose any more men."

Squires had promised the Metis and Cree many horses, rifles, and firewater if they would follow him to the white man's town, then into the mountains. The map Bate Baker had been forced to give him was accurate. The map had been crudely drawn on deer hide, but it showed the river crossings and the trail to Crow Killer's valley. He had readily promised the Indians horses if they would help him steal the white woman. Squires had no idea he would lose so many men chasing after the woman. Indians, even the half breed Metis, could not understand any man taking a chance on getting killed over a mere squaw. Women, especially Indian squaws, were too easily bought or stolen on the frontier. Squires knew the Indian mind and when a fight was in their favor, they were willing and great fighters. But when danger or death presented itself, they would take what they could and return home to their women and lodges.

Squires had to finish this fight quickly before the Metis, in their superstitious ways, persuaded the Cree to turn on him. Including their leader Batiste, the Metis and Cree had lost many men since leaving the Gallatins because Squires had promised them great plunder if they would follow him east after the woman. He knew the warriors following him had already spotted the many horses grazing on the valley floor and they studied the woman, his woman. He was afraid they would turn on him and his men, take the woman, then take their scalps, horses, and rifles, and ride back north to their home villages. Squires had lived and traded with the Metis and Cree for many years. He knew their minds were like children and they could change on a whim. They would consider the woman, horses, and rifles would be better than the chance of getting any more of them killed.

Staying out of rifle range of the cabin, Squires had the warriors dismount and encircle the cabin. Several shots were fired as lead rifle balls tore into the thick-walled cabin but the rifle fire couldn't penetrate the thick logs. He would have to set fire to the cabin, but not during the daylight hours when they would be perfect targets for the sharpshooters inside. Leaving two guards to watch, the trapper pulled his men back away from the cabin to wait until dark. Building a small fire across the creek, Squires watched as the Metis and Cree sat by the fire as they talked among themselves.

Knowing he had to lighten the mood, Squires sent Nobles and another hunter to look for fresh meat. Perhaps a good meal would get the Metis and Cree in better spirits. Anything to get the enraged warriors' minds off him, his men, and the woman.

Pushing Ellie to the ground next to the fire, Squires sat down beside her and grinned. "Well, lady, it was a hard ride but I finally got you." The big hunter pulled Ellie to her feet. "You're my woman now."

"I'll never be your woman."

Only the hard blow from the back of his huge fist could be heard as Ellie was flung backward to the ground. "You're mine. It might take a little persuasion, woman, but you'll learn who's the boss."

Pulling herself to her feet, Ellie wiped the blood from her tore lip. "Never."

Again, the big hand was raised but Squires grinned and dropped his arm. "I like a little fight in my women. Now, you gather more wood for this fire."

Looking out the cabin window, Wilson cussed loudly as he watched two of the white hunters leading his beloved cow across the stream. Throwing the door wide open, the farmer raced toward the creek and his cow. Little Wound threw his arms around Wilson's legs and hung on to the wild thrashing body. Two rifle slugs from the Metis guards tore up the ground around the two struggling men before Jed could help Little Wound drag Wilson back behind the table.

"We've got to get inside the cabin, Pa." Jed pulled the screaming man to his feet as another bullet took a piece of wood out of the oak table. "Come on."

"My cow, those heathens are fixing to eat her!" Wilson swore.

"I'm sorry, Pa, but she's gone now. We'll get another cow." Jed pushed Wilson ahead of him. "We can't stand out here while they're shooting at us."

"Not another one like she was."

"We'll get you another cow, Pa." Jed pushed the farmer through the door. "I promise."

Falling inside the safety of the cabin, Wilson shook his head sadly. "I'm sorry, Jed. I should be worried about Ellie, not the cow."

Jed patted Wilson's shoulder. "It's okay, Pa. I understand."

Jed looked toward the creek as he turned back to the door. The black mule, as usual, had followed the cow. Jed knew most Indians liked mule and horse meat as well as buffalo. So far, they had ignored the mule, but he knew when the cow meat was eaten, they would turn on her. There was no way he could help her now, but he knew how Wilson felt. He had grown fond of the mule over the years, mainly because she belonged to the Silent One.

"I'm sorry about the cow, Pa." Jed tried to calm him down. "We'll get another one for you."

"They'll pay! Every one of them red heathens will pay." Wilson sat down heavily in a chair, and then noticed Jed's side was bleeding again. "You're bleeding again, boy. I'm sorry."

Blood covered Jed's hunting shirt. Earlier, the initial shock and burn from the bullet had subsided and the blood had started to clot. Fighting with Wilson, trying to pull him back into the safety of the cabin, had reopened the nasty tear in his side. Placing a bandage over the wound, Little Wound bound Jed's side tightly.

"It will be painful for a few days, but not serious." The warrior finished binding the wound. "You know they have taken my sister?"

"I know. They won't hurt her for now." Jed looked out the door. "They're too busy with us. We'll get her back."

"I don't see her. She must be with the others that retreated across the creek." Wilson spoke up.

"I don't see Squires either but he's probably keeping her back out of harm's way." Jed added.

"Soon as dark gets here, they'll be coming." Hatcher looked out the window toward the smoke from Squires' campfire. "Squires knows he has to kill us here so we can't follow him and Ellie."

"What'll you reckon they'll try, Lige?" Jed asked the old scout.

"Hard to say, but the white man leading that bunch knows, as well as I do, he has to do something and quick. That is if he plans on keeping his own hair." Hatcher seemed clearheaded, as if he had recovered his senses.

"You think the others might turn on old Squires?" Jed looked at Little Wound.

"Sometimes, the Metis and Cree can get crazy." The warrior explained. "They have lost many warriors on this trail and have nothing to show for losing so many."

"And?"

"I think they will turn on him quick if he doesn't kill us." Little Wound continued. "I think if we stay alive, the white man may die."

"It'll be hard for them to penetrate these walls with their rifles." Jed looked around. "And we have plenty of food and water."

"I figure they might try to burn us out." Hatcher turned back to the window. "That's my opinion for what it's worth."

"I'd say it is a good opinion, Lige." Jed nodded. "That would be their only chance of getting to us."

"I swear if he harms Ellie, I'll drink his blood." Hatcher's voice was cold. "No matter how far he runs."

"They sure couldn't burn the cave, providing we can get to it." Wilson stood up and walked to the window. "And there's plenty of rifles, lead, and powder there."

"That would be running and I ain't running from them heathens." Hatcher declared.

"We're outnumbered and vulnerable inside the cabin, Lige." Jed spoke over his shoulder. "We can't help Ellie if we get burned up."

"I reckon you're right about that, Jed." The old scout agreed.

Looking around inside the snug cabin, Jed thought about Squires burning it. He and Bright Moon had spent many happy moments there, but like the cow, the cabin could be replaced. However, their lives could not be replaced and Jed knew he couldn't rescue Ellie if he was dead. Wilson was right, the cave would be the perfect place to seek refuge. Surrounded by large boulders, the cave couldn't be burned, but anyone trying to reach it would be easy targets for their rifles. Four men on that narrow, rock-sheltered path could hold off a hundred attackers. Jed had his mind made up, as soon as dark overshadowed the trail, they would make a run for the cave.

"I figure they'll move in to burn the cabin as soon as it gets dark." Jed looked around at the faces. "That's when we'll retreat to the cave."

"Their watchers sit outside." Little Wound studied the creek banks. "I have only seen two watching us."

"Two can see as well as many." Hatcher shook his head.

"Gather your possibles, rifles, and all the dried meat you can carry." Jed looked over at Wilson. "Is there any water inside the cave?"

"I put a fresh barrel in there a few days back."

"Good, then we're ready." Jed looked at Little Wound. "Exactly where are the watchers?"

"They wait on the creek bank, one on each side of the lodge."

"We'll go out the back window." Jed pointed at a larger window barricaded with a heavy beam. "I made it especially for a way out to get up on the roof."

"They'll never know we're gone." Wilson grinned. "When we get to the cave and get ready for them vultures, maybe we can sneak back down the trail and pick off a few of them."

"Maybe we'll do just that, Ed." Hatcher laughed.

"We must get Ellie clear before we do any more killing," Jed warned. "We don't want the Metis and Cree to take out their revenge on her."

"How we gonna do that, Jed?" Wilson spoke up.

"That I don't know." Jed looked up at the bright sun. "It's still a few hours until sundown, then we'll pull out."

"Well, maybe something will turn up." Hatcher checked the priming of his rifle. "I know y'all are right about the cave, but right now I sure ain't in the running mood."

"I'll study on it some." Jed knew his wound and the long run had weakened him. Looking at the tall brush bordering the creek, he wondered if he could slip into their camp after dark and rescue Ellie.

From the doorway, Jed watched as several Cree and Metis warriors rode toward the band of horses grazing out on the flat meadow. However this turned out, he knew they meant to have the horses caught and ready to cross back over the mountains to the northwest. His horses, especially the stronger ones, were highly prized by every horseback tribe. The horses in his pasture were well-blooded animals, truly magnificent, bred for strength and endurance. Most Indian mustangs were smaller animals, hardy, but not strong and swift like the ones out on the meadow.

Shaking his head, as a Cree warrior placed his rawhide rope around the neck of a rangy bay horse, Jed tightened his fingers, but he was afraid to take the shot. His fear was for Ellie's safety, he couldn't fire. Right now, Ellie was much more important to him than the horses. He worried what would become of her if the Cree and Metis took their vengeance out on Squires.

Squires sat back and studied Ellie. Temporarily, he had satisfied the Metis and Cree. They were content after they had gotten their stomachs full of Wilson's cow. After eating, several of the greedier warriors were busy on the valley floor, gathering the band of grazing horses. Looking out across the valley floor, he nodded. At least the horses kept the warrior's minds from him, his men, and the woman. He knew the warriors were preparing to leave the valley whichever way the fight turned out. He wanted the men in the cabin dead, but getting the Cree to attack the log structure could be dangerous. If they lost one more of their companions, in their rage, they just might turn on him.

Red Hawk sat the spotted horse high on the southern ridge, over-looking Jed's beautiful valley. The valley was long, but even from this great distance, he could hear gunfire sounding out on the far northern end of the valley. Looking down the steep mountain trail, his sharp eyes located what he searched for. Walking Horse and his caravan of riders were just emerging from the trees lining the valley floor. Firing his rifle to get their attention, Red Hawk circled the spotted stallion several times so he would be recognized. He hoped Wilson heard his rifle fire also, so he would know help was on the way.

Seeing the riders below had stopped and were looking up the mountain, Red Hawk kicked the stallion and started his descent. Several minutes later, Walking Horse smiled in relief as he recognized Red Hawk, Ice Walker, Long Leaper, and several others dropping onto the valley floor.

"It is good to see my friend, Red Hawk." Walking Horse extended his hand as the Crow reined up beside him. "You have made good time."

"We came as fast as we could." Red Hawk looked over at Little Antelope and Bright Moon. "Are the women and children safe?"

"Yes, they are safe." Walking Horse motioned for Bright Moon. "These are the children of our brother, Crow Killer."

Smiling, Red Hawk studied both babies. "They are beautiful children, too pretty for Arapaho, they should be Crow."

"I thank Red Hawk for coming with his warriors." Little Antelope greeted the Crow warrior. "It is good to see you again."

"It appears you did not need us." Red Hawk smiled at Little Antelope. "We saw the bodies of the Comanche and the burial scaffolds of your warriors."

"We were lucky, but we lost a great warrior." Walking Horse referred to Big Owl but did not say his name. Speaking of the dead, for any reason, was taboo among most tribes. "We lost several great warriors."

"Yes, he was a great loss, but he will always be remembered around the Arapaho fires."

"And in our hearts." Little Antelope added. "It is good that Red Hawk has come here."

"This one said the Comanche's were after you." Red Hawk nodded at Ice Walker, then smiled at Little Antelope. "I couldn't let anything happen to my favorite Arapaho."

"Uh-huh." Little Antelope shook her head. "Same old Red Hawk, I see."

Turning serious, Red Hawk looked toward the end of the valley. "The noise of many rifles comes from Crow Killer's lodge."

"Gunfire?" Walking Horse looked to where Red Hawk was watching.

Red Hawk nodded. "From down here, the rolling meadows and tall grass muffle the noise. We must ride there quickly."

"The women?"

Red Hawk looked around at his warriors, then at Walking Horse "Long Leaper and Ice Walker will go with us to see what causes the noise."

"You must hurry and see if the white father of Crow Killer is in danger." Bright Moon spoke out. "Hurry warriors."

"Crazy Cat will keep you safe here." Looking at the Cheyenne warrior, Walking Horse nodded. "Hide His Face, Iron Oak, and the other warriors will stay here and help him protect the women and children until I return with news."

"I will protect them, Walking Horse." Crazy Cat nodded.

"Hide them in the tall cedars." Walking Horse lifted his huge arm and pointed. "Do not come out until one of us comes for you."

Kicking the spotted horse, Red Hawk, with Walking Horse and the others, started toward the northern end of the valley. Topping a high knoll, they could make out the noise of rifles firing sounding in the distance to the north.

"The sound of many rifles is on the wind, my friend."

"We must hurry." Walking Horse agreed.

Racing the horses in a hard run, the four warriors crossed the valley riding up and down the knolls of the big meadows until they were within a short horse run of the cabin. Reining in, they watched as several mounted warriors were busy rounding up loose horses on the valley floor.

"The rifle fire has become silent." Red Hawk studied the warrior's intent on capturing the horses. "We may be too late to help the white man. He may be dead."

"What tribe are they?" Walking Horse didn't recognize the dress or markings of the Metis and Cree.

"It doesn't matter. They are the enemy and they will die." Red Hawk removed the leather sheath that covered his rifle. "They may have killed the white and now they take our brother's horses."

"They have us outnumbered, my chief." Long Leaper looked nervously at the warriors.

"If you are afraid, Long Leaper, return to the women." Red Hawk was furious. He was ready for battle. "Today, we may die, but we fight!"

"This is not what I meant, my chief."

"They have not seen us yet." Walking Horse studied the eight warriors that were preoccupied, busy trying to round up the black mule. "Red Hawk, take Long Leaper and go to the right of the lodge. Ice Walker will ride with me and we will hit them from the left."

"We go." Red Hawk turned the stallion. "Be strong, my brother. We will meet in the middle of these warriors."

"You do the same."

"I will let them see me and Long Leaper, then we will wait until you and Ice Walker get in position to attack them in surprise."

"It is a good plan." Walking Horse shook his rifle. "Hokahey!"

Loping the spotted stallion across the flat meadow, Red Hawk reined him to a stop almost within rifle range of the warriors rounding up the loose horses. The raiders, engrossed in catching the prize horses, didn't see Red Hawk and Long Leaper sitting their horses. Only when the black mule whirled and ran, in Red Hawk's direction, did the Cree and Metis become aware of their presence.

"Hee yah, enemies." A Cree warrior whirled his horse and pointed across the meadow.

All six Cree and two Metis turned their attention on Red Hawk and Long Leaper who sat their horses quietly out on the meadow. One of the Cree raised his rifle and fired. No movement came from Red Hawk or Long Leaper as they calmly watched the strange warriors.

"Two scalps and a beautiful spotted horse have been given to us. Who follows me?" The Cree yelled and fired his rifle wildly as he charged.

Hearing the rifle blast out on the meadow, Squires lunged to his feet and looked to where the Cree were screaming their war cries. Raising her hand to block the sun's rays, Ellie looked out on the meadow in the direction Squires was looking.

"Who's out there, Squires?" Scarface looked across the flats. "They're not our warriors."

"It's too far to tell." The words were hardly out of his mouth when the Cree and Metis yelled their war cry and kicked their horses toward the two lone figures.

A smile came to Ellie's face when she recognized the great spotted horse as the afternoon sun rays glistened off his shimmering hide. Even though far off, she knew it was Red Hawk and his magnificent animal as they returned the war cries and charged toward the oncoming Cree. Squires hollered in frustration as he watched his warriors riding forth, charging the two warriors. He knew it had to be a trap since the two warriors weren't running, instead, they were charging the oncoming Cree. Suddenly, from far behind the cabin, two more riders rode into view, closing in on the screaming Cree who were unaware of the oncoming danger.

"What'll we do, Squires?" Scarface watched as the two forces clashed together with their rifles spitting fire and death. "Those fool Cree of ours are being cut to pieces."

"Look at that magnificent fighter out front." Squires couldn't believe his eyes as Red Hawk had already unseated two of the Cree fighters. "That one on the spotted horse is a devil."

"He's something alright." Nobles agreed. "He's worth four of ours."

Looking at Ellie smiling, Squires turned red with jealous rage. "Is that one Crow Killer?"

"It is too far to see who he is." Ellie shook her head.

The remaining Metis and Cree sitting around the fire finally became aware of the fight out on the valley floor. They mounted their horses to ride to the relief of their brothers.

Squires waited until all the warriors cleared the camp before turning to Scarface and the other white hunters. "Saddle the horses, we're leaving here quick."

"That's the smartest thing you've said in a while." Scarface and Harve raced for the hobbled horses. "Let's get."

Ellie, seeing Squires' attention riveted on the fight in the flats, turned to run. Grabbing her from behind, Squires grinned down at her with his yellowish teeth showing from his curved back lips. The whitish eyes seemed dead as he pushed her toward a hobbled horse.

"Not so quick, girl, you're coming with me."

"Let me go, and Crow Killer may not follow you."

"He follows me and you're a dead woman." The big hunter cackled as he laughed hysterically. "You're mine now, woman, don't forget it."

Jed stood watching from the doorway as the Cree and Metis raiders focused their attention on catching the loose horses out on the meadow. Darting from the grasp of a warrior, the black mule whirled and focused her attention to the east and let out with a long bray. Dropping behind the wooden table in the yard, Jed followed her gaze where two figures sat their horses like statues atop a knoll on the valley floor.

Even at a faraway distance, the sun glistened off the magnificent black and white markings of the spotted Appaloosa which made him unmistakable. Jed sighed a sigh of relief, knowing it had to be Red Hawk since no other rode such a marked animal. Bright Moon had a son of the great spotted Appaloosa, but Jed knew he was with Bright Moon back in the Cheyenne village of He Dog.

Smiling, he hollered at the others. "It's Red Hawk and another warrior. I don't know how he happened to be here, but there's no mistake it's him."

Rising from behind the table, Jed dropped one of the Metis as they charged toward the fighting out on the meadow. With a long shot, Hatcher knocked another warrior from his racing horse.

Reloading his rifle, Jed raced to the creek with the others close behind him. He hadn't spotted Ellie or Squires so he figured she had to be across the creek in the raider's camp. Wading the creek, he heard the sound of several horses, then watched as four white men, leading Ellie's horse, raced away in flight toward the north pass. The big figure leading her horse was no doubt, Squires. Raising his rifle, Jed tried to get a sight on Squire's broad back, but with Ellie being led behind the others, Jed couldn't fire for fear of hitting her. Turning his attention on one of the other hunters, Jed fired as Harve mounted his plunging horse. Flung sideways, the hunter stumbled several steps and fell into the short grass. Weak from loss of blood, the run from the cabin had exhausted Jed, making his hands shake. Looking around for a loose horse, but finding none, Jed shook his head in disgust, then turned his attention to the meadow. The fighters engaged in horseback warfare moved closer to the cabin, coming within rifle range. From this distance, Jed could clearly make out Walking Horse and another warrior as they joined the fight. The fourth fighter, fighting two Cree, looked like the young warrior, Ice Walker, but Jed couldn't be certain.

The Cree and Metis were not cowards and the fight out on the meadow was savage. They were brave fighters. Outnumbered now, about ten warriors to four, Red Hawk and Walking Horse were pushing forward, making a fierce fight of it. The battle raged hot and savage, and there was no time to reload the rifles. The combatants fought hand to hand with war axes and knives. Red Hawk seemed to be everywhere, pushing the great Appaloosa forward into the smaller horses of the raiders.

Hatcher's rifle spoke again dropping another Cree. Eager to get into the fight, Little Wound raced toward the battle. Afraid Red Hawk would not recognize the Gros Ventre, Jed hurried in pursuit as fast as he could run.

"Stay here and use your rifles." Jed hollered over his shoulder at the two older men. He didn't want them too close to the fierce fighting. "Stay here."

"That suits me just dandy." Hatcher laughed, and then fired his rifle again. "Just like a turkey shoot back home, ain't it, Ed?"

"More like cold-blooded murder." The farmer fired again, missing his target. "Well, it would be, if'n I could shoot straighter."

Hatcher laughed. "Just hold your breath and touch her off slow and easy."

Jed hollered for the excited Little Wound to wait for him, and together they moved toward the fight. Ahead, Jed watched as Ice Walker was knocked from his horse by a Metis fighter. Aiming deliberately, Jed knocked the screaming Metis from his horse. Again, Little Wound charged ahead and raced to where a Cree was fighting with another warrior against Red Hawk. The Cree never saw Little Wound as the young warrior with a mighty leap landed on the plunging horse behind the Cree, toppling both man and horse to the ground. The razor-sharp hunting knife of the Gros Ventre quickly ended the Cree's life.

Seeing they had lost so many warriors and the whites from the cabin were almost on them, the remaining Cree and Metis raced toward the south end of the valley. Hatcher and Wilson hadn't listened to Jed as they had run forward to engage the enemy raiders. A fleeing Metis pulled his fractious horse to a stop and took deliberate aim at Hatcher. The bullet didn't miss as the old scout was knocked sideways to the ground. Seeing Hatcher fall, Jed raced to the old scout's side and turned him over.

"That one got me good, Jed." Hatcher smiled slightly. "I should have listened to you, boy."

Jed looked down at the old face. "I suspect it did, old hoss. I'm sorry."

"Don't be sorry, every dog has his day to go under." The grey head nodded. "Reckon this is mine."

Little Wound knelt beside Hatcher and held his arm. "Our people will speak of your bravery in battle, my father."

Grabbing Jed's arm tightly, Hatcher looked up into the dark eyes. "Get Ellie back, boy, and kill the swine that took her. If she's hurt, you skin him alive. You hear me?"

"I hear you, Lige. I hear you."

Looking at the Crow, Jed noticed blood dripping from Red Hawk's arms and shoulder. About to speak to Hatcher again, he felt the strong body go limp and the last breath of life passed from the old scout.

"Are you hurt bad, my brother?"

"It is nothing. Where is Medicine Thunder?" Red Hawk looked down at Hatcher. "She should be here with Rolling Thunder."

"The whites have taken her. They ride with her back to the north pass." Jed nodded. "I wish she were here."

Walking Horse rode up and looked at Red Hawk and Jed as he dismounted. "My brothers you are both wounded, but you are alive. The young Cheyenne warrior, Ice Walker, has gone to meet his ancestors."

"We will grieve over them later. Now, there is no time. We must go after Ellie." Jed looked up at Walking Horse, then at Long Leaper. "How many of the enemy got away?"

"Six flee to the south." Long Leaper pointed to the far end of the valley. "The rest are all dead."

"We will follow them later. Now, we must ride after the whites." Jed stood weakly to his feet. "We must go after Ellie."

Red Hawk looked at Long Leaper. "Go after the horses and bring them here quickly."

For once the young Crow didn't argue. "What about the women?"

Jed's head snapped at the question. "What women?"

"My warriors, led by Crazy Cat the Cheyenne, are guarding the women. They have Bright Moon, Little Antelope, and the children hidden back near the south pass." Walking Horse watched as Jed laid Hatcher gently back on the tall grass. "They will be safe with Crazy Cat."

"Bright Moon is here with the children? What is she doing here? She was supposed to be in He Dog's village." Jed looked at Walking Horse.

"Your woman is a hardheaded woman, my brother." Walking Horse explained. "She refused to stay behind in our village."

Looking to the south, then back to the north pass, Jed looked to where Wilson stood silently. "Pa, take care of Lige and Ice Walker."

"Of course I will. Where are you going, Jed?" The farmer asked.

Clenching his teeth, Jed grabbed his side, then pointed to the end of the valley. "I must see to the safety of my wife and children first. Then, I will follow Squires to the north after Ellie."

"Who is this one?" Red Hawk looked to where Little Wound stood over Hatcher. "He saved my life today."

"His name is Little Wound. He is the son of Rolling Thunder and the brother of Medicine Thunder."

"Rolling Thunder's son?"

"He is Gros Ventre." Jed nodded. "His lands are far to the west in the Gallatin Mountains."

"You are a great warrior, Little Wound. Would you honor me and ride by my side after Medicine Thunder?" Red Hawk swung up on the spotted horse and looked down at the Gros Ventre. "If he rides with me, Walking Horse can ride with you to where the children and your wives are waiting."

Little Wound nodded. "I will ride with Red Hawk."

"How many guard the women and children?" Jed questioned Walking Horse.

"Crazy Cat, Hides His Face, Iron Oak, and three other warriors. They are safe with Crazy Cat." Walking Horse assured him.

Long Leaper led four horses to where the men stood talking. "This is all I could catch."

"They are enough, Long Leaper." Jed nodded. "Thank you."

"Long Leaper will ride with you and Walking Horse. Hurry and protect the women and children." Red Hawk looked hard at Jed. "Are you strong enough to ride, my brother?"

"I can ride." Jed took a long-legged bay horse and quickly fashioned a rawhide bridle out of the rope Long Leaper handed him. "Pa, stay watchful. We will return shortly."

"We go." Red Hawk looked down from the spotted horse and nodded at Little Wound. "Good hunting, my brothers."

Little Wound swung up on a Cree horse that was covered in blood. Nodding at Jed, he turned to the north after Red Hawk.

"When the women and children are safe, I will follow you."

"See to the women and children, Crow Killer." Red Hawk hollered back over his shoulder. "We will return Medicine Thunder to you."

Jed nodded. "Ride safe, my brothers."

Turning the bay, Jed kicked him into a hard lope to the south end of the valley. From no work, the horse was fresh and wanting to run. Jed knew they were many miles away from the south pass so he held the animal in, reserving his strength until they caught up with the enemy Cree or found the women. Walking Horse passed Jed and took the lead as they neared the far end of the valley. A heavy line of trees covered the end of the valley where the south trail over the mountains started.

Reining in, Walking Horse dismounted and studied the tracks left on the sandy ground. "Six horses have passed up the trail."

"And the women?"

"They should be in there." Walking Horse's huge arm pointed to a heavy growth of cedar and scrub brush at the base of the mountain. "That is where we left Crazy Cat."

The warrior hardly had pointed when a lone rider came toward them in a hard run. Crazy Cat, watching from the trees, recognized Jed and Walking Horse. Riding to meet him, Jed reined in as the Cheyenne raced up to them.

"Are the women safe, my brother?" Walking Horse was relieved to see the warrior.

"They await us there in the trees." Crazy Cat looked at Jed's bloody hunting shirt. "You have been in a fight?"

Nudging the big bay, Jed hurried to where the women waited. Sliding from the horse, he grabbed Bright Moon in a tight bear hug. Feeling her cringe, he loosened his hold on her and looked down at her bloody side.

"You are hurt."

"It is a small thing, now that you are here, my husband." Bright Moon smiled. "We are all safe, thanks to Crazy Cat and these warriors watching over us.

Grabbing the shoulder of the Cheyenne, Jed nodded. "We will always be in your debt."

"It is nothing." Crazy Cat smiled, then turned to where Little Antelope held the babies. "Bright Moon and Little Antelope are the real fighters here."

Seeing Jed's bloody hunting shirt, Bright Moon frowned. "You have been wounded, my husband."

"Like you said, Bright Moon, it is nothing." Jed smiled in relief.

"The Cree and Metis are good shots, but not good enough to kill the great Crow Killer." Walking Horse took Little Antelope's arm and smiled at her.

"We have lost good friends today." Jed saw Crazy Cat looking around for more warriors to appear. "We lost Ice Walker. I am sorry, Crazy Cat. I know he was your nephew."

"Did my nephew die well, Crow Killer? Did he die the death of a Cheyenne Dog Soldier?"

"He died bravely fighting against the Cree and Metis renegades. He counted coup, on many enemies." Jed replied sadly. "Ice Walker was a brave man."

"Losing one like him is always sad." Crazy Cat nodded solemnly. "But, there is no need for sorrow, he made us proud."

"Yes, he did." Walking Horse agreed. "He was beside me when he fell. Our fires will sing great songs of him."

Turning to where Little Antelope approached with the babies, Jed took Eagle's Wing in his hands and lifted him to the sky. "They have grown so much while I've been away."

Looking around at Walking Horse, then at Long Leaper, she questioned them. "Where is Red Hawk and the rest?"

"The whites have taken Medicine Thunder captive." Walking Horse looked into Little Antelope's face. "Red Hawk has gone after her."

"And your father?" Bright Moon took Eagle's Wing from Jed. "Does he live?"

"He lives." Jed nodded at Walking Horse. "We will talk of these things later. Now, we must return quickly to the cabin."

"We watched as several Cree and Metis warriors passed below. They sat their horses for a while at the bottom of the pass, then started up the trail over the mountain." Crazy Cat pointed to the mountain pass. "I think they knew we were here but were afraid to come near."

"Will we pursue them?" Hides His Face spoke up.

"No, Red Hawk may need our help more." Jed swung stiffly on the bay. "Come, we go quickly to the cabin."

"I will follow these warriors to the east." Long Leaper turned his horse. "We do not want them returning."

Jed knew grown warriors did as they wanted. "Go then, but be careful, Long Leaper, and thank you, my friend."

"Long Leaper should not follow these warriors." Crazy Cat held up his hand.

Iron Oak and two other young Crow warriors followed Long Leaper as he loped toward the mountain trail.

"Long Leaper wishes to save face with Red Hawk this day." Crazy Cat shook his head as he watched the warriors race across the valley floor.

Jed was curious as he looked at Walking Horse. "What does he mean?"

"We will speak of it back at your lodge." Walking Horse knew Long Leaper had proven his bravery in battle this day. There was no use bringing up things that had happened back near the big river. If Jed insisted, Walking Horse would speak more of it later, after everyone was safe.

Standing behind a huge oak near the creek, Ed Wilson watched as several riders crossed the long valley and approached the cabin. Recognizing Jed and Walking Horse in the lead, Wilson hurried back to the cabin to help the women dismount. He could see from the strain on their faces, they were nearing exhaustion.

Helping the wounded Bright Moon dismount, he lifted Eagle's Wing from where his cradleboard hung from the saddle and smiled down at the baby. Looking up, he stared in shock to where Little Antelope held another baby in her arms.

"Two?" The farmer grinned from ear to ear. "Is there any more?"

"Just two, Pa." Jed sat down heavily at the table, then looked to where the two bodies lay wrapped in blankets. "I believe that's enough."

Noticing Jed staring at the wrapped bodies, Wilson tried to apologize. "I didn't know whether you wanted them buried or raised on burial scaffolds."

"You did right, Pa." Jed looked to where Walking Horse was holding Little Ellie. "I think we'll put Lige up on a scaffold. He'd like that."

"We have lost many great warriors on this trail, Crow Killer, and we may still lose more." Walking Horse shook his head sadly.

Pulling Bright Moon away from the others, Jed looked into her eyes. "I must ride after Red Hawk."

"I know he is your brother. You owe him much, but is my husband strong enough?" She asked him.

"I owe him more than I could ever repay." Jed smiled at Bright Moon. "Yes, I am strong enough."

"Then ride, my husband. Bring our sister home safe."

"Walking Horse says you have killed many more enemy warriors."

"They rode against us back at the big river crossing." Bright Moon smiled sadly. "A mother will always protect her babies."

"You might have been killed." Jed chided her. "Then the babies would have no mother, and I, little mother, would have no one to share my life with."

"I wasn't killed. Everything is good now." Bright Moon looked down at her bloody side. "The Comanche's spear came close, but I still live, my husband."

"I must ride. You stay here at the cabin and don't leave." Jed pointed at her beautiful face. "You hear me?"

"This time my ears will listen better." Bright Moon nodded. "I almost lost our children by my hardheadedness, and I got many warriors killed."

"It wasn't all your fault. It's over with now." Jed smiled down at her. "I'm leaving Hides His Face and the other warrior here with you. With Pa, you'll be safe enough until I return."

"Walking Horse and Crazy Cat will ride with you?" Little Antelope walked to where they stood.

"Yes."

"With the three greatest warriors in the tribes riding against them, your enemies will flee before you." Bright Moon smiled.

"I hope so, that is after we get your sister away from them." Jed continued. "I just hope Red Hawk doesn't get careless when he catches up with the whites."

"I think the Crow likes our sister." Little Antelope smiled coyly. "And perhaps, she likes him."

Bright Moon laughed lightly. "Maybe she will be the one to tame him."

"She just might." Jed had seen how agitated Red Hawk had become when he found out Squires had taken Ellie. "If he can be tamed that is."

"No mere squaw will ever tame that one. He is too wild." Little Antelope laughed.

"You know, my husband." Bright Moon laid Eagle's Wing on a blanket near the cabin. "His father, Plenty Coups, might not like him marrying an Arapaho."

"Plenty Coups would accept her for a daughter-in-law without blinking." Jed smiled. He knew how partial the old chief was to Ellie. "She is as his daughter already."

As one of the Crow warriors brought fresh horses into the corral, Jed had Walking Horse pick a fresh mount since his sorrel had been ridden many miles from Arapaho lands.

Bright Moon walked to where her spotted horse stood, then led him to Walking Horse. "You will ride my horse. You will be better mounted than my husband."

At first, Walking Horse refused the reins of the young Appaloosa, but not wanting to hurt Bright Moon's feelings he reluctantly accepted the horse. "Thank you, my sister. He is indeed a great animal."

"We go." Jed swung up on his paint horse and looked over at Wilson. "Take care of all of them, Pa. Keep them inside the cabin."

"You bet I will." Wilson smiled. "You better hurry. You're three hours ride behind Red Hawk."

Walking Horse laughed. "Maybe we are, but now we have stronger and fresher horses to run them down with."

CHAPTER 10

S quires and his men hastily retreated up the north trail. Fearing for their lives, they hadn't waited around to see how the fight on the valley floor ended. No matter which side won the battle, he and his men would be in the crosshairs of anger from both sides. He had pushed his horses hard for more than a day to reach the Snake River Crossing without slowing to check behind him for any sign of pursuers. He knew without a doubt they would follow. If Crow Killer lived, he would come for the girl. If the Cree and Metis won, they might follow for revenge and his scalp. He had caused the death of so many of their people and they would be hungry for vengeance against the one that led them into this folly. Squires and his men had to reach the safety of Fort Bridger before whoever followed him and his men could catch up. Squires knew Bridger's reputation and the old trader had given orders there would be no fighting or killing around his trading post. Bridger would protect them at least for as long as they stayed within the confines of the post.

For now, no one in the settlements knew he had taken Doc Zeke's daughter. Hopefully, he would be far to the east, way past Bridger, when word got out. To go to Baxter Springs would be disastrous since the woman would be recognized immediately. Going any further west would only let the Cree and Metis pursue him easier. No, Bridger's Post was the only place to seek refuge, as a temporary place of sanctuary, for him and his men. Only Nobles and Scarface remained of his white hunters. Both Pete and Harve had been killed in the fighting, back near the cabin. Squires had left the other hunter, Sugar, behind in Baxter

Springs to watch for the woman and the one called Crow Killer. He hadn't been seen since so Squires figured Sugar was dead too.

"Our horses are played out, Squires." Nobles looked at the trapper and frowned. "They've got to rest or they'll drop in their tracks."

"I know they're done in." Squires snapped back at the hunter. "We'll cross the river first, then let them graze a bit and rest."

"You reckon anyone's after us?" Scarface looked behind them nervously. "My neck is itching."

"Your neck is always itching." Nobles complained. "A good bath would cure that."

"Well, it is. My neck always itches when danger's near." Scarface shook his finger. "And you watch your mouth, Nobles, you ain't so clean yourself."

"We'll cross the river, and from there, we can hold off anybody trying to cross." Squires looked across the water. "One thing though, either way the fight ended, I doubt either side could have many warriors left."

"That's a gamble you're staking our lives on, Squires." Scarface frowned and looked sideways at Ellie. "But, I for one, am not counting on it."

"I agree with Scarface for once." Nobles added. "We ain't sure what took place back there after we left out."

"Ran out, you mean?" Scarface blurted out. "Like whipped dogs, all on account of one female."

"All that talk of the bear killer's luck has got you and Nobles spooked." Squires lashed out. "You're both running scared of one Arapaho."

"Dang right, it has." Noble's eyes flashed fire. "I knew Billy Wilson and I've heard about the grizzlies. Wilson was a bad actor and now all of them are dead. Probably many more we ain't heard anything of."

"Yeah, and I remember that Nez Perce Injun say how many great warriors Crow Killer has put under." Scarface added. "We'll be next."

"Never figured you two to be yellow." The big hunter pointed his finger at the two hunters. "You're yeller cur dogs, both of you."

Nobles turned red at being called a coward. "You heard as well as we did what that Nez Perce back at Baxter Springs said about him."

"You mean the ugly one called Squirrel Tooth." Squires laughed wildly. "I heard him, so what?"

"Yeah, he was scared to death talking about the Arapaho." Nobles remembered how nervous the warrior looked when he mentioned Crow Killer's name. "Something about spirits and bad medicine."

"You were the first to run back there, Mister Squires, so don't you be calling us yeller." Scarface glared at Ellie. "This is all because of that woman. We could all be drinking and gambling in Baxter Springs safely right now."

"Shut up with that nonsense and let's get across." Squires looked at Ellie. "Get a tight hold, woman. You fall off and I'll let you drown."

"I say we turn her loose, here and now." Scarface had been watching their back trail. "Woman, you reckon they'd let us go if'n we turned you loose now?"

"And what if the Cree won back there?" Squires growled, not giving Ellie a chance to talk. "They'll take her scalp and keep after us."

"I ain't scared of the heathen Cree or Metis." Scarface shook his head. "But I'm telling you, it's the grizzly killer coming after us. Word is out, no one can stand against him and his bear medicine."

"You can't fight a spirit person, Squires." Nobles chimed in.

"Shucks, Nobles, you sound like you're believing all them stories about him." Squires laughed weakly.

"I do believe them."

"Every tribe in these mountains believes them. Yeah, I believe them too." Scarface frowned again making his face pucker. "I say we leave her here. He'll kill all of us for sure if we keep her."

"Shut up, you dang coward, and let's cross." Squires glared at the scar-faced one. "Like I said, you're yellow like a cur dog."

"No, Mister Squires, I'm just smart." Scarface looked at the woman. "Turn her loose and we may get away with our hair. You hang on to her and we're all dead men."

"I ain't leaving her and that's final." Squires swore. "I gave up too much for this little gal."

"That's true you have, but we're all still alive." Scarface shook his head in disbelief. "How can you be so stupid, Squires? I'm telling you this, when we get back to civilization, me and you are quits."

"So, that's the way it's gonna be?" The big hunter scowled. "You're just cutting out on me and Nobles... that right?"

"That's it in a nutshell." The scarred face frowned.

"Well, that's terrible, us being friends and all."

"We ain't friends, Squires." Scarface kicked his horse. "We never have been. We're just trapped together is all."

"Now, Scarface, you've done gone and hurt my feelings." Squires pretended to pout.

"Maybe, but if'n this bear killer catches us with the woman that's not all that's gonna be hurting you."

Squires turned his crazed eyes on the other hunter. "What say you, Nobles? You want me to turn my woman loose too?"

Ignoring the last question, Nobles took the lead as they walked the horses into the current of the Snake. Scarface rode in the middle with Squires and Ellie following. Scarface hadn't reached swimming water when the roar of Squires' big Hawken rifle erupted, knocking Scarface sideways into the river.

"What the...?" Nobles whirled, looking behind him. "Have you took complete leave of your senses, Squires?"

"My gun went off accidentally." Squires grinned sourly. "I feel real bad about that."

Nobles watched as Scarface's dead body floated downstream spilling blood into the water. "I sure hope it ain't gonna go off again by accident."

"That depends. You understand this... I'm not leaving the woman behind." Squires looked at Ellie. "Now, you get your skull around that."

"You know, you just cost us a rifle that we may need pretty quick."

"Scared as he was, old Scarface wouldn't have been much help if a fight broke out." Squires' horse was almost in swimming water. "Sides, his rifle is still hanging on his saddle horn. Lead out."

"I'm leading." Nobles didn't like turning his back on the crazed hunter, but he had no choice in the middle of the river. "And I wasn't talking just about the rifle."

Riding out of the river, their horses were finished, trembling from the hard run from the valley and long swim. Squires had Nobles hobble the horses and turn them loose to graze along the riverbank. Careful not to turn his back on the crazy hunter, Nobles started to unsaddle the horses.

"Don't unsaddle them you dang fool." Squires hollered. "We may need them in a hurry."

Shaking his head, Nobles grumbled. "Hurry? These horses couldn't outrun me in their condition, and he calls me a fool."

"You." Squires pointed at Ellie. "Toss together some wood and start a fire."

"Out in the open, where all can plainly see?" Nobles questioned.

"It don't matter none. If they're coming, they'll know where we are." Squires glared at Ellie. "I said build a fire, woman. Now!"

"If I don't, are you gonna shoot me too?"

"It's a thought alright." The big hunter raised his hand as he stepped toward Ellie. "You're the cause of this whole dang mess. Now, move!"

Ellie glared at the crazed hunter. She knew better than to argue with the man in his unbalanced condition as he just might lose what mind he had left and shoot her as he had Scarface. She was a doctor and she had seen men lose their senses before so she knew this one had completely lost his mind and was capable of doing anything. The last few days of running, fatigue, and being afraid of what followed them had the hunter hitting back at everything like a wounded animal.

Piling some loose driftwood together, she looked at the unkempt man. "I'll need some flint and steel."

Nodding, Squires tossed his small possibles bag at her feet. "Now, that's better. You'll learn to do as you're told soon enough."

Squatting beside her, Nobles looked across the drifting water. "He's gone loco, crazy as a bat. You be careful, woman. He'll bite anything that crosses him now."

"I figured that. I believe our Mister Squires knows he's a walking dead man." Ellie shook her head.

"So, you reckon your man is following us?" Nobles glanced sideways to make sure Squires didn't see him talking with Ellie. "Providing he's alive."

"One thing you can bet on, mister, he's following, and another thing I'll bet money on... he's alive." Ellie warned.

"Is he now?"

"He is and I'll tell you something else." Ellie worked with the fire, keeping her eyes on Squires who was preoccupied with watching the far bank. "So far, I'm not hurt, but if anything happens to me, he'll skin you alive. I mean that... he'll peel your skin while you're still alive."

"How can you be so sure he's alive?" Nobles looked at Squires. "That was a pretty big fight back there on the flats. Lots of shooting and yelling."

Ellie smiled as she struck sparks into the small pile of squaw wood. "Because of his great bear medicine, Crow Killer can't be killed."

"You're a white woman and you believe that malarkey?" Nobles laughed lightly. "It's just an Indian belief is all."

"The Arapaho part of me does." Ellie pushed more twigs onto the small flame. "Matter of fact, the white side does too."

"What, what are you saying, woman?" Nobles' head jerked around like he had been shot. "You're part Arapaho?"

"Half."

Only a snort, then a chuckle came from the filthy hide hunter. "Old Squires don't know he's done got himself killed over a half-breed squaw."

"Well, that's what I am alright."

"Well, now, if that don't turn the kettle black." Nobles grinned. "I can't wait until he finds out, that'll cook his goose."

"You ain't gonna tell him?" Ellie looked at the yellow-stained teeth as the man grinned.

"Shucks, no, squaw." Nobles shook his head. "I don't want to end up like old Scarface. And lady, if'n you're smart, you won't either."

"Why not?"

"I tell you why, missy." Nobles was about to laugh himself sick. "Old Squires loves the womenfolk, he surely do. Right now, he believes in his sick mind that he got all these men killed and lost us a pile of money for a white woman. That part is okay, but when he finds out you're a breed... "

"That's what I am." Ellie blinked, this was the very first time she had actually thought of herself as a half-breed. Somehow, the thought made her feel warm inside, proud. "Half Arapaho and half white."

"Lady, he's crazy loco now." Nobles warned. "You tell him that and we're probably both as good as dead."

"What are you two palavering about, Nobles?"

"I was just trying to find out from your woman how long we have before company could arrive." Nobles lied.

"And what did my woman say?"

"She don't know if anyone is coming."

"She's lying." Squires walked to the fire and glared down at Ellie. "They're coming alright. I can smell them."

"I don't know how you can smell anything from your own stench." Ellie mumbled under her breath.

After making coffee and heating some food, Ellie sat down away from the fire and studied the river as the two hunters gulped down their food. She hadn't told Nobles the truth and wondered who might come after her or if anyone was. She knew Jed had been shot near the cabin. Red Hawk and his men had been badly outnumbered. She didn't know how the fight ended.

"I'll tell you this, if our Metis and Cree had come out on top, they would have caught up to us by now." Squires tossed the dregs from his coffee cup and stood up. "Well, let the horses rest the night, then we'll pull out first light."

"We sure can't go back to Baxter Springs, dragging her along." Nobles eyed Squires' rifle. "Where we headed?"

"We'll ride to Bridger's Post, then cut north to Assiniboine country." Squires studied Ellie whose attention was on the crossing. "We'll be safe enough, providing we can get into Canada."

"Will we?" Nobles shrugged. "From what I've heard about this Crow Killer, he'll follow us to hell and back for her."

"I say we'll be safe in the mother country."

"I'd say that depends if any Metis or Cree get back alive to tell their story." Nobles didn't dare rile the crazed one too much. "Wouldn't you?"

"You remember old Scarface?" Glaring at Nobles, the big hunter took his rifle and stomped away. "You tell me to leave her here, Nobles, and I'll kill you."

"It don't matter." Shaking his head, Nobles leaned back against a tree trunk and whispered. "Fact is, I believe this old son is already dead."

Two sets of dark eyes stared from across the river, watching as Squires stalked up and down the bank nervously.

"Little Wound, your sister, Medicine Thunder, does not seem hurt." Red Hawk pointed his chin at Ellie and smiled.

"That is a good thing, but hurt or not these whites are dead men."
The young warrior glared across the river with hatred at the white
hunters. "These whites have killed many and caused much trouble in my
lands."

"Why would these whites come this far, all the way into these
mountains, just to steal a woman? It is hard for me to believe."

"Why? I have heard Red Hawk rides into Comanche lands to steal
women."

"I go to take horses and the women just happen to want to come
home with my warriors."

"Well, she is a very beautiful woman." Little Wound stared across
the river.

"Yes, she is, and a strong-willed woman." Red Hawk nodded. "I
agree, but aren't there many women in your lands?"

"Not white women with my sister's beauty."

"She is beautiful but she's not white, and she is a handful at times."
The Crow smiled.

"A challenge for a warrior to tame." Little Wound could tell the way
Red Hawk was watching Ellie that he thought much of his sister.

"Maybe too much of a challenge." Red Hawk grunted. "Maybe a
headache would be a better word."

"Any warrior knows the harder a horse is to break and the greater his
spirit, the better the horse will be when tamed."

"We're not talking about horses, Little Wound." Red Hawk seemed
to blush. "We're talking about Medicine Thunder, your sister."

"I am." The Gros Ventre grinned. "I've found women and horses are
about the same. Difficult to handle sometimes, but with kindness and a
tender touch… "

"You have a woman?"

"How will we cross the river and rescue her from the whites?" The
young Gros Ventre quickly changed the subject. "They might kill her if
we are discovered."

"The big one, walking the bank, watches his back trail nervously.
Even from here, I can smell fear in him." Red Hawk nodded at Little
Wound, knowing he had asked the warrior about a sore subject. "I believe
they will rest their horses tonight, then leave this place with the new sun."

"Crow Killer said three whites ran from his lodge with my sister." Little Wound looked across the river at the smoking fire. "I have only seen two white hunters, but there are four horses in their camp."

"Perhaps one is hiding, watching for us, or has walked ahead to check the trail." Red Hawk nodded. "But, I do not think so. Something is wrong here."

"I think this too, their horses are tired and need rest badly." Little Wound agreed. "I do not think the missing one would have left his horse and walked away on foot. Where can he be?"

"This I do not know. We just have to watch closely for him." Red Hawk looked across the river. "I will ride upstream and find a place to cross the river."

"And what would you have Little Wound do?"

"Stay here." Red Hawk looked up at the overhead sky. "With the coming of the new sun, walk out where they can see you."

"If they know we are here, will they not kill my sister?" The Gros Ventre shook his head doubtfully.

"No, if it is as you say, the big hunter has come too far after Medicine Thunder to kill her." Red Hawk retreated from their hiding place and stood up. "With the coming of the new day, I will be in place. Walk out and show yourself, but be careful, my friend. Their long rifles shoot far and these whites are very good shots."

"What do you think they will do when they see me?"

"I think the big white hunter is a coward. He is crazy in the head like a rabid wolf. Still, he desires Medicine Thunder and would not leave her behind." Red Hawk looked toward the river. "I believe he will leave the other whites behind at the river to keep you from crossing."

"Would the others be so stupid to stay so he can escape?" Little Wound asked. "What would they have to gain?"

"If they see only you, they may think only one of us survived the battle and follows them." Red Hawk explained. "The others will keep you from crossing the river long enough, for the big white to escape with Medicine Thunder, then they will flee after him."

"I know whites, they do not have much loyalty for one another." The young warrior shook his head. "Why would they do such a thing?"

"Fear, Little Wound. If there is only one other white hunter left, he knows if he does not obey, the big hunter might kill him." Red Hawk shrugged. "Maybe that was what happened to the third white hunter that we do not see."

"Why would the big white kill one of his own men?"

"This one is touched in the head." The Crow shrugged. "Maybe the missing white tried to take your sister away from him. Be careful, my friend, we do not know what happened. The other white might still be over there hiding."

"If your plan works, the big white will ride right into your ambush alone with only my sister?" Little Wound asked.

"This is what I hope for." Red Hawk nodded. "Then maybe I can get Medicine Thunder away from him unharmed."

"And the white that stays behind?" The black eyes snapped.

Red Hawk looked at the young warrior. "He is yours, or if two still live, they are yours. The horses, rifles, and their scalps are yours."

"I will wait until the sun returns to the sky, then I will show myself as you ask."

"When he fires at you swim the river while he is reloading." Red Hawk smiled. "With luck, my friend, he can only get off two shots at you before you are across."

"This is a good plan." Little Wound laughed lightly. "That is if he misses and I swim fast."

"In the water, you will be hard to hit." The Crow reached out his hand. "Yes, swim fast, my young friend, very fast."

Swinging up on the great spotted horse, Red Hawk turned downstream, out of sight of the crossing. He knew finding a good place to cross the river might take time. The banks along this part of the Snake were sandy and steep with no access down to the water. Trying to take the horse down these banks could cause them to cave in under the horse's weight and injure them both. There weren't many natural places to ford the Snake. Four miles further down the river from the crossing, Red Hawk finally found a place to cross. It would be a dangerous, rough crossing, as the river narrowed and the current was much stronger, but it was the best place he could find. He hoped he wouldn't injure the stallion as he slid down the steep sandy bank into the swift, perilous current. He had no choice since he didn't have time to look for another crossing. Letting the Appaloosa pick his way carefully down to the edge of the sandy slide, he nudged the stallion forward until the steep sandy bank started him sliding down into the deep water. Hitting the water with a noisy splash, the horse went completely under, then came up swimming hard, fighting across the swift current toward the far bank. Lunging up the sandy bank on the north side of the river, Red Hawk swung back on the spotted horse, then rode him to the top of the ridge overlooking the river.

Slipping from his horse, he quickly checked the stallion for any cuts or bruises. Looking down at the rough water, he patted the Appaloosa fondly on the neck and smiled. Only a great horse like the spotted one had the heart to make such a swim in the treacherous current of the river. When the horse slid off into the river's deep current, he hadn't been able to keep his rifle above water when he and the horse plunged beneath the surface. His bow and arrows didn't matter, but his powder had to be dry or the rifle would be useless. Quickly dumping out his wet powder and cleaning the touch hole of the rifle, Red Hawk had to wait until the rifle pan was completely dry before adding his powder to prime the weapon. Once dry, he opened his horn powder flask and dumped a fresh load of dry powder in the weapon. He remembered when Crow Killer had first insisted he use the white man's weapon. Until then, he had been satisfied with the age-old bow and arrow. Now, after learning the weapon, he would not part with the Hawken.

Perhaps on the trail, if he was lucky, he wouldn't need the rifle. For the safety of Medicine Thunder, he preferred to fight hand-to-hand combat with the white, before the man had time to turn his rifle on the woman. Red Hawk had no doubt the white hunter would kill Medicine Thunder before he would allow her to be taken away from him.

The sun was setting and time was against him. Satisfied the weapon was ready, Red Hawk swung up on the spotted horse and turned him back toward the crossing. Riding through the rock-strewn, timbered riverbank in the dark would be slow and dangerous.

The early morning sun was beginning to show as Red Hawk located and moved out onto the small trail that led north to the immigrant road. He remembered the terrain from when he and Crow Killer rode to the white village of Baxter Springs on their way to Shoshone lands. Smiling lightly, he remembered when Crow Killer said that was going to be their last war trail. However, here he was, riding after an enemy he didn't even know, but he knew the woman, Medicine Thunder, and she would be rescued at the peril of his own life. He also knew Crow Killer would follow and soon be there to help.

Early dawn had barely spread across the lands when Jed, Crazy Cat, and Walking Horse heard the discharge of a heavy Hawkin rifle just ahead of them. Jed knew this trail well, and the crossing was less than two miles ahead. They had pushed their horses hard, making good time as they hurried to catch up with Red Hawk and Little Wound.

"The shot came from the crossing ahead." Jed reined in the sweating paint horse. "Red Hawk and Little Wound have caught up to Ellie and the whites."

"Only one rifle was fired." Walking Horse cocked his ear, listening for another shot. "Where are the other whites?"

Seconds later, again the blast of a heavy rifle went off. "Come, they may need our help."

Awakened from a deep sleep, Squires almost fell face first in the river's sandy bank as the heavy burst from the first rifle went off just beside where he slept. Tangling his feet in some loose pieces of wood, he cursed as he kicked himself loose.

"What the…" The big hunter rubbed his face, then looked around in fear. "Nobles, what are you shooting at?"

"They're across the river." The buckskin-clad arm pointed. "Over there, I seen them plain as my nose in the morning light."

"How many?"

"I only seen one, but that don't mean there ain't more of them buggers." The hunter pointed his rifle. "I aim for them to stay over there or take some lead in their brisket."

"Catch up the horses, quick."

Turning to where Ellie was staring across the river, Squires frowned. "You see anything, woman?"

"No."

"You telling the truth or are you lying again?"

"I didn't see anything." Ellie lied. In the early morning light, her sharp eyes had spotted Little Wound several seconds before Nobles had seen him. "I think your friend is just jumpy is all."

"Maybe so, but we ain't waiting around here to find out."

"You jumpy too, big man?"

Only the hard slap of his open hand was heard as Ellie was thrown back across the fire. Seeing her fall, Little Wound let out a war cry from the river's south bank. Whirling, Squires snapped off a quick shot at the elusive, moving target.

"I see one of them, Nobles." Squires took the reins of two horses from Nobles.

"What'll we do, Squires?"

"I'll leave you the strongest horse." Squires jerked Ellie to her feet. "Give us a good lead and keep them at bay over there, then catch up to us."

"How long?" Nobles was skeptical since he didn't trust Squires. He knew the big hunter would leave him to die just to save his own skin and the woman.

"Just keep them from crossing for an hour, then come on the run as fast as that plug will carry you."

Nobles studied the far shore where he had seen the Indian. The lone warrior hadn't shown himself again. Maybe, Squires had hit the man with his shot, but he doubted it. Anyway, he wasn't arguing with Squires. With the Hawken rifle, he could keep anyone from trying to cross the river. Watching as Squires threw the woman roughly on her horse, then mounted himself, Nobles had a bad premonition as they rode away.

"You're a fool, Nobles, a blame fool." Talking to himself, he turned to see if the Indian would show himself again.

Little Wound watched as the big hunter forced Ellie onto her horse, then mounted his own. Red Hawk's plan was working out as the warrior had planned. Bending low, Little Wound made his move toward the river in a zigzag run.

Raising the rifle again, as the warrior started for the water, Nobles touched off the hard shooting rifle. Little Wound was thrown sideways as the heavy ball tore his leg. Rolling behind a drift log, out of sight of the white man, the warrior looked down at his leg. Hearing the sound of horses racing up, he turned to see Crow Killer, Crazy Cat, and Walking Horse dismount and race to where he lay.

"You hurt bad, Little Wound?" Jed asked.

"No, it bleeds but the wound is just a scratch." The Gros Ventre shook his head. "I did not move fast enough."

"You are right, it is not serious." Jed checked the leg where the bullet had barely grazed it. "Where is Red Hawk and your sister?"

"Red Hawk crossed the river during the dark time. If he is in time, he waits ahead on the trail for the big white."

Peeking over a log, Jed sighted Nobles behind a drift log with his rifle pointed across the river. "Walking Horse, Crazy Cat, keep the white busy while I cross the river."

"You will be a good target, my brother."

"Not if you keep him pinned down." Jed handed over his rifle. "Shoot straight and fast."

"She is my sister, Crow Killer, I will go." Little Wound started to rise.

"Not this time, my friend." Jed pushed the Gros Ventre back down. "If I fail, then you can try."

"Good luck, my brother." Walking Horse sighted down the barrel of his rifle. "Keep your head down and swim fast."

"Now!"

Jed raced for the river as a rifle ball kicked up sand right behind him. Diving into the shallows, he swam underwater several yards before surfacing in the deeper part of the river. He could hear the thunder of Walking Horse and Crazy Cat's rifles as the two warriors fired across the water at the white. Water splashed in his face as another rifle ball missed him by mere inches before he slipped beneath the moving current. Again, he surfaced, but this time he was able to take in air and submerge before Nobles had time to sight in on him. He was almost to the far bank when the white's rifle sounded again and missed.

In his fear and anxiety, Nobles knew he had fired too quickly, missing his target several times. He had been a fool to listen to Squires, and now more warriors were massing on the far bank. The whining, thudding bullets being fired at him were keeping his head pinned down behind the log so he couldn't take time to get a good bead on the one in the water.

Jed didn't know, but Little Wound, despite his leg wound, had raced to the river and was swimming across downstream from him. Closing the distance to the bank, Jed suddenly rose to his feet, dodging and ducking as he ran. Another explosion came as Nobles tried to get a sight on him. Hearing the rifle fire and feeling the ball as it breezed by him, Jed raced to where the white hunter had risen from the log and was trying to mount his skittish horse. Flinging himself over the log and into the frightened horse, Jed grasped the muscular hunter, dragging him from the saddle. Raising his sharp skinning knife, Jed looked down into the frightened face.

"No, he is mine." Little Wound came running up from the water. "I claim this one as my blood right. He is mine."

"Alright, Little Wound."

"Be careful, Crow Killer, there may be another white hunter nearby."

Jerking the rifle and knife from Nobles, Jed stepped back from the downed hunter. Looking across the river where Walking Horse and Crazy Cat were bringing the horses to the water's edge, Jed motioned them across. Little Wound stood over the frightened man, looking down calmly as Nobles cringed away from him.

"You remember me, white man?" Little Wound knew the hunter understood his words. "You remember my uncle?"

"It wasn't me, it was the crazy kid, Dibbs Bacon, that did for him." Nobles' eyes grew wide.

"You lie, white man." Little Wound pulled his knife. "It was you and the other four whites you rode with that welcomed him to your camp. You gave my uncle the firewater of the whites, then killed him. Then you stole his furs and scalped him for the bounty it would bring."

"No, I'm not lying, it was the killer, Bloody Hand Bacon."

"Two of the others had an easy death, but yours, white man, will come much harder." Little Wound turned to where Jed stood with Walking Horse. "You, Crazy Cat, and Walking Horse go help Red Hawk rescue my sister and leave this one alone with me."

"You are weak from your wound, my friend." Jed looked down at the bleeding leg. "Maybe one of us should stay here with you."

"Leave us, my wound is nothing." Little Wound waved his hand. "This is mine to do alone. Go help my sister."

Nodding, Jed and the two warriors swung up on their horses and turned north toward the immigrant trail. Looking back, they saw Little Wound dragging the whimpering Nobles to a tall willow tree.

"What will he do to that one?" Walking Horse watched as the Gros Ventre started stretching the hunter's arms to the tree limbs. They hardly cleared the river bottom when a hideous scream came from behind them.

"I don't know, but I've heard from the Bacon kid that the Gros Ventre were a vengeful tribe when they have been wronged."

Crazy Cat smiled. "I don't think this will be good for the white."

Again, an agonized scream came from behind them. Jed kicked the paint into a hard lope, wanting to get out of hearing range of the screaming man. Jed had killed many times, but he had never tortured or brutalized any of his enemies.

Jed was curious, Little Wound didn't seem cruel. "I wouldn't have thought the young one would torture a man."

"When a man has been wronged, you never know what he will do." Crazy Cat added. "If Bright Moon had been killed what would you have done to the Comanche?"

Jed only shrugged as he pulled the horse back to a slow lope.

Red Hawk sat the spotted stallion behind a large cedar tree, watching as Squires led Medicine Thunder's horse up the sandy trail in a hard trot. Red Hawk had heard the rifles in the distance so he knew the white was aware his men were under attack back at the river crossing. The white hunter, in his fear and hurry to escape, was more worried about what was behind him and never considered more enemies might be waiting ahead on the trail. Kicking the spotted horse, Red Hawk rode out onto the trail in plain sight, only fifty yards from where Squires led the horses.

The bright morning sun shone brightly as it glimmered off the Appaloosa. Red Hawk's muscular body seemed to shimmer as the morning rays brought their strong light to bear on him. The lone feather sticking out from his scalp lock, the long black hair flowing down his back, and his broad forehead made the warrior look like a statue. Only a breechcloth covered him, leaving his strong chest and flat stomach bare, showing his well-formed body that rippled with muscles. Ellie blinked, as she had never looked this close at the Crow warrior. Even with the danger she was in with Squires, she was astonished. Before her, sitting ramrod straight was a Crow warrior with the body of a Greek god, like she had seen in books back east.

Squires reined in abruptly and stared at the apparition sitting before him. Fear seemed to freeze the big hunter in his saddle. His hands shook as he studied the still, imposing figure before him. His eyes blinked in disbelief. Was this a man or the demon the bear tales were told of?

Mumbling to Ellie, who sat behind him, Squires could only squeak. "Is this the one you call Crow Killer?"

"No, Mister Squires, that is Red Hawk of the Crow people." Ellie could plainly see the big bore of the Hawkin's muzzle staring right at her. "Magnificent looking isn't he."

"I thought you belonged to Crow Killer?"

"I belong to no one."

Squires studied the imposing figure sitting the spotted horse. "You belong to me. You're mine, woman. If I can't have you, nobody will."

Ellie heard the loud click of the rifle's hammer being cocked. "You pull that trigger and your gun will be empty and useless."

"And you'd like that, wouldn't you?" Squires growled. "That would save your man there."

"He's not my man. I told you, no man owns me and certainly not you." Ellie retorted. "I would rather be dead than be in your filthy hands. Go ahead, shoot me, then you will die."

"You'd like me to empty my rifle, wouldn't you?" Squires glared at Ellie. "You don't want your man killed. No, I'll kill him first, then I'll teach you who's boss."

"You know what the Crow do to their enemies… the ones captured alive?" Ellie warned him.

"I have heard, but I ain't been captured yet, woman." Sweat rolled down the big man's scraggly beard.

"Then go ahead, pull the trigger, and you'll seal your fate." Ellie laughed in the man's face. "You better decide quick, Squires, here he comes."

Whirling in the saddle, Squires whipped up the rife and fired as he heard the hard-charging warrior send out his shrill war cry. The mighty spotted stallion was coming hard right at him, less than thirty yards away. The heavy slug tore into Red Hawk's rifle stock, knocking it from his hands. The heavy bull-hide covered war shield deflected the ricocheting bullet, preventing it from hitting the man or horse. Yelling his fierce war cry, Red Hawk closed in on the hunter as he tried to reload the rifle. Only the noise from the spotted horse's body as it shouldered into Squires' bay horse was heard as both horses went down in a pile under the impact.

Rolling quickly to his feet, Red Hawk pulled his war axe and moved toward the stunned white man. Shaking his head to clear it, Squires, seeing the imposing figure advancing toward him, staggered unsteadily to his feet. Rage filled Red Hawk as he swung the heavy war axe, slashing at the retreating hunter. Trying to use the rifle as a club, Squires parried the heavy blows reigning against his Hawken. Slobber dribbled from the man as fear gripped him and panic set in across his face. Finally, in despair, Squires dropped the rifle and turned away, trying to run from the menace before him. Grabbing the fleeing man's leather hunting shirt, Red Hawk pulled the terrified white man back to him and slammed the heavy axe into his head.

Ellie turned her head as blood and gore spewed everywhere from the man's split skull. Starting to pull his skinning knife, Red Hawk looked at Ellie, then shoved it back in its sheath. Walking over to Ellie, the warrior stopped before her.

"You are alright, Medicine Thunder?"

"I am now." Smiling at the warrior, she slipped trembling from her horse into his arms. "Thanks to you, Red Hawk."

Hearing the Hawken's blast, Jed and Walking Horse rode their horses up the trail in a hard run, reining in as they saw Red Hawk and Ellie standing near Squires' bloody body.

Sliding to the ground, Jed took her by the arm. "Are you okay, Ellie?"

"Thanks to Red Hawk, I am now." Ellie looked down at the dead body and seemed to go limp for a second. "He was crazy."

Looking at Squires, Jed shook his head. "He won't be bothering you anymore."

"I told him to turn me loose and he might live." Ellie placed her hand on Red Hawk's arm. "I warned him."

Jed looked into Ellie's eyes. "No, he was a dead man when he came into my valley to steal you. If Red Hawk hadn't killed this one, I would have."

"Well, it's over with now."

"Yes, it's finished now." Walking Horse added.

"And my father and the others?" Ellie looked at Walking Horse.

The tall Arapaho warrior averted his eyes. "My sister, we have lost many of our friends and loved ones today."

"My father?"

"Your father died trying to help your brother and his friends." Red Hawk nodded solemnly. "Now, he will hunt in the big meadow above with his father and their fathers. His was a good death."

"Mourn your father, but do not feel sorrow." Walking Horse looked into her eyes. "Now, he will forever be happy."

"And my brother, Little Wound?"

"He waits at the river crossing for us."

Nodding sadly, Ellie turned and walked back down the trail toward the crossing. Wrapping a rawhide rope around Squires' feet, Jed mounted the paint and pulled the body off the trail and into the brush. After picking up Squire's weapons, Jed noticed the rifle had a big B carved in the stock as Dibbs had said. Walking Horse gathered the loose horses, then turned and followed Ellie and Red Hawk. The procession was solemn, and not a word had been spoken as they neared the river crossing where they found Little Wound waiting for them. Jed looked around the area quickly for Nobles' body, but it was nowhere in sight. Jed breathed a sigh of relief. He didn't want Ellie seeing the body. He didn't want her knowing how her brother had killed the white and what his body probably looked like now. He knew she had seen enough death to last her a lifetime.

"Ellie, your brother needs a little doctoring." Jed dismounted and walked to where Little Wound sat on a drift log.

Examining the flesh wound, Ellie ripped strips from her shirttail and bandaged the wound. "We will fix it properly when we return to the valley."

Little Wound shrugged. "Thank you, Sister, but it is nothing."

"I've heard that many times before." Ellie smiled and touched the young warrior's shoulder, then turned to Jed. "Let me see your side."

Red Hawk and Walking Horse looked about curiously for Nobles but there was no doubt the hunter was dead, as the bloody scalp of the dead white hung from the Gros Ventre's bow. They could see Little Wound was still damp from bathing himself in the river, washing away the victim's blood. Jed only hoped Ellie hadn't noticed the drying scalp.

"My young brother has collected many horses and rifles today." Walking Horse smiled at the dark face of Little Wound.

"I take nothing from these dogs, but the hair from the one who killed my father." The dark eyes went to the bloody scalp.

Red Hawk looked around the campsite, then at Little Wound. "You did not find the other white?"

"No, he was not here with the others."

"It is as I thought... the big hunter must have killed him or maybe he was wounded in the fight in the valley and died from his wounds." Red Hawk surmised.

"Let's go home." Ellie nodded and looked away from the dangling scalp. "Enough talk of killing. Now, I've got some babies to go see."

The crossing of the Snake was made without mishap as the horses splashed up the sandy bank. Jed smiled and nodded at Walking Horse when he noticed Ellie riding in close to Red Hawk with her knee touching his as the horses started toward the valley. They couldn't help notice the looks that passed between the two. As they rode, Ellie reached out and took the warrior's hand.

"I think our friend, Red Hawk, is finally finished with his wild ways." Walking Horse smiled. "Medicine Thunder has looked at him."

"But, has Red Hawk looked back?"

"See for yourself, my brother." Walking Horse grinned as he nodded at the two holding hands. "I believe our brother's raiding and fighting may be finished."

"Perhaps you are right, but I'll have to see that for myself." Jed laughed. "But, I believe you are right about one thing. If anyone can still the wildness in his heart. Ellie may just be the one."

"I never thought I would see Red Hawk holding hands with a woman." Walking Horse shook his head. "Wait until I tell Little Antelope. She will not believe it."

"My sister is a beautiful woman, my brothers." Little Wound smiled. "Many warriors would want to hold her hand."

"That's true." Jed smiled.

Bright Moon raced across the cabin grounds toward the small creek as she sighted the small party coming down the mountain trail. Smiling and waving, she giggled as Jed lifted her onto the horse in front of him. Wiggling back against him, she looked up at him and seemed to shiver.

"You are home, my husband." The round dark eyes glowed with warmth as she looked into his eyes. "You are home safe."

"I am home, my lady." Jed hugged her to him. "This time for good."

"We hope." Bright Moon laughed with happiness. "But, we have heard that before."

"Yes, we have." Jed knew she spoke the truth. "The children?"

"They are fine."

"They have grown since I have been away."

"They wait to greet their father, the great Crow Killer." Bright Moon laughed, leaning back against Jed. Noticing Ellie riding close to Red Hawk, she looked curiously at the pair. "My sister rides very close to the Crow."

"Very close." Jed smiled.

"Is this good, my husband?" Bright Moon frowned. "Red Hawk is so wild, too wild for any one woman."

"If I'm not wrong, his wild days may be over."

"I'll have to see that to believe it." Bright Moon shook her head. "That Crow's wild spirit will never be tamed by any woman and I don't want my sister hurt."

"I don't believe she'll be the one getting hurt."

Dismounting before the cabin, Jed took in a deep breath and smiled. They were home. Jed picked up the babies one at a time, and held them high, smiling at their little faces. Walking Horse took Little Ellie from him and smiled. Jed nodded to Bright Moon when he noticed Red Hawk and Ellie had walked away together, down the trail toward the creek. He wondered, maybe Ellie could tame the wildness that coursed through the Crow's blood. Next to Walking Horse, Red Hawk was his best friend and brother. Jed hoped the wild, untamed heart of the Crow would be calmed down a little, if not tamed altogether. Several times in the following three days, since they all returned to the cabin, the two walked off by themselves.

Little Antelope, catching Jed out of hearing of the others, questioned Jed. "Is this a good thing, my warrior?"

"They seem to be in love, little one." Jed shrugged. "What could be wrong about it?"

"But he is Crow and she is Arapaho." Little Antelope was doubtful. "Can she live with his people? I know Red Hawk. He will not live with the Arapaho, and you know how wild and reckless the Crow is."

"The Crow people think much of Medicine Thunder for saving the life of Plenty Coups." Jed assured her. "She will be welcome in the Crow villages."

"And Red Hawk, will the Arapaho welcome him?"

"Walking Horse will make him welcome in his villages." Jed nodded. "But, like you said I doubt they will live with the Arapaho."

"It is customary for the man to move into the village of his wife." Little Antelope added. "This has always been the custom."

"You know Red Hawk, he makes his own customs." Jed smiled. "One day, Red Hawk will take the place of Plenty Coups, and be Chief of the Crow people."

Little Antelope frowned. "Yes, I know Red Hawk."

"It will be alright, little one." Jed smiled. "You will see."

"Still, for two people to marry that have been hereditary enemies, it doesn't seem right." Little Antelope watched as the couple moved out of sight across the creek.

"What will be, will be." Jed laughed at her worries. "You know Ellie is a strong-minded girl."

"I wonder if she is strong-minded enough to tame the beast in that one."

"Only time can tell, but it could be a good battle alright." Jed laughed.

"I hope you are right." Little Antelope, carrying Eagle's Wing on her hip, idly stroked the baby's coal-black hair.

"How have you been?" Jed looked down into her beautiful face.

"I am well now that you and my husband are both home safe."

"Walking Horse has been a good friend and brother." Jed looked to where two riders were coming toward the cabin. "But I ask about you, Little Antelope, how have you been?"

Looking down at the baby, she smiled. "I am happy for you and Bright Moon. They are beautiful babies."

"One day you will hold your own baby." Jed knew her thoughts.

"Will I, my warrior?"

"You will." Jed smiled down at the pretty woman. "I'll bet you have several beautiful children."

"I hope this is so." The little woman smiled sadly. "For my husband Walking Horse's sake, I hope this comes true."

Walking Horse and Little Wound rode up to the cabin with a freshly killed deer. Walking Horse grinned broadly as he looked at the young Gros Ventre. "My brother, Little Wound, has made a great shot on this deer with his father's rifle."

Little Wound looked embarrassed at all the attention. "It was a lucky shot, but we will feast tonight."

Jed knew Walking Horse had been working with the young Gros Ventre and the rifle of Lige Hatcher he had found among the rifles of the dead Metis. Walking Horse was proud of the clean shot Little Wound had made on the deer.

Jed remembered the first days when he and Walking Horse had ridden together while the Arapaho was teaching him the ways of the warrior. At first, Walking Horse's dislike for the young Jed was plain for all to see, but then it had turned into a strong bond, stronger than true brothers. Their lives had been intertwined together, each holding the other's life in his hand many times. They had been in many fights together against their enemies, each one bonding them closer together.

Then their blood had been mixed together by the old Arapaho Medicine Man, White Swan, and they were as one.

Supper was finished and everyone was sitting in the yard around the oak table, drinking coffee when Red Hawk led the spotted stallion from the corral and stopped in front of Little Wound. His mane and tail were braided and ribbons decorated his braids. Red paint covered the stallion in circles and depicted the great bison's skull and horns.

"I have come to ask for your sister to be my wife. Today, I offer this great Appaloosa horse for her." Presenting the Appaloosa to the astonished warrior, Red Hawk smiled.

"Me? You are asking me?" Little Wound looked around the table shocked. "Why me?"

"Her father rests now with his ancestors, so Walking Horse, her other brother, says I am to speak with you about her bride price. He says you are her father now."

Looking at Ellie, Little Wound stood up and took the reins of the great stallion. "Is this my sister's wish?"

Taking Red Hawk's arm, Ellie smiled and nodded quietly. "It is, my brother."

Shaking his head sadly, Little Wound returned the reins to Red Hawk. Rubbing his hands down the great neck of the spotted horse, Little Wound only smiled. He was honored as the offer of the great spotted horse was the greatest gift Red Hawk could give in marriage.

"Is he not enough for your sister?" Red Hawk was confused.

"He is more than enough, my brother." Little Wound smiled. "But, this great spotted horse belongs only to the great warrior Red Hawk of the Crow people. I cannot accept this great gift. He would not be happy being ridden by a lesser warrior as I. My sister is yours, and may your days be many and happy."

"Little Wound will come to my village for the wedding. There you will have plenty of horses to choose from." Red Hawk looked proudly at the stallion. "Comanche horses and many young Crow maidens."

"Red Hawk!" Ellie scolded the warrior.

"No, thanks to my sister, my wound no longer bleeds and is almost healed." Little Wound shook his head. "Tomorrow, I must leave for the lands to the west and go to my people."

"And we must return to our villages." Walking Horse smiled at Little Antelope.

"So soon?" Bright Moon looked around the table.

"Yes, I have been away from my village far too long now." Walking Horse smiled. "We must leave with the coming sun."

Jed looked at Little Wound. "I will ride with Little Wound and make sure you get past the white village safely."

"It will be okay, I will ride alone." The Gros Ventre laughed. "A few whites will not find me in the dark as I pass."

"Are you sure, Little Wound?" Ellie shook her head. "It is a long and dangerous journey back to your lands."

"No more dangerous than being here with all of you." Little Wound laughed. "You people live dangerous lives."

"He's right about that. I will go with Little Wound." Jed offered.

"No, Crow Killer, you must stay here and enjoy your new family." Red Hawk shook his head. "You have been away far too long now."

Looking out across the meadow, as the little mule brayed, Jed reached for his rifle, then recognized Long Leaper and two Crow warriors as they neared the cabin. Six horses were being led and Jed could tell the young Crow warriors had been in a fight. Scalps, rifles, and small bags were tied to the saddles of the led horses.

Red Hawk held Ellie's arm as Long Leaper reined in his grey horse and looked down at them arrogantly. "We have returned, my chief."

"You have been in a fight, Long Leaper?" Red Hawk looked up at the mounted warriors behind Long Leaper.

"We caught up with the Cree and Metis from the western lands." Long Leaper looked back at the young Crow warriors. Both of the young men raised their shields and howled. "Here in a strange land, they were lost. They did not know where to run to so we showed them the way to their ancestors."

"Where is Iron Oak?" Crazy Cat looked behind the warriors. "His horse is here, but he is not."

"He rests along the great river." Long Leaper averted his eyes. "He died bravely in battle. He counted many coups on his enemies."

Red Hawk's teeth gritted. Iron Oak was the son of Wild Elk a good friend of his. He had practically raised the young warrior in his own lodge since he was a young boy.

"That won't be much comfort to Wild Elk. The young warrior who died was his last living son."

"I am sorry, Red Hawk, but he died a warrior's death." Long Leaper shrugged. "We will sing his praises around our fires."

Taking Ellie by the arm, Red Hawk walked toward the creek. To stay longer, facing the haughty Long Leaper, would lead to another death. Red Hawk had never liked the young warrior nor his father Wild Wind, but to kill him would be wrong. No leader or chief of the Crow Nation was allowed to harm another Crow. Walking away from the warrior until his temper had cooled, avoiding more words with the arrogant Long Leaper was all he could do.

Ellie looked sideways at the scowling face of Red Hawk. "The dead warrior was a friend?"

"Almost like a son."

"I'm sorry, Red Hawk."

"Crazy Cat said he had told Long Leaper not to follow the Cree to the east." The warrior grabbed a rock and flung it across the water. "The foolish one just wanted to count coup and make a name for himself. Now, our village has lost a great warrior and I have lost a good friend."

"What troubles, Red Hawk?" Long Leaper looked at the troubled faces surrounding him and shrugged as Red Hawk stalked off. "We have won a great victory today and taken many scalps."

Crazy Cat stepped forward, staring hard at the young Crow. "You have lost a better warrior today than you are. I myself, told you not to go."

"Sometimes there are losses in battle." Long Leaper glared at the Cheyenne. "And no Cheyenne tells a Crow what to do or when to do it. Never!"

Jed stepped between the two warriors as Crazy Cat in his anger started forward. "Long Leaper has spoken enough today."

"We will make camp until Red Hawk tells us what to do." Long Leaper swung up on his horse and motioned toward Wilson's cabin. "Over there."

Walking Horse stepped forward. "By the look of Red Hawk's face, it would be best for all of you to return to your village now."

"We are not welcome here at your lodge, Crow Killer?" Long Leaper looked down at Jed. "If this is so, say it and we will depart."

Jed looked up at the warrior. "I will not turn away any of Chief Plenty Coups' people from my lodge. You make camp here and you may eat with us at my lodge, but keep your mouth still. Not another word about your battle or Iron Oak's death."

"It will be as you ask." Nodding, the young warrior turned his horse toward Ed Wilson's cabin and corral. "We will be over there."

"Camp anywhere you wish, Crow." Crazy Cat hissed between closed teeth. "One day, we'll meet again."

"Not here, my friend, not here near my lodge." Jed shook his head. "Today, let this one live."

"I would not bring shame on my brother." The Cheyenne looked at the retreating backs of the three young Crow and shook his head. "That one is bound for trouble."

"He is that." Jed agreed. "But, he is proud, like most young warriors."

"Sometimes pride can get you killed, my friend."

Walking Horse watched the riders move away, then turned to where Little Antelope was playing with the children. "We will prepare our things for an early parting with the new sun."

"You'll have something to eat before you ride from our lodge." Bright Moon insisted. "I will have your food ready with the new sun."

Walking Horse smiled. He wasn't about to argue with her. "Yes, we will eat before we go. Thank you, my sister."

Red Hawk and Ellie returned to the table and took their places around the large fire that had been built. The warriors pulled out their pipes and stared into the light. Tonight, their last night at Crow Killer's lodge would be a peaceful time, a time for smoking and telling of stories. Red Hawk was in great demand in the Crow Nation for telling tales of bygone battles and tales of the spirit world. With his winning personality and handsome face, he could hold his audience spellbound for hours at a time. However tonight, with the news of Iron Oaks' death, he was not in the mood for stories.

Bright Moon and Little Antelope moved about the oak table, pouring coffee for the men and passing out hoecake they had baked for the occasion. The hardship and danger of the past days were finished, and now they could relax and enjoy themselves. Their losses had been great and many a warrior had gone to their ancestors on this trail.

"Red Hawk has something to say." Ellie looked at the gathered faces, then turned to the warrior. "Tell them, Red Hawk."

Long Leaper and his warriors had strolled back over to the fire and found a seat on the ground. Not speaking, they sat back without saying a word. They didn't know if they were welcome at the fire or not. Red Hawk glared at the three warriors, then dropped his eyes.

"The brother of Medicine Thunder and Walking Horse rides west toward the village of the whites with the new sun." The warrior looked back at Ellie. "Medicine Thunder wishes to tell her grandfather of our marriage. I know the trail from the last time Crow Killer and I rode across the great rivers to the village of the whites. It is a dangerous trail and the whites are many. Medicine Thunder and I have decided to ride with Little Wound and help him get past the white's village, then we will visit her grandfather and tell him of our plans."

"This is a good plan, my friend." Jed nodded, giving his approval of the plan. "There is safety in numbers and you know the trail."

"And I will go with them." Ed Wilson spoke up.

"You're leaving the valley, Pa?" Jed looked at the older man. "Why?"

"To bring back a cow and help Red Hawk get past the whites." Wilson replied. "You know west of here could be dangerous for him as well as Little Wound."

"It is a good plan, Crow Killer." Little Antelope refilled the coffee cups in front of the men. "The Crow might get lost in the dark."

Red Hawk looked at Walking Horse and smiled. "Your woman, my brother, has a sharp tongue."

"Yes, she does." Walking Horse laughed lightly.

"You promised me a cow and I'm going after one." Wilson thrust out his chin. "The babies will need milk and coffee ain't much count without cream."

"You just be careful, Pa." Jed was worried about the old farmer. "We don't want to lose you."

Red Hawk nodded and looked over to where Long Leaper sat quietly. "I will see that he gets back here safely."

"Good, now that's settled." Wilson smiled.

"Providing, I don't lose my way." Red Hawk had to jab at Little Antelope. "You make good coffee for an Arapaho."

"Well, thank you, Red Hawk." The little woman smiled. "I didn't think a Crow would know good coffee from bad."

"It is good coffee." Jed intervened stopping the argument.

"Will we ride with you, my chief?" Long Leaper spoke up.

"No, you will ride with Walking Horse and Crazy Cat, and help them watch for the Comanche." Red Hawk stared hard at the warrior. "Then ride on to Plenty Coups and tell him what happened. Everything!"

Dropping his eyes, Long Leaper could only mutter. "Yes, my chief."

Early daylight found the cabin in a quiet mood. Everyone had their horses loaded and were sadly saying their goodbyes. Little Antelope couldn't bear to tear herself away from the babies. Few words had been spoken as breakfast finished and both parties prepared to depart. Red Hawk to the west to Baxter Springs, and Walking Horse to the south to Arapaho lands. Shaking hands with his friends, Jed took Eagle's Wing from Little Antelope and touched her shoulder.

"Good-bye, Medicine Thunder, we will see you at the wedding." Walking Horse looked up at Red Hawk. "Tell me, Red Hawk, where will the wedding and the feasting be?"

"We will have a huge gathering of the tribes on the banks of the Yellowstone." Red Hawk laughed. "There will be dancing, singing, and much food to eat."

Jed nodded. "Sounds like it'll be a good day to marry."

"I will send warriors to escort you and Bright Moon to the river." Red Hawk looked over at Ellie and smiled.

"Good-bye." Little Antelope took Ellie's small hand and kissed it. "Take care of my babies, Bright Moon."

"I promise."

"We will see you when you and Red Hawk return from the white village, Ellie." Jed looked at Wilson. "Be safe, Pa, and bring back your new cow."

Red Hawk nodded, then kicked the spotted horse. "We will bring him back to the valley safely."

Jed watched expectantly as Red Hawk had a few words with Long Leaper and the other two Crow warriors. He could tell there was very little cordiality among the Crow this morning.

Finally, the time to depart arrived, and everyone shook hands before turning their horses away from the cabin. Jed and Bright Moon, each carrying a baby, walked a little way out onto the valley floor, waving good-bye to their friends and loved ones. Slowly, with the passing of the horse's hooves, the rider's backs diminished in the early rays of the morning. The small black mule had followed the riders a short way to the south end of the valley, then brayed. Tears rolled down Bright Moon's cheeks.

"Do not be sad." Jed smiled. "We'll see them again when they pass back this way, and then at your sister's wedding."

"I am not sad, my husband." Bright Moon smiled. "I couldn't be happier. I have the greatest and most handsome warrior in the land for a husband and two beautiful children. One which was foretold to become a great warrior himself one day. How could I be sad?"

"I'm not sure I like old Spotted Panther's prophecy this time." Jed was worried about the medicine man's predictions of the future.

"Spotted Panther is a great medicine man and his prophecies always come true." Bright Moon beamed. "Our son, Eagle's Wing, will be a great warrior and nothing can change what was foretold."

"Yes, but that is a long way off. For now, we will look forward to things that come sooner. Like Red Hawk and your sister Medicine Thunder's marriage on the banks of the Yellowstone. We will all be there to watch their marriage and enjoy a great celebration." Jed smiled. "It will be a wonderful day for us."

The long, lonely cry of the great lobo wolf sounded high on the mountain. Once again, things were good, and Crow Killer was at last home in his beloved valley with his beautiful family.

The End

CPSIA information can be obtained
at www.ICGtesting.com
Printed in the USA
BVHW040617070221
599461BV00010BA/952